LET THEIR SPIRITS DANCE·

ALSO BY STELLA POPE DUARTE

Fragile Night (Stories)

LET THEIR SPIRITS

A NOVEL · STELLA

DANCE ·

POPE DUARTE ·

· rayo ·

An Imprint of HarperCollins*Publishers*

HarperCollins books may be purchased for educational, business,
or sales promotional use. For information, please write: Special
Markets Department, HarperCollins Publishers Inc., 10 East 53rd
Street, New York, NY 10022.

FIRST EDITION

Designed by JUDITH STAGNITTO ABBATE / ABBATE DESIGN

Printed on acid-free paper

Library of Congress Cataloging-in-Publication Data
Duarte, Stella Pope.
    Let their spirits dance / Stella Pope Duarte.—Rayo 1st ed.
    p. cm
    ISBN 0-06-018637-2
    1. Vietnamese conflict, 1961–1975—Participation, Mexican
American—Fiction. 2. Vietnamese Conflict, 1961–1975—
Registers of dead—Fiction. 3. Vietnam Veterans Memorial
(Washington, D.C.)—Fiction. 4. Mexican American families—
Fiction. 5. Washington (D.C.)—Fiction. 6. Phoenix (Ariz.)—
Fiction. [1. Soldiers—Family relationships—Fiction.] I. Title.
PS3554.U236 L48 2002
813'.54—dc21
                                                    2001057879

ISBN 0-06-018637-2

02 03 04 05 06 BVG/QW 10 9 8 7 6 5 4 3 2

DEDICATED TO THE MEMORY OF

SGT. TONY CRUZ AND ALL LA RAZA

WHO DIED IN VIETNAM.

We hear you ...

Acknowledgments •

Primeramente, gracias to John Gutierrez who sat with me at a Starbucks and said, "Why don't you let our Chicano guys talk to the nation from the Vietnam Memorial Wall?" and thus was born *Let Their Spirits Dance*. Making the trip to Albuquerque with me, sharing the history, the ghosts, the treasures, then together searching out a new title. For everything, John, gracias.

To John Ruiz, gracias for the trip across the nation with my son John and me to the Wall, marking the journey, fleshing out the characters, embracing America, and for watching videos on the war with me, so many we could have rewritten the history of the Vietnam War.

De veras, warm thanks to the family of Sgt. Tony Cruz, to his mother Maria Escoto, his sisters, Gracie Valenzuela and Christina Cañez, his brother Joe Cruz, and his best friend, David Reyes, for sharing Tony's belief with me that one day we would read about him in a book. Someday a story would honor los Chicanos who went across the sea and never came back. Gracias.

For the guys who shared their war days with me, especially Robert Ramirez, Rayo Reyes, Joe Little, Ted Lloyd, Frank Diaz, Ernie Chavez, and Henry Villalobos. Thank you, guys, I know you did it for all the others. And for Danny Alday, who told me the story of his brother, Frank.

For Tony Valenzuela who gave me the story of Francisco "Pancho" Jimenez, Congressional Medal of Honor recipient, born in Mexico, gracias. To Lionel Sanchez of Arizona State Representative Ed Pastor's office, gracias for the suggestion that I visit the Wall at night. Yes, there is sacredness there.

For Ruben Hernandez who made the journey to the Wall with me, so we could see it at night, in freezing weather, gracias. Also, for leading me to Rosalio Muñoz, a piece of Chicano history, in person, in L.A. And for being my first copy editor, you were there for me.

Great thanks to Natalie Zeitlin for introducing me to her brother Dr. Jack Shulimson, whom I interviewed in Washington, D.C. Gracias, Dr. Shulimson, for sharing your expertise on the Tet offensive with me.

I owe a debt of gratitude to Tom and Carol Miles, who took my son John and me to Vietnam. Gracias for showing us the way, and helping us cross the busy streets of Ho Chi Minh City! Especially, Tom, for all the insights into the war, you knew it well. You did two tours.

My Vietnamese tutors, Chau Pho and his wife Thom Pham, who tutored me for six months, patiently, *cám ơn*, thank you.

Ron Carlson. Where do I begin? Ron sat with me at a Starbucks, shoes off, chomping on a cookie, drawing a choo-choo train for me so I could understand how to structure the final draft. He is amazing! "Cut and paste," he told me, and he gave me this unbelievable confidence that I could do it all. Ron, gracias.

Friends, there are so many for whom I extend mil gracias. Kathy Muñoz Tellez, for coming to see me the first time I read in the Valley, when it was storming outside, a freak storm that flooded the city. Her face was all I knew as I read, and after that she never failed to be there— no matter what. Belen Servin, since high school days she has been there to lead me out of the dark pits I have fallen into. Her faith is what has opened the way for me, time and again. Martisa and Mike Vignali, their belief that my book would soar kept me writing sometimes when I felt I could not go on. Ann and Andrew Thomas, jewels, ever confident that God would lead the way and the book would tell the story the way it should be told. For Maria Alvarado, long-time amiga who has shared the journey, and brightened the vision. I will not forget Lisa Ruiz, fellow writer, who shared trips to D.C. and Little Saigon with me, and kept telling me I was doing everything right. And for her sister, Marisa Ruiz, my first-grade student all grown-up who lent me her apartment in D.C. Angie Camarena, like a sister, who listened to all my crazy babbling, the stories inside me that ran in circles, and still, she listened. Phil Mandel, who told me what I had to do next, "Get an agent!" I'm glad I listened.

For Severiano Rodarte, amigo, fellow storyteller and an inspiration for our community.

Diane Reverend. I was blessed to have Diane as my first editor at HarperCollins. Truly, her insights made the book what it is today. I salute you, Diane, and gracias for your heart-open acceptance of my work. For Loretta Barrett, my agent, who was dedicated to the Vietnam era long before I knew her. So many miracles, and one of them has been having Loretta for my agent. Gracias y abrazos to René Alegría of RAYO, my editor, who told me so many beautiful things about my book, I actually started to believe them!

Gracias and overflowing love to my children Vince, Monica, Deborah, and John, and to my grandchildren, Angelo, Alyvia, Elaine, Gavin, and Marcelo for the "I love you's" along the way, that meant the world to me! And for my in-law children, Valerie, Paul "Rocky," and Miguel "Nacho." For my sisters Rosie, Mary, Lena, Lupe, and my sisters who went ahead of us, Linda and Sophie, and for my brother, Frank. I believe in us as a family, in who we are to each other, and to the world. Without you, the journey would have been bleak, the road unbearable.

Gracias, for so many others who have brought this book into existence through their encouragement and support. Kent Franklin, librarian at Carl Hayden High School, Betsy Lehman, librarian at Cesar Chavez, my wonderful friends at Phoenix Union High School District, my students from the University of Phoenix and Arizona State University, Writers Voice of Arizona, the Arizona Commission on the Arts, and people all over Arizona who have cared for me, shown me their love.

My father. Francisco Moreno Duarte, yes dad, for the dream that led me to see that I was destined to write, gracias del corazón.

My mother. Rosanna Pope Duarte, Irish Latina beauty who sealed my heart with her love, and taught me, "Dios obra en todo," God works through all things. And He does, Mom, He really does.

I CAME FROM THE SEVEN CAVES,

THE FIRST PLACE, WHERE MAGIC RULED,

MY FOOTPRINTS LEAD FROM THERE,

WHERE THE TRIBES BEGAN.

"Song of the Mimixcoa" • *Poems of the Aztec Peoples*

Contents •

LET THEIR SPIRITS DANCE·

1968 ·

T he passion vine bloomed until late November the year
Jesse died. Amazing. Every morning I walked out on
the rough slab of concrete that led to the wooden trel-
lis leaning against the side of the house to check for
blossoms. Warm September days in Arizona fueled the vine's growth, and
the cool days of October should have signaled it to stop. Still, in 1968,
truth was suspended in midair, and the passion vine forced blooms into
the cold, gray days of November. Each blossom lived one day. All that
beauty for just one day.

Early missionaries saw the mystery of Christ's passion in the flower's
intricate design. The petals symbolize the ten apostles at the Crucifixion,
the rays of the corona are the crown of thorns, the five anthers the
wounds, the three stigmas the nails, the coiling tendrils the cords and
whips, and the five-lobed leaves the cruel hands of the persecutors. The
flower was fully open, a purple-white disc, translucent in the gray dawn.
Dewdrops shone on the petals. I felt around the flower's delicate stamen,
feeling pollen under my fingertips; the petals felt thick, rubbery. The
smell of dead leaves, wet earth, and moist wood hung in the air.

I shivered in my flannel nightgown and bare feet. My face felt numb.
I knew my nose was turning red. The evergreen tree in the front yard
and the skinny chinaberry tree growing by the woodshed glowed in the
early morning light. Across the street, Fireball, the Williamses' rooster,

crowed. El Cielito, my old barrio, was coming alive—awkwardly, like a dinosaur rising to its feet.

I spotted Duke, our old German shepherd, walking toward me from the backyard. Jesse had named our dog Duke for the song "Duke of Earl" that we practiced dancing to in the living room. We made the old 45 go round so many times the needle cracked. It was worth it, because all our dips and spins matched perfectly, and Jesse felt so good about his dancing he even asked Mary Ann to dance with him at his eighth-grade graduation party.

Jesse said Duke was seventy-seven years old in dog years. That was two years ago. Poor Duke, no wonder he was walking so slow, dragging around over seventy years of chasing cats and cars. He padded toward me in silence, yawning once. Seeing me there was no surprise. Duke picked a path parallel to the water hose that ran along the hard-packed earth to a row of hedges that grew against the chicken-wire fence, separating our property from our neighbors, the Navarros.

Duke came up to me, brushing along the side of my leg. He nuzzled the hem of my nightgown with his wet nose. I saw patches of bald spots on Duke's brown back, and his tail wagged like a melancholy pendulum between his back legs. "Good dog," I said patting him. "Sit, Duke. Sit here." I pointed to the spot next to me. Jesse had taught Duke how to sit, jump on lawn chairs, retrieve a baseball, and scare the mailman.

With Duke at my side, I stared at the tangled passion vine and through its spidery web of stems and leaves at my mother's bedroom window, blocked off from the outside world by curtains that had faded in the sun. I knew my mother was in her room crying. Crying was all my mother did after Jesse was killed in Vietnam.

I hardly recognized her anymore. I had grown used to every expression of her face, all the ups and downs of her eyebrows, and the way the tiny wrinkles on her chin smoothed out when she smiled. I couldn't describe her face anymore. I didn't want to. I had to make myself stop wanting to hear her sing in the mornings while she made breakfast for me, Priscilla, and Paul, got coffee ready for my dad, and clattered the dishes around until we all got up. I couldn't even talk to Jesse about it, this whole worry about my mom, unless I went out to the passion vine.

I knew my father wasn't in the bedroom with my mother. How could he be? He could only take so much of her tears, then he pulled back, retreating into his own thoughts, into the circle of smoke made by cigarettes he forgot to finish smoking. He let his coffee, café con leche, get cold. Cigarette ashes got all over the kitchen table. When he felt the cigarette burn his fingers, he put it out in one hard motion in the ashtray, then he gulped down more coffee, but he wouldn't go back into the bedroom with Mom. My parents lived in the same house as strangers long before Jesse died.

There was more between my parents than Jesse's death. There was Consuelo. Since I could remember, Consuelo's name was whispered, shouted, and swept out of our house over and over again, and it reappeared, a spider's web stubbornly clinging to a dark corner of the living room. The spider's web stood up to blasts of air spewing from the swamp cooler that made wheezing sounds when the humidity was up. It was a reminder to me that Consuelo was there, entangling us in a web of lies and shame, holding us captive, hexing my father, Tía Katia said, with his own photograph and a pin pushed right into his heart.

Anger was a balled fist between my breasts. It made me want to rip the passion vine apart, reach for my mother right through the glass, and make her stop crying. No one was around except Duke, keeping guard. It was too early for El Cielito's winos to begin their morning trek down the alley to the liquor store. It was two hours before I had to catch the bus to Palo Verde High School to finish my senior year. It was an hour before neighbors who worked in construction had to get up. I wanted to tear the vine apart, destroy the blooms that told the story of suffering and death with Duke my only witness.

Yet, the passion flower I held in my hand fascinated me. How could anything so beautiful be filled with the memory of so much suffering? Thorns, nails, blood, so long ago, Christ, ripped from his human existence. Why? Why all the suffering? The question grew inside me, pressing in me, forcing my hand to close over the flower, over the evidence of a murder. My body was wound tight with sobs that made my throat ache and my stomach jerk. I cried into the back of my hand, letting go of the flower. It was the first morning I chose not to crush it. The bloom lived on in the cold November morning, firm evidence that suffering was alive and well. Later, I was glad I hadn't crushed the flower, because it was the last bloom the passion vine gave that year. After that, the vine wilted away and slept through the winter as it should have done in the first place. I turned around and got on my knees, encircling Duke in my arms. "Good dog, Duke. Yes, taking care of me, like Jesse did." Duke stood perfectly still, and let me cry into his furry neck.

El Cielito •

The dream about my left ear was what started the whole thing. It came just before Christmas 1996, two nights before my mother heard the voices and I had a showdown with Sandra. The dream revealed a spot in the middle of my head I had never seen before. The spot was a microscopic reservoir of clear, watery liquid that ran out my left ear. It reminded me of the water from the Salt River, El Río Salado. I almost drowned in El Río Salado when I was seven, and I thought maybe I still had water in my ears—imagine after all these years! Dreams are that way. They show you a time in your life you forgot existed, a time you got stuck inside yourself and never came up for air. It was good, the dream; it wiped my ear clean so I could listen, listen hard to what I couldn't see. It cleared my head thirty years after Jesse's death and unplugged the thoughts I had hidden away, so secretly, so painfully. The dream made me brave and reckless, but I didn't know it then. I had been so used to stagnant pools inside myself, I didn't know how to live in water that was full and wild, teeming with life, so the dream set out to teach me.

• THE STREET IS DARK, a cavern I could lose myself in if it weren't for strings of Christmas lights on neighbors' front porches and the star of

Bethlehem blinking over Blanche Williams's house to show me the way. Mist hangs in the cold air, thick enough to make street lights on opposite ends of the road look as if they're miles away. I have no idea why there's moisture in the air—El Cielito is nowhere near water.

The hazy air makes it hard for me to see, or maybe it's tears starting. I reach for the Kleenex on my lap as I drive up to the front of my mother's house. I press the Kleenex up to my bruised lip, cursing Sandra and Ray. Blood oozes from inside my lip, saturating the wad of Kleenex. Pain shoots into my jaw.

So clearly, I see Ray in my mind on stage at the Riverside. His shirt is open at the collar, unbuttoned midway down his chest. At close range, the hairs on his chest stick out, sexy, unruly. He cradles the guitar in his arms, a loaded weapon he soothes and urges on, strums soft, strums hard, until the instrument explodes in his hands, making the speakers over the stage vibrate with the salsa sounds of Latin Blast. Ray's face changes colors. The blue stage light is one color, then his face turns to red, purple, and amber, colors reflected from openings in an aluminum globe suspended from the ceiling, spinning over the dance floor.

I wasn't there that night to see him perform with Latin Blast. I was there to see her—Sandra, the woman I was tired of hearing about. The woman Ray swears is only another groupie, an ugly, no-name woman who pays to see him play. I found out Sandra isn't ugly, and besides that, she's showy and defiant about Ray. I watched Ray thrust his guitar in the air, Elvis-style, a flourish, as the band took a break between songs. I noticed Sandra at a table nearby take a drink of her margarita. A woman shouted, "Hey Sandra, Ray wants you on stage!" Both women laughed and Sandra said, "Tell him I'll be there in a minute!" She took another drink of her margarita and was laughing so hard she spit it out. I suddenly saw only one color before my eyes—RED. A flash of red illuminated Sandra, and I jumped at her, tackling her to the wooden surface of the bar, punching her in the face as she fought back. I grabbed her by the hair and got her cheap hairspray all over my hands. It was as bad-smelling as her perfume, and sticky, too. People were screaming. I heard glasses breaking. We fell between bar stools. Sandra hit me in the mouth, then took her fingernails and carved three gashes on each side of my face. By this time, I was whaling on her, pounding away all the hurt and pain of my husband's betrayal, and the years of Consuelo owning my father. I heard my dress rip, then straddled my legs over Sandra's middle and ripped off her dress, neatly, like it was coming off a hanger. Her breasts were exposed and I wanted to laugh at Sandra's small breasts sticking up in the air, her nipples nothing more than two brown nodes, small disc-shaped circles on her chest. I couldn't imagine Ray, Mr. Breast-Man himself, interested in her! My mouth burned with pain, and I couldn't make my lips form a smile. The smile would be fake anyway, obscene even, considering how humiliated I felt. A security guard stopped us, pulled us apart. The manager of the place ran out and shouted at Ray, "Get your women under control, or I'll cancel your contract!"

"No need for that," I told him. "You'll never see me in here again!" It made me mad, the manager's words—"your women"—as if there was an audience full of women who wanted Ray. I turned my back on all of them and didn't even stop in the bathroom to take care of my face. Somebody handed me Kleenex. As I walked out. I heard a man's voice yell, "Don't drive like that, you'll be stopped by the cops!"

"Let them try!" I yelled back. I gunned the motor and made it out of the parking lot, oblivious to people milling at the entrance, watching me tear away. Looking into my car's rearview mirror in front of Mom's house, I make out the scratches Sandra's fingernails left on my face, three red gashes on each side that angle down my cheeks. The set on the left almost touches my lip. Will I need plastic surgery? I'm certain my blood crusted under Sandra's fingernails, because her blood crusted under mine. I shake off strands of her hair from the front of my dress as I stop the car and turn off the ignition. My hands are shaking so hard I have to hold them together to make them stop. I smooth my hair down and remember I left my sweater at the Riverside. I'm glad for the darkness and haze.

There's a light on in the house next to Mom's. The house used to belong to Ricky Navarro's family but has now been taken over by a bunch of shiftless renters who barely manage to pay the rent. For once, I'm glad Ricky and his mother, Sofia, aren't living there anymore. Ricky was my boy-prince, the kid I planned tea parties with behind gnarled bougainvillea and miguelito vines. It was hard to imagine Ricky belonged to the rough world of El Cielito when I watched him balance a teacup delicately between his thumb and forefinger.

Ricky came back from Vietnam in '66, crazy Ricky everybody called him. He brought back ten Zippo lighters he had collected from dead U.S. soldiers. There were burns on his hands and up his arms, and it didn't seem to matter to him. He picked at the scabs, opening up fresh wounds. Ricky was a twisted, distorted figure, rough and unshaven when he got back from Vietnam. No one could convince me it was the same Ricky I knew. He didn't look at me anymore when we talked. His green eyes stared over my head or around my shoulder as if he was waiting for something to happen. "Los Chicanos are like ducks in a row in Nam, waiting for the next bullet, Teresa," he said to me. "We're so glad to serve, and for what? To come back here and be treated like scum. Nothing's changed!"

Eventually, Ricky moved to California, to get away from the cops who stopped him from fighting when he was stoned on pot or high on pills. They hauled him back and forth to jail so many times, his fatigue jacket got to be two sizes too big from all the weight he lost. There were rumors that Ricky had joined a hippie commune in California. Ricky's mother was a barmaid who worked over at La Casita Restaurant, and she didn't put up with his shit. Still, she loved him so much, her green-eyed, baby Ricky. One day she disappeared and everyone said she had followed him to California.

Cholo, the family mutt, is barking in the front yard, running in circles, crouching low, barking again. He's the opposite of slow-moving Duke, who barked like he was coughing up phlegm.

"It's me, you dumb dog, stop barking!" Cholo snarls, crouches, barks again. I drop the wad of Kleenex as I struggle to open the padlock on the gate. For a minute, I wonder if I have the right key. Is this the right house? Why is the dog barking at me, he should know better. My hands are trembling as I wiggle the key into the lock again. Maybe my mother changed the lock and didn't tell me. Finally, it gives way, and I walk into Mom's front yard with Cholo jumping all over me, making it harder for me to hang on to my dress. I look down, searching for the wad of Kleenex and can't find it.

The light is on in my mother's room, but the rest of the house is dark. What happened to the porch light? There's no Christmas tree at the window. Mom hasn't put up a tree since Paul left home. The house looks as dark as the cave in Bethlehem. I see the edge of the curtain move, a simple flutter, but I know Mom is peeking out. It's more than she did years ago when I stood outside her window, staring at the faded curtains through the tangled web of the passion vine. I look at the barren spot where the passion vine once grew, and where Duke joined me on mornings I held a private vigil for Jesse. The passion vine was blown away years ago, how many, I can't remember exactly. A fluke blew it away, a storm that resembled a hurricane swept through the Valley, unearthing anything not rooted deep enough or held down by concrete. I look at the spot, and it sends a shock wave through my body. Jesse is there, watching me come home, remembering how I crushed out suffering for him, one blossom at a time, until I gave up and the passion vine went to sleep on its own, making suffering stop in its tracks for the winter at least.

I rush to the kitchen door with Cholo at my heels. I have the key in the lock and open the door before my mother walks into the kitchen. I used to sneak in so quietly as a teenager. Sometimes Priscilla would leave the door unlocked when she wasn't mad at me. And now all this fanfare. All I need is a drumroll.

"Mija!" My mother gasps and strains to balance herself on her cane. Her hair is a maze of white, wispy tangles all around her face. Her nightgown dangles to her heels, exposing the white socks on her feet. Her hand is on her mouth, staring in horror.

"It's nothing Mom . . . nothing at all." I feel my swollen lip shaping each word. Syllables catch like tangled threads in places where my lip feels numb.

"How . . . mija . . . what happened? Dios mio!"

I kick off my heels and let my dress slip off my body. I'm standing in front of Mom in my bra and slip.

"You'll freeze," Mom says. "Go get my robe in the bathroom." I walk down the hall into the bathroom, talking to Mom over my shoulder as I reach for an old bathrobe hanging on a nail. The robe is quilted, pink rayon with a frayed ribbon at the collar.

"It's OK, Mom, just some trouble over where Ray plays . . . at the club."

"With Ray? Did he do this? Call the police!"

"No, Ray didn't do this." I walk back to the kitchen sink and soak paper towels, pressing them up to my face.

"I thought you were here because you saw Jesse!"

"Jesse!" The paper towels freeze in midair over my face. Saying my brother's name raises the hair at the back of my neck. His name comes out of me like a shout. I look at Mom, half expecting to see Jesse standing behind her. She's smiling. The wrinkles on her chin have disappeared and her eyes look as if she's staring at a newborn baby—soft, tender.

"I heard his voice—tonight! Ay, it's as beautiful as ever. You remember, don't you, Teresa?"

Mom has her hand on my shoulder, shaking it, trying to make me believe what she just said. She doesn't know I've never forgotten Jesse's voice. I recorded it in my mind when it was still a boy's voice and not a man's.

"Ouch—Mom, my shoulder hurts."

"Ay mija! How could this happen to you, and tonight, why tonight?"

"I don't know, maybe it's part of a big plan. It doesn't matter; she got the worst of it."

"Who? Sandra? Don't tell me you were fighting in a bar with that woman!"

"Not a bar, Mom, the club—the Riverside."

"But fighting . . . mija . . . she's bigger than you. Did you hit her a few good ones at least? May God forgive me!"

"She'll remember me the rest of her life! I ripped off her dress too, the bitch, she had it coming."

"Don't cuss, mija! Ray's like your dad, another woman at his side. Sandra's your Consuelo."

"Don't even say that woman's name, Mom! I don't want to hear it." Mom pulls me by the arm. "Look, let me show you . . . your brother is visiting us tonight!" I walk with her as she balances herself easily on her cane. I haven't seen her walk this fast in years.

"Be careful Mom, you'll fall." She ignores me and walks into her bedroom with me trailing at her side. The room is lit by veladoras flickering before the image of El Santo Niño de Atocha, a fancy name for the Christ Child. The Christ Child is dressed in a simple blue robe with a brown mantle over His shoulders. In one hand he holds a stalk of wheat, in the other a scepter topped with a globe of the world. His dark, wavy hair is down to his shoulders and frames His small, somber face. The picture is propped on top of a white-draped oak dresser. My mother decorates an altar in honor of El Santo Niño every Christmas and prays a nine-day novena. The candlelight is white, friendly. It hushes me, yet I feel the need to dispel its shadows and reach for the light switch.

"No, mija! Spirits don't like bright light."

"Spirits?"

"Look." She leads me to the window and lifts a corner of the drapes. "What do you see?"

"Nothing but Cholo acting like he's got the rabies."

"Look carefully." My mother's voice is urgent.

I look intently. I'm glad there's nobody around to see me next to Mom. My face is red and raw. The pink rayon bathrobe is tight around my shoulders, its frayed ribbon sags at my collarbone. I can't imagine what my fellow teachers at Jimenez Elementary would say if they saw me now. It's so ironic after the whole school worked on a unit on nonviolence. I'm already worried my face won't heal in time to make it back to my second-grade class after Christmas break.

Trees are still, not a leaf blowing. Through the misty air, I see the star of Bethlehem blinking over Blanche's house across the street. Its light is multicolored, red, blue, yellow. I make out the white fence posts of the wooden pen in Blanche's backyard that used to belong to her proud rooster, Fireball. After El Cielito was zoned "industrial" by the city, Blanche had to get rid of all her animals, including Chiva, the black and white goat that gave up her milk for Blanche's kids. Fireball was gone long before that, captured and made into chicken soup by a local who got tired of being woken up at four in the morning.

A souped-up Malibu with a muffler that sounds like a motorcycle pulls up into the driveway of the shiftless renters next door. A man opens the door and creeps out.

"I see a guy getting out of a car next door."

"Never mind about him," Mom says, exasperated that I don't see anything else. "They come and go at that house all night long."

Cholo is standing in the spot where the passion vine used to grow, barking at me as I look out the window.

"Stop, you mangy dog!" The dog runs around in a half circle and barks toward the chain link fence, cringes, snarls, barks again.

"What's wrong with the dog?"

"He sees Jesse's spirit. Los animales see the spirit world."

Cholo's barking gets all the dogs in the neighborhood going. One by one, the dogs start barking, some louder, some softer, until an eerie howl sounds, and the last dog stops barking.

"This is spooky."

Mom is insistent. "Do you see my mijito? Is he wearing his uniform?"

"No, Mom, I don't see Jesse." I'm looking hard, scanning the dark, expecting what?

"I heard his voice tonight. Jesse's voice!"

"You were dreaming."

"No! My eyes were open. I could barely hear him, but it was him talking to someone—other men. Voices. He promised me, don't you remember, Teresa, promised me at the airport that I would hear his voice again!"

"Con calma, Mom. Calm down. Jesse said all kinds of things. He said we'd read about him in a book, too."

"If only I had listened harder. I don't know what he was trying to tell me." My mother bursts into tears. The curtain slips from her hand. Cholo stops barking and is now whimpering. A solitary dog barks in the distance, then stops.

"Ay, he's leaving!" Mom turns and walks slowly back to bed, holding on to my arm. Suddenly, she is weak again, frail. I help her lie down, easing her head back on the pillow. She's crying, her shoulders heaving with every sob. I take a Kleenex from the box on the nightstand and hand it to her, switching on the lamp. In the light, I notice her face is flushed. I put my hand on her forehead, and it feels warm. I know the pain in her legs is excruciating, but she's stubborn and won't take prescribed pain pills. I'm wondering if I should call Dr. Mann and tell him Mom's hallucinating. There's a part of me that wants to think this whole thing is a nightmare and I'll wake up soon.

"Ay, Teresa, your face looks horrible! You need to see a doctor."

"Don't worry about my face. You feel hot. Do your lungs hurt?" I look closely at her for signs of the weariness I've come to identify as the pneumonia she's battled with twice this winter.

"Mom, you were dreaming. Go to sleep."

"No! I heard your brother's voice."

"Why would Jesse be waking you up?" I play inside my mother's head. It's no use trying to force reality. The real and the invisible are clouds my mother moves in and out of without noticing the difference. She looks matter-of-factly at me.

"Why would anyone wake me up at night? Jesse has something to tell me. Him and his friends."

"Friends?"

"Voices . . ." She searches the dark again, straining to hear.

"What were they saying?" I ask her.

"Who knows? They were whispering! Ay, Santo Niño help me!" she cries. "What is it I have to do?" She looks over at the image of El Santo Niño and tears start again. I brush them off her face and feel I'm the mother, and she's the child. I'm wondering if Elsa, my oldest daughter, will someday feel the same way about me. She'll look at me and think I'm crazy for waking her up in the middle of the night.

"Something in my chest is heavy, mija. There's something I have to do."

Since Jesse's death, my mother feels all her pain in her breastbone. It travels through the center of her chest and meets in her back between her shoulder blades. She holds on to the pain with one hand.

"Don't think about it. You need to rest."

"How can I rest when there's something I have to do? Didn't you hear anything?" She holds my hand and listens one more time. The action makes me cock my head to listen, too. If only I could hear my brother's voice, now, in this house! I would cup my hand around it and seal it forever into the grooves of plaster on the walls.

"Do you think Jesse forgave me? Ay, mijito! He suffered so much for me, que pena! Why didn't I throw your father out?" She sits up and starts coughing, gasping for air.

"Mom, stop accusing yourself! You're making yourself sick." I pat her back and give her a drink of water.

"Is the room warm enough for you?" I look over at the orange coils of the electric heater. "It's so cold in this house! Just like my dad to go off and die and never fix anything."

"It doesn't matter, mija. The other world is catching up to me anyway, just think, I might have to put up with your father and Consuelo after I die. God knows, I should have buried their bones together!"

"They're probably in Hell, Mom. You'll never see them."

"Maybe I will, and maybe I won't. God knows what He will do with those two. May they rest in peace, even though they never gave me any peace!" She touches my aching face gently. "See, here's my nightmare . . . your face, to tell me I should have left your father years ago. Why didn't I fight them both? That's why Jesse went to Vietnam. He couldn't stand it anymore! Will my son ever forgive me?"

"Mom, he's forgiven you. Stop this! Look at me. Do you think I'm proud of what happened tonight? Mom, it was wrong, but I lost control. I've kept things inside for so long, and Jesse's part of it, too."

"You remind me of your nana. Remember how she argued with Consuelo at church? Can you imagine . . . and on the day of Our Lady! Ay que mi ma! Here, let me help you, mija. I have medicine in the kitchen, peroxide."

"No. Mom, you need to rest. I'll get the medicine. Don't worry, I'll rest, too, in my old room."

"What about the kids? And Ray, mija. Are you leaving him?"

"For good this time, Mom. I'll talk to the kids tomorrow. Cisco's been wanting me to leave his dad for a long time. Lisa and Lilly are only fourteen. They're so young to be going through all this. And Elsa—well, she'll be mad at me."

"Elsa's closest to Ray. Es su consentida. Remember how he cried when she was born? She's always defended her dad."

"Just like I did sometimes."

"Did you want me to leave your dad?"

"Mom, that was a long time ago. Stop making yourself miserable." As I say the words, the phone starts ringing.

"It's Ray, already," Mom says.

Will this night ever end? I glance at a picture of St. Rita hanging in the hall as I make my way to the phone. St. Rita, the saint for desperate cases. St. Rita's face has the pious look of someone in deep suffering. She was famous for putting up with her cruel husband. So great was her love for Christ's passion that she asked to suffer in the same way he had. In answer to her prayer, a thorn from Christ's crown struck her on the forehead and caused her terrible pain until the day she died. Imagine wanting to suffer! I brush my forehead with my hand, probably the only spot on my face that doesn't hurt. I'm far from wanting a thorn stuck in it. St. Rita won Heaven for all her troubles. The only thing I feel I'm winning for my troubles is Hell.

I grab the wall phone and hear Ray shouting on the other end. "Thanks for the big scene you made at the club. The manager canceled my contract! What a bitch!"

"Canceled it? You liar! You'll be playing there next weekend with Sandra at your side. Don't give me that shit!"

"If you'd listen . . ." I slam the phone down and unplug it from the wall. Ray always accused me of not listening to him. In my mind, he never listened to me. I never told Ray the dream about my left ear, and the fact that tonight I was listening in the dark for voices my mother says she heard. I've never told Ray any of my dreams. I tried a few times, and he only half-listened as if he was hearing a news report he didn't care about. There are tears at the corners of my eyes, brimming over, falling down my face, stinging the swollen, cut places.

I open the kitchen door and Cholo runs up to me, wagging his tail and jumping on my legs. Cholo's ears are pointed straight up and look like the tips of my mother's pruning shears. He's furry like an Alaskan husky and short like a cocker spaniel. His fur is the color of straw except for a white *x* on his chest that looks like the work of an artist's paintbrush. I remember Duke and the melancholy swish of his tail, slow-moving Duke who lived to be a hundred in dog years. Cholo's jumping, sniffing at my legs. "Down boy, get down!" He runs to the oleander bushes growing against the back fence and starts barking again.

"You're not Duke! You didn't even know Jesse!" I'm shivering, trying to stop my teeth from chattering. It's dark, just like the mornings after Jesse's death. I still can't believe the passion vine bloomed until November the year he died.

"Jesse?" I whisper his name. A breeze blows through the pink rayon bathrobe.

"Mom's sick, Jesse. And look at me. Ain't I a sight for sore eyes! Ray and Sandra. You remember Consuelo? Well, like mother, like daughter. I've got Sandra." I taste tears dribbling down my swollen lip. I do a pantomime in the dark, searching for the invisible with my hand. Pretending I've found Jesse's hand, I hold on tight until my knuckles turn white. I look up at the sky. Clouds are huge ink spots floating overhead. Everything is quiet. Whatever was out there is gone. I hear a gunshot go off in the distance, once, twice. It scares Cholo, and he howls. Welcome back to El Cielito, the place I said I'd only come back to visit. Jesse would be surprised to know the old neighborhood sounds like Vietnam these days with everybody owning a gun.

I walk by Mom's room on my way to bed. She's wide awake. The glow from the veladoras makes her look ghostly.

"Did you find the peroxide? And ice, mija, don't forget an ice pack. All this trouble, but Ray will get what he deserves. Remember all the bad things your father went through. Sandra will never compare to you, mija. Ray will regret all this, le va poder. Try to sleep now. Jesse will keep his promise."

I want to ask her what promise he'll keep, but don't say anything. After all these years, Mom doesn't know I kept Jesse's secret, like St. Rita's thorn lodged deep in my flesh. Mom's voice sounds far away to me.

"El Santo Niño will let me know what all this means in the morning." I look at the image of the Christ Child and wonder what *His* voice sounds like.

Solitary Man •

El Cielito passes by as we ride down Buckeye Road to Sky Harbor Airport, the first week of January, 1968. Nana's sitting in the front seat between Mom and Dad. Jesse's sitting in the back between me and Priscilla with Paul on his lap. Paul's nine years old and Mom says he's too big to sit on Jesse's lap. Dad grunts and says there's nowhere to put him, unless he sits in the back of the station wagon on top of Jesse's baggage.

Jesse's dark like my dad and not much taller than me. He was always a skinny kid who wore plaid shirts to make his chest look broader. His shoulders eventually filled out and toned up when he got into boxing. His eyebrows are two smooth, straight lines, not shaggy ones like Dad's. When he talks, his voice fits into my ear like a seashell.

"Just think, Los Tres Reyes are delivering gifts at the house right now," Nana says. "We'll have to open them later and mail yours to you, mijo," she tells Jesse. It's Nana's way of trying to make us smile.

"Yeah, the Three Kings," Jesse says. "I forgot about them . . . sure, Nana, mail them to me."

The morning is cold, dark, looks like rain, or maybe it's tears starting. I don't know if what I'm doing now is part of Jesse's funeral or his welcome home.

Ol' man Perez is sitting outside his dry-cleaning shop on a lawn chair. He looks like a mannequin wearing a Stetson hat he dry-cleans once a year.

"The cheapskate," Dad says.

"Pobrecito," Mom says. "How old is he anyway?"

"Who knows. He's been there a hundred years."

"Wasn't his daughter a little run-around, una cabroncita who went after anything in pants?" Nana asks. I know she's giving my dad una indirecta, talking about Consuelo without really saying her name. Dad says nothing, just keeps his hands on the steering wheel.

"She's married," says my mom.

"No!" says Nana. She says the word like it's a big joke.

There's El Rancho Drive-in, where you can chain your car up to a speaker and watch the latest thriller. Guys with cars are the lucky ones. They get to take their girlfriends to the old El Rancho, nicknamed El Rancho Grande, and fake watching the movie. All they really want is to make out and find out how far they can go. It's pretty easy to tell who's gone too far. The girlfriend drops out of school and pretty soon we see her working at Woolworth's so she can make enough money to pay for diapers and formula, and if there hasn't been a shotgun wedding, her boyfriend is back at El Rancho Grande with another girl.

Neighborhood kids stand on rooftops and watch the movies all night. They make up dialogues and jump from rooftop to rooftop looking for the best angle to watch the movie. Chicano spidermen, they have the cartoons memorized. On nights when the moon is full, they play astronaut and fake a landing on the moon. Below them, the grown-ups sit on lawn chairs, sipping beer or Kool-Aid and talking about the time a big canal flowed right where the middle row of speakers now stands. It's a wonder, they say, that the speakers don't electrocute everybody, for sure there's water down there.

"What's showing?" Jesse asks. "Hey, what? What does it say?"

He really wants to know. I stoop low to watch the marquee from the window of my father's Ford wagon. "Huh, D-A-R-K, oh, *Dark Shadows!*" I tell him.

"Gotta see it when I get back," he says and smiles. "Relax, sis, relax."

The Golden Gate Gym is up ahead. The building looks wet in places where the paint is discolored. The door isn't open yet. I can't see the ring where Jesse used to box. I remember the sour smell of boxing gloves and tennis shoes.

"Didn't those guys ever wash their feet?"

"Some of them didn't even have soap to wash them in," Jesse says,

"Oh, by the way, tell Trini I'm gonna kick his butt when I get back. He won't mess with a sarge!" Then he laughs. "Love that ol' man. He sure got me some good fights."

"What good fights?" Mom asks. "What about that scar from Andres El Animal?"

"It was a fair fight, Ma."

"Can I touch it, Jesse?" Paul asks. "Go ahead." Paul traces the faint outline over Jesse's left eyebrow with his finger. El Animal's handiwork when Jesse was El Gato and boxed featherweight in the Golden Gloves.

Pete's Fish 'n' Chips is whizzing by, but it's closed until eleven o'clock. "Gee, and I wanted some fish and chips," Jesse says.

"After all those tamales last night?" Priscilla asks.

"Yeah. Wish I could wrap those tamales and take them with me to Nam, Baby Doll."

Priscilla smiles because Jesse still calls her Baby Doll, even though she's a freshman in high school.

"I'll send you some at Christmas, mijito," Nana says from the front. She keeps looking at Jesse in the back seat through the rearview mirror. Jesse waves to her. "Hi, Nana, Hi! Love that little viejita!" He reaches over and rubs her neck. Mom grabs his hand and kisses it, turning around as far as she can to see him dressed in his Army green. "You look so handsome, mijo. Don't let those big gabachos run you over. You know how those white guys can be."

"Nah, Ma, I got lots of friends in there, besides Chris. We all have the same thing to do so we gotta stick together."

"Did Armando get back from Vietnam?" Dad asks.

"Who, Betty's son? Quien?" Mom asks.

"Yeah, he did," I say. "I talk to his sister at school."

"Was he Army?"

"No," Jesse says, "Air Force."

"Just what I told you, Jesse. The Air Force is the best. That's how I made it through World War II. We blasted the hell out of 'em before the Army even got there."

Jesse sighs. "Yeah Dad, you told me." I see my dad's jaw set squarely down. He won't fight now. I know that. There's too much in the air, there's no room.

"Remember when the people went out to the train station to say good-bye to the men going off to World War II?" Mom asks.

"They would light fires all night long waiting for the trains to come in," Nana says. "Everybody hugged everybody and women gave La

Oración Del Justo Juez, the prayer of the Just Judge, to the men for protection."

"You were there, Alicia," Dad says, "to say good-bye to me. Remember the song?"

"What song?" I ask Mom.

" 'Sentimental Journey,' " Mom says. "We all sang that song. Everybody was sentimental back then, even people who didn't have men leaving for the war."

"Nobody sang it like your mom," Dad says. "I left with her voice right here." He points to his heart. Mom looks over at Dad. Nana shrugs her shoulders.

"Sing it, Mom," Paul says.

"Maybe later . . . later."

"When I get back," Jesse says. He looks at me. "What's Armando's sister's name, Teresa?"

"You mean Annie?"

"Yeah, Annie. She's cute. Tell her to write to me."

"Espi's gonna write to you."

"Espi's your friend. I've known her all my life."

"Didn't her brother Ray come back from Vietnam?" Mom asks.

"He just got back three weeks ago. He's starting up his band again."

"You're blushing," Jesse teases.

"Why? I don't like Ray. He's too old!"

"Yeah, right!"

"Was he Air Force?" Dad asks.

"He was Army."

"He should have gone Air Force."

"Write to us, Jesse," Mom says, "every day if you can, mijo." Her voice trembles. Both women start crying.

"What is this? Both of you quit it!" Jesse puts one hand on Nana's shoulder and one on Mom's.

Nana starts a wail, "Ay mijito . . . Ay Dios, why didn't you stay in college? You're so smart!"

"Don't start, Mama," Mom says.

"La Oración Del Justo Juez. Do you have it, mijo?" Nana asks.

"Yep."

"Keep it in your pocket. Don't forget the prayer. God will protect you. Your enemies won't even see you. Porque la guerra? I don't even know any Vietnamese. Why do you have to go there?"

"I'm patriotic, Nana . . . listen, *Oh, say can you see by the dawn's early light* . . ." Jesse sings the first line of the "Star Spangled Banner." "This is one Chicano they'll remember, you'll see. I'll make up for all those guys who've been blown away."

Mom and Nana cry louder.

"Bad timing," I tell him.

"It'll be OK, Mom," Jesse says, trying to raise his voice above the crying. "Look, there's Herrera School."

"Ya, mujer, quit it, will you?" Dad says to Mom. "I met him—Sylvestre Herrera himself. He won the Medal of Honor in World War II. A great man."

"Their baseball team was good, but ours was better," Jesse says. "We beat them so many times in baseball, remember, Teresa? Chris went there when he first came to Phoenix, then he got some sense into his head and went to Lowell with us. Knucklehead. It took him a while. Remember that game I pitched, a no-hitter, those escamones were terrified. They had never seen such lightning hands."

Jesse grabs Paul in a bear hug, and they both laugh.

"Chris wanted to dance with you last night, Teresa, but you acted all pesetuda, like you didn't give a damn about him. I told him, Ah she's just a snotty cheerleader, thinks she's got enough guys to throw up in the air."

"You didn't!"

"Chris drinks too much," Mom says, blowing her nose on a tissue.

"Just last night, Ma. You know how that goes. The vato's cool."

"You don't like him, Teresa?"

"Maybe I do and maybe I don't."

"He wants you to write to him."

"I'll think about it He's too good-looking for his own good. Every girl wants him."

"I wish I had that curse," Jesse says, laughing. Then he leans over to me and whispers, "I don't think I'm coming back, Teresa. Take care of Mom."

I feel as if someone just plunged a needle into my arm.

"What?"

"What's wrong, Teresa?" Nana asks. She catches a glimpse of my face in the rearview mirror. "You look like you just saw the devil."

"Nothing," I answer. My hands turn cold.

Jesse wrestles with Paul as if he didn't say a thing to me, both of them laughing. He puts one finger up to his lips for me to see.

"Hey, guess what, everybody," he says out loud. "Someday I'm gonna be famous. You're gonna read about me in a book. I'm gonna make history!"

"Really, mijo?" Mom asks. The crying turns to sniffles.

I pull Jesse's sleeve. "You'll be back!" I whisper, trying not to attract Nana's attention. He whispers back, "I don't think so, play it by ear." I want to scream, *Dad, stop the car and let me out, NOW. I can't take this anymore.* I press Jesse's hand into mine. "Yes, you *will.*" I insist. I know what he wants. This is a secret I have to keep.

"Your hand is cold." He squeezes my hand, warming it up in his own.

"Yeah, Ma, I'll be famous, you just watch."

We all laugh because nothing is real. We don't even know what the inside of the airport looks like. We've never been there. Everybody we know lives in Arizona. We're on our way to St. Anthony's, or to the Japanese Gardens to get my mother some sweet peas.

"How far is Vietnam?" Paul asks.

"On the other side of the world, what do you think?" Jesse says. "The people walk upside down. That's why they wear those cone hats, to keep themselves balanced!" We all laugh, like it's the funniest joke in the world, even Dad.

We're passing the Smitty's Jesse and I rode our bikes to on Sundays just to get a Coke from the machine. The Black Canyon Freeway loops to the south of the store, just a few feet away from Food City, the cheapest place in town to buy food. It's seven o'clock in the morning; traffic is picking up. The sun is climbing over the freeway, making the day come alive.

My dad brakes at the stoplight, and we see Tortuga crossing the street.

"Roll the window down, Teresa. I gotta say bye to Tortuga." Jesse shouts through the open window, "Hey, hey Tortuga, don't you know me ese?"

Tortuga is wearing a fatigue jacket over a pair of Levi's. He looks every bit a turtle with his neck sunk into the collar of his jacket. The green jacket looks like a shell over his scrawny back. He's got on army boots with no shoelaces. He walks up to the window and looks in. Tortuga's face is inches away from mine. His breath smells like a stopped-up sink.

"Buenos dias! Look at this, the whole Ramirez family! How's everybody today?"

"What's with the fatigue jacket, Tortuga?" Jesse asks. "I'm the one going to Nam."

"Orale, Jesse, you really headed for Nam?"

"Check out my rags. Where'd you get your jacket?"

"My nephew, you know Leo, he's over there. He sent it to me."

"You mean Leito? The little kid? I thought he was only seventeen."

"Naw, Jesse, he turned eighteen and enlisted."

"I'll be damned."

"Hey, Jesse, do me a favor. Tell him his mom is going to pieces over here watching the news. He better come home quick before she does herself in. . . . You got a couple of dollars on you, Jesse? My ol' lady threw me out on the streets last night, esa vieja pinche!"

"Don't cuss at your wife, Tortuga," Nana says. "She's a good woman."

"She's a little devil, Abuela, you don't know her."

"Here." Jesse pulls a twenty-dollar bill out of his pocket. "Take it, buy some food for Mauricio."

"Muchos thank-yous Jesse, you were always the best! Hey, man, don't forget El Cielito, OK? Come back to us, hermanito." Tortuga's eyes fill with tears. He walks around the car and starts running down the sidewalk.

"Can't wait to get his bottle of wine," Dad says.

"Pobre," Mom says. "His son Mauricio must cost him a fortune. He weighs about 200 pounds! Can you imagine? Tortuga drinks his life away, and his son eats himself to death! What a pair!"

"I see Mauricio at school, Mom, and all the kids make fun of him," Priscilla says. "Poor Mauricio, he doesn't even fit in his desk."

"Poor, nothing," Nana says, "Quien le manda. Nobody forces him to eat like a pig."

Up ahead we see the sign: SKY HARBOR AIRPORT. My stomach does a Ferris wheel turn. Mom and Nana start the tears again. I hold on to Jesse. He pats my arm. "Relax, sis. It's OK, Teresa." I watch his every move. I want him to wink. I want him to show me a sign that tells me what he said to me isn't true, but he doesn't. He only smiles. I want to grab his face in my hands and make him look into my eyes and tell me he's coming back. I know he doesn't want me to. I hold on to his hand, Priscilla holds on to the other. Paul wraps his arms around Jesse's neck.

"Didn't know everybody loved me so much," Jesse croons. "Love, love, love . . . hey I loves you, too!"

Dad parks the car. For a few seconds, we sit motionless watching

Army men, Marines, a few Navy go by. We listen to Nana and Mom's sobs. Nobody wants to be the first to get out, then Dad opens his door, and all the other doors fly open at the same time. We are wooden figures, stiff-knees forcing ourselves out. Jesse grabs his bags from the back and gives the smaller one to Paul.

Father Ramon, round and red-faced, is already waiting for us with three of the Guadalupanas, Nana's friends, old ladies who look like gray swallows. They are the sisterhood from St. Anthony's Church who venerate the dark virgin, La Virgen de Guadalupe. They look like birds circling to land, swallows chirping out the singsong prayers of the rosary. They know what they have to do. They are here to pray, to make sure Jesse is covered over with God's blessings.

Mom's best friend, Irene from across the alley, didn't come. She's Jesse's godmother, his nina. Her heart is broken, grieving over her son, Faustino, who was killed in Vietnam only last year. It was all she could do to talk to Jesse on the phone before he left. Irene still sleeps with the American flag from her son's coffin under her pillow and a veladora burning for his soul in front of the image of the Sacred Heart.

I look around to see who's staring at the Guadalupanas and see Chris with two other guys. He said good-bye to his parents in Albuquerque then flew into Phoenix so he'd be on the same plane with Jesse. He waves to us. We wave back. Everywhere there are women holding on to their men. We press around Jesse. He lifts both bags onto a loaded flat bed. An army man arranges the bags on top of the stack.

"Are they labeled?"

"Yep."

"You're set."

We pass the big bronze sign at the entrance: WELCOME TO PHOENIX ARIZONA THE VALLEY OF THE SUN. Women everywhere are crying, or getting ready to cry. The men are mostly standing around looking miserable. White tissues and handkerchiefs wave like miniature banners.

The airport's walls are painted with murals of the colonization of the Southwest. The Spanish conquistador Cortés, in full armor, greets the Aztec emperor, Moctezuma, who is dressed in an elaborate robe and a huge plumed headdress. Another scene shows the ancient Aztec god of war, Huitzilopochtli, luring his victims in for the kill over a sacrificial block atop a pyramid. Waiting at the top of the pyramid is a black-hooded executioner brandishing an obsidian knife. A few yards from the scene is Padre Kino in black robe and sandals holding up a crucifix, blessing an Indian peasant who kneels at his feet. Next to Padre Kino are rugged pioneers in covered wagons traveling into a distant view of sky-scrapers and busy highways. Senators Carl Hayden and Barry Goldwater stare down at us. The background is saguaros, cholla, barrel cactus, a colorful sunset, and a roadrunner fleeing a coyote. Last of all is a painting of the Grand Canyon, the pride of Arizona. The airport is crowded, people are rushing everywhere. I smell breakfast cooking and coffee brewing from the fast-food shops. THE COPPER STATE SOUVENIR SHOP boasts copper planters for sale and copper ashtray souvenirs.

Mom is kissing Jesse, stroking his hands one by one, kissing each finger, then the inside of his palms. She leans into his chest to hear his heartbeat, smoothes back the stiff uniform around his shoulders and only lets him go long enough to let my dad hold him tight. I hear the drone of the Guadalupanas, the penitents, making amends for the war, searching out God's ear. "For this one, for this one man. Yes, keep him safe, por favor Virgencita, Justo Juez, Father God. Holy Mary Mother of God, pray for us sinners now and at the hour of our death. Amen, amen . . ." The wrinkles around their lips barely move. Their chanting makes the whole place sacred. I can almost smell incense, seeping in through the air-conditioning vents, making a fragrant cloud appear to ease God's war-torn spirit and defy the Aztec war god's feathered talons.

We are a funeral procession, walking, hoping not to get to the place where we will have to say good-bye. Jesse is crying now. He brushes his tears away with the back of his hand. Mom is still holding on to him for dear life. I hear a wail beginning to sound from Nana. She sways to and fro as if she's rocking Jesse to sleep.

"Keep the prayer close to your heart, mijito. La Oración Del Justo Juez. Don't forget how much we love you. Ay Dios mio! Ay mijito!" She makes little crosses in the air with her thumb, blessing Jesse over and over again. Jesse holds me tight one more time. I take a deep breath to inhale the scent of my brother forever, to hold his spirit deep inside.

"Don't forget what I told you," he whispers. "Take care of Mom." I nod. My hair gets caught in one of the buttons of his jacket. We laugh.

"I love you." We say it at the same time.

He looks into my eyes. "It's just something I feel, OK, maybe I'm wrong." He smoothes back my hair. "Don't worry, things will be all right."

I want to argue with him, convince him. "Jesse, please come back . . ." He turns around to kiss Mom, then goes down on one knee to hug Paul. Paul hides his face in Jesse's shoulder. Jesse takes his cap out of his back pocket and puts it on Paul. "See, you're a big guy now. It's OK, tough guy. Just remember, take care of the little guys and help Mom." He gets Paul to do a little sparring with him. "Yeah, you got the right stuff! Talk to Trini about Paul, Mom, he'll be a good boxer, too."

Priscilla and Nana hang on to Jesse as he stands up. "Don't cry, Baby Doll," he says to Priscilla.

"Don't go," Priscilla sobs.

"I have to, but you know I love you. I gotta have a letter from you every chance you get! And keep playing sports, maybe you can even get Teresa to throw a ball around every once in a while."

Jesse turns to Nana. She's holding her handkerchief up to her nose. She's not wearing her glasses.

"Nana, where are your glasses?" Jesse asks.

"In my pocket, mijito. I don't need them. All I want is to see you come back home again! Every second I will pray for you, always. Keep La Oración Del Justo Juez close to you. I gave the prayer to Chris, too."

"Ay que mi, Nana, don't cry so much! I don't want to cause you any more white hair!"

I reach for Jesse before he goes back to Mom and Dad. "Jesse, you'll be all right?"

He looks at me. "Yeah, you bet!" He smiles big. His smile makes me feel good and I smile back.

Now he's in Mom's arms again. "Mom, Mom . . . God, Mom, stop crying so much! Everything will be fine. I love you . . . you're the best Mom a guy could ever have. Mom . . ." he kisses her forehead.

"Ay mijito, my son . . . you're my world. Ay mijito, you have to come back to me! The war doesn't matter. It's you I want back in my arms! It's your voice I want to hear again!"

"You will, Mom, I promise you, you will."

Now Dad is holding Jesse, patting both shoulders gruffly. "Grow eyes in the back of your head, mijo. Don't depend on anyone to look out for you. Run like hell if you have to. I don't want no war hero, I want my son."

"Yeah, Dad . . . OK, take care of everybody, especially Mom." He looks into Dad's eyes, and Dad knows Jesse wants him to stay away from Consuelo.

"Yes, mijo. Seguro, sure. I'll be there for your mom." They both smile at the same time. It's the first time I've seen them look at each other eye to eye and separate as friends.

We start walking again, Mom and Dad on either side of Jesse, me next to Mom. Two women walk by dressed in identical flowered pantsuits. They're saying good-bye to a Navy man. We pass them by. Jesse, Mom, Dad, Nana, Priscilla, Paul, the Guadalupanas, Father Ramon, all of us walking together until we have to let Jesse go. Father Ramon steps ahead of us and raises his hand over Jesse's forehead to give him the official church blessing. He draws a big cross in the air. Father Ramon looks like Padre Kino blessing a convert. I look around to see if anybody's staring at us. Everyone is busy with their own good-byes. Girlfriends and wives are hanging on to their men. Jesse wanted Mary Ann to come to the airport, but she didn't want to. He tried so hard to have a girlfriend, but never did.

Outside the huge windows, I see the plane waiting: US AIRBORNE. It is a commercial airplane, and will make two stops before heading for Vietnam. The Black Canyon Freeway stretches out in the distance, bordered by the purple ridge of the South Mountains. Chris walks up to me and gives me a big hug. He is tall and I have to reach up to put my arms around his neck. His face is fair, his features chiseled to perfection.

"Teresa, you're the most beautiful girl I've ever seen!" he whispers. "Write to me—yes?"

"I will." I answer without thinking. Chris flashes me a smile that gives me goosebumps. Priscilla gives me the look that says "I knew you liked him!"

"Sorry about last night," I say.

"Sorry for what?" We both laugh and he kisses me good-bye, a simple kiss, the kind you can give in front of your parents.

Father Ramon stands next to Mom as Jesse and Chris walk away. Chris turns back, waves to me, blows a kiss. Everybody waves back at the same time. I blow a kiss. It's so natural. Everybody's doing it. Jesse waves to all of us, smiling, walking backward like he's balancing on a tightrope. Then they both disappear into a group of civilians and a scattering of green uniforms, mute figures, prey for the god of war. I can't tell which one is Jesse anymore.

Everybody rushes over to the windows to see the men board the plane. We can pick out Jesse from the others now, because they're walking in a line, and he's shorter than most of the other guys. I see dark clouds moving in from the east and worry that the plane will get caught in a thunderstorm. The plane's flattened wings lie dormant. It looks unreal, a grounded paper airplane with black slots for windows. The plane's red lights are blinking. Jesse climbs up the steps and turns one last time to wave toward the windows. He can't see us but he knows we're there.

"Ay mijito, my son, my son . . . oh God, my son!" Mom is chanting her own lament.

She stops abruptly and starts digging into her purse, She grabs my arm, "Run, Teresa!" she yells. "I forgot to give Jesse el cochito." Jesse's favorite cookie is wrapped in a paper napkin, gingerbread in the shape of a little pig.

"The plane's leaving, Mom. They won't let me give it to him." I can't imagine trying to explain el cochito to the pilot.

"Try, mija, try!" My mother is crying, pleading. There's nothing left to do but hold tight to el cochito and do a zigzag run up to the man standing at the gate. By the time I get there, everybody's staring at me.

I'm catching my breath in gulps. "I have to give something to my brother! He's on the plane to Vietnam!"

"I'm sorry, but they've already boarded the plane." The man gives me a big smile.

"You have to give this to my brother. My mom's going crazy!" I hold the cookie up to him.

"What is it?"

"A little pig."

"A what?"

"A little pig . . . like a gingerbread man . . . except it's a pig. It's my brother's favorite cookie. He's on his way to Vietnam." I'm talking so fast I can hardly say the words.

The man looks at me like I've lost my mind. "I'll try," he says. I hear him on the two-way radio. "I've got something for one of the men headed for Nam. Ah, can you send someone out to get it? . . . Over."

He opens the paper napkin and stares at el cochito.

"Roger. What is it? Over."

"A pig. Over."

"A what? Over."

"I mean it's in the shape of a little pig. It's a cookie, Ralph, for crying out loud! Ever hear the story of the Gingerbread Man?" I see him smile again. "Anyway, his mom wants him to have it real bad. Over."

"Who's the guy? Over."

"Sergeant Jesse Ramirez," I say.

"A Sergeant Ramirez. Over," repeats the man.

"Roger, sure for a sarge, I'll do it. Over and out."

We wait a few minutes. My mother is frozen in position, my dad at her side. I can almost hear a drumroll sounding as we wait for an airline stewardess to appear. People are staring at us. The man hands the little pig to the stewardess.

"A little pig," she says, "How cute!"

I smile back. "Thank you."

The stewardess turns and walks away. A hush falls over the crowd gathered at the windows. We wait until the stewardess boards the airplane and the plane taxis down the runway, lifting itself up into the darkening sky. I hear sobs starting again and people talking. We're actors on stage, and nobody knows what to do next. Slowly, people start moving away from the windows. I look over at Mom. Her knees bend suddenly, as if she just sat down in a place where there should have been a chair. For the first time in my life, I see my dad pick my mom up in his arms like she's a little girl.

• LATER THAT DAY we laughed because Jesse stalled the plane to Vietnam. If we had known any better, we would have kidnapped the pilot and turned him into a real pig. Instead, we went home and turned on the evening news that told us the war was escalating with no end in sight. I bit off my fingernails. I was trapped between a raging war and Jesse's words. I put his words away and told myself it wasn't true. It couldn't be true. He was just saying that just in case. I couldn't see the end of Jesse. I had watched him from my cradle, tracing his features in my mind before I learned to talk.

"Turn it off!" Dad yelled, "Turn the damn thing off!" Priscilla and I stayed in our room the rest of the night listening to "Solitary Man," Jesse's favorite song.

Tlachisqui •

The night Jesse's plane soared into Vietnam, Don Florencío, El Cielito's old seer, said he saw a flock of bats fly out of La Cueva del Diablo. They were in a frenzy, screeching, darting across the sky, and circling the face of the moon four times. The bats were seeking the four directions, Don Florencío said, north, south, east, west, black, blue, red, and white, searching for blood.

"I shouted at them, mija, with all my might! Go, you bloodsuckers, chupones de sangre! Go, go, fly to Vietnam . . . ALL! ESTA MI RAZA! And they flew, mija, and there was nothing I could do but chase them screaming like a madman with my arms flapping in the air. And I cried, big tears, an old man's tears to make God look at me. If he looks at me, it will break His heart, I reasoned, and He will stop the war."

• DON FLORENCÍO WAS the only visionary Jesse and I ever knew. He lived along the banks of El Río Salado, and nobody ever visited him unless they were sick, and needed relief from one of his ancient remedies, or had bumped into his shack in the dark in a drunken stupor. The old man was dark-skinned, small-boned, his body hardened by miles of walking, climbing, living by his wits. His long black hair smelled like ashy mesquite wood. His legs were bowed a little and he always wore boots. He said his legs were living proof of all the burdens his people had been forced to carry for the Spanish patrones. Don Florencío could speak Nahuatl, the language of the Aztecs, which used to be called mejicano, the same language Malinche taught Cortés when he landed in the new world. Don Florencío claimed to be a direct descendant of the Aztec people, declaring himself a tlachisqui of the Mexicas, la gente de razon, the people of reason, as they were known. He told Jesse and me stories of magic, visions, men who could turn themselves into animals, and the power of invisible forces both good and evil.

The old man's shack faced east on the rocky banks of El Río Salado. La Cueva del Diablo, a huge, hollowed-out hole at the base of a rocky hill, faced north. La Cueva del Diablo was boarded up many years later, condemned and dynamited out of existence, but when we were kids, it was a black, yawning gap spewing out the stench of bat droppings.

La Cueva del Diablo produced nothing but dark, flinty rocks and peals of laughter from scoffers who mocked the men who had gone through the trouble of taking pick and shovel and laboring for days in the hot sun, searching for gold. Pan for gold by the banks of El Río Salado, why don't you, the scoffers said, and some people did. Don Florencío said they were all fools like Cortés's men. There were no Seven Cities of Cibola, cities of gold as the Indians had related. The dead were the last to laugh after all. The land was the gold, but the Spaniards couldn't see it.

Everyone said La Cueva del Diablo was occupied by a ghost who slept by un entierro, a stash of gold someone buried and forgot about, or was murdered before he could return to claim it. Why a ghost needed money was a mystery to me. Yet, for years the ghost had taken possession of the land and the cave and el entierro. People were afraid of the ghost and stayed away from La Cueva del Diablo and Don Florencío's adobe shack. The old man only laughed and said we were descendants of people who had once made their homes in seven caves, living in harmony with all living things, in Aztlán, the land of whiteness, the land of the Aztecs, la gente de razon. Aztlán was north of what we now know as Mexico, and no one has ever been able to determine how far north its boundaries extended.

Tata O'Brien, my Irish grandfather on Mom's side of the family, befriended Don Florencío. Tata O'Brien's cohort of old-timers included Indians, Mexicans, full-breeds and half-breeds who stuck together for the single purpose of defying modern times. Aliens to the code of progress, the old men crouched in circles in our backyard, passing around Don Florencío's ironwood pipe with the sculpted faces on the stem, filled with tobacco, sweet-smelling stuff, fragrant sagebrush. In the winter, they hid in the folds of thick blankets woven by their Indian wives and warmed themselves before fires blazing with mesquite logs. Sometimes their women came with them and sat in the alley next to our house with their children, passive Indian faces unmoving. Some of the old men had warred with Geronimo, or Pancho Villa, or Zapata. By then the lines of rebellion were blurred and having served in any war was better than not having served at all. They were descendants of warriors, after all, legendary warriors who fought to the death for the privilege of riding on the crest of the rising sun.

Concrete, iron, and steel didn't impress the old men. They had lived between mud bricks in adobe houses that kept them warm in the winter and cool in the summer. They traded with Tata O'Brien mesquite wood, blankets, and ceramic pots for vegetables and chili from Tata's famous Victory Garden, named for the miraculous harvest it produced during the years of the Great Depression. Tata was fascinated with growing chiles. He grew jalapeños, chiles japones, chili de arbol, serranos, chili pequin, and chili tepin. The last two always sounded the same to me. He fussed over the plants, and worried they wouldn't be hot enough, or the crop would suffer damage through cold and frost. He wanted me to grow up and be the U.S. ambassador to Chile. He figured a country with a name like "Chile" would grow only the very best chiles. "Bring back the pods, Teresa, that's where the seeds are. I'll do the rest."

When Tata O'Brien lay dying, Don Florencío came over and built a small fire in the backyard. He hunched over it, throwing sacred meal into it every once in a while and smoking his ironwood pipe with the little sculpted faces on the stem. The sweet, pungent smell of tobacco blended in with the mesquite wood of his fire. Don Florencío made an offering of smoke to the four directions for Tata, north, south, east, and west, and to the sun and moon. He said in the old days his people stopped at every river before crossing it and the huehues, leaders of his tribe, blessed the river, toasting it with aguardiente, asking its permission to cross over. "It's always wise to salute nature," he said, "especially when the spirit of a friend is about to join it." Dad said Don Florencío was smoking peyote and that he smoked the pipe to dream about the other world the way the Chinese used opium. I never believed him, because everything Don Florencío said to me and Jesse made perfect sense.

Jesse and I were the only kids from El Cielito who visited Don

Florencío at his adobe shack. Mom didn't like it, but Tata never wavered. What kind of disrespect was that? he said to her, the old man was one of his friends. Jesse and I couldn't stay away, the old man was our lure, his crackling voice answering the burning mesquite wood. Our own medicine man, Jesse said. Sometimes Don Florencío threw sacred meal into the campfire, making purple-orange sparks appear that sputtered and danced before our eyes. And we danced too, Jesse and I, although we didn't know actual Indian dances. Still, we jumped around the campfire while Don Florencío played his wooden flute. We were powerful, we were the visions people have in the night of ghosts and nahuals who throw their spirits into animals and walk in the woods at midnight.

Don Florencío believed in Aztlán. He told us the history of Aztlán while he tended his small campfire in the evenings and smoked his ironwood pipe. We sat on burlap mats. Don Florencío's legs were sturdy stumps under him. He sat stiffly on an old wooden chair with a seat made of straw, held together with twine. He lit his ironwood pipe and began.

"It was like this, mijos, oh, so many years ago, I can't even think that far, but God knows. Our people were living peacefully in seven caves in Aztlán, somewhere north of Mexico. The Aztec they were called, the Heron people. Later, they became the Sun People. There was war among them, mijos, one god against another, but more than that, it was evil men trying to gain control of the tribe, frightening the people into slavery. Quetzalcoatl was cast out by the god of war, Huitzilopochtli. The priests of Huitzilopochtli were madmen who spoke for the god. They wrapped his body like a mummy and told the people they were now the voice of the god. What stupidity! The people might have questioned why they had to leave their beautiful homeland, but the priests by then had gained power over them. Go south, they told the people, south, until you see the sign, an eagle perched on a cactus, with a serpent in its beak, there build your city. Can you imagine how far they must have traveled? Pobre la gente de razon, with little food, huddling like sheep, listening to their god. When they saw an eagle sitting on a cactus with a serpent in its beak, they knew it was the place to build their city. This happened in the year 2-House. In our time, it was 1325. They named the city Tenochtitlán, and today we call it la capital de Mejico. Later the Mexicas tried finding Aztlán again and to this day they are still in search of it.

"It was at that time that Quetzalcoatl, the Aztec god of peace, Sky Serpent also called Ce Acatl Topiltzin, Our Lord I-Reed, was tricked by evil deities into committing incest, a terrible thing, and finally fled the shores of Mexico vowing to come back. In 1519, when Cortés arrived on the shores of Yucatán, the Aztec emperor Moctezuma believed him to be Quetzalcoatl, the fair-skinned god who would return to take over his empire. Do you realize what that meant, mijos? Moctezuma thought Cortés was a god! If they had only seen clearly, ay, mi gente, they would have seen that he was a demon instead!

"It was time for the empire to be destroyed anyway, mijos. Huitzilopochtli was bloodthirsty. He consumed human hearts. Many of my ancestors had already fled the capital and settled in the mountains, joining other Indian tribes. Later, centuries later, I left to cross the border myself and search for Aztlán."

"Did you find it?" I asked him.

"Find what?" he asked, as if he had just forgotten what he had said.

"Aztlán!"

"No, mija, I'm still searching for it. Maybe you and Jesse will be the ones to find it, you're Mexicas, too. And look," he said, pointing to Jesse, "Your brother has an Ixpetz, a polished eye, that can see through the nature of things and find their true meaning. In the old world, he would be celebrated for his bravery and fearlessness."

Jesse pounded his chest, "Aii! Aii! Does that sound like a warrior? What do you think?"

"Good try," I said.

Don Florencío said he knew this about Jesse, because he had seen the spirit of a warrior rise in the fire when he fed it alum the day Jesse was born.

"The flames rose so high I became frightened, and in the center, I saw a warrior with a plumed headdress. Just then, your tata arrived at my house to tell me Jesse had been born!"

• THE DAY AFTER Jesse was killed, I walked to Don Florencío's shack, forcing myself to put one foot in front of the other. Don Florencío was sitting outside his adobe shack on his old wooden chair. The sun was setting, Don Florencío was facing east. He had a fire going, burning copal. I knew it was copal because it was aromatic, sweet. The smoke was cleansing the air around him of evil spirits.

He saw me trudge up to his shack and never said a word. He was smoking his ironwood pipe with the sculpted faces on the stem. My voice was gone. A whine began from deep within my breastbone. I had never heard it before. I moved toward the old man and knelt by his side.

I clung to his neck, holding on to him for dear life. Over and over again, I let out the tone of a melody that never varied. The pitch was the same, and it came in great gulps. Again and again it came, and the birds answered me, chirping in the distant cottonwood trees.

"You cry like our ancestors," Don Florencío said to me. "They cried with their souls, not their eyes. That is the way to mourn, to mourn with all your heart. They accused us, mija, of sacrificing to the bloodthirsty god of war, our priests who carved out human hearts. A horrible thing to do, not in keeping with the teachings of the true God and his mother Tonantzin that you call La Virgen de Guadalupe. But look, there are men now, greedy for power, like the priests of Huitzilopochtli. They sacrifice our young, your brother and many others to war, war that has no hope of ending—bloodthirsty, ha! And they said we were bloodthirsty! But never mind, Jesse will return, mija, in a new form. Our people have always walked the earth."

I thought about Don Florencío's words when we met Jesse's coffin at the airport after days and days of waiting. The Army said they had sent his body to the wrong address. Even in that, they betrayed us, treated us less than human. I stared at Jesse's body through the plastic lid, dressed in Army green. I had no words to say how I felt, only shouts, tones, and pitches I had never heard anyone else make.

Don Florencío made me a tea from a flower he said was shaped like a heart, yoloxochitl, the yellow flower of the heart that heals tlazotlaliste, the sickness of attachment, the fever of affection. I drank it and the cry inside me went away, and eventually I was able to speak again.

We buried Jesse next to Tata O'Brien. Later Nana was buried with them, and after her, Annette, Priscilla's six-month-old baby. Don Florencío died months later in one of the caves that bordered the hills close to his shack. It was right that he died in a cave, that's where he said we came from, like Christ, birthed in a cave. He was taken off in a body bag like the guys in Vietnam. Since there were no relatives to bury him, the neighbors who knew him pitched in and bargained with Murphy's Funeral Home for a cheap burial. The Murphys were competing with Phoenix First Funeral Home for all the bodies coming home from Vietnam, and those left here dying of heartache. Because of their greediness, God punished them, and Phoenix First Funeral came out ahead in the end. It all happened because Murphy's didn't close Esteban Luna's head after his motorcycle accident and a pinkish fluid oozed from the crack around the circumference of his skull. After that, nobody wanted to be buried by Murphy's because they didn't want to be oozing in their coffins, even if they were dead.

When Don Florencío died, the Murphys were on a campaign to win back their business. The whole family smiled together at his services. They were like a string of flashing Christmas lights. When one was winking, the other was blinking. They dressed in black as a rule, and only broke the color code by wearing navy blue on occasions when people died during the holiday season. That was their most festive attire. Their daughter, Marie, was a scandal. She had wild red hair that was shocking to the other family members. At funerals, in broad daylight, it looked like it had been set on fire. Finally, Marie hid her hair under huge hats, and that comforted the family.

The Murphys buried Don Florencío in an old pioneer cemetery for only fifty dollars as a service to the community. The cemetery was overgrown with weeds and short, stumpy trees with misshapen limbs. They marked his grave with a wooden cross, and eventually the cross was blown away by the wind. It was fitting. Don Florencío wasn't in his grave anyway. Neither was Jesse. *A new form* . . . I had forgotten Don Florencío's prophecy.

• I THINK BACK, now, at what Don Florencío said, the words of an old man steeped in legend and magic. Jesse, a warrior? Perhaps. I don't believe warriors are made in the womb, no matter what the old man saw. There are plans, evil plans that take over the minds of men and search the deepest recesses of where hatred lurks, ready to spring. The beginning of a war may take place in an office building with windows overlooking the White House, or in the meanest hovel deep in the jungle. Soft, manicured hands can sign decrees of death and war, as can dirty, blood-crusted hands in villages where people no longer expect the sun to rise. War is the battleground of the human heart where avarice, hatred, greed for power, for money, for land, are allowed to thrive. The Godless man begins to sense that in the entire universe his right to live in the manner he chooses is the only way to live. The disorder in his soul is the beginning of war.

Private War •

Morning comes and goes with no word from El Santo Niño. My old bedroom has warmed up enough to make me want to stay under the covers. If my face didn't hurt so much, I probably would. The adrenaline that ran through me last night is gone, leaving in my body a tender, open wound. I have plans to search the house in broad daylight and convince my mother that the voices she heard were only a dream. I'm wondering if it's me I'm trying to convince. I find out by way of a weather report that the mist hanging in the air the night of the voices was a low pressure point, a cloud that dangled too close to earth. So that explains the hazy air—but what about the rest?

My mother's always been a dreamer, dreaming dreams for everybody, why not this time? Mom's good at seeing the insides of things. Maybe she's like Jesse, seeing with an Ixpetz, a polished eye that looks through flesh as easily as seeing through glass. She could see my father's weakness, the darkness in him that led him away from her to find his match in his lover, Consuelo. He could never be Mom's equal. He was earth, flinty rock. She was wind, an invisible stream he could never hope to touch. She knew us, too—her children—stole glances into our souls. If she knew Jesse would never come back, she didn't say it. That was one line of truth my mother never crossed.

Mom's got a good memory, too. She didn't forget anything Jesse told us at the airport. I've tried to forget what he said for the last thirty years. I never understood why he told me he'd never come back. His words got caught in the chambers of my heart and flowed out to every cell in my body. My head, eyes, feet, skin, every part of me knew. My mind battled the truth and a war began inside me. There's nothing worse than a private war going on inside you every day. I should have climbed on the plane with Jesse, I would have been better off in Vietnam, at close range, waiting for the words to come true. I was in my own Vietnam anyway, whether anyone knew it or not.

What do you want from me now, Jesse? I couldn't do anything to help you in '68. But I'm here taking care of Mom. Isn't that what you wanted me to do? That sounds like I'm mad. Maybe I should have been here a long time ago, should have put my life on hold and come back to this freezer of a house—cold in the winter, hot in the summer. Dad had the gall to die before he got proper heating in the house, just like him to miss something so obvious. So now I'm talking to spirits! Already this house is taking me over, and I'm acting like a kid.

Jesse's voice is no clearer than the voices already in my head, not to me anyway. Maybe to Mom. She's the one who believes in Houdini, in handcuffs breaking off just before Houdini starts to drown in the sea. Out pops Houdini, alive and well. The Great Escape Artist Numero Uno; but not in death, the Great Houdini couldn't escape death. He sent his wife a message from the beyond, something that had to be deciphered by a medium. Is that what Jesse's doing, sending us a message?

My mother is patient like Houdini's wife. She wasn't always that way. She was a meek mouse when I was a kid, to keep peace in the house. Still, I knew she could be as fiery as Nana Esther and her sister, my Tía Katia. Jesse's death changed all that. There was a part of her that got on the plane with Jesse and never came back. After Jesse was killed, she didn't care anymore if my dad came home or not. She never sang songs anymore, Mexican ballads when she cleaned the house, soft songs when she held me in her arms, and loud Spanish hymns at church. Her voice was a warm hand in a soft leather glove when she sang. It fit perfectly into my soul. According to her, she could shush my worst colic attack as an infant with a simple lullaby. That's how I know I heard my mother sing before I was born. Jesse wasn't there—nothing mattered to her. Slowly she came back to life, months and months, two years, a mummy uncoiling. When it was over her eyes were two blank holes the Egyptians forgot to seal.

She didn't talk to anyone in particular the whole time, mostly she sighed. Eventually she learned to shout again, like she did at Jesse when he fought with Ignacio just before he left for Vietnam. Ignacio, Consuelo's oldest, drove down the alley every other day in one of the cars he had resurrected from the pile of junk in his mother's front yard. He was a hungry wolf, lean and bony like his mother. He drove down the alley next to our house to whistle at me. Ignacio wore a small black hat cocked to one side and a perpetual smile that said, "Hey, what can I say, your old man is sleeping at my house!"

Jesse was on leave from Fort Benning when he saw Ignacio's brown '55 Chevy with the missing hood creep down the alley. The next time the car went by, Jesse was at the end of the alley, hiding in a tree. He jumped out from the tree onto the car's roof and dented it right over Ignacio's head, knocking off his hat. When Jesse's temper unraveled, every muscle had its own name. His boxer instincts took over and his energy screwed this way and that like a jackal darting bullets. He was El Gato again. I was glad I was his sister and not his enemy.

Before Ignacio knew what was happening, Jesse had jumped off the roof of the car and slugged him right through the open window, making Ignacio miss the turn into the street and run into Irene's chicken-wire fence.

My mother yelled at Jesse at the top of her lungs. "You want to get yourself killed? There's three of them for every one of you!"

"He's the one over here! I'm sick of my dad's shit! Tired of letting him run all over you!"

"Your father's not worth it! Do you see me crying? It doesn't matter. Your father will pay someday. God isn't blind!"

It took a long time for my mother's words to come true, that God wasn't blind. Years later, my father got cancer on the same hip the U.S. Air Force had operated on after World War II. My dad said they didn't know what they were doing, pushing pins into his hip like he was a slab of meat hanging in a freezer. It got so painful for him as the years went by that in his old age he couldn't get himself to Consuelo's house unless he crawled there. Consuelo went to see him in the hospital when we weren't there.

"Let her," my mother said. "She's dying, too. What can they do except hold hands and pray that God will forgive them?"

I want to fold up into a fetal position in my old bed and shut all the memories out of my head but can't, because my face hurts if I lie on my side. I want to hear my mother sing again, now! It's been so long since she sang solos at St. Anthony's. It was a hot, humid day in June when we were told Jesse was gone. The electric fan in the choir loft barely moved the air around us. Then everything turned icy cold, death rose before us, bigger than the cross of Christ, jeering at our stubborn faith. My mother's voice froze in her throat, and she never sang again.

The morning is cold today, brutal. Invisible fingers point my way, accusing me of losing at the game of life. I vow to put a restraining order on Ray so he won't show up at Mom's. In the next instant, I vow to go to Sandra's house and tell her what a whore she is. Then my thoughts cross paths, and I vow to leave Sandra and Ray alone so they'll die like Dad and Consuelo did. I make a pledge to call Priscilla and tell her she's a hell of a daughter, coming over once a week to look in on Mom. I vow to yell at Paul and tell him the next time he breaks his probation he'll get nothing from me. I vow to stop thinking about sleeping with Ray. Hail Mary, Holy Mary, Virgen de Guadalupe, pray for me that I won't freeze in this house so Ray won't have the pleasure of burying a blue corpse with Sandra standing by my coffin laughing. The bitch would have the laugh of her life! God forgive me for thinking this way. I really want to be good. I never wanted to get my Holy Communion dress dirty. Where did that memory come from? Never! It wasn't my fault I dropped a cup of punch on it and stained the silk material under the layer of lace. What a pity, my mother said, now Priscilla won't be able to wear it. Maybe that's why I did it. Forgive me God, I really want to be good!

I feel the top of my head with my hand. My hair is cold from the draft seeping in under the drapes. My chest is aching. I've learned how to hold pain in my breastbone like Mom does. Mom's good at letting the invisible creep in and crawl into her lap. I watch the invisible from afar, marking its movements with caution, afraid to let it move in too close. Thoughts spin circles in my head, long tails lashing, collecting fragments of other thoughts, unfinished sentences that refuse to become whole. The impossible is frightening to me. I don't want to struggle with things I don't understand. Yet I can't deny there was an energy in the house last night, something tangible in the air, not powerful like a bolt of lightning but steady and absorbing space like raindrops that never fell to earth. I didn't hear voices as Mom did, but I wanted to. For a few seconds, I was able to suspend logic in me and quiet the part of me that doubted my sanity. I scanned the air with my left ear, the one washed clean in my dream. I was afraid I'd hear something and disappointed when I didn't.

The memory of my brother fighting Ignacio was only the beginning of an avalanche of memories that would assail me at Mom's. Memories would elbow in, demanding my attention, making all the secret places where I hid my brother's death rise and erupt in me like the watery explosion I saw in my dream.

• THE NEXT MORNING I call Lisa and Lilly, my fourteen-year-old twins. They're just getting up and don't know their Dad and I split up.

"I'm over at Nana's. Start packing your stuff. We'll talk about it later."

"Why?" Lilly asks.

"I'll tell you later."

"Tell me now." She's as stubborn as Mom.

"Let me talk to Lisa." The girls are fraternal twins, alike in so many ways, except personality. Lisa is easier to talk to, more open to reason.

"Hold on. I've got a call on the other line."

Finally, I talk to Lisa and halfway explain they'll be staying with me at Mom's.

"There's lots of reasons. Nana's sick, too."

"You and Dad are splitting. We've known it all along. Is Cisco coming, too?"

"There's no room. He can stay with Dad until I get us a place."

"Elsa's gonna get mad."

"Elsa doesn't control me. She'll have to get over it."

Lisa sighs. "Are you all right?"

"No, but I'll get better. Don't be surprised when you see me either. You might say I've been in a little accident."

Two days after Christmas, a deputy sheriff dropped by to serve a subpoena on me for assault charges.

"I should be charging her! Look at my face, does this look like I fought by myself?"

"I don't know anything about it, ma'am," he said, uninterested. "All I do is serve subpoenas."

"I'm a schoolteacher. I've never had any trouble with the law."

"Nobody's a criminal until proven guilty, if that's any comfort. If I were you, I'd get pictures . . . of your face . . . you know, before and after. You got any witnesses?"

"I can't think of any."

"If it's your word against hers, it'll be hard to prove," he said, handing me the papers.

Miniature Islands •

M y mother doesn't hear the voices again, unless she does but doesn't tell me. She tells Priscilla and Paul about it and Irene, who believes in everything, including rumors of sightings of La Llorona. Who knows if her son, Faustino, wasn't one of the men talking to Jesse that night, Irene says. My mother agrees, yes, of course, Faustino and Aurelio Dominguez, the boy who lived two streets from us. His folks moved back to Mexico after his death. Actually it could have been more, Mom says, there were so many! My mother's mind is closed to anything Paul, Priscilla, or I tell her that doesn't fit in with what she has decided to believe.

There's no way I can hide my face from anybody. Paul says I've joined his ranks . . . the ranks of street fighters who aren't afraid to take on an enemy in public. I look at my face in the mirror and apply the cream the doctor prescribed, three times a day. The welts are now purple scabs. I feel powerful and ashamed at the same time. What am I teaching my children? What example am I setting for my daughters, especially Elsa, her husband Julio, and my three-year-old granddaughter, Marisol? Elsa will be mad, Lisa says. Of course she'll be mad, she's daddy's girl. Now I'm wondering if I would have gotten mad at Mom if she had ever left Dad, and I wasn't even daddy's girl, maybe Priscilla was. It must hurt to see your parents separated, no matter how hard life is between them.

Paul says I was right to jump Sandra, but I'm not so sure. Is there ever a time when violence is the *only* way to deal with a situation? Then again, isn't that what war is about? Nations forget common sense, common interests, and make public enemies of each other.

• IRENE CHECKS UP ON Mom daily by phone and walks over at least every other day, but she's got her own health problems, varicose veins that run like purple cords down each leg. She wears thick, flesh-colored stockings, even in summer when the temperature goes over a hundred.

Priscilla says Mom needs a full-time nurse to take care of her. I tell her Mom would never allow anybody to take care of her who isn't family, but she insists. If I had told her I was getting Mom a nurse, Priscilla would have argued that only family could do the job.

Priscilla, three years younger than me, is short and slim, with tight knots of muscles up and down her calves. When we were kids, nobody ever looked for us in the same place at the same time. In high school her hair was short and shiny, coiling into two curlicues at her cheeks; mine was down to the middle of my back, with waves of hair I soaked with hairspray so they wouldn't bunch up at the top of my head. Atoms of space between Priscilla and me were dot-to-dot outlines that connected us with identical profiles, foreheads, and eyebrows that looped over each eye with uneven scatterings of hair we plucked away with tweezers. I always thought Priscilla's eyes were closer together than mine. We ended up measuring the space between our eyes with a ruler, and the measurements were always the same. Priscilla criticized my height and I laughed at her short legs, telling her models were tall with slim, slick bodies men drooled over. I made the cheerleading squad at Palo Verde in my sophomore year, and she played varsity tennis, badminton, and softball.

"You're Priscilla's sister. I see the resemblance." Everyone said so, and behind Priscilla's back they always said I was the prettiest. After Jesse's death, the dot-to-dot pictures that connected us got split up. If I moved right, Priscilla moved left, if I visited Mom, Priscilla stayed away. If I stayed away, Priscilla went to see her. We were always passing each other by, and I didn't know why. "Why can't you get closer?" Mom asked. "She's your only sister." Then I'd try, because I still remembered combing Priscilla's hair and letting little strands of hair at the end of her ponytail tickle my lips. I remembered evenings we'd sleep with Mom in her bed, one on each arm, watching the pattern of light from veladoras flicker overhead, making rings like halos for saints we named after our dolls. Sometimes we'd tangle our arms around Mom's neck, pinching each other to try to make one of us lose our grip. We kept it up until my mother said we would end up choking her to death, then she would push both our arms away.

There were times Mom insisted I call Priscilla, and finally I would. One of her boyfriends would answer. There was always someone new, and it started a knot growing in my throat. I wanted to yell at her to get some sense into her head and make her stop searching for love. I knew if I yelled at Priscilla over the phone, she would hang up on me like Mom hung up on Tía Katia when they got mad at each other. By that time, Priscilla had her son Angelo and had lost her baby Annette. Losing Annette almost cost Priscilla her mind. The baby was six months old when she died, apparently without cause—crib death, the doctor said. Everything Priscilla had gone through with Jesse's death came back to her when Annette died. It was as if time had not passed for her, and Jesse had never gone to the war. We buried Annette next to Nana Esther and Jesse. When Priscilla saw Jesse's grave, she knelt down and hugged the head-stone and lay her head on it, as she had laid her head on Jesse's shoulder at the airport.

Paul, the youngest of our family, doesn't have much of an opinion about Mom's health. He figures we women will take care of everything. A few years ago, he spent time in prison for possession of drugs. Before Jesse died, Paul was this normal kid, loving life, playing pranks on Priscilla and me, growing up safe, Jesse's little brother, thinking about being like Jesse. When we lost Jesse, it was as if Paul had been thrust into a cage. That's the way I saw him in my mind, locked in a cage of chicken wire, looking out, his eyes mournful, the dark lashes stuck together with tears. He turned into a disturbed kid at school, one that had to see the school counselor. After a while, teachers lost patience with him, his naughtiness turned into all-out rebellion, and his pranks became criminal acts: van-dalizing the school, riding around in stolen cars with his friends, and buy-ing liquor when he was still a minor. Paul's life was a turbulent storm, thundering and out of control.

Ironically, Paul's son, Michael, is gifted. He was tested at school and came out with an IQ of over 120. Summertimes, Michael spends his time studying in a special program for brainy kids in Scottsdale. Michael's got big, gray eyes and a bottom lip that protrudes over his top lip when he's thinking hard about something. His hair is short and spiky at the top. Recently, Michael had braces removed from his teeth. His dental work was donated free of charge, by a dentist who suffered with crooked teeth all his life and wanted to help kids in a similar situation. I have to credit Priscilla for taking Michael to all his dental appointments, and there were many. When Michael graduates from the eighth grade next year, he'll be sent to a summer program at the University of Arizona to study science and math. Michael's mother was someone Paul knew in high school. Neither one of them graduated. Paul eventually got his GED in a prison program. The two met years later and struck up a relationship. By that time, Tina was living on her own. She had been a foster child for years, a hard life for her. After she had Michael, she turned him over to Mom and Paul, saying she needed to move on, and she'd be back. To this day, we've never heard from her. I wonder about Michael, the product of an ex-con and a foster child. Where did all his intelligence come from? Life is uncanny. Appearances are only an illusion. Intelligence is not a birthright after all, but a gift. Michael talks like a university professor, and I have to keep reminding myself he's a kid and my nephew besides. Another one of life's unanswered questions: How did Michael get so smart when his dad's been in and out of trouble with the police all his life? The relationship is hit-and-miss, with Paul gloating over his son's brains, and at the same time frustrated at not being able to deal with a child so bright that family members consider him a genius. When Paul was in prison, Michael lived with Priscilla and was like a brother to his eight-year-old cousin, Angelo. Now he refuses to live with Paul and treats Priscilla as if she is his Mom and her boyfriends are his uncles.

Paul's lived with Donna for the past four years. She's an ex-addict my mother nicknamed "la gringita." Donna surprised Paul the last time he was picked up for parole violations by joining the First Assembly Church of God and giving her life over to Jesus Christ. Now Paul is preached to every day, and it's hard for him to go on using drugs. He threw her out twice, saying she reads the Bible too much and prays in weird languages. Then he went looking for her at church because he felt guilty for throwing her out just because she was trying to be holy. "Ay, la gringita," Mom always says. "She's so white she looks like a ghost."

"Except for her tattoos," I remind her. Donna adores Mom, and no matter how many times she splits with Paul, she's at the house checking up on Mom. The pastor from her church set her up with doctor's appointments to start the process to remove her tattoos. Donna says she wants to be clean inside and out. I've gotten used to Donna's tattoos, especially the tiny unicorn on her left shoulder that seems to spread its wings when she moves her arms up and down. I'm making plans to call Donna and have her help me take care of Mom.

Tía Katia was helping Mom before she had a stroke that paralyzed her and eventually took her life. Mom sat with her, helpless, sometimes with Irene at her side, chanting the rosary, watching her only sister die, wishing out loud that she could take her place. Tía Katia suffered months on end, and there was nothing her brood of kids could do except spray her mouth with water, because she couldn't swallow whole drops. Her kids argued over who was doing what for her until finally she wouldn't accept water from any of them. Her tongue got flat like the wooden stick a doctor uses to check your throat, and the whites of her eyes turned yellow.

Jesse and I always considered Tía Katia's husband, Bernardo, our favorite uncle. He died two years before Tía Katia did. The bones on his back formed a mound of cartilage that made it hard for him to breathe. Then one day he had a seizure that threw him flat on his back. The shock of the fall made Tío Bernardo spit up phlegm that he couldn't clear from his throat. This stopped his breathing entirely, and Tío Bernardo died as he always said he would, with his shoes on. I still remembered Tío's half-smile, lopsided, gentle, his fingers long and tapered, the hands of a musician, only his deformed back never allowed him to play an instrument. His fingers, warm and comforting, slipped through mine at Jesse's funeral and steadied me as I walked back to the white limousine that whisked us away to the funeral home.

• THE SAME PICTURES look down at me every day from the walls at Mom's house, brown faces, with black pits for eyes, haunting me. Jesse in his uniform, Priscilla, Paul, Mom and Dad, an assortment of wedding pictures. And there are religious pictures too, the Sacred Heart of Jesus, the Guardian Angel walking the children over the bridge, St. Rita, La Virgen de Guadalupe, El Santo Niño de Atocha, St. Michael the Archangel. Sometimes the faces seem to feel sorry for me, other times they seem to be mad at me or laugh at me, mocking me for what happened with Sandra. Ray's betrayal—didn't I see it coming? Couldn't I smell it like the mothballs stuck in Mom's closet? Who was I really fighting that night—Sandra or the ghost of Consuelo? I think now I was fighting myself, punching myself awake, making the pain surface, letting the explosion I saw in my dream go off like dynamite in my head.

We were a family back then, the pictures show it—even though we lived under the shadow of Dad and his lover, still we were together. The storms were something we lived through together. It all ended after Jesse was killed. Jesse was the fiber that welded our family together. We were rudderless without him, drifting on separate rafts. Sometimes we drifted so far from each other we became miniature islands. We lost sight of each other, gliding into dark waters and a sullen, empty sky like the one Jesse flew into when he left for Vietnam.

The last thing we did as a family was wait for Jesse's body to come back from Vietnam. The stillness of Mom's house at night reminds me of how we waited. We waited so long, we almost lost hope. The Army had sent his body to the wrong address. It was Lent at our house back then. The statute of Our Lady of Sorrows with the dagger piercing her heart and the big cross of Christ were in procession through every room. I understood her pain now, the pain of Our Lady of Sorrows. In my mind's eye, I still see the candle I lit for Jesse at St. Anthony's—the candle he asked me for in his letters. The candle's thin flame flickered so small in the huge dark church, I was afraid it would die out, and I'd never see Jesse again.

I don't remember if we ate anything while we waited for Jesse's body to come home. I know Dad drank coffee and tequila and smoked. I know Nana rocked back and forth in her rocking chair and wrung her hands in despair. I know Mom sank into her bed, draped the windows with blankets and didn't light the veladoras. She was getting ready for the worst migraine of her life, the first after she had been healed at Brother Jakes's revival when Jesse and I were kids, and the last she would ever have. After that, Mom kept the pain of Jesse's death deep inside her breastbone, until the day she died. Priscilla, Paul, and I didn't have the strength to talk on the phone to friends. Dad told them we were asleep. My voice was gone. Where? How did it disappear? The hole that appeared when my mother was sick with her migraines came back again. It yawned dark and menacing in the kitchen. I put my hands over it and felt its vibrations, icy cold. I went around it, and my dad asked me if I was crazy.

El Ganso •

At Mom's, I walk into Jesse's old room. There are boxes stacked up against the walls, old towels, kitchen supplies, plastic bowls and plates, a pair of metal tongs sticking up from one box, picture albums in another, a box of old *Life* magazines, bathroom rugs, mismatched toilet seat covers, shower curtains with color-coordinated plastic rings, kids' books from the Lowell School Library, and textbooks from Palo Verde. In a plastic bag are Jesse's letters, bound together with rubber bands.

Some of Dad's clothes are hanging in the closet. The smell of mothballs assaults me when I slide the closet door open. Mom's still taking care of Dad's clothes. Jesse's clothes are gone, Mom gave them all away after a year of holding on to them. She kept his school letter sweater with patches of baseball insignias sewn into the front, RAMIREZ 1965 under the left pocket. She kept the sweater and hung it in her closet behind all her clothes. The floor is bare, dusty, beige vinyl tile squares. Drapes hang at the window, the design is diagonal lines, brown and yellow. Mom thought they looked like curtains for a boy's room. I always thought the design looked like lightning bolts, all the wrong color. I lift a corner of the drapes and stare at the chinaberry tree in Mom's backyard. The tree is a fixed part of the scenery. It outlived Jesse and Dad.

I lock the door and read Jesse's letters as if I'm doing something forbidden. Opening the past all over again.

January 20, 1968

Dear Sis,

It's not what it looks like on TV. It's worse. The place is filthy, nowhere to go to the bathroom out in the bush, ants crawling all over the place, mosquitoes at night. I'm trying to write as much as I can but it's so hot, I'm sweating all the time and thirsty. Sorry about the letters. I know they look like I dropped them in puddles. I can't tell you how thirsty you get out here, it's like you've been walking in the desert. Walking with no place to go. Hills have a number out here. Sometimes the big shots get mixed up and don't know which hill we're on. Most of the guys out here are OK, but there's some assholes, like Major Cunningham, a gabacho who likes to volunteer for all kinds of action. I told him, stop volunteering our platoon, pendejo, what do you want, to see us all dead? We got enough to do. The vato wants to be a celebrated hero. He makes the rules in the rear and you know us, los Chicanos we're out there, front lines. I tell the guys shoot, cover yourselves, but it's hard when you look at the Vietnamese in the face. They're farm people, they look like a bunch of mi-grants bending over the rice paddies. They look so pathetic. Gabachos who have been here for a while say it's all a cover. They punch them around, beat them up, even the women. I can't, sis, it would be like hitting my nana or tata. I'm watching for Charlie but they all look the same.

I'm sending you a picture of the Mekong Delta. It's gray water all over the place. The jungle is so thick you could be a few feet away from somebody and still they couldn't see you. They count on that, the VC. I'll be damned if I didn't think of El Ganso the other night. Remember his long neck and how he swam with you back to shore when you almost drowned in the Salt River? He looked like a big old goose, que no? I was shaking back then, thinking Dad was gonna haul ass on me, even after I saw you were OK. Here I was walking in water up to my elbows. I laughed out loud and one of the guys pushed my head under the water cause he thought I had gone nuts and forgot Charlie was watching us from everywhere. I would have given everything I had to see you and El Ganso all over again.

Check out the red fingerprint. The dirt is red here. It's like the red rocks of Sedona. Remember when we went to Slide Rock? We counted stars from the back of Tía Katia's station wagon on our way back to Phoenix. Phoenix. I tell guys I'm from Phoenix, Arizona and it sounds like I'm saying I'm from Mars. Then I say El Cielito and they get the idea, cause los Chicanos always come from a barrio—Sierra Vista, El

Watche, Los Molinos, lots of others. I can't believe I was ever a kid play-
ing in the dirt in El Cielito.

*   I'll be writing as much as I can. Don't tell Mom what I tell you. I*
don't want her to worry, you know her. Light a candle for me at St.
Anthony's. You can't ever be wrong lighting a candle. And don't think
about that stuff I told you at the airport. There's no way I want to end
up a statistic, and if I do, I know I can count on you to take care of Mom.
Don't take it hard, sis, I don't know how to say things, I've never been
in a war before. You're the best sister, ever.

SWAK,
Jesse

P.S. Chris says to write. He's got a girl in Albuquerque, so my advice
is to write if you want, but don't let the vato fool you, sis. Tell Espi to
write to me.

I got to know my brother through his letters, the inmost parts Jesse
hid so well in the States. I got to know SWAK meant "Sealed With A
Kiss." I knew he was lonely, even though there were guys all around him.
He told me later it was better for him not to make too many friends, as
they could be dead tomorrow. His idea of what it meant to go to war
wasn't anything like what they taught him in training. He was fighting
people who looked like people we knew. He was visiting villages with
makeshift hootches that didn't look like enemy headquarters. There were
cameras and reporters all around. The VC were blowing the hell out of
them. The Tet offensive was raging and guys were still posing, talking to
their Moms from the jungles. They were so young. No surprise, that
America was making a Hollywood movie out of a tragedy.

Jesse remembered El Ganso in his first letter, but he forgot to men
tion Inez.

• I ALMOST DROWNED in the Salt River the time we went on a picnic
with Tía Katia, her hunchbacked husband Bernardo, and their five kids.
I was seven, Jesse was nine, and Priscilla was three. Mom was pregnant
but not with Paul. Her belly was rising like a small ball of masa under her
blouse that stayed too small, then went away. It was the only baby we
never got to see. "Something's wrong," Doña Carolina told her. "The
baby won't hold on."

Doña Carolina was El Cielito's curandera, and midwife, an expert in anything that pertained to giving birth. Her fingers were short and flat, and the tips felt warm on our skin when she gave us her own version of a physical. "Fingers have a mind of their own," she told me one day, "it's like being plugged into ten electrical wires." Doña Carolina's ten electrical wires sent her the right message about Mom, because she lost the baby I had named Inez. I knew she had to be a girl because Doña Carolina had tested my mom to find out what the baby was by swinging a needle on a string over her belly button. If the needle went clockwise the baby was a boy. If the needle went counterclockwise the baby was a girl. The needle spun around from left to right, so I felt good about naming the baby Inez.

Maybe Mom lost Inez because she suffered un miedo, a fear that gripped her when she heard that I had almost drowned in the Salt River. Fear, as Doña Carolina said, could claim a life by freezing it into place. Maybe that's why she prescribed a drink of water right after experiencing a fear to keep things moving. For once, water wouldn't have worked for me. I had already swallowed too much of the Salt River, and the only thing left to do was to spit it back up.

I had waded into the shallow part of the river with no problem until my legs got tangled in reeds that grew close to the bank. The reeds gripped my skinny legs like ropes, pulling me into deep water, and I started swallowing buckets full of the Salt River before anyone noticed. My cousin, Alfonso, nicknamed El Ganso for his long, goose-like neck, dove in after he saw me disappear behind a clump of reeds. It was the only time El Ganso's neck came in handy for me. I hung onto his neck for dear life and actually rode on his back as we made our way to shore.

"You were all wila, wila," he said. "So skinny you weren't bigger than one of the reeds. I saw you go down, down and when I didn't see you come back up, I figured I'd go in after you. Si, si, that's what I did." El Ganso talked like he was singing. Everybody said he was from a part of Mexico back in the mountains where everybody sang instead of talked.

El Ganso made it sound like everything just happened to be happening, and he never took credit for saving my life. He just yawned and went on playing cards with the rest of the men. He didn't care that he was a hero. El Ganso died two years later, when he was only twenty-five, in an accident at Jones's Granary. They said he fell into a reservoir full of grain and suffocated before anyone could help him. I thought about that and how unfair it was after he had saved me from drowning. Already death was crowding into my life, snuffing out Inez and suffocating El Ganso.

Jesse was waiting for me on the bank with a towel after the rescue. He threw the towel over me and tried to wrap me up like a cocoon. Maybe he thought he could squeeze the Salt River out of me. He never left my side the whole time. Tía Katia compressed the area under my ribs with the palms of her hands to make me cough up all the muddy water. "Ay Dios mio! Help me!" Tía Katia was shouting and calling on God, His Mother, angels, saints, and anyone else in Heaven she could think of to help me. I could feel Tío Bernardo's hands on the back of my head. I looked up at his face and saw tears running down his cheeks. It hurt to force up the water, and I could hear the Salt River rushing in my ears long after I was pulled out.

There were tears in Jesse's eyes as he held me close, patting my hair dry with another towel. "It's OK, Teresa. You're all better now. Don't cry anymore. Look, El Ganso's over there laughing and playing cards. It wasn't that bad." He was dripping wet, shaking, partly from being scared I would die and partly from thinking how he would explain it all to my mom and dad.

Mom and Dad didn't take it lightly when we told them. "We used to play there as kids," my dad said, "and nobody ever fell in." They were ready to jump on anyone who hadn't watched me close enough and yelled at Jesse for being the oldest and not preventing me from falling in the first place. My dad was already fingering the buckle on his belt, and Jesse was putting on his macho face. Once my dad's anger was flying there were few rules. I stood close to Jesse, knowing that if blows started I would be pushed away. Still, if I could have taken even one of his blows, I would have done it. My mother's light complexion turned a deathly white. She stood between Jesse and Dad, holding Priscilla in her arms.

"It's Katia's fault! Will you beat your son because my sister is crazy?"

The next thing Mom did was call Tía Katia on the phone. She yelled at her so loud Tía Katia hung up on her. No more than two weeks after my mother suffered this miedo, she lost Inez. Night after night, I dreamed about the Salt River and felt El Ganso's long neck encircled in my hands. More than once a plastic baby rode with me on El Ganso's back and I was sure it was Inez. Two blue, glassy eyes, like my doll's eyes, looked at me. "I'm sorry, Inez. I didn't mean it." There was no answer. I held on tighter to El Ganso's neck, hiding from Inez. Each time I woke up from the dream with a jump before El Ganso reached the riverbank. That was the first of many dreams I would have about the Salt River and El Ganso, except in my dreams I called the river El Río Salado.

• • •

• By 1968, we were all drowning. La raza was submerged by mainstream America, a submarine drifting under a sea of politics, prejudice, and racism. Barrios like El Cielito, ignored by the U.S. government, suddenly appeared on Uncle Sam's map. Chicanos who had never been thought about before were on the list of draftees. Uncle Sam's finger was pointing at them, ordering them across the ocean to war, a war that the President kept saying was a "conflict." Minorities always attract attention when there's a war, and Chicanos, descendants of Aztec warriors, have always made it to the top of the list. This was more than la jura, the police, picking up our boys on Saturday nights and pumping up charges against them to "teach them Mexicans a lesson." This was a game that said, We're gonna pay you for being over there, and if you don't want to go, we'll draft you anyway. So why don't you join up and avoid all the trouble? You know you don't want to stay in school, anyway. And lots of guys didn't. They had families to support, they had buddies over there. They couldn't pack up and run.

Everybody was on the move in the sixties. The Chicanos, the Blacks, Native Americans, flower children, drug addicts, demonstrators, everybody had something to say. Hearts in El Cielito were being plundered. La Llorona quit haunting El Cielito at night looking for her children. She flew over the Pacific to Vietnam and finally quenched her thirst for the children she had drowned so long ago. She wrapped her ghostly shroud around Chicanos and other Latinos who were being ripped apart from their bodies every day in the war and was satisfied at last.

We had depended on the smoke of candles lit before sacred images to reach God's nostrils, to touch the heart of Justo Juez, the Just Judge, and end the war. Instead, the twirling smoke turned into an obnoxious vapor that cast stagnant shadows everywhere. It wasn't anything formal or planned, it was haphazard evil, playing with our lives. El Cielito was a hearse, black, smooth, and silent. We saw skulls staring at us from the windows, grimacing. President Kennedy's death had not been enough, there had to be more. More deaths that we saw as blows against the poor, Martin Luther King, Jr.'s death and Robert Kennedy's, Che Guevara, and there were more.

Coffins kept coming home from Vietnam wrapped in American flags. We could have tolled death bells from one end of South Phoenix to the other. Our guys didn't stand a chance. Most of them didn't have money to go on to college. They were sitting ducks for the draft.

The Tet offensive raged on in Vietnam, making my mother quieter and more helpless than she had ever been before. She never stopped thinking about Faustino Lara, Irene's son, killed in '67. She had stood with Irene at her son's open grave, and now she stood alone waiting, keeping her thoughts to herself. Irene was no help because every time she saw my mother she burst into tears. "Ay, Alicia, may God spare you what I've been through! I pray every day for Jesse, mi hijado, si todos los dias, for God to stand by his side. May God listen to me. I'm his godmother! But why did God take my son? Why, Alicia, why?" She pounded her fist in the air, and my mother looked away. Mom never answered Irene's question.

Ray Alvarez, Espi's older brother, came home from the war in '67, the same year Faustino was killed. I met him when I was still a kid in grammar school and he was starting his freshman year at Palo Verde. He looked so tall and sophisticated to me, I never thought for a second I'd marry him. He was always hanging around when I spent the night at Espi's house. I talked to him about Jesse, and he described the way things looked in Vietnam. He didn't see much action because he stayed at base camp most of the time working as a mechanic. Ray wasn't crazy like Ricky Navarro. Every time I talked to him, I felt like Jesse would really come home. "I made it, Teresa," he said. "Jesse's no fool. He knows how to watch his back."

Ray played guitar and sang in nightclubs. Espi said he had women watching him all the time, women with false eyelashes, rhinestone earrings, and strapless dresses who wanted to go to bed with him. Espi told me Ray never showed much interest in women until he met me. At first I couldn't believe Ray was interested in me. He was suave, experienced, a man who smelled of English Leather and tobacco. On stage, he sometimes wore a white panama hat, which made him look like a Latin movie star. I could see myself hugging Ray, but I couldn't imagine kissing him, until later. There were so many times I wanted to be close to Ray, because he was somebody who had made it. Maybe I could learn something from him that would bring Jesse back home. Espi was the only person who knew what Jesse had said to me before he left—that he wouldn't be back. After Ray and I got serious, Ray was the second person to know. I told myself Jesse's words were only a warning, something he said just in case. Still, the secret gnawed at me from the inside, festered in me. I was seeing Paul again falling from the mulberry tree in the backyard after

Mom told me to watch him and make sure he didn't fall. Paul went too far, climbing out on a bare, brittle limb. I saw the fall coming and froze with fear. El susto took over my body, and I knew I'd never be able to save him. By the time I got there, Paul was lying face down in the dirt, his lip a bloody mess. If I told Mom Jesse wasn't coming back home, I worried she might experience a susto so great, she would die like Baby Inez did.

To make matters worse, Ricky Navarro from next door started sleeping outside on a cot almost every night. This worried Mom, and she wondered if Jesse would come back just as crazy as Ricky. There wasn't enough room in his house, Ricky said. For some reason space was real important to him after he came back from Vietnam, and he didn't like feeling crowded. "The world's crazy, Teresa," he told me one day. "La vida loca is everywhere. It's not any different here than in Vietnam. Those sons-of-bitches tried to kill me at the airport! Our own U.S. citizens, protesting the good, old American way! If I had known those fuckers were so ungrateful, I would have never gone!"

I hated the demonstrators. They were totally ungrateful. Didn't they know my brother was over there doing battle for their asses? President Johnson with his Southern drawl nauseated me. "Our boys are holding their own in Kee Sung." He couldn't even pronounce the names right. I wondered if any of his relatives had served in Vietnam.

There were times I watched the news on TV and looked for Jesse's face to show up with all the other boys running into trenches, walking through ditches and jungles. I wanted to see him to know he was alive, a movie star fighting for right when everything was all wrong, defending people who ran back to their villages every chance they got and played both sides to stay alive. If we were right, then that meant the Vietnamese were wrong. The twisted power of war dictated that those in the wrong had no right to obstruct those in the right, there could be no rules, right must always win.

• CHICANOS, HALF AZTEC, half European, hearts pounding, warriors from the past, sacrificed to Huitzilopochtli, god of war, were writing their names in blood so the sun could be fed and move over into tomorrow. That was Vietnam for us, for the Mexicas of Aztlán, la gente de razon, as Don Florencío would say.

Jimenez Elementary •

W e're starting a unit on Vietnam, boys and girls. Does anyone know anything about Vietnam? Let's brainstorm." Questioning faces look up at me. A few hands go up, the Vietnam War, the Vietnam Wall, rice paddies, cone hats, China, war, Li Ann's family is from there, they sleep when we get up. "I saw *Born on the Fourth of July*," says Andy. "Were your parents with you?" I ask. Andy shakes his head. The second grade has brainstormed itself out. My assistant Lorena Padilla and I arrange the children into small groups to research facts about the country. We agree that late January is the best time of the year to do a unit on Vietnam. We can go over information on Tet, the Vietnamese New Year's holiday celebrated in late January. Lorena doesn't know that living at Mom's has brought Vietnam back to life for me. Jesse's letters are telling the story all over again. Vietnam, so far away, sinister yet beautiful, sealed my brother's fate in its red earth. I trace over red smudges on Jesse's letters carefully with my fingertips. Having Li Ann Nguyen in class will help make things real for the kids. She was born in the U.S., but her mother was born in Vietnam.

I watch Lorena sifting through our picture files for any pictures related to New Year's celebrations in Vietnam and China. Lorena looks like she's twenty, though she's actually in her thirties. Most days she wears a ponytail, blouses tucked into jeans, and tennis shoes. I owe Lorena big time these days. She helped an assortment of substitute teachers the first two weeks of January while my face was healing. She likes to tease me about what she had to put up with: people who looked homeless, she said; one who brought in a trained parrot perched on his shoulder, a woman who everybody swears is the bag lady they see on their way to work, and a huge man, a dead ringer for a serial murderer advertised at the post office who ended up being the favorite of the class. All these people paraded through my classroom while my face returned to normal. There are still faint lines someone might notice if they tried, but I keep them concealed with Cover Girl make-up.

The assault charges are still pending. I've talked to an attorney named Sam Diamond. He was recommended to me by a friend at school who said that he defended her brother when he got into a bar fight. She said his nickname is Slick Sam, and I'm hoping his reputation will work in my favor. Slick Sam assures me that besides the embarrassment of it all, what else can happen? For sure, they won't give you time, he assures me. A beautiful woman like you, he says, an upstanding citizen, a schoolteacher for God's sake, a role model for the community who lost her cool in a fit of rage, a crime of passion. Yes, everybody understands passion, look at President Clinton! "Let me look at your face," he says, then gets so close I can smell his toothpaste. "Marvelous skin," he says. "Have you ever done any modeling?"

Outside the classroom windows, I see Orlando Gomez heading for recess with his first-grade class. They must be doing their "Snowman Project," as Orlando calls it. I notice some of the kids are still drying their hands on their clothes, always a sign that they're working with paint or glue. After the Snowman Project, the kids will make valentines to hang around the room and blow up red and white balloons. After that, they'll get ready for windy March by constructing paper kites with tails made of yarn. It's like clockwork in Orlando's class, the Snowman Project, the valentines, the balloons, the kites, and finally a huge caterpillar they build for the book *Inchworm,* which leads them into spring. Everybody says Orlando should have been a watchmaker because everything he does runs like hands on a clock, which doesn't say much for days when Fireman Bob and his famous Dalmatian, Spotty, visit the school for their fire drill presentations. On those days, Orlando holes up in the teacher's lounge and sends his assistant Millie to the auditorium with the kids. Today, obviously, he's happy, there are no interruptions, only routine duties.

The weather is still cold, although I know it will turn hot very quickly. For now, it matches my heart, cold, hard. I've filed for divorce.

Ray was served papers at the All Pro Auto Parts Shop where he's a store manager. I knew it would make him mad to get the papers in front of his employees, a taste of Sandra's subpoena at Mom's. Besides, I couldn't find an officer who would take the papers into the Riverside while Ray was performing. That would have been the best revenge. So cruel, he would say, what are you trying to do, ruin my career? And I'd tell him he deserved it for everything my dad did to Mom, for Consuelo the cobweb who never disappeared from our house, for Sandra, the Latin Blast groupie who clung too long, clung too strong.

Maps of Vietnam go up all over the classroom, with tagboard sentence strips, labeling important information in Spanish and English. Crayon drawings of Vietnam scenes are posted here and there. The children find out that waving good-bye to a Vietnamese really means "Come here." Last names are first in Vietnamese, and calling someone with your finger is an insult because that's the way animals are called. Lorena helps the children construct Vietnamese hats suitable for working in imaginary rice paddies. The children have plans to make mudholes out on the playground to try out their new hats, but I talk them out of it and promise I'll talk to their parents to get permission for them to make mudholes at home.

I tell the children about my big brother, Jesse. Real name, Jésus Antonio Ramirez. He always went by Jesse. He was killed in the middle of a battle right outside Saigon. I point to Saigon, Ho Chi Minh City, on the map. It was when all the crazy fighting was going on in 1968 after Tet, Vietnam's New Year's holiday.

"Wow! That was almost thirty years ago, Mrs. Alvarez."

"Yes, Brandon, but it seems like yesterday. When you lose someone you love as much as I loved Jesse, the years are nothing. Nothing." The last word leaves me shaking my head. I look around the classroom at the pictures of Vietnam, a setting sun against palm trees on one, a house on stilts on another, jungle and more jungle on the rest. He was there. The pictures hit home. No deserts, no Río Salado, no El Cielito, a world he never dreamed he'd live in. I can't imagine Jesse drinking from a coconut, sleeping in the pouring rain, much less aiming to kill. My brother a killer? I wonder if he ever did it. Really killed somebody. I'll never know, although I would if he were alive. Jesse told me everything.

Word gets around to Mr. H., our principal, that I told my class about Jesse. Mr. H.'s name is William Horowitz. His last name sounds so much like the word "horror" to the children that he has asked to be called Mr. H. Some of the kids and teachers say the *H* stands for Hell.

"Telling the children about your brother might be too much for them and even for you, Teresa. A bit too personal," he says as we talk in his office one morning. He runs his fingers through strands of unruly hair on the top of his head. He has aged visibly in the three years since he has taken over the job as head of Jimenez Elementary. His face is thin, his nose sticking out of it, sniffing the air for danger. His clothes are one size too big. What used to be fat is now flab.

The "ousting committee" at the school, headed by a teacher nicknamed Annie Get Your Guns, is partly to blame for Mr. H.'s pitiful appearance. The committee is a group of teachers who run the school no matter who's principal. Some of them have been in the district so long they can walk through the school blindfolded and never bump into anything. Because of the committee's success with the school board and parents, Mr. H.'s chances of staying in his position are getting slimmer by the day. Members of the committee are faithful to their commitment when working on a campaign and meet daily at someone's house or keep in touch by phone. Each day they build momentum in the push to free themselves of a "tyrant who will soon grovel," as they put it. He didn't look very tyrannical to me standing in his office, balancing a coffee cup, with a pencil stuck over one ear.

"What do you mean, 'too personal'?" I ask. "It's the truth."

"Yes, but children are so susceptible. Remember the ones who got hit by the car two years ago? Kids are having nightmares to this day."

Ironically, the school is named for the Medal of Honor recipient Lance Corporal Jose Francisco "Pancho" Jimenez, U.S. Marine Corps. Jimenez was born in Mexico City on March 20, 1946. He came to the U.S. legally at the age of ten and was raised in Red Rock, Arizona. Later he attended high school in nearby Eloy. The large Chicano community surrounding the school voted unanimously for naming the school after the war hero, who was killed on August 28, 1969, in the vicinity of Quang Nam province. Jimenez single-handedly destroyed several of the enemy forces and silenced an anti-aircraft weapon. His heroic actions saved several members of his company. He was buried in Morelia, Michoacán, Mexico, and is the only Medal of Honor recipient of the Vietnam War who was born in Mexico.

"Mr. H., who is this school named for?" I ask.

"I realize all that. And that's paying honor where honor is due. Of course that's not saying your brother wasn't a hero. Don't misunderstand me, Teresa. We also have to consider Vietnamese students at the school."

"I have Li Ann Nguyen in my class." My throat starts to ache. I'm surprised at the insane thoughts going through my mind. Little weasel. That's what he looks like. An albino weasel who stayed home protesting the war when my brother was fighting in Vietnam to save his flabby ass! Calmate. Calm yourself. My fingers turn ice cold. I breathe in, holding the ambush of thoughts at bay. I shift in the chair. He looks pathetic, the little weasel. I'm a sucker for the underdog just like Jesse was.

"Suppose I get support from Li Ann's family. Would that make you feel better?"

"It's not what makes me feel better, Teresa. It's what's best for the children and their parents. We don't want all-out war on the playground, no pun intended. Everything I say these days seems to bug somebody, no matter how I say it."

"I can't believe I'm hearing this!" I stand up. I notice the pencil stub stuck over one of Mr. H.'s ears. It looks stupid. It brings me back to the moment, dissipates the past, so I can talk to him without going for his throat. "There's a pencil stuck on your ear."

"Oh thanks, Teresa. I was working on some bubble sheets. Deadlines—there's so many deadlines! We just got through with state testing, and now they want us to restructure all the district tests. You wouldn't be interested in working on the committee, would you?"

"I was on the committee that made the ones they're restructuring! A fine thank-you for all the work we did. But I guess they have to spend district money somehow before the year's over."

I listen to angry voices in the next room. Shirley, the school secretary, walks in dragging one of the fourth-grade boys by the arm. I secretly thank God I'm not a fourth-grade teacher.

"Oh, no, not Jason again!" says Mr. H., spilling coffee on his white slacks.

"He was out fighting again at recess. Eric is in the nurse's office. Jason gave him a whopper of a bloody nose." Jason squirms out of Shirley's grasp as I walk out. His reputation for notorious behavior is known throughout the district. Last year, teachers from other schools in the district pitched in and paid his mother's rent so she wouldn't move into their area. The fifth-grade teachers have already drawn straws to decide who will get Jason next year, and there are rumors that the loser is resigning. The other teachers are thinking of picketing to stop the resignation.

I watch Mr. H. stick the pencil stub back on his ear. Keeping the assistant principal busy is another ploy used by the "ousting committee" to overwork Mr. H. More power to the "ousting committee" and Annie Get Your Guns!

I walk out into the school office and see the huge glass cabinet with mementos of Pancho Jimenez. In one of them, he's standing in a cowboy outfit with his mother, Basilia Jimenez Chagolla, and his younger sister, Maria del Pilar. He was the only son of his mother. His father was killed in an accident months before Pancho was born. Pancho could have received a deferment as a sole surviving son but refused to do so. There's another picture showing President Nixon presenting Pancho's mother with the Medal of Honor in 1970. Pancho's gravesite in Mexico was not decorated with the headstone of a Medal of Honor recipient until many years later due to the unpopularity of the Vietnam War. Pictures of Arizona's three other Medal of Honor recipients, Jay M. Vargas, Maj. U.S. Marine Corps, Nicky D. Bacon, Sgt. U.S. Army, and Oscar P. Austin, PFC U.S. Marine Corps, also hang on separate frames on the wall. A real uniting of Arizona's best in Vietnam.

Clara, the office assistant, hands me a pink telephone message as I walk up to the front desk. "Your husband, I mean your ex–husband-to-be, called an hour ago and said he needs to talk to you before you leave school." I take the message, crumple it, and throw it in the trash. Instantly, I am filled with remorse as I watch Clara's eyes glitter with anticipation of new gossip.

"By the way, Teresa, do you want to be called Mrs. Alvarez, or *Ms.* Ramirez?" She puts an inflection on the word "Ms." Clara reminds me of a vulture asking its dying victim if there are any last words.

"Mrs. Alvarez for now. It would be too hard for the kids to try to call me anything else so late in the year. Next year I'll use Ramirez."

"Must be hard. I mean the divorce and all . . . but I'm glad you made it back in one piece. I mean you look great . . . I guess what happened over the holidays was a real nightmare, maybe . . ." Her voice trails off as if she wants me to fill in the blanks.

"Yeah, it was hard." All of a sudden I feel tired. Tired of thinking about the divorce, Ray, Sandra, the kids, my mother, and now Jesse.

Clara loves rumors, thrives on rumors. I read the words of the latest gossip on her face: *Ray's living with that hot little number he picked up at one of his gigs. Always a younger woman, ain't that a damn shame, after all you've been through with him. What can you expect from men anyway?* All she really says is, "I'm here if you need my help, Teresa." Right. Help from the Rumor Queen.

Two Doors Gospel •

y mother keeps Jesse's medals hidden away in a cabinet where the ballerina with the purple sprinkles is frozen in a perfect pirouette. The ballerina has her own story to tell. We bought her from a descendant of Carlos Peña Arminderez, the patriarch of a band of gypsies who owned an empty field west of the railroad tracks. The gypsies never stayed very long anywhere. When they were gone for more than three years, the Black brothers of Two Doors Gospel Church thought that meant they had abandoned the property. Two Doors Gospel took over the land, claiming it as church property, until a city slicker from Buffalo came by flashing authentic-looking land deeds. He swore he was a direct descendant of Carlos Peña Arminderez and that the land belonged to him. He set up a store on the property and sold imported knickknacks of windup porcelain ballet dancers that spun around in glass containers filled with liquid sprinkles. He didn't make any sales on the ballet dancers and reverted to selling beer until the Black brothers from Two Doors Gospel convinced him that the only door left for him, for all eternity, was the one leading to Hell. They preached so loud and so righteously and sang so many songs that the descendant of Carlos Peña Arminderez finally took off in the middle of the night, leaving all the ballet dancers behind. For the longest time, we had one of the figurines standing on a shelf my dad built. Every once in a while I would wind it up and turn it upside down to see the purple sprinkles float around the delicate ballet dancer. Years later, Mom transferred the ballerina to the glass cabinet she bought for Jesse's medals at the secondhand store. The ballerina doesn't dance anymore, but if you turn her glass container upside down the purple sprinkles float over her head and make you think she's watching over Jesse's medals.

• IN THE SUMMER OF '57, Brother Mel Jakes set up a big canvas tent on the field vacated by the Arminderez clan. I was nine and Jesse was twelve. Under Brother Jakes's direction, the congregation sent evangelists in pairs to scour the neighborhood looking for sinners, mostly homeless people, to fill up the tent. The revival was a call to repentance, a time for the brothers to usher in candidates who might walk a few yards down the way and join the Two Doors Gospel Church after the revival was over. The tent was a circus attraction, except it had no man on the flying trapeze for the crowd to ooh and ahh. Instead, Brother Jakes told the crowd what would happen to pleasure-seekers who passed their time away looking for excitement while forgetting to prepare for life beyond the grave. The part about worms crawling out of dead people's eyes stayed in my mind the night we went over to hear Brother Jakes preach.

"It's as easy as one, two, three to be free!" Brother Jakes shouted, sticking his fingers up in the air for emphasis. "There are two doors, two gates, and two pastures where yo' all can end up. And some of yo' all may already be penned up where you ain't supposed to be! There ain't no use trying to hide. Once you is in the wrong place there's no way out!"

Brother Jakes's tent was off-limits to me and Jesse, because we were Catholic. We were supposed to be suspicious of tambourines and people who jumped around speaking gibberish and falling all over the place, but our curiosity got the best of us. On regular Sunday evening services, we spied on the congregation through the open windows. Jesse sometimes gave me a step up with his hands crossed one over the other so I could get a better look.

Looking over the windowsill, I searched for Hanny, an enormous Black woman who lived next to Wong's Market. Chong Wong's backyard faced Hanny's dilapidated shack. Chong Wong had secured it with a six-foot chain-link fence and his own brand of burglar alarm, his Doberman, General Custer. Chong Wong's son, Willy, was one of Jesse's best friends. Willy had read the history of the United States to his father, translating it into Chinese. Since Mr. Wong loved the part about General George Custer and how the Indians surrounded him at Little Big Horn, he named his Doberman General Custer. Neighbors asked daily, "How's the General, Chong?" Chong Wong would answer, "He vely fine. Eat much meat, chase injuns all day!" Then he would laugh and show all his black teeth. I wondered why his teeth were black when all the rice they ate was white. His wife Xiu had gray teeth that never went all the way to black. I watched them sometimes, having dinner in the store, with their rice bowls poised right under their noses. They used the chopsticks like shovels, pushing the rice into their mouths a mile a minute. In between, they would talk Chinese that sounded like they were arguing with each other. Willy's real name was Willard and he hated it. His father said he named him Willard because it sounded like the name of an American president. Willy's parents made him wear suspenders, and none of the other kids wore suspenders. I felt sorry for Willy when I saw him wearing his older brother's pants, held up by two red suspenders.

The Wongs were fans of *The Ed Sullivan Show* and watched it every Sunday night. They loved to see Sammy Davis, Jr. perform and wanted Willy to imitate him. They bought Willy a suit with a fake carnation on the lapel. Willy sang into a broomstick microphone, "I Left My Heart in San Francisco" and all kinds of old-fashioned songs. Chong Wong and Xiu clapped for him, but his brothers and sisters only laughed. Willy told me later that the only good thing about the suit was that it covered up his suspenders. The Wongs finally gave up on Willy and said America would never accept a Chinese Sammy Davis, Jr.

The Wongs saved some of their money in the bank, and some of it Willy said in the big walk-in refrigerator that kept their meat cold. "It's a big secret," Willy said. "Don't tell anybody, Teresa." I told him the refrigerator was a weird place to hide money. "My dad says if they break in they'll take the meat and forget to look for money. That's the Chinese way. Let them think they're winning!"

Willy did lots of things other Chinese guys didn't do. He signed up for the Marines right after Jesse signed up for the Army, even though Chong Wong told him the Chinese had already been to Vietnam and nothing good had come of it. It was un escandalo, a scandal in their world when Willy signed up with the Marines. In America, the Chinese were known for using their brains, not their fists, to make a living, but Willy only wanted to be like one of the vatos from El Cielito. Chong Wong kept a picture of Willy in his Marine uniform at the cash register and never stopped saying, "Dis boy tink he Amelican. Dis boy find out in Vietnam, he vely Chinese!"

On their way to Wong's Market, neighbors could hear Hanny in her shack stomping and clapping out the old church melodies. The smell of cornbread baking and chicken frying issued from Hanny's shack and made everybody's mouth water. One day, I asked my mom what Hanny's real name was, but she said that was all that had ever been given to her by her folks down South. For all I know, there's a tombstone somewhere with HANNY written on it.

Hanny always wore the same huge straw hat with ostrich feathers around the brim to church. I loved the graceful waving of the ostrich feathers and wanted to touch them, but Jesse said no. No matter how much Hanny clapped and stomped her feet, the ostrich feathers kept their own fluid movement around her face. I figured they had been plucked off an ostrich's tail while it dug its head in the sand.

"Bring them po' Mexican chil'en in . . . Jeeesus loves them, too!" Hanny had seen me peering over the windowsill. She motioned us with her hand, and one of the brothers was kind enough to oblige her by bringing us in, except Jesse and I had already run off into the night. Running away from the Two Doors Gospel Church was like walking out of a real live movie screen into an empty theater. It took a few minutes to clear our heads of the rush and movement of the congregation.

Jesse and I compared notes on what we had seen. One brother's eyes were ready to pop when he cried out "Hallelujah!" and claimed that "the ol' tempter has done left my soul." The kids were dancing and hollering right along with the adults. The whole place was lit up, packed and swaying with sweaty bodies that leaped, jumped, danced, and lifted their hands up to an enormous bare cross. Jesse said the cross was bare because they couldn't find one with a black Jesus.

We got to see the congregation up close the night Mom went with our neighbor, Blanche Williams, to Brother Jakes's revival services. Blanche had convinced Mom that the only way she would ever be rid of her migraine headaches was through the power of Jesus Christ. My mother tried to hide the pain of her headaches from my father, because she knew he had no patience for any pain except his own. Doña Carolina treated my mother's migraines with yagaby leaves simmered into a tea. Willy Wong always said that in the Chinese world, Doña Carolina was the ying and Don Florencío was the yang of the neighborhood because they were male and female, old folks who knew lots of secrets. Don

Florencío never recommended yagaby leaves for Mom. He said her problem was right in front of her face, and later I found out what he meant.

The yagaby tea helped Mom but at times the fury of the headaches was so intense we ended up taking her to Dr. Camacho, who had a small office off skid row. The only remedy for her then was to get a shot that put her to sleep. Dr. Camacho gave shots for everything, for colds, flus, cuts, and even ingrown toenails. Mom slept for two days after the shot. Jesse and I made sure Priscilla had enough to eat and something to wear. We tiptoed around the house and closed all the curtains, because my mother's eyes hurt when she looked out into the sun. There was a hole in the house when Mom got sick, right in the middle where she sang, cooked, and cleaned. The hole had power to suck me into itself and hold me prisoner. My dad never noticed it, but I could tell you exactly where it was and how I felt when I put my hands over it and didn't feel the floor underneath.

My parents were opposites in almost everything, which was probably why my mother got her migraines in the first place. Energy spun around her in circles as she tried to please my father. Sometimes the path of energy went right to her head like the picture of a muscle man I once saw, slugging away at a heavy weight and making it go all the way to TNT. The muscle man won the prize when the alarms went off and the red lights were blinking. My mother won her migraine when she tried to get my father to stay away from Consuelo and couldn't do it. Then she gave up and let all the energy fly up like electric sparks to her brain where it turned into a migraine.

When my dad heard my mother was having "another one," he came home from Consuelo's house. Consuelo reminded me of the Old Woman Who Lived in a Shoe. Her limbs were stiff from the six children she had carried at her hip. The last two everyone knew were definitely Ramirezes. Consuelo walked like a wooden soldier with knees that never bent as they should. When my dad went over to Consuelo's he said he was only going to visit his brother, Tío Ernie, who lived next door to her. When we saw him at Consuelo's, he said it was because the poor woman had no one to fix her broken windows, seal her leaky pipes, and nail down the tar paper on her roof that the wind had lifted up at the corners.

Consuelo's house sloped down on one side, making one of the windows almost level with the ground. Her six kids used the window like a door. I wondered why they didn't just put a doorknob and hinges on it.

Her front yard looked like a cemetery of old cars, some with their hoods and doors missing. Her kids played in them. One time one of them was bitten by a black widow spider that made its home in the worn-out seats. Nana said Consuelo's yard was puro yonkie, nothing but a pile of junk.

"I'm going over to your Tío Ernie's" were the words that started the strange energy in my mother. They started something in me and Jesse, too. One part of us said, "Get on your knees and beg him to stay," the other part said, "Jump him." It was as if he had just marched Consuelo into our kitchen and sat her at our table. There was nothing we could do but watch him go. Sometimes Tío Ernie would visit us. He was jolly and loud like a Santa Claus, but his eyes were shifty, and he couldn't look Mom in the face, because he knew. He wanted everyone to think he was good, very good, giving us sticky candy suckers, but there was a bitterness to it all and a sense of life gone bad.

My father was dark and stocky with rounded shoulders that had once been muscular and a limp that favored the hip the Germans shattered with an exploding grenade. The government had a surgeon stick pins into my dad's hip, then the doctor said he was healthy enough to go to work. Under his shaggy brows, my father's black eyes were alive, alert, penetrating every face, taking in everyone else's eyes. My father could do that. He could absorb your eyes into his until you were only a reflection in his pupils. I guess that's how he held on to Mom. She could only see the world through his eyes. If he couldn't capture your eyes, he didn't want anything to do with you. Power was a thread stretching taut and brittle between my parents, a tug-of-war that went in my dad's favor. The struggle ended when Mom walked away shaking her head, wringing her hands.

Mom's skin was light with a few freckles on the soft flesh under her arms. Her hair was sandy red. After Kennedy was elected president, she dyed it dark brown and brushed it into a flip to imitate her idol, Jackie Kennedy. Her head came up to my dad's slumping shoulder and her body smelled like Frosted Flakes. She wore different colored aprons, fringed by a collection of safety pins around the hem. Mom said you never knew when you would need a safety pin. Mom noticed everything. She saw dust bunnies under the dresser and the crooked part down the middle of my hair that looked like a road crew's idea of a joke.

"God is God, no matter where you go." I heard it with my own ears. My dad said this to Mom when he gave us permission to go to the Two Doors Gospel Church with Blanche. He sat at the table with a full plate of chili con carne and beans. I could tell my mom was getting ready for

World War III by the way she went from one end of the kitchen to the other doing nothing more than picking up plates putting them back down again and rearranging forks and spoons. This was the nervous energy of her migraines. My dad was sullen, quiet, his mustache drooping. His attitude was "I don't care, leave me alone." So careless. I looked closely at him and knew he was ready for another trip to Tío Ernie's. I glanced out the window, but there was no rain in sight. "Construction crews don't work in the rain," was one of the excuses my dad used for visiting his brother. Jesse took odd jobs all over the neighborhood to help support Mom and us when my dad was over at Tío Ernie's. We depended on Jesse for so many things, we forgot my dad was supposed to be the man of the house.

One night, I heard Tía Katia yell at my mother "Divorce him! Leave him, the lazy good-for-nothing. Que se vaya a la chingada! Look at Bernardo, he doesn't do that shit to me."

"Bernardo's afraid of you, Katia. Besides, you know Pablo's hip is bad, pobre. He's got pain in his hip. He wasn't always like this."

My mother's defense of my father was solid. "We married in the Church. I'll pray to Santa Rita, the patroness of women with evil husbands. I'll light another candle to El Santo Niño. If all else fails, I'll call on St. Jude for impossible cases."

Tía Katia said Consuelo was good at one thing, and that was opening her legs. "She's opened them so many times, you'd think she was riding a horse." When I thought of Consuelo's six kids, I knew there was truth to what Tía Katia said. The last two kids looked like us, except their voices didn't match ours. They spoke like they had just blown their noses and didn't get all the snot out. The girl's name was April, because she was born in April. April looked a whole lot like me except her hair was dark like Consuelo's and mine was light like my mom's. I don't know why they didn't name her brother January, because he was born in January. Instead, they named him Federico, but everybody called him Fufu.

April sometimes pushed her doll carriage down the dirt sidewalk in front of their house. The brat sometimes waved to me and wanted me to play dolls with her. I imagined one day turning into Tarzan and whipping from one telephone pole to another, snatching her doll carriage and stomping it to bits. I'd gouge out her stupid dolls' eyes, too.

Every time I saw April and Fufu, I wanted to do crazy things like set fire to my father's tool shed or grab his electric saw and cut off the posts holding up the roof of the garage so the whole thing would fall on his car and crush it. All I really did was walk backwards in the yard sometimes and make myself fall in holes in the yard so my mother would worry and show my dad all my bruises. I wanted her to say, "See what you're doing to mijita, she doesn't care if she lives or dies!" Then I'd say, "Kick his ass out, Ma! Let him go live with Consuelo and her stupid kids. You don't need him! Why don't you stand up for yourself!"

After I said all that, he'd look at me and maybe slap me across the face, then my mom would have to stick up for me. Then he'd leave Consuelo for good and stop humiliating my mom, and she'd stop roaming all over the house, cleaning and re-cleaning things that were already clean. But I couldn't stand up to him either, and there were times I didn't want to, times when he hugged me and told me I was his one and only. His neck smelled like sweat mixed with sawdust from the wood he hauled around at the construction sites. I wanted to set the table for him and rub his shoulders and make him feel good so he'd never go back to Consuelo.

The night we went to Brother Jakes's revival, I washed up and got into my oxfords, white blouse, and dark skirt and let my mom brush my hair and make a clean part down the middle that nobody would laugh at with two smooth-as-silk ponytails hanging on either side. Jesse had to wear his clean Levi's and tennis shoes and the checkered shirt my mom liked but he hated. He was on a baseball team and wanted to wear his cap. Blanche said that was disrespect to the Lord's house.

Jesse was agile, lean, his muscles taut. Energy in his body surged to the surface, surprising everyone around him. I saw him release it, like a bottle cap popping when he hit a home run that nobody expected from the "poor little guy." He defied the odds against him, winning at King of the Hill when everybody thought he'd never make it halfway up. He'd smile when he was at the top, showing two rows of perfectly formed teeth that I envied because I had a crooked one toward the top back, but it didn't show much unless I wanted someone to see it. People underestimated Jesse's skinny body and didn't suspect that behind the shy smile there was an intense power that could bring down the most formidable opponent.

"Hope nobody mistakes him for one of los negritos at Two Doors," my dad said. Jesse looked right through my dad like he hadn't said anything at all. It was no use fighting with him. Nobody ever won a battle with my dad. When he told me I was gonna quit school and marry the first man who told me he loved me, I said "Yep, you're right, dad," then he shut up. All he wanted to know was that he was right.

"Don't be sceered of them ol' holy rollers," Blanche told my mother.

"They all be's in the Lord and are harmless as flies." She assured mom that the "ol' Devil of headaches is gonna meet his match tonight!" All this happened before Paul was born so he doesn't even remember. Priscilla was only four years old, and we left her with Tía Katia.

Blanche came by for us that evening with her four kids. They were all spruced up and shined up. Jesse didn't feel so bad when he saw that his friend Gus, Blanche's son, was going too, along with his two older sisters and brother, Cindy, Betty, and Franklin. They all stood on our front porch, and it was all I could do not to laugh, because they all smelled like hair grease. Gus and Franklin had on ties that made them look like miniature preachers. Gus was called Gates because people said he was as big as a gate and twice as strong. He was almost as tall as Franklin, even though Franklin was five years older. I asked Mom if Gates looked like his father, but she said Blanche's husband was a skinny negrito who had arthritis all over his body and showed every rib through his shirts. Gates was big and had a light complexion. Blanche said it was nobody's business who his father was, because she had turned her life over to Jesus Christ and repented after she kicked her husband out and got rid of all his heating pads and pills. Gates wasn't afraid of anybody or anything. When Jesse took off for the Army, Gates had already done training in Special Forces and got as close to wearing a green beret as he could, except he kept getting into trouble and bringing his rank down.

We walked three blocks to the church, and all the while I kept comparing Mom to Blanche, watching their flowered dresses sway around their hips one step ahead of us. They dug their white high-heeled shoes into the soft dirt and balanced their walk with purses they dangled on their left arms. Blanche was tall and slim and dark, but not exactly black. She wore a small hat with a shiny red pin stuck in the middle. On days Blanche wasn't wearing her Sunday best, she wore an apron over her dress tied around her waist. Blanche always smelled like clean clothes hanging in the sun even when she was out back feeding the chickens and her proud rooster, Fireball.

Mom was shorter than Blanche, and her creamy skin gleamed smooth and silky in the darkening shadows. Every now and then, I saw the soft, red tone of rouge on her cheekbone as she turned to look at Blanche. She had left her lace veil at home. I couldn't imagine what a Catholic priest would have done if he had seen us walking to the Two Doors Gospel Church. Maybe he would have sprinkled holy water on us to bring us to our senses.

Everyone in the neighborhood watched us as we walked by, but nobody came out from anywhere, because they didn't know what to say to us. "Hello" wouldn't have been enough. They would have had to go into details, and nobody wanted to do that. The Ruizes' old dog stood out on the front yard and barked at us. He was the same dog who chased cars and was later killed by one of them.

I noticed gallons of ice cream out on tables as we walked up to the big tent and wondered how they would hold up in the warm night. The sisters of Two Doors were making Kool-Aid in huge plastic containers. They cut up lemons and threw them in. The lemon slices collided with ladles that bopped up and down on the surface of the water. All through the service, I worried about the ice cream and wondered if the Kool-Aid would be cold. The tent was different from the church. Fold-up chairs were set up on bare dirt and Brother Jakes stood on a wooden platform with other members of the church sitting in a row behind him. The three front rows of chairs were taken up by the choir, who burst into song every now and then, whether it was time for them to sing or not. The choir sounded so good you'd think you were listening to a long-playing record set at full volume. Hanny was a member of the choir. She came by and gave us a hug and the ostrich feathers on her hat tickled my face. " 'Bout time yo' all came by!"

Brother Jakes spoke into a microphone, but I didn't think he needed one. His voice carried all the way down to the end of the block. There were rough-looking people there that night, people Jesse and I didn't see at the Sunday services. I later found out that the brothers had gone down to skid row and visited places under the bridges looking for lost souls in need of conversion. These were brought in and made welcome. I think most of them were waiting for the ice cream and Kool-Aid.

After two hours of singing, preaching, and touching each other's chairs for electricity, we were told that everyone who was sick should go up to the front for prayer. By this time, Blanche was in tears, and her hat was on backwards with the shiny pin on the back instead of the front. Lots of other people were crying, and I thought maybe they were sorry for all their sins and wanted to go in through the right door. I spotted the ostrich feathers on Hanny's hat as we shuffled up to the front. By this time, Mom was crying too, and I was holding on to her purse trying not to lose her in the rush to get prayed over by Brother Jakes. I glanced at Jesse next to me looking serious like he was gonna get Mom's headaches settled once and for all. We were probably the only people in the whole place who weren't Black and that caught Brother Jakes's attention. He put the microphone down and started mopping his forehead with a big white handkerchief. Every time he wiped his sweat away, new drops showed up, and he had to do it all over again. I was hoping he'd roll up his sleeves so he would cool off. He put his handkerchief in his shirt pocket and walked right up to Mom.

"Speak, sister! What do you ask of the Lord?" My mom answered, "My head hurts, I have migraine headaches."

"Not anymore!" he shouted. "In the name of Jesus Christ, sister, I deliver you from migraine headaches!" Voices from the congregation answered "Amen!" "Jesus is the Healer! Turn your faith loose, sister!"

Brother Jakes barely touched Mom's head with one of his huge, shaky hands, and Mom fell back like she had been hit by a bolt of lightning. She landed in the arms of Blanche, who was standing behind her. My heart jumped to my throat. Jesse and I were over Mom in a flash. "She be all right," Blanche said. "It's the power of the Lord what knocked her down." All around us people were getting knocked down by the same power. I grabbed Jesse's hand tight. I figured if I went down I'd bring him with me.

Mom got up and was still crying, holding on to Jesse as she made her way out. I became a believer of the Two Doors Gospel Church that night, because Mom never had another migraine in all her life, except after Jesse's funeral. Then I think it was more than that. It was all her heartache bursting inside that made her hurt so bad she stayed in bed for two weeks.

When guys in El Cielito were being drafted to Vietnam, Brother Mel Jakes took a position as a conscientious objector and refused to allow his son Rufus to go to war. Rufus eventually went into the ministry and was just as successful as his father in rounding up souls for the congregation. Besides his skills at convincing people to choose the right door, Rufus played guitar like Jimi Hendrix and that made it easy to attract a crowd.

The Two Doors Gospel people had the right idea about the ice cream. By the time the service ended, it had melted down and was ready to spread over peach cobbler that the sisters had baked in huge pans. It was the sweetest dessert Jesse and I ever had. We were so happy, kicking up loose dirt in front of the revival tent with Cindy, Gates, Franklin, and Betty and watching Mom standing out in the warm summer evening with her headache gone, eating a dish of peach cobbler with the Black sisters of Two Doors Gospel.

•   •   •

• THE BALLERINA LEFT BEHIND by the descendant of Carlos Peña Arminderez hasn't slept a wink in thirty years. Her beady eyes are locked into the distance. She doesn't know anything about medals or war. She is the lithe figure on the top shelf of the cabinet with the little glass doors that my mother bought at the secondhand store. One of the doors has a missing knob. You have to put your hand in through the door above it, then push out from the inside to get it to open. There aren't any more medals to put in the cabinet, so life there is very quiet.

If the medals talked to the ballerina, they would frighten her away. She doesn't understand that for them to be there, somebody had to bleed or die. If it weren't for them she wouldn't be there either, because the cabinet was bought to display them many years after my mother decided she was the mother of a veteran like all the other American Legion Gold Star Mothers. For years, my mother wouldn't even look at the medals. The medals have names too, Silver Star, Bronze Medal, Purple Heart, Good Conduct Medal, Air Medal, and two from the South Vietnamese government that have no names. The ballerina also has no name. We didn't care enough about her to give her one.

The medals don't tell the story of why my brother had to die. They are the evidence, the passion flower opening, its stamen sticking out from the center and the white-lobed petals blurry through my tears. It surprises me that the medals and the ballerina are dusty. Crevices, I suppose, between the little doors. Everywhere there are crevices, life is like that.

Yoloxochitl •

ast night I dreamed the roof was leaking, leaking right through the vent over the stove. First it was slow, then fast, faster, until it was a shower. There were other people in the room. I asked someone, "Is the Río Salado flooding?" and the person answered, "No, we don't know where this water's coming from." A man came in who was going to repair the leak, but he said he couldn't because he had to go make love in a hurry, then he'd go up and do it. I watched the leak go from a drip to a small shower and I kept thinking, isn't that dangerous, with the electricity from the stove and all. Maybe the man was more dangerous, his need to make love was urgent. He was more dangerous than electricity, than fire, explosions, and death.

• "Is it OK if I take Jesse's medals to my classroom, Mom?"

Mom's leaning on her cane in the doorway of the living room. She's looking at the glass cabinet fitted stiffly in its corner of the living room.

"Now?"

"No, tomorrow. We're learning about the country of Vietnam. I have Li Ann in class, una chinita. She's from Vietnam." I think of Li Ann's face, a small valentine someone forgot to color red. Her face is the color of ivory. Beads of sweat on Li Ann's forehead appear clear, color-less. When she smiles her lips loop over her small chin, making its trian-gle tip go flat. When Li Ann smiles she is like any other second-grader. When she is solemn, she is not like any of them. A serious look from her starts a chain reaction in her body that ends in quiet, fluid movements. You might expect her to float up over the heads of the other children and land on your lap. They're like that, the women of Vietnam, phantom-like. I've seen them in pictures wearing graceful ao yais, delicate silk clothes that free up their midriffs, hang loose around their legs and tight around their tiny breasts. Jesse mentioned how they dressed in one of his letters and told me about a village girl who was teaching him Vietnamese. In pictures I've seen of Vietnamese women, their hair always seems to match the sheen of the silky clothes they wear, long or short it's kept neat, never wild.

Did Jesse fall in love with one of them? So different from our warm, round bodies. Their faces tell you nothing, our faces tell you everything. Some of them became whores. War always plays havoc in women's lives. Hard to imagine the delicate bodies raped and bruised. I know Jesse saw whores. They're the product of war, man's violence erupting from his sex splitting a woman in two, any woman, anywhere in the world. He gets even with the enemy by pinning his woman under him. He enters her, tempting fate with the hard rod of his body thrust between her legs. He is coming to the end of himself in her and doesn't even know it. The white flag of surrender is his. Jesse's too? I've never thought about it.

"Mom, do you remember that call you got from Saigon, three years after Jesse was killed?"

"What about it? I never knew who it was."

"Suppose it was a woman. Somebody Jesse knew in Vietnam."

"Why would she call me and never say a word?"

"Maybe she didn't speak English."

"Ay, mija, that's not possible."

"Why? The Vietnamese women are beautiful."

Mom sighs loudly. "I can't think about that now, mija. I have to get them ready."

"Get what ready?"

"The medals. Didn't you ask me for the medals?" She's standing in the middle of the living room, smoothing down her apron with one hand, leaning on her cane with the other. Her apron is clean, unsoiled by grease spots and food stains, not like when Jesse and I were kids. The safety pins are still stuck around the edge. My mother's always on the hunt for new aprons at secondhand stores, Goodwill, and St. Vincent de Paul's, where she still buys old furniture and clothes, dishes, and knick-knacks. She now uses some of the safety pins on her apron to hold up her clothes. I can't get her to understand that she's not a size 16 anymore. She's an 8. She tells me she doesn't like men staring at her in tight clothes, and I wonder if she means the toothless nomad who hangs around the Goodwill store with a shopping cart, staring at everybody who walks in.

"I hate those medals!" she says suddenly, with such anger that I close the book of poetry I'm reading.

"They never brought him back! Those men, what did they know? Pendejos! They said, here, take these medals in place of your son. What were they thinking? I never wanted the medals. I wanted my son!" Her legs are shaking. There are no tears, only anger.

"They're just medals, Mom." But I feel it, too. We were taken, cheated, lied to. What Jesse did in Vietnam doesn't matter to us. We weren't there. All we know is that he never came home, only the medals came, the colored ribbons stiff and new. No one asked us, "Do you women want to release your loved one to us?" They just took him away, and what we wanted didn't matter. Then again, they never asked us, "Do you want the medals?" They just sent them. The war ended for us when Jesse was killed. For others, it went on and on. On TV—we looked away. On the radio—we turned it off. In magazines and newspapers—we flipped them upside down. Every time it was shoved in our faces we closed our eyes. The war was Jesse's coffin, it had nothing to do with winning or losing.

"Yes, yes, mija. Take them if you want." She walks over to the cabinet and opens the door that has the working knob. Putting in her hand she opens the door under the ballerina. She takes out the medals one by one, brushing them off with her apron. There are tears now. "My poor mijito! Look at all he won! And he wasn't even there a year." She gives them to me one by one. I trace over the letters of his name on the Good Conduct Medal with my finger, *Jesse A. Ramirez.* I'm looking into La Cueva del Diablo, disturbing the bats that hung upside down. If he knew, why did he go? Did he have his own death planned? How could he do this to me, to my mother? My hair, caught in the button of his uniform before he left, tangled me up in his death before he even boarded the plane.

"Remember, Teresa? Remember el cochito and how you ran to give it to Jesse at the airport? It was the last time he got to eat un cochito." The scene is alive in me, as I run up to the man at the gate, the stewardess takes the cookie telling me how cute it is, everyone is staring. I want to tell my mother that Jesse isn't coming back. I hide his words in my breast-bone, the same place my mother hides all her pain. The words are a fiery ember, burning. If I tell her now, what will she say? Why did he go, then? How could he do this to me when he knew I loved him so much? I won't be able to answer her. Maybe it's too late. Maybe it's not important any-more. Don Florencío knew, Nana knew. She saw it in the way I lived, hiding like a bandit from conversations about Jesse's death, not wanting to know more than I had to.

The ember inside my breastbone is fanning itself to life the longer I hold on to Jesse's medals. I've carried a secret, more a wound that pools with guilt. It's like the time Paul fell out of the tree and I wasn't there to stop him. Jesse's words are like the picture before the fall. I was waiting to hear the words come true, and when they did, all I could do was point to myself and say, "I knew."

"Here, mija, take the medals before I get them all wet with my tears. Show them to the children, tell them what a good person your brother was. Tell them that when a son dies, his mother's heart goes with him."

I lay Jesse's medals down on the coffee table. My mother walks slowly down the hallway to her room, leaning heavily on her cane. I'm right be-hind her, shadowing her shuffling steps.

• MY CONVERSATION WITH Mr. H. does nothing to make me change my plans. I figure he's on his way out anyway. I walk the thin line be-tween truth and consequences that all teachers walk. You dance to the principal's tune during evaluation time, then shut the door after he's gone, give the kids the pizza you promised for good behavior, and go back to teaching your way.

I bring in pictures of Jesse, of me, Priscilla, Paul, Mom and Dad. What does it mean to say good-bye? To see a person you love one day, then never again? The children don't know. There's a child in fifth grade whose mother died in a traffic accident last year. He knows. The child's name is Gabriel, some kids say, like the angel at Christmas. Gabriel is sad now, not like the child he used to be who played soccer and got in trou-ble once in a while. Now he's nervous and thin. At times his eyes open wide in alarm, then suddenly shut down, as if the pupils have been rubbed raw and there's nothing left to reflect. I wonder if that's the way I looked when Jesse died. Everybody walked around me on tiptoes like

I had the flu. My friends wanted to carry my books for me at school. A girl I hated let me keep one of her sweaters, because she said she didn't need it anymore. I never said a word, I just put it on and walked away. I listened, I passed my classes, graduating like the rest of the kids, but I don't remember what I heard or what I learned or if I went to the prom that year or not. Maybe I did, but I don't remember. Gabriel won't remember either. His brain is spinning thoughts that get trapped behind his eyes, then fade away.

• MY MOTHER PACKED Jesse's medals in white tissue paper and put them carefully into a plastic bag. There are teachers in the lounge who want to see them before I bring them into my class. Orlando Gomez tells me his brother Ed served during the Vietnam War. A cousin too, who later died of a drug overdose. "He came back a full-blown drug addict from Vietnam," he says, "died in an alley where his mother found him on her way to the store in the morning." Edna and Vicki, two sixth-grade teachers, start their own horror stories about friends who came back and others, they say, who never made it.

"I remember your brother, Teresa, he went to school with one of my cousins," Edna says. "Smart, oh, he was smart! Wasn't he in the National Honor Society?"

"Yes, he was in all that."

"What a shame, I mean to lose someone who could have done so much for society."

"You still have another brother, don't you, Teresa?" Vicki asks. She's tall and pale, with dark hair hanging to her waist and dark circles under her eyes. She reminds me of a fantasma, someone who isn't real. Her question makes me mad. I think of Paul, and all the trouble he's caused.

"Don't you, Teresa?" she repeats herself. "Don't you have another brother?"

"One brother can't replace another."

"Oh, no, sweetie, I didn't mean it that way. I only mean you still have a brother."

"Right." The word squeezes past my lips. My fingers twitch. A couple of other teachers come in with coffee mugs in hand. I wrap the medals up and have them packed in the plastic bag before they make their way to the table. The morning is like any other for everyone but me. Coffee is brewing and cool air drifts into the lounge from outside every time someone opens the door. My hands are ice cold. I've never had a part of Jesse with me at Jimenez Elementary. I've brought him into the teacher's lounge, and already his name has been said so many times I'm starting to regret I brought his medals in. Questions are being asked, so many of them. What year was he killed? How? Where? The war was a farce, wasn't it? America's biggest mistake. Weren't the baby killers of My Lai court-martialed? The U.S. are the real terrorists all over the world, look at what we did in Vietnam.

People go quiet as I walk out. I hear the bathroom flush. They're waiting for me to close the door. *She looks like she's gonna cry. Hard for her, she probably shouldn't be doing this, but you know Teresa, she'll do anything to teach a meaningful lesson.*

I know, but I can't stop myself. I'm the man in my dream. The leaks in my life have caught up to me.

Lorena helps me clear the work table of glue, scissors, and construction paper before the children come in. We set up Jesse's medals on a white linen cloth I have stored in my classroom for special occasions. Lorena watches me closely. Working together for five years, she knows all the ups and downs of my face, like I know Mom's.

"They're beautiful, Teresa. I've never seen medals up close like this."

"Good experience for you."

"Are you OK? You look sad."

"What do you expect, Lorena? You know how close we were."

"Maybe you shouldn't do this. Mr. H. might . . ."

"Never mind about that asshole! What does he know about any-thing?" My voice rises several pitches. Lorena stands up and looks out the window.

"Look, there's Andy, waving at us." I look out and wave back. Andy's dressed in his Phoenix Suns sweatshirt. He wears variations of the Phoenix Suns most every day. He lives with his dad and gets to go to all the Suns games, ASU games, and everything that has to do with sports. It's amazing the kid can keep his eyes open at school after being out so late most nights.

"Cute kid, I wish I had five others like him." Without knowing it, Andy has relaxed me, for the moment.

The room looks like America in the '60s. I've cut out pictures of President Johnson, Kennedy, Martin Luther King, Jr., Robert Kennedy, Cesar Chavez, Nixon, the demonstrators, the Vietnam Wall. A few war scenes dot the room. Under the picture of the Vietnam Wall is information the children copied from a book. There's only one misspelling. The "y" is missing on the word "unity."

The Vietnam Wall forms a chevron-shaped angle like a V that connects the Washington Monument and the Lincoln Memorial. Ms. Lin designed the wall to create a unit between the nation's past and present. It is made of black granite and each name is etched on the surface in white. People visit the Wall and look for the names of people they know. They take a paper and put it over the name. They use a crayon or pencil to get a rubbing of the man's name to take back home with them.

The children constructed a mural of the Vietnam Wall and taped it to the brick wall just outside the classroom door. A long strip of butcher paper is colored entirely with black crayon, a background for names that are etched in with a popsicle stick. The first name on the wall is Jesse A. Ramirez.

I stare at the medals over and over again from wherever I am in the classroom. Houdini escaping death, the voices my mother heard, El Santo Niño's solemn face staring at me from between the flickering veladoras, Don Florencío's prophecy, *your brother will come back in a new form*, now this. I'm pinned under the medals, wearing them when I don't want to, caring all over again about something I couldn't do anything about.

The children come into class. *Oooo . . . Ah! Look at Jesse's medals. How many did he kill, Mrs. Alvarez? POW, POW!* Juan, Andy, and Brandon are pointing imaginary guns at one another. "Did you know the AK-47s were better than the M-16s?" That's Brandon talking. His dad is a know-it-all, and they talk about everything.

"My uncle went to Vietnam, and my mom says he's crazy," Julissa says.

"Did you see anything, Li Ann?" Charlotte asks. "Anything?"

"She didn't see anything," Lorena says, putting one arm over Li Ann. "She was born in America. Her mother, her grandmother saw it all."

Li Ann's mother Huong (her name means perfume in Vietnamese), walks in behind the children, bringing in a medal given to her uncle by the South Vietnamese Army. She's not too much taller than the children. My arms tingle like a draft of cold air just hit me. I feel my body go rigid and force myself to walk up to her, smiling, putting out my hand to touch her shoulder. I wonder if she looks like the woman Jesse knew in Vietnam. I want to ask her if her family knew any American soldiers in

Vietnam. As soon as I think about asking her, I change my mind and don't say a word.

"That why my family come here," she tells me. "Communist kill. Dey kill if you don' do what dey say. My uncle was killed fighting like Jesse." There are tears in her eyes, but she's smiling. I know it's the Asian face masking tragedy.

"Come share with us," I tell her, even though I don't feel so bad that her uncle died. She's one of the ones my brother fought to protect, and where did that get him? I know her answer will be no. She shyly hands me her uncle's medal so I can display it with Jesse's medals. The next day she sends us a Vietnamese dessert that reminds me of arroz con leche, except there's no brown sugar in it. She explains it is simmered in coconut milk.

I start a private dialogue with the medals while the children settle into their desks.

It's Ray's fault I'm like this, Jesse, the son-of-a-bitch took everything I had and ran with it as long and as hard as he could, then threw it all in the garbage. Maybe I turned to him to forget you. Married him because he was there and you weren't. Why did you go, Jesse? What were you thinking? Was the war more important than us? I can't make it here anymore, Jesse. Take me away from here to wherever you are. I trust you. Yes, Jesse . . . please say yes."

"Mrs. Alvarez? Are you OK?" Lorena is leaning over me. I'm sitting at my desk, staring at the attendance sheet without writing anything down. My breastbone is aching like somebody just hit me in the chest. I want Lorena to hold me tight, to take all the pain out of my breastbone, but I don't want to prove Mr. H. right, the little plastic doughboy, all protected at home while my brother did all his dirty work.

"I'm leaving . . . I mean . . . I'm going to the bathroom. Uh . . . have the kids start working in their groups." Lorena looks closely at me.

"Let me ask someone to cover the class."

"No, hell no," I whisper, "and have Mr. H. find out?"

I make it to the door. Li Ann is watching me. I see her tiny face staring at me while the other kids are oblivious to anything except Lorena's voice, telling them what to do next. Li Ann knows. She looks deep into my eyes, her pencil poised in her hand, not intrusive, just knowing. I smile, weakly. She only stares, never changing the contours of her heart-shaped face.

I'm out the door, out into a February morning that has turned gray. I brush up against the Vietnam Wall mural, unsealing the taped corner closest to Jesse's name. I pause to fix it, running my fingers over Jesse's name. Everything else is a blur. *Please God, don't let anyone be around. Don't let anyone see me.* I walk as normally as I can into the teacher's lounge, then race into the bathroom, locking the door behind me. I run the water full blast and cry into a paper towel. My whole body is aching.

Your mouthpiece, Jesse. Your mouthpiece—where was it? Did you fall and break all your teeth? And me nowhere near to help you. Oh, Jesse—where was the wound? The wound that took your life? The hole in your body that made you bleed to death. Where were the medics, the bandages, the helicopter? Why didn't they move fast enough? Saved my brother. MY BROTHER! I'm sorry about everybody else's brother, but that was MY BROTHER fighting for political monsters who could give a shit if he lived or died. MY BROTHER brought back in a sealed coffin with a plastic lid. Your body all swollen, your face disfigured. Too many days. So sorry. He was sent to the wrong family. Can you believe the bastards didn't even get our address right! So sorry. The U.S. Army apologizes for such a tragic error. APOLOGIZES! What a trip! They should have gotten on their fuckin' knees and begged our forgiveness. And don't ever let me find out it was friendly fire, that some asshole from our side murdered MY BROTHER! Oh, God, I can't take this anymore.

I remember their faces, family friends—who is she? That one, over there. The one screaming like that? That's his sister, Teresa. She was the one closest to him. The paper towel is in shreds. I wring my hands together, pretending one is Jesse's. *Pray for me, Don Florencío, tlachisqui of the Mexica Nation, pray for me, Virgen de Guadalupe. I need some tea, Don Florencío, the tea from the yellow flower, yoloxochitl, to heal my broken heart! Now, oh God, I need it now!*

I'm ready to start the wail Don Florencío said was the sound of my soul weeping. I feel it catch in my throat and swallow hard to make it go away. Someone is knocking on the door. It's Lorena. I let her in, and if it hadn't been for Lorena Padilla that day, I would have proven Mr. H. right.

• THERE WAS A balance owing in my life that day—a debt of tears, pleas, cries, energy pushing to the surface. How can you owe a debt to the universe? But I did. And the universe wouldn't be conned into taking anything less than the cold chill in my heart, strange payment for the warmth that was to follow.

La Manda •

Irene is sitting across from me at the kitchen table. Mom's at the sink washing dishes. Irene's there almost every day visiting Mom. The two ward off loneliness by talking about the old days and comparing aches and pains. Irene has her legs massaged at least once a week by an old man who advertises himself as a "sobador." Irene has diabetes and says she needs massages on her feet to keep the blood flowing. Who knows, without the sobador she might have to have her feet cut off, especially with crazy doctors who don't care whose feet they cut off as long as they make money.

Irene says Doña Carolina would rise from her grave if she knew how much the old sobador is charging. "They're not healers anymore, Teresa, they're in it for the money. Doña Carolina would die twice if she knew how this old man works. He never says a prayer when he gives us medicine. I pray anyway when he's massaging me with ordinary lotion, Jergens, can you imagine, that he buys at Walgreens! He's as bad as the crazy doctors who killed Lencho by giving him so many pills. They poisoned him!"

My mother and Irene used to dance at the park on the 16th of September for Las Fiestas Patrias in the old days. I can't imagine them light on their feet, clicking castanets between their fingers. "Cree lo,"

Irene says, "Believe it. We were young once before your father and Lencho made us get old."

Irene wears the same medallion my mother does, the image of La Virgen de Guadalupe, engraved on a gold-plated disc. They'll be Guadalupanas until the day they die, the sodality is that strong. The women are a comadrazgo, a sisterhood bound together by spiritual ties to the Church and to La Virgen de Guadalupe. Nana used to point to the picture of La Virgen's image hanging in our living room. "She's the only woman who has ever been given the sun, moon, and stars by God Himself," she would say. "Look at her face. Have you ever seen anything more beautiful?" I didn't say anything because Nana was right. La Virgen's face was small and peaceful. Her eyes were partly closed but I wanted them to be open. I wanted big, brown pools of eyes I could swim in and see God from the inside out.

Legend holds that the sacred image miraculously appeared on Juan Diego's rough woven poncho, which in Spanish is called a tilma, centuries ago in the mountains outside Mexico City. The Mother of God appeared suspended in the heavens, a crescent moon at her feet, clothed in a mantle of stars like an Aztec princess. She presented Juan Diego with roses that grew miraculously on the cold, barren ground. He collected these in his tilma. By the time he showed them to the bishop, the image had impressed itself on the rough cloth and remains so to this day, hanging at the Basilica of La Virgen de Guadalupe in Mexico City. Besides the gold medallions, the old women wear ribbons on special occasions, listónes, red, white, and green that hang like tassels over their shoulders. Nana told me that a Guadalupana wears her medallion and listón even in her coffin and is accompanied by una guardia, one woman at the head of her coffin and one at the foot until her body is lowered into its grave.

Nana Esther was president of Las Guadalupanas for years. As a child, I watched the old women proceed down the aisle of St. Anthony's, black shoes laced up to their ankles. The younger women, those under seventy years old, stepped lightly in black or white pumps. Long skirts and dresses hung over stockinged legs, short legs, most of them, extending from lumpy hips exhausted from bearing many children, instead of just one like La Virgen. Here and there, you caught the glint of eyeglasses on a wrinkled nose, the whiff of perfume from the younger women, and the bland smell of aged skin untouched in widowhood by husbands' hands and children at the breast. The air was filled with the authority of many women's hearts beating at the same time for the same reason. The soul of motherhood, the hidden treasure of la raza, was passing by on its way to the altar set with red roses, white linen, and candles. Not even a demon shot from hell would have dared disrupt the shuffling swaying procession of mothers united in the victory of La Virgen with Nana at the head. I heard the opening verse of "Paloma Blanca" and broke into tears. The lusty voices of el mariachi and their Spanish guitars released such a rush of emotion, I held onto the pew with one hand for support. Pride burst inside me over my brown skin and my regal Indian Mother.

On Sundays, I drive Mom and Irene over to St. Anthony's, where they go to mass. On special days, they still walk in procession with other Guadalupanas behind the silken banner of La Virgen. They look like they did at the airport when Jesse flew out to Vietnam, gray swallows weighed down by earth's gravity, measuring their progress in slow, sacred steps. I walk in with Mom holding on to the arm that's free of her cane. The singing is loud, and everything moves slow like in the old days. The songs are the same, "Paloma Blanca," "Adios Reina Del Cielo," "Las Mañanitas." I look around and wonder if Las Guadalupanas will run out of old ladies to replace the ones who have died. It doesn't look like they will. Women live longer than men, into their eighties, their nineties. My mother is seventy-nine.

My twins, Lisa and Lilly, are not so patient with Irene and Mom. They can't stand it when Irene comes over, looks at them unblinking, and says things like, "If I had dressed like that to go to school, my father would have beaten me with a club."

"It's not the old days, Irene," my mother says. "Girls nowadays have babies at the age of fifteen. May God forbid that happens to the twins!" She makes the sign of the cross over herself, then into the air, blessing Lisa and Lilly whether they're in the room or not. I was glad when the girls went in for the "baggy look." Irene feels better when they wear loose clothing.

I'm watching my mother wash dishes, something she insists on doing by herself even though it takes her a long time to finish. She drags the dishrag over each dish and utensil, barely wiping its surface. Her elbows lean heavily on the white enamel surface. Her face is not too many inches above the soapy water. Poor circulation causes great pain in my mother's legs. Her heart medication controls the swelling, but there is always stiffness and pain, sometimes numbness in her feet and toes.

"Mom, let Lisa and Lilly clean up the kitchen. They're coming here after school today. They'll be moving in soon anyway, so they might as well get used to it."

"No, mija. They have so much homework. I hate to bother them."

"Well, then let me help you."

"No, you're busy, too. Every night you bring work to do. Ay, mija, why do you have to work so hard?"

"The curse of being educated, I guess." I've got papers stacked on the table, spelling tests, book reports, crossword puzzle worksheets I'm grading.

"The truth is your mother wants to do the dishes herself, Teresa," says Irene. "She's been stubborn all her life. Me? I let my daughters do them. What are they there for anyway? They never helped me when they were young."

"Manuel called for you today, mija," my mother says. "Pobrecito, he's always liked you, since you were children in school. Remember, Teresa? That stepmother of his, Matilde, curse her for all she did to him! Now she's sick with her bladder. He told me she had an operation on her bladder. I said to him, tell her to drink agua de maize. Cut off the fibers on the ears of corn, those long threads, el pelo del maize, that's what you boil. What did our ancestors live on if not corn? They said it was the gift of the gods. She should add sugar if she has to, that will open her kidneys and help her pee. Manuel says the doctors have her convinced she has to take these big, red pills that look like they should be given to an elephant. That's the way doctors are, always doing something unnatural and laughing at our remedies. I guess it's not her fault she listens to them. She's ignorant, la tonta."

"I had a horse once who was the same color as those pills," Irene says. "Terrible horse too, he bucked me off three times, no wonder Santiago was born blue, that horse messed up my womb when I was a girl. The cord, el ombligo, got tangled up inside me and Santiago almost choked on it."

"He did not!" says Mom. "You were too old, Irene, that was your problem."

"Don't tell me about being old—why—"

"What did Manuel want, Mom?" I interrupt Irene, knowing their argument will end up in a stand-off. Neither one ever admits to defeat. I grip the red pen tighter. "Can't he take no for an answer?"

"Don't be mean to him, mija. He was an orphan. He's always been good to you. He joined the choir at St. Anthony's just to be near you."

"How could I forget?"

Mom had a thing about kids who had been orphaned. The truth was that Manuel did have a mother, but she ran away with a heroin addict when Manuel was still a baby. His aunt Matilde and her husband adopted him and loved him all the way up to the fourth grade, when his aunt delivered her own baby. After that, nothing Manuel said or did was better than Eliseo, their real son. They started ignoring Manuel and regretted adopting him in the first place. It was a sad life for Manuel. Besides all that, his mother was never found. Some suspected she had ended up an addict herself and died of an overdose.

Manuel was nicknamed Casper by his aunt Matilde, because she said he was always disappearing. Disappearing to where? Matilde and her husband didn't really care. Later, Manuel told me he would hide in the boxcars of the Santa Fe freight trains and play marbles by himself. He met all kinds of hobos, and one time took such a long nap that he ended up in Flagstaff and didn't know where he was, until one of the hobos woke him up just in time for him to jump on the other track and come back to Phoenix.

"His ex-wife Regina already has a boyfriend," Mom says, "and it's only been a year since they divorced. Poor Manuel, he was never the kind to run around. His daughter, Maria, helps him now in his accounting business. He's always been such a hard worker, pobrecito, not like your father. That's the kind of man you need, Teresa. Good, hardworking."

"First of all, what does being an orphan have to do with anything? And can you imagine me with Manuel? From a musician to an accountant!"

"Give people a chance, mija. Don't close your heart."

"Oh, Mom, please. Just thinking about another man makes me sick. Manuel knows I'm getting a divorce. He's biding his time to see if I'll give in to him."

"You still love Ray?"

"I don't know. I don't know if I ever loved Ray, but I know I've never loved Manuel. He's a friend, that's all."

"Muy mulo," Irene says, "like all men, stubborn. Look at Lencho, he never let me go, and your father never let your mother go either. Men don't like to lose."

"In the old days you women didn't have much to say about anything. Men chased you, and caught you like you were some kind of prize. Manuel isn't right for me. He's just a friend. Besides, I thought you wanted me to stay here with you, Mom."

"Yes, mija, but I won't last forever. Look at me, I can barely walk. I'm glad Consuelo's not around anymore. I would have hit her over the head with my cane!"

"No, you wouldn't. You sent her soup when she was dying."

"Yes, admit it," says Irene. "You had pity on her even though she went after Pablo Jesús. If it were me, I would have put rat poison in the soup, cree lo."

"I had to feed her, she looked awful. She was a stick by the time she died. Don't you remember? And all her worthless kids standing around with their hands in their pockets waiting to take the house right from under her feet."

"Talking about kids . . . my kids at school really liked Jesse's medals."

"What did they say, mija?" My mother stops wiping the dishes and turns around to look at me. Two safety pins stuck onto the frazzled edge of her apron jiggle slightly.

"That he was brave. They didn't even touch them. That's how much they respected them." I don't mention the comments about the AK-47s and the M-16s. "They drew a wall like the real Vietnam Wall and put Jesse's name first." I reach under one of the stacks of papers I'm working on and pull out a photograph of the Vietnam Wall I cut from a calendar sent to me by the VFW.

"Look, here's a picture of it." I walk up to her, holding up the photograph. Remember the wall they have here in Phoenix with the names of our guys on it? Well, this is the big one in Washington."

My mother is looking at the photograph, poised in position over the sink full of dishes. She drops the cup she's holding and it clatters down onto the sink's white enamel. I'm always thinking strokes and heart attacks. I react instantly, putting my arm around her.

"Mom, what is it? Are you OK? Mom?" She lets the dishrag slip back into the water and presses her hand up to her breastbone. She looks up at me.

"Que pasa? What's wrong, Alicia?" Irene is up on her feet.

"That's it, mija! That's it!"

"What's it?"

"The Wall, mija. Where is it?"

"In Washington, D.C."

"I have to get there!" Suddenly, her eyes are the same ones I saw when she hid surprises for me and Priscilla behind her back when we were kids, teasing, joyous.

"Mom, it's too far away! You can barely get to the doctor and back. Mom, what are you saying?"

"Remember the voices?"

"What voices?"

"At Christmas! The voices I heard in my room. It was my mijito! It was Jesse and his friends, the ones on the Wall!" She points to the picture. Irene crowds in next to her.

"Faustino's name is on there too!" she says, pointing to the picture. "He was talking with Jesse that night."

"Nobody was talking to anybody! Mom, they're only names!"

"It was him, Teresa! It was Jesse. Don't you remember he promised me I'd hear his voice again?"

"When?"

"At the airport! Don't you remember? Your nana was there, too."

Irene is crying now, nodding her head. "Of course, there's your answer, right there on the Wall."

My mother clasps both hands to her heart. "I vow this day, before all the hosts of Heaven, before God, una manda. I'll get to the Wall before I die and touch my son's name. If it's the last thing I do on this earth, I promise I'll touch Jesse's name!"

"Cree lo," Irene says. "God will get us there!"

"*Us?*" The word sends a chill down my spine.

Parallel Universe •

emember the man who married Doña Elodia and Doña Azusena, the one Nana said looked like Mutt?" Mom's sitting on a wing chair in her room. I'm rubbing her feet, slowly, gently, kneeling on a small carpet. Her feet are swollen, painful, even though I've given her medications that should work to open up her blood vessels.

Images of the two ladies Mom's talking about focus in my mind. I first saw Doña Elodia Beltran and Doña Azusena Gamez shuffling up to the altar at St. Anthony's in line with the other Guadalupanas. In my mind, they were saints. They reflected the same long-suffering look I had seen on saints' faces on calendars at home. I never wanted to serve them coffee when they came over to see Nana, fearing I'd drop a cup of hot coffee down one of their backs and they would sit there, taking in all the pain, forgiving my clumsy ways, eyeing me with pity for being a modern girl, crude and undisciplined. Nana surprised me when she told me a little of their histories after one of their visits to our house.

"Don't let them fool you, mija," Nana said. "Look at their holy faces, parecen la pura verdad, but I remember when they ran away from home. One went one way and the other went in the opposite direction and both ended up marrying the same man anyway. Ay Dios, can you believe it? One of the Robles brothers, who looked like something out of a cartoon." Nana was an avid reader of the comics. "Remember Mutt and

Jeff? The man's name was Feliciano or Felipe or something, I don't remember, but he looked like Mutt. He was a talker though! First he married Azusena, then afterwards decided he had made a mistake and
married Elodia. Las dos tontas, both of them were stupid for marrying
him in the first place. Then when he died, there they were, crying over
his coffin. Hardheaded, both of them! Your mother should learn something from them." Hearing the story of the two old ladies that day made
me want to grow up and join the procession of solemn women and mar-
vel at the mysteries of God and La Virgen, and most of all, find out who
ran away from home when they were young.

"Nana always said the Robles brother looked like Mutt. You remember, Teresa. Ay que mi Ma! Anyway, he made a manda once, a
promise to go to Magdalena in Mexico to the church of San Francisco
Xavier. People went there in the old days to see a statute of San Francisco
in a big casket laid out like he was sleeping. They put their hands under
his head and tried to lift him and if they did, it meant they would get
their prayers answered. If they didn't, that meant God wasn't listening to
their prayers, maybe they didn't have enough faith, or something. They
still go there, faith isn't dead, you know. Well, this dimwit of a man made
a promise and didn't have the sense to keep it as he said he would in one
year. That's why he died the way he did, mija, screaming with pain in his
stomach. He said he had swallowed a needle he was threading for one of
the Doñas. The doctors kept telling him the needle would have stuck in
his throat before it got to his stomach, but he insisted it had disappeared
down his throat. He finally went to Magdalena five years after his promise and look at what happened—he couldn't even budge the saint's head.
That's when he knew he was headed for the grave. And look, he died as
soon as he got back to Phoenix."

"That's a sad story. Nobody gets healed by lifting up a ceramic statue,
Mom. It's all in people's heads."

"It's not the statue, mija. It's faith in God that matters. I believe you
can lift up anything in this world if you have faith."

"You do?" I look up at her. The collar of her flowered blouse is
tucked in under her neck. Strands of gray hair fall over her eyes.

"Your hair's getting long."

"I know." She hands me her socks. "That's enough, mija." I look
around for her shoes, slip-ons she bought at the Goodwill. I'm putting
them on, hurrying.

"I have faith I'm getting to the Vietnam Wall," she says.

"Now that's something we should talk about! The airplane tickets are expensive, Mom, more than $200 one way, and it's a five-hour flight to get from here to Baltimore, then from there we have to take a shuttle into D.C." My mother stares at me, then starts laughing.

"Oh, no, mija, we're not going by plane. We're going by car!"

Now it's my turn to laugh. "Car! Mom, you've got to be kidding! It'll take a week to get us there, and with you sick, it'll take two!"

"Me and Irene have never gotten on a plane. God forbid we get on a plane, tempting God by flying into the clouds!"

"The two of you are going?" I can see them in my mind. My mother with her cane, Irene with her thick stockings, looking up a sobador in D.C., and the two of them wearing their medallions of La Virgen.

"Mom this isn't a joke. This is a long trip!"

"Don't worry, mija, El Santo Niño will get us there. He walks around in his sandals all over the place. Haven't you heard?"

"Mom, how can you believe in that? That's just a story! It's something people made up to make themselves feel better." I'm up on my feet, reaching for the plastic pitcher on the nightstand. "I'll go get you some water."

"God can do what He wants, Teresa. If He wants to get me to the Wall, He will."

"How? Can you tell me how? For one thing, we don't have the money; for another thing, you don't have the strength. Doctor Mann will never let you leave town. Do you want everything and everybody to stop just so you can get to the Wall? I'm working, and the kids are in school. And if that's not enough, I'm waiting for the divorce to be final, *and* for my court date with Sandra. So now, how are we getting to the Wall?"

"Don't yell, Teresa. I'm not deaf."

"I'm not yelling!"

"You *are* yelling, and you're mad, too."

"If I'm mad it's because you're so stubborn!"

"Too bad I can't get to Magdalena to San Francisco's Church to find out if God's listening or not."

"Yeah, right, that would help us! Maybe I should check with El Santo Niño, too. Just think, he might lead the way to the Wall in his little sandals."

"What do you think Jesse wanted to tell me that night?" she asks as I'm walking out with the pitcher.

"How should I know? I never heard anything."

• • •

• IT'S RAINING the day I call a family meeting with Priscilla and Paul, raining on a Sunday in March. Doesn't the saying go *April showers bring May flowers?* In Arizona any rainy day is a miracle, so people don't complain much when it rains. I run my thumbs along my bedroom windowpane tracing two trails of raindrops falling on the opposite side of the glass. Two smudges appear on the glass. Mom and Jesse separated by a thin layer of reality. I'm caught in the middle.

I look into the backyard made lush green by the steady rain. Pomegranates appear ruby red between the plant's boughs and leafy maze. New tendrils sprouting from the honeysuckle vine curl into white blossoms that look like bells. Tata's Victory Garden is a sodden mess, its furrows extinct. Oleanders along the fence are overgrown, with branches bending under the weight of raindrops. I make a mental note to have Cisco cut them down. Oleander dust can be poisonous. Cholo lies crouched under my Honda, the white *x* on his chest hidden under his shaggy coat.

I see Irene's back door through the chain-link fence. Irene is in the house, probably resting her head on the pillow with the American flag under it, the flag her son, Faustino, won with his death. Keeping the flag close to her is Irene's way of holding on to her son. The ancient shack is the same tottering structure I remember as a child, except it has a shingled roof and real glass on the windows. There was always a question as to what Irene did with the $10,000 she got for Faustino's death. Mom says she handed it over to her husband, Lencho, and he bought a brand-new car and a fancy tool chest. He bought her new carpet, too, a shag green that looked like poor Irene had moved into the Vietnam jungle. Lencho wanted the tools so he could do side jobs at home and quit plaguing his flat feet by running all over the neighborhood playing delivery boy. I never heard of a single family who prospered from the money they got for their son's death. It was as if they wanted to get rid of it as soon as they could.

Reminds me that I never found out what my mother did with the money she got for Jesse. I make a mental note to ask her about it. I know there were repairs made on Consuelo's house, probably my dad using some of the money (the gall of the man!). A washer and dryer were bought for the first time ever, and lots of trips to Mexico were made to visit old relatives and help them with money. My mother never said anything more about it. It took her three years to display Jesse's medals in the cabinet with the ballerina. The money and the medals meant nothing to her.

• I FEEL LIKE we're a secret clan making plans behind closed doors instead of a family trying to figure out what to do with a stubborn old woman. We're sitting in the living room. Mom's resting in her room. Lisa and Lilly are on the phone in their bedroom, Cisco's watching a baseball game on TV in the next room.

"It's your fault," Priscilla says. "You're the one who took Jesse's medals to school. You're the one who showed Mom the picture of the Wall. All this is getting to her. I don't even know why Jesse's name is all over the place these days. Why can't we just let him rest in peace?"

"Get a life, Priscilla! Did I stage the voices she heard at Christmas? That's what started the whole thing. Do you honestly think I want her to make the trip? And as far as Jesse's concerned, it looks like he's the one disturbing the peace."

"You got the money?" Priscilla asks. "Must be a fortune you're getting for selling that house."

"I don't have any money, you know that. Why don't you try telling Mom she can't go, huh? Or you, Paul?"

"Nobody can take care of things as good as you can, right, Teresa? Why should we try?" Priscilla says.

"I'm surprised you don't remember how you felt when you lost Annette. Mom has felt that way for years."

"That has nothing to do with this!"

"It has everything to do with it. Pain is pain, no matter whose pain it is. You should sympathize with Mom instead of trying to sabotage the trip."

"Sabotage it? I'm trying to help her get back to reality! She's risking her life going to the Wall."

"How do you know? Maybe it'll bring her peace, something she hasn't had for years."

"It'll be too much for her—you watch. Mom can't take this."

"Speak for yourself!"

"Get off my back. I don't need any advice from you!"

"Who's up to bat?" Paul yells at Cisco.

"Baltimore."

"Screwballs."

"Paul, are you listening to all this?" Donna asks.

"Sure, I'm listening. I'm hearing that you girls want to get Mom to the Vietnam Wall when she's practically on her deathbed. Great planners all of you!" Paul's holding Donna's hand. I can make out the last part of the letters, *onna,* tattooed on his left arm. He was lucky the girl's name he tattooed on first was named Anna. All he did was go back to the same guy who tattooed *Anna* on his arm and had him redo the name and make it *Donna.* Now he's running around with an *A* that looks like a capital *O.* Donna's got tats that are small flowers and stars, one on her hand, one on her ankle.

"It's not what we want to do, Paul. It's what Mom wants. I can't get her to change her mind."

"You can't leave the state anyway, Teresa. You've got a court case pending—you've joined my ranks, a common criminal. I can't believe it, my holier-than-thou sister charged with assault!"

"You weren't there. She provoked it, so why don't you back off."

"Some example you're setting for Elsa and the twins."

"I can't believe you just said that, Priscilla, considering how you've lived your life."

"Where's Elsa, anyway?" Paul asks.

"She's not here. She's pissed off," Priscilla says, "mad as hell with Teresa for the divorce."

"At least I have a marriage to get a divorce from, not like some people I know who live together like rats in a maze." Priscilla glares at me.

Paul's son, Michael, is sprawled on the carpet reading a road atlas. He's following lines of numbers on the page, marking distances with a red pen. He's concentrating hard, his lower lip pressing tight over his upper lip. The spiky part of his hair looks like it's grown out, and he swishes away a loose strand. "It's 2,350 miles from Phoenix to Washington, D.C.," he says. Angelo, Priscilla's son, is next to him, coloring with fat Crayola crayons on a Disneyland coloring book. He's scribbling over Tinkerbell's face. Angelo is chunky, his face full. When he smiles, he shows front teeth that haven't finished rounding off yet.

"Look," Michael says. He points to a red circle he's drawn on a chart and shows it to Priscilla.

"I can't see it," says Priscilla, "the letters are too small."

"Hey, Einstein," Paul says, "quit all the research, your nana's not going there, pal, unless you want to pay for her funeral."

Michael looks closely at the atlas. "I can chart the whole way and build us an itinerary. It would be easier if Nana went by plane, of course; she'd be there in five hours."

"Look at that, my own kid making plans like a travel agent," Paul says. He sits next to Michael on the floor. "A kid who doesn't want to live with his poor old man even though I've been following the rules like a damn priest." Paul gets on his knees. "Please forgive me, a sinner! But, na, I'm not good enough for you, right, Michael?"

"I spoke to your parole officer yesterday and explained my side of the story," Michael says. He keeps his eyes on the atlas.

"You talked to Mindy? Doesn't that beat all! Probably bad-mouthed me for all you're worth! She probably thinks I'm not fit to be your dad—a real snake-in-the-grass is what she thinks of me."

"She says you can't force me to live with you. I've got my rights, too."

"The only rights you have is to a beating. I should take my belt to you—using your brains against mc! How did I get stuck with a kid like this?"

"Yeah, use your belt, Paul. The right solution. Didn't you learn anything from watching Dad get mad all the time?" Priscilla asks.

"Stay out of this! You're the one encouraging this kid to make me look like Jack the Ripper. All this brainy stuff is leading him nowhere!"

"Leave him alone!" yells Priscilla. "Just because your brains are gone doesn't mean Michael should be ashamed of his. You should be proud of him, but you don't even have the sense to do that!"

Donna bends down and yanks Paul's shirt, making him sit next to her again. "He's gifted, Paul. You know that," Donna says.

"Gifted, shifted, this kid's just a smart aleck."

"You should be nice to me, Dad. You never know if I'll have to defend you in court someday."

"Defend me? You'd probably send me to the electric chair!"

"Capital punishment is by way of injection these days, besides I don't want to be a lawyer, I want to be a cosmologist."

Paul slaps the side of his leg. "I knew this kid had some La La in him. See what you're doing to him, Priscilla—making him a sissy. A cosmetologist! What do you say about that?"

"If you'd listen to the word, asshole, you'd know what he said."

"Don't call me asshole."

"A cosmologist is a scientist who studies the universe, the cosmos, in case you didn't know," says Michael.

"I knew," says Angelo, "and I'm only in third grade."

"Tell him what a cartographer is, Angelo."

"A person who makes maps."

"He's brainwashing Angelo," Paul says.

"I want to be the first Chicano cosmic cartographer in the world. I'm gonna be like our ancestors the Mayas. They were astronomers like the Egyptians, way back in 1500 B.C. You'll be coming to me to find your way to Pluto, Dad, and I don't mean Mickey's dog either."

"What do you think I am, stupid?"

"Actually, you might have learned about some of these things if you had used your time to read while you wasted taxpayers' money in that institution. Where were you? Maximum security, cell block B?"

"Let me at that kid!" Paul stands up and so do I.

"Stop it! Both of you!"

"I'm leaving!" Priscilla yells. "I'll be damned if I let Paul insult Michael in front of my face! That's child abuse!"

"Will you both stop! What am I, some kind of a referee?"

"Paul, please," Donna says. "We're here for your mom."

"Exactly, we're here for Mom. *Thank you, Donna!* We're here to figure out what to do about all this. She wants us all to go with her to the Wall. I can see why now. Jesse was the only one she could count on for comfort."

"What does that mean, Miss Know-It-All? That I'm not any comfort to her?" asks Paul.

"Don't even go there! All you've ever given her is heartache!"

"OK, OK, we all know that," says Priscilla. "I want to get this whole thing settled about Mom so I can leave."

"Just *like* you, Priscilla, not to want to stay very long when somebody's sick. Someone waiting for you?"

"Wouldn't you like to know!"

"Is Baltimore down?" Paul yells.

"Yep," Cisco shouts back.

"A real kangaroo court, all of us! Mom's sick, we all know that. How much more time she has, we don't know." Everyone is quiet. Nobody looks at anyone else. "She wants to get to the Wall, and she wants to take Irene with her. She won't fly, neither one of them will, so that leaves us to go by car. If any of you think you can stop her, well then go ahead and try!"

"She'll never make it," Priscilla says.

"She'll make it," says Donna. "Your mother is the strongest woman I've ever known."

"Stay out of this, Donna," says Priscilla. "She's not your mom. I know one thing, if anything happens to her, I'm going after *you*, Teresa."

"How? With the acrylic nails you just got? You might get them damaged!" Priscilla grabs her purse and stands up.

"Sit down, Madonna!" says Paul. "You ain't going nowhere until we get this thing settled."

Mom walks into the living room with Lisa at her side. "All this yelling woke Nana up," Lisa says.

"Here, Alicia, sit here," says Donna, leading Mom to the rocker. "Now, where were we?"

Paul kneels next to Mom. Donna stands behind her with her hand on Mom's shoulder.

"Por favor, please, don't fight, any of you. I just want to go touch my mijito's name on the Vietnam Wall. It's a promise, una manda I've made with God. I have to go now . . . don't you see?"

"You're too sick to go, Mom," Paul says. "Jesse would understand, and God won't get mad either."

"Go by plane," Michael says enthusiastically. "It's safer than going by car."

"No, mijito, your nana can't do that. I'm too old to fly. The only wings I'll ever have are those God will give me if I ever make it to Heaven."

"Mom, it's over two thousand miles," says Paul.

"You remembered!" says Michael with a smirk. Paul glares at him.

"Don't be mad at him, Paul. Your son's a genius, pobrecito, he can't help himself."

"Mom, I don't want you to go there. It'll be too hard for you."

"But I heard your brother! I heard Jesse—I know it was him!"

"It's the parallel universe talking to you, Nana," says Michael. "Things we can't see jump into our orbits and start traveling with us."

"You can't believe everything you read in books, knucklehead," Paul says.

"How do you know that?" I ask Michael.

"I read about it, Tía, and I believe it's true. It's like when somebody loses a leg and they still feel pain where the missing limb used to be. Energy can't be created or destroyed; Einstein proved that. It only changes into another form. Tío Jesse is out there somewhere, and maybe the energy of his soul crossed orbits with Nana's."

Don Florencío's words flash through my mind . . . *a new form, our people have always walked the earth.*

"The kid's crazy!" says Paul.

"No, Paul. Don Florencío told me years ago—that—" Paul doesn't let me finish.

"That crazy old man! He should have stopped smoking peyote. He was stoned half the time."

"You're one to talk about being stoned! I never saw Don Florencío stoned, *you* I've seen stoned."

"I have to do this, mijo," Mom says to Paul. "I've made a manda, don't you understand? Do you want me to end up like the Robles brother?"

"What Robles brother?"

"Some guy who never kept his promise to God and died screaming in pain."

"Mom, that won't happen to you," says Paul. Mom grabs Paul's hand and starts to cry. "Please, mijo, your mother is asking you for something, please take me to the Wall. God will do the rest." Paul is holding Mom in his arms, and she is openly weeping. The rain is splattering on the roof, my mother is weeping, the phone rings in the bedroom, and Lilly yells for Lisa. Cisco walks in. His face is relaxed, as if he just finished yawning. He looks at me like he's throwing me a lifeline.

"What's so hard about getting Nana to the Vietnam Wall?" he asks. "She wants to go, we'll get her there."

Of course, so reasonable, so simple. Cisco's like Tata O'Brien—nothing to it. We'll get Mom to the Vietnam Wall and I'll be the ambassador to Chile and bring back chili seeds for Tata to plant in his Victory Garden.

"We'll get you there," Donna whispers to Mom. "Don't cry, Alicia, we'll get you there, won't we, Teresa?"

"Sure, Mom, yes we will." There's nothing else for me to say. Priscilla stares at me, then looks out the window.

"Can you imagine being together all those days?" she asks.

Rothberg •

I t was pretty scary this morning. I slipped into a pair of Priscilla's shoes. They were in the closet, way in the back. They looked like they were a pair of white sandals I used to wear. Instead, I put on these soft, white leather shoes, flats with small, satin-embroidered oval openings just over the toes, very feminine. Priscilla bought them when she was coming to terms with herself as a woman. What surprises me is that the shoes fit me. Priscilla wears at least one size smaller. Now I'm worried my feet are shrinking, or maybe I've lost so much weight it's affected my feet. Everyone says the divorce has been good for me. I look sexy again. I can feel my hip bones, something I was forgetting I owned. My shoulders are taking form, the bones curving into smooth muscles, and my legs are getting skinnier than I want them to get. But my feet? I wear Priscilla's shoes to school that day just to prove to myself that I can. It's strange to walk around in somebody else's shoes, it makes you wonder if you could ever live out that person's life, or if you would want to. I think of my mother's shoes and the things she's walked through, of Ray's, Paul's, of Jesse's, and El Santo Niño's sandals. I'm imagining walking in Priscilla's white leather shoes all the way to the Vietnam Wall. Isn't white the color of mourning in Vietnam? Crazy thoughts come into your head when you're wearing somebody else's shoes.

• • •

• "THERE'S A BONA FIDE REASON for everything in the world," says Brandon. He's talking to Juan, and making himself feel good because his "Word of the Day" is *bona fide,* and he's just used it in a sentence. Most of the classroom is packed away, bulletin boards are blank, construction paper is neatly stockpiled on the shelves, pencil marks in textbooks have been erased, and tomorrow the children will scrub their desks. The usual hustle and bustle of putting things away for summer vacation has started. New shoes the children wore in September have long been outgrown, the squeaky leather now a sagging gray.

A few people told me they liked my shoes, Priscilla's shoes, actually. "Cute, feminine. Are they comfortable?" asked Vicki. "Sure, if you consider I wear an eight and these are a size seven." I'm still wondering how they fit in the first place, when I get a call over the classroom intercom.

"Your Mom called, Mrs. Alvarez," Clara announces. "She wants you to call her at lunchtime." Clara's voice sounds matter-of-fact, but I know she's dying to know what this is all about. My mother never calls the school.

"Is it an emergency?"

"No." she says. "It's about a letter."

"A letter? Never mind, I'll call her later."

"What letter, Mrs. Alvarez?" asks Julissa.

"Oh, I don't know, sweetheart, probably something she got from an office or a doctor. My mother gets confused sometimes and needs a little help."

Lorena's washing off paintbrushes at the sink. Her plastic apron is streaked with colors that look like an outlandish finger painting.

"Just like Clara to announce everything to the world," she says. "All she had to say was that it wasn't an emergency."

"Can you imagine? Half the school will know about the letter by lunchtime. Is there anything we can do about her?"

"Clara's been transferred from two other schools. They couldn't do anything about her either, outside of taping her mouth shut. Three's the charm, though, Mrs. Alvarez, the buck might stop here."

By lunchtime Priscilla's shoes are feeling tighter. My toes are starting to bulge out of the satin oval openings. Stupid of me to think I could wear them all day. Clara is standing at the front desk talking to Shirley when I walk in at lunch.

"Did you call your mom, Teresa?" Clara asks.

"Not yet. This is the first time I've had a break all day." She's standing next to Shirley with a box of envelopes in her hands.

"Mail-out?" I ask.

"End-of-the-year stuff," says Shirley. "By the way Teresa, I hate to break the news to you but Mr. H. is thinking of vacating your room and Mrs. Allen's for the new developmental first grades. Both of you would be moved to the next building."

"Getting back at me for not working on the stupid CRTs, is he? I told him we just revamped them last summer, and now they're district scratch paper."

"We're just running out of room," she says.

Shirley's hair is dark gray, almost blue in some places. She looks like Aunt Bee on *The Andy Griffith Show*, minus the apron. Shirley should be in a kitchen making cookies for the neighborhood kids, not at Jimenez Elementary trying to keep Clara busy. The only thing Clara wants to stay busy with is other people's business. She's got a perpetual smile on her face and eyes that invite you to spill your guts. When you're having a bad hair day, it's all you can do not to come in and confess to everything you've ever done, including the time you sneaked out expensive bond paper from the office for your personal use.

"He can't make Mrs. Allen do anything. Annie Get Your Guns is her best friend."

Clara's eyes light up. "Annie's so vocal!"

Shirley shoots a look at her. "Just finish the mail-out, Clara."

I walk into the workroom and place a call home. On the other end, my mother explains that she has a letter from the Veterans Administration in Washington, D.C. She's reading the return address.

"Veterans Admin . . . something . . . Veterans of Four Wars."

"It's probably Veterans of Foreign Wars, Mom, there's only been two world wars, unless I've lost count."

"Do they know I want to get to the Vietnam Wall, mija?"

"No, Mom, they don't. I can't imagine what this is all about. Who is the letter for?"

"For me, mija, it's addressed to me."

"Did you tell the lady who answered the phone here at school about the letter?"

"Ay, mija, she's a busybody. She wouldn't stop asking me questions, la metichi."

"OK, Mom, don't worry. Is Paul there, or Cisco?"

"No one."

"Just leave the letter for me, and I'll read it after school."

As I say the last words, Clara walks in to use the paper cutter.

"I thought you were doing a mail-out."

"I have to get these sheets cut into halves for the PTO meeting tonight. Did you find out what the letter is about?"

"What letter?"

"I thought this was about a letter?"

"Oh, you mean the one from Social Security?"

"Is that all it is?"

"Yep." Disappointed, Clara walks out with a few sheets cut in half.

"Not very many parents coming tonight."

"I just remembered the PTO meeting is tomorrow night."

"Right."

• BY THE TIME I walk into Mom's after school, I'm holding Priscilla's shoes in one hand. Maybe my feet grew from morning to afternoon, or maybe I found out that no matter how hard I try I'll never be able to fit into Priscilla's shoes. Why would I want to?

"You should have worn nylons, mija. You're not supposed to wear dress shoes without nylons. You'll sweat and ruin the shoes. Priscilla won't want them back now."

"I don't like nylons. It's too hot to wear them, besides I don't care if Priscilla ever wears these shoes or not. Serves her right for leaving them here."

"I'll get her another pair if she gets mad."

"Mom, who cares! You're always trying to save us from getting mad at each other. Priscilla will do what she wants no matter what you do." My mother's got rice boiling on the stove and meat simmering in gravy with potatoes. She finishes stirring the pan of meat.

"Look on top of your dresser, mija, the letter is in there."

I dump Priscilla's shoes into a corner of the bedroom, cursing them for starting blisters on my feet. I pick up the letter with the insignia of the Veterans Administration. What do they want now? Paul's not a veteran, so it's not about that. It's not for Cisco, he's already signed up for the Selective Service. I want to tear the letter open, and at the same time I want to rip it into shreds. How dare they send us a letter! They have the life of one Ramirez. Isn't that enough?

I'm waving the letter in one hand, standing barefoot in the bedroom, slipping out of my blouse and skirt. I hear the stump of Mom's cane coming up to the bedroom door. She's looking at me in my underwear, angling her head for balance. She peers at me like she's looking over the edge of a blanket.

"You're getting too skinny, Teresa. I remember when I was that size, and it wasn't just your father who was after me either. There were a few others."

"Then why did you choose my dad?"

She ignores my question. "What's in the letter?" She sits on the edge of the bed. I put the letter up to the light coming in from the window, and notice space between the edge of the letter inside it and the end of the envelope. I tear open the end of the envelope that's free of the letter.

May 23, 1997

Dear Mrs. Ramirez,

In reviewing the records pertaining to your son Sgt. Jesse A. Ramirez, it has come to our attention that an alteration of the money granted to you on August 25, 1968 for your son's untimely death in South Vietnam is currently under investigation by this office. We apologize for any distress this notification may cause you and hope to resolve these concerns as quickly as possible. Please contact our office at your earliest convenience.

Sincerely,
Kenneth J. Rothberg
Accounting Specialist, Veterans Administration

"Another letter of apology? These fuckers can never get enough."

"Don't cuss, mija."

"What do you want me to say? I can't make heads or tails of what this means. They're experts at twisting the truth."

"What truth? Something about Jesse?"

My heart is racing and my hands are suddenly ice cold. "Yes, something about Jesse—but I don't know what it means. What time is it?"

"It's after four o'clock. Why?"

"There's a number here for me to call in D.C. but it's a three-hour difference. The office is closed by now. I'll have to wait until tomorrow."

"What do they want with my son?" My mother is already in tears.

"Mom, don't cry, this bastard Rothberg probably made a mistake, like they always do. I'll find out tomorrow."

"The meat, mija!"

I run to the stove in my underwear, grabbing an old T-shirt on my way out. I'm just in time to turn off the pan with the meat and potatoes as the last bit of gravy is disappearing and the meat is starting to burn. I race back into the bedroom and my mother is sitting with the letter in her hand staring at Jesse's name. Under my breath I'm cursing the pain in my feet, red blisters on each little toe from wearing Priscilla's shoes.

El Niño Comes Through •

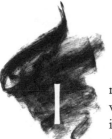 need a tlachisqui, a bona fide seer, to use Brandon's word. If Don Florencío were alive I'd run and ask him if what's happening now is part of Jesse coming back to us in a new form. What does it mean, this whole mistake, turned inside out. I'm wearing seamed edges on the outside instead of the inside. There's a surface I haven't seen yet, a rough, invisible something coming into focus. Don Florencío would probably nod his head and say, "The soul can't be rushed, mijita. It's not like plunging headlong into a river. It all starts with listening."

Did the listening start with the explosion in my dream, or with the voices my mother heard at Christmas? Were the voices only the chirping of birds nesting on the pine branches of the evergreens? Not in winter, when all the birds are gone, the sound so close to my mother's ear, it woke her up. And Cholo barking, yet crouching low, afraid. Of what? Does belief start with asking questions? I believe in the hereafter? I believe in Heaven and Hell. I'm a good Catholic daughter, brought up in the tradition of punishment and reward, of chains rattling on the limbs of tattered souls struggling in Purgatory. How do you chain up a soul anyway? How can a soul be destroyed in fire? It has to be symbols, everything is symbolic. We're floating in universal parallels like Michael says, touching other realities we know nothing about. It's standing in my way, whatever it is, eager to show me—what?

My phone call to D.C. is part of it all. It is shocking. Rothberg lives up to his name. He sounds stuffy to me, white-collar all the way, and so does his voice over the phone. I place the call at lunchtime. My mother is sitting on a chair, listening to every word, the letter still in her hand.

"Er, Mrs. Ramirez?"

"No, this is her daughter. I don't think my eighty-year-old mother would be up to answering your questions."

"Your name, ma'am?"

"Is this an inquisition? It's Teresa Alvarez, soon to be Ramirez again."

"I see . . . this is rather difficult to explain, somewhat a bit of a problem . . . not for you in any way, Ms. Alvarez. It's the U.S. government that's blundered."

"Wow, that's news!"

"When your mother received the money given to her as part of your brother's death in 1968, she didn't receive the full amount. Perhaps you recall, Ms. Alvarez, that your brother's body was originally sent to an incorrect address?"

"Don't remind me!"

"I'm sorry about that."

"Yeah, that's what they said back then, too."

"The family, Ms. Alvarez, of the veteran where the body was initially sent, received half your brother's money, namely five thousand dollars. Amazing, I realize, but it was done. Your brother's name and this other veteran's name were the same except for the middle initial. Your brother's was *A* and his was *R*. We have addressed this issue with the veteran, who is now in one of our hospital facilities, and he states he has no knowledge of the money."

"Of course he won't admit anything! Why should he? Did the government think Jesse was a twin? The address was different, for God's sake! How could all of you be so stupid?"

"Don't cuss, mija," Mom says.

"What does all this mean?"

"Are you sitting down, Ms. Alvarez?"

"I wasn't sitting down when we were told my brother was killed. Just give it to me, Mr. Rothberg."

"The government now owes your mother in excess of ninety thousand dollars. Interest compounded annually brings the exact amount to $92,401."

The phone drops out of my hand, as if a bolt of lightning had run through it.

"What!" yells my mother. "What is it?" She is on her feet without her cane.

"Mom, how would you like to go to the Wall? You've got the money now! God knows you've got the money, ninety-two thousand dollars!"

"How?" My mother's eyes open wide. She has managed to straighten her back up so she is almost eye-to-eye with me.

"They made a mistake, Mom! Remember when Jesse was sent to the wrong address? They paid that family half the money and didn't give you the ten thousand dollars they owed. Now they owe you five thousand dollars plus all the interest! They've been our bank all these years, and we didn't even know it!"

"El Santo Niño! La Virgen! I told you God would find a way! I'm telling Irene." She hobbles toward the door.

"Wait, your cane!" I'm holding her cane and grabbing for the phone receiver on the floor.

"Hello . . . hello?"

"Ms. Alvarez . . . are you there?"

"Listen, I can't explain, I gotta run after my mom. When will the check come?"

"You'll receive it within a week."

Mom is heading down the alley yelling for Irene. I run after her and put her cane in her hand. I race up to Irene's back door while my mother is still calling for her at the top of her lungs.

Irene opens the door slowly, then throws it open all the way, fear coming over her face as she sees my mother walking down the alley yelling, "Irene, Irene, comadre!"

"What's wrong with your Mom, Teresa? Did somebody die?"

"Yeah, years ago." I'm smiling, and Irene is totally confused.

"El gobierno, Irene, el gobierno made a mistake on my mijito's money. They owe us . . . tell her, Teresa . . . tell her how much!" My mother is out of breath, gasping.

"Ninety-two thousand dollars!"

"Dios mio!"

"Cree lo," I say, using Irene's own words. "Believe it!"

"Ay mi Virgencita." She reaches for the medallion on its gold chain and kisses the image.

"Let's go pack, mija," says Mom. "See? El Santo Niño told me the truth at Christmas."

• • •

• I SWEAR I'LL NEVER doubt El Santo Niño or lifting up San Francisco's head in Magdalena, or marching behind the banner of La Virgen with its magical image of roses, or anything that has to do with crazy things I don't understand. I say this to myself, then start forgetting all about it as reality hits and the trip to D.C. starts to take shape. Mom wants Jesse's friends to go, Willy, Gates, and Chris. She wants Manuel to go so he can take care of the money. Who could do it better? She doesn't trust Paul with the money, and none of us would be able to get past him to get our hands on it anyway. She wants everything to be figured out all at once, and us to be on the road. Irene, of course, is coming. I try to explain to her about my job and that I have one more week at school, the divorce is pending, the sale of the house is on my back, and if that's not enough, there's a court date for the assault charges in five days.

"Mom, I can't go right now," I tell her. "In three weeks . . . yes, wait three weeks, everything should be clear."

"No!" Mom is unmovable. There's a feverish energy that takes over her, a scurrying I've never seen before.

"Mom, what are you in a hurry for?"

"I have to get there, mija . . . la manda. I don't want to end up like the Robles brother."

"Three weeks, Mom. That's nothing!"

"I'll be dead in three weeks!"

"No, you won't! Don't threaten me with that. You're so selfish! People can't put everything on hold just for you."

"Stay then, Teresa," she says coolly. "Stay if that will make you feel better. Priscilla and Paul can go with me, Jesse's friends, Manuel, Irene."

"They'll put a warrant out for my arrest if I don't show up in court!"

"They will do nothing to you! Do you think God is blind? This is His plan. Sandra will drop the charges."

"Sandra hates me." I'm watching Mom rummaging through her dresser, pulling out underwear she'll take on the trip. She pauses for a second.

"Let her hate you, just don't hate her back," she says, then goes back to picking out underwear.

• IRENE'S KIDS BUY LUGGAGE for her at Wal-Mart. I buy Mom's luggage at Dillard's. Why not? She's got the money for the expensive stuff. Neither of the ladies has ever traveled. The only things they've ever packed are plastic clothes baskets with their family's laundry. Blue, green, maroon luggage, we have a choice. I call Irene's kids to make sure we don't all buy the same color and mix the ladies up on a grand scale. Manuel is looking into car rentals—two vans, one for him, me, Mom, Irene, Lisa, and Lilly and another for Paul, Donna, Priscilla, Michael, Angelo, and Cisco. Elsa's staying at Mom's house with her husband Julio and my granddaughter, Marisol. She's upset over the divorce, and says she'll stay behind to make sure her dad has a square meal once in a while. Ray's got Elsa convinced that Sandra's the one who's after him, and he's tried to get away from her for the longest time. I went crazy, he says, for no reason. I'm full of bad memories. I've got screws loose. Why should he have to suffer for what my father did to my mother? Elsa listens, something I would have never done, and that's how Ray holds on to her.

Willy and his wife Susie will ride in a car with Gates. We'll pick up Chris in Albuquerque, and he'll get in wherever he can find room. My mother's crazy energy is enveloping us all.

The day after the money arrives, Channel 5 News descends on the house. They spoke to a family member by phone, they said, who gave them permission to conduct an interview with Mom. We later found out it was Michael who called the station and alerted the news media to the mistake the U.S. government had made.

In between stories of natural disasters and graduation parties gone awry, the news people decide the story has merit. Neighbors are standing outside on the sidewalk next to the van with the letters CHANNEL 5 NEWS on it. I'm in the house with Paul, Donna, and Michael.

"Nice touch, Einstein," Paul tells Michael. "What were you thinking about? Trying to make your nana nervous with all this shit?"

"Nothing wrong with a little publicity. People will follow us all the way to the Wall. I'm working on a web page for Nana. I'm putting her on the Internet. You've heard about the web sites, haven't you?"

Michael is working on a laptop computer he's been given to use over the summer by the gifted program at school. They also gave him a cellular phone so he could connect with the Internet.

"Michael, why are you doing this?" I ask him.

"Publicity, Tía! Nana is now www.jramirez68.com. There are people out there who know Tío Jesse. Watch, they'll be in touch with us."

"In touch with you, wise guy," says Paul.

"Leave him alone. He's right. A little publicity is just what we need. A Chicano soldier from el barrio, unknown just like all our guys who went over there and were never appreciated. They emptied the barrios during the Vietnam War, and you're complaining about some recognition?"

One photographer and a redheaded reporter walk in to interview Mom. Mom sits in her rocker wearing her best blouse, a blue one with huge white buttons and a pair of navy blue slacks, two sizes too big. She's at ease talking to the woman, a redhead with long legs who sits on the couch with a small yellow pad and pencil. She's trying to look official, then her cellular phone rings.

"I can't talk right now, call me later. . . . No, I never said that, you took it wrong." She looks at Mom. "Excuse me." She rushes out to the front porch and talks heatedly to somebody.

"Probably her boyfriend," Paul says. "But I'm free. Hey redhead, I'm free." Donna gives Paul a dirty look. "Just kidding, babe."

"Sorry, Mrs. Ramirez." The redhead is back, and I notice the light on her cellular phone is out. Her face looks flushed.

"Don't worry about men," Mom says. "They make trouble, but they can't live without women."

The redhead smiles. "I think you're right about that." She signals the camera to start rolling. "Now, what about this money you received from the government, Mrs. Ramirez? Ninety-two thousand dollars, my goodness! Was it a shock?"

"No. I was expecting to get some money. I knew God would send it to me. I need it to get to Washington, D.C."

"You mean to see our capital and the president?"

"No, to get to the Vietnam Wall to touch my son's name. I promised to do it before I die."

"Promised your family?"

"I promised God. That's why I got the money."

The redhead shuffles her long legs, uncrosses them, then crosses them again.

"So, you believe in supernatural intervention?"

"In what?"

"In super . . ."

"Never mind about all that," I tell her. "Mom has lots of faith and believes we are meant to go to the Vietnam Wall."

"Tell them, Teresa, about the voices and El Santo Niño."

"What voices?" The redhead looks confused.

"A dream Mom had."

"No! It wasn't a dream, it was my son and his friends talking to me."

The redhead is curious. "What did they say?"

"I don't know. That's why I tell my daughter here, that El Santo Niño will let us know."

"Who is El San . . . to Ni . . . no?" She signals the cameraman to stop.

"God," my mother says.

"It's her faith in God," I say.

The redhead looks at me. "Do you believe this?" Her blue eyes are boring into mine.

"I don't know what to believe . . . my brother, Jesse, the Vietnam vet, told her she'd hear his voice someday, and he told us we'd read about him in a book, and . . ." I stop myself before I announce to her he told me he'd never come back.

Paul looks at me. "You don't have to tell her anything."

The redhead purses her lips. "I'm not trying to pry, I'm really interested."

"In what?" Paul asks. "In a story for the six o'clock news? My brother's body was sent to the wrong address, the sons-of-bitches couldn't even get that part right! Why don't you put that in your story, Miss Six O'Clock News."

"Don't cuss, mijo!" my mother says.

The redhead stands up. "I'm sorry, I didn't know this was so disturbing. I had no . . ."

"It's OK, Miss Red Hair," my mother says. "My mijito got his prayer answered in Heaven, and we're leaving for the Vietnam Wall in a few days."

There are tears in the redhead's eyes. "My cousin died in Vietnam. He was like a brother to me—Robert O'Connor, 1969." Paul walks away without another word.

"Was he Irish?" I ask her.

"Yes."

"So was my grandfather, William James O'Brien, my mom's dad."

"God bless you, pobrecita," my mother says. "We'll touch his name, too." The redhead walks out crying into a Kleenex, followed by the cameraman, who unplugs his camera and thanks my mother for the interview.

• ON THE SIX O'CLOCK NEWS that night we saw a head shot of Mom and the redhead, the front of the house, and neighbors around the Channel 5 van. We heard the part about the money, nothing about la manda or El Santo Niño. No surprise to me. We heard the redhead we found out was named Holly Stevens tell the audience that the Ramirezes, family of the deceased Vietnam vet Sgt. Jesse A. Ramirez, were on their way to the Vietnam Wall, made possible by a huge blunder made by the Veterans Administration in 1968. The government's mistake is the Ramirezes' good fortune, she said. Miracles can and do happen even in this day and age, she added, smiling big into the camera.

Sacred Meal •

The next day Espi and I drive up to the old house on East Canterbury, the house Ray and I lived in for over fifteen years. It's better than the apartments we lived in the first few years of our marriage, not counting the duplex Ray invested in with his friend Steve. Steve's nothing but a con artist. Ray knew it but never admitted it, even when Steve ran off with the rent money and ended the campaign against roaches in the duplex by leaving all the fumigating solution in Ray's pick-up. "I guess he never finished the job," Ray told me. "Never finished? He never got started, you idiot! He took you for everything you had!" Ray says Steve's one hell of a drummer, and he still lets him drum out beats for Latin Blast. If it were me, I'd have exchanged his beloved drums for the fumigating solution.

"I'm glad I don't have to worry about your brother's business investments anymore, Espi. We almost lost the house because he owed so much on the duplex."

"Amen to that."

I double-check the carport to make sure Ray's pick-up is gone.

"We bought the house because I liked that tree." I'm pointing to the huge carob tree that engulfs the front yard. The tree is an evergreen sprouting dark green leaves year-round. The tree won't produce the sphere-shaped carob nut until spring, when the hard nut bursts from its brown shell and falls to the ground, untouched. I've never known anyone who harvested the carob nut. It's not like pecans or piñones. The nuts fall everywhere, casting a strong, sticky smell that borders on the unbearable on summer evenings when the heat of the day, like invisible waves, rises from the asphalt streets. All you do is rake up the mess under the tree. If you love trees like I do, you run your hand over the gnarled trunk, amazed at the tree's dark, green beauty and pungent smell.

This year the yard is a dismal yellow, the grass has gone unwatered. The FOR SALE sign is hanging out, inches from the sidewalk, announcing to the neighborhood that the marriage between Ray and Teresa Alvarez is over. Everybody knew it before the sign went up. It looks sad, the sign. I glance at it once coming in and once going out.

Inside, the house is desolate. Most of the furniture is in storage, leaving only the pieces Ray and Cisco will need until the house sells: the couch, TV, kitchen table, chairs, bedroom furniture, and a desk in Cisco's room. We're here to look at the girls' room to calculate how much furniture we should move to Mom's.

"Look at this mess, Espi! Your brother must be crazier than I thought. How does he expect to sell the house? And now we're leaving for the Wall. It'll take at least two weeks for me to get back and start cleaning up."

"You know how men are, anything is OK for them. They have no sense of the right thing to do. I'll help you when you get back. Just think this is the most exciting thing that's ever happened to your family. Jesse's reaching for you from the Vietnam Wall!"

"Or my mother's reaching for him . . . or they're both reaching for each other. Either way, it'll be a long trip, you know how we are as a family. We only get together for Mom's sake." I'm standing in the dark hallway. It feels like I'm in a confessional. "I can't ever go back to your brother, Espi, not after the whole thing with Sandra."

"It must be hard for you. I don't know why my brother got mixed up with her. I'm glad Tommy doesn't run around."

"Tommy? I can't imagine it! Remember when he and Manuel joined the choir at St. Anthony's just to be close to us?" We both laugh, remembering how Yolanda Escalante, the organist, scolded them for being off-key. Yolanda couldn't get rid of them, because they were the only boys in the choir and we needed their voices. We both get quiet.

"You OK?"

"Yeah. What can I say? All these memories all over the place. I don't know how much more I can take, Espi. But, I'll tell you the truth about

Sandra. I don't think she started the problems between me and your brother."

"Then why did you fight her? I can't believe you went that far. You might even end up with a prison record!"

"Don't get dramatic. I fought her because she was laughing at me—no shame, just like Consuelo, you remember, Dad's mistress? But I think everything started before that, Sandra's just the last thing that happened. Ray and I hardly talked anymore. He wanted to watch baseball on TV and live on beer and peanuts when he wasn't working. A far cry from the man who got involved with the Brown Berets when they came to Phoenix. Ray was an activist, don't you remember, Espi? He went to Denver in '69 when los Chicanos proposed El Plan Espiritual de Aztlán. They were saying we had a history. We were descendants of the Aztec nation, but we were different, too. We were a people searching for our own mythical land, our own Atlantis. Then I don't know what happened to Ray. He just quit. He wouldn't go with us to the Chicano Moratorium in East L.A. He said we were crazy."

"We *were* crazy in those days, Teresa. We could have gotten ourselves killed. I still can't forget that reporter the L.A. sheriff killed—Ruben Salazar. They murdered him in cold blood!"

"Don't even remind me. It makes my blood boil."

"I still have nightmares over it."

"Maybe you've got a form of PTSD, Espi—you know, post-traumatic stress disorder. You can suffer for years over some trauma that's happened in your life. Now, I'm wondering if Ray didn't have PTSD. I read about it. Lots of guys who served in Vietnam suffer from it. They live the war out in different ways and it doesn't end for them until they come to terms with what's happened to them. Ray never told me one thing about Vietnam, even though I asked him lots of times. The war was so brutal, then coming back here was just as bad with people blaming them for the whole thing. Now that I think of it, Ray might have been going through depression, but you know your brother, he never wanted anybody to help him."

Pictures are all over the walls as we walk into the family room.

"I told the girls to take all these pictures down and pack them in newspapers."

We browse around looking at the pictures. There's Elsa and Julio sitting with Marisol in front of a fireplace, last year's Christmas photo. Elsa's petite, a little elf. Her thin hair hangs down around her shoulders.

My life was gray inside when Elsa was born in early '71. Nothing had color. Losing Jesse did that to me. Made me a blank sheet. I held Elsa and it was better for me, feeling flesh and blood, a little heart pounding through her lumpy chest. She was beautiful and always smelled of the fabric softener I used for her baby clothes. She was pink like her blankets and slept on my chest many nights curled in between my breasts, making them squirt milk when they were full.

"Look, there's Priscilla with Angelo and Michael." Espi's pointing to a photo of Priscilla, Angelo, and Michael at Disneyland. "Michael's such a brainy kid."

"He's a real *Jeopardy* candidate. He's in a special school in Scottsdale, the only Chicano kid from the Southside over in rich man's land."

"More power to him. I wonder what he'll be when he grows up."

"Ask him. He'll tell you. You'll feel like you're talking to a university professor."

"Wish I had a kid like that!"

"Really? Some people are scared of kids like that. Paul can't stand him, his own son! They get into arguments all the time."

Espi's staring at a photo of Paul. "It must be hard for Paul, having a brother like Jesse who did everything right. Jesse was your mother's favorite, for sure."

"I don't know about that. Paul's the baby, and you know how moms feel about their babies. Mom loves us all. I don't think she ever made a distinction between us, but then again, if you ask Paul, he'll tell you Jesse was Mom's favorite."

Espi's voice and mine bounce off the half-empty rooms. It's like we're walking in La Cueva del Diablo, not the house I used to live in. The angel with the flaming sword found something wanting and is sealing the place up. There's a sore spot inside my chest I can't reach. I open the door to the girls' bedroom and stare blankly at their twin beds, stripped of blankets and sheets. The twins' identities split off in amazing directions, just like Priscilla's and mine did. Lilly is all sports, She made varsity basketball in her freshman year. Her body is supple and strong. She winces at wearing jewelry and dresses. Her hairdo is nothing more than a short bob. She's more Priscilla's daughter than mine.

Lisa is me all over again. Her nose is always in a book, memorizing poetry, reading the latest authors. She's in drama, auditioning for Squanto's wife this year, and last year for the lead female in *Tom Sawyer*. She's almost plump. I'm hoping she won't have a weight problem like some of her cousins, who weigh in at 200, if they were to tell the truth.

"I'll leave the chest of drawers and come back for the dresser. They've got beds at Mom's, so we'll have to put the beds in storage. The girls would hate it if I sold them. And look at all these clothes still hanging in the closet. Most of it they never wear. I'm gonna bag it all and give it to the Goodwill."

I glance into my old bedroom as we walk by. Ray wouldn't bring Sandra here, not now anyway. Maybe later when he gets a place of his own. I glance at the bed. The pillows are lying on top of each other. The comforter's in a heap in the middle of the bed. The bed's been pushed up against the wall, instead of being centered in the middle of the room like Ray used to like it. I'm looking at the bed of a woman I don't remember anymore. Was it really me in bed with Ray? When? I can't even remember the smell of us together that made me catch my breath when we were first married.

There was a warm, sacred part of Ray, a hand that held mine all night when I cried for Jesse. It was warm blood I felt when I pressed my fingers gently on the artery in Ray's neck. It was something I had wanted to do for Jesse, to feel for his pulse. I felt Ray's heartbeat over and over again to make up for not hearing Jesse's.

Walking down the hallway, I hear Cisco's stereo playing in his room. He loves music and dancing like Ray. Names for his CDs are unpronounceable to me, 2-Pac, Aaliyah, Ice Cube, Bone Thugs, Jodeci, Lighter Shade of Brown, Snoop Doggy Dog, and the only one that makes any sense to me, Gloria Estefan.

"Are you awake? Cisco?" I'm knocking on his door; after a few seconds he opens.

"Oh, hi, Mom. I didn't know you were here." He's half-asleep, running his hand through his thick mop of hair that ends in a ponytail when he combs it out. Cisco's taller than me by several inches, and so handsome I don't want to take my eyes off his face. He's got several girls on his trail. He's half Ray, half Tata O'Brien. His lean, muscular body is light cream. He wears a small gold earring on his left ear that I like but Ray hates. He's standing in his boxers, rubbing his eyes.

"What's up, Mom? Are we ready to get on the road?"

"Not yet! Your nana wants me to invite Gates and Willy and there's a hundred other things to do. I'm just checking around to see what needs to be done here. Espi's with me."

"I'll be up in a little while. I've got wrestling practice."

I'm already down the hall on my way to the kitchen. The stove is greasy. Food stains, multicolored blotches, show up on the stainless steel surface. The floor looks like somebody tried to mop it and missed a few spots. The trash can's overstuffed with beer cans. I make a mental note to tell Ray to hire someone to clean up the place. I open one of the cabinets in the kitchen and find two tiny silver spoons that belonged to the girls when they were babies, a baby shower gift.

"OK, Espi, we can go. I found what I'm looking for." I'm holding up the silver spoons.

"That? That's what you came here for?"

"No, but that's all the energy I have left for right now. Just enough to pack these little silver spoons into my purse. I might even take them to the Wall. They leave all kinds of things there."

I'm surprised at my tears, at how fast they pool at the corners of my eyes, as I put the silver spoons into my purse. Espi's not surprised, she saw them coming before I did.

• ON OUR WAY back to Mom's I point my Honda toward the river bottom, deciding, suddenly, to follow the road that leads to La Cueva del Diablo and Don Florencío's old shack.

"Where are we going?" asks Espi.

"Just cruising down to Don Florencío's old shack. I want to see how things have changed."

"Things have changed for the worst. What do you expect, a brand-new tract of homes? Most of it is a landfill now. Homeless people, that's all we'll find there. Who knows if they won't jump us and go off with the car."

"They're homeless, Espi, not criminals!"

I glance at Espi next to me. Everything's changed, not just the landscape. She's lost weight, her hair is dyed, smoothed back behind her ears. Her nose used to remind me of a small brown doorknob. Now it looks rounder, flatter. She doesn't have that devil-may-care attitude in her eyes anymore. They're serious looking with worry lines at the corners.

"What did you see in that old man, Teresa? He was so strange."

"He was strange to us because we don't know who we are. He knew who he was and he knew one other thing, too. He knew Jesse wasn't coming back before I told him what Jesse said to me the day he left."

"How?"

"He was a tlachisqui of the Mexicas—that's us. He interpreted the invisible world for them."

"What did I tell you? He was a curandero, maybe from the dark side."

"Never! That old man never hurt a fly. If anything he was a dreamer, a visionary who followed the old ways to the letter. He even spoke Nahuatl, the language of the Aztecs. People don't know that the word *Chicano* is an Aztec word, except it was spelled with an *x* instead of a *ch*. His ancestors split from the Aztec nation centuries ago because they didn't believe in human sacrifice. He made his way north to search for Aztlán, which is how he ended up in Arizona."

"Did he find it—Aztlán?"

"No . . . not that I know of. North of the Gulf, in a marshy land, the land of the herons . . . all kinds of things are said about Aztlán, even that it was a mythical island or that it went all the way up to Wisconsin!"

"Give me a break!"

"We came from somewhere, Espi. We had to have had a home somewhere. According to legend, we left a land flowing with milk and honey and journeyed south to what is now Mexico City."

"Kicked out of the Garden of Eden, huh?"

"Maybe, with an angel and a flaming sword. An angel who said, 'Out!' Wonder what we did wrong?"

"*We*? Maybe they just ran out of water."

"With the Río Salado and Río Grande running full blast? No, it had to be something else. Didn't I ever tell you—Don Florencio saw Jesse in the flames of his campfire outlined like a warrior on the day he was born. Can you imagine? The old man saw him as a warrior, and Jesse had barely been born!"

"This is getting spooky! Do you believe in all this?"

"Who knows? My mom heard something in the house at Christmas, but she didn't see anything. She said it was Jesse and his friends talking. Don't you believe in spirits, Espi?"

"I believe in God. He's a spirit. A keeper of spirits too, I guess. Can you imagine if somebody heard us talking like this, Teresa? They'd say we've gone off the deep end."

"So what's new? They said the same things about Don Florencio. Places change, but people stay the same. Nothing's sacred. Ray was like that, too. After he quit marching with la raza, he started criticizing everything. I told him, he'd regret it when his own kids forgot where they came from."

I'm driving slowly now, turning the last curve of the road where I know we can get off and walk up the rocky incline.

"Hope the car doesn't pick up any nails," Espi says. "All we need out here is a flat. I can just hear Tommy saying I tempted God."

"So, that's where all the gray hairs are coming from. Tommy better loosen up!"

I stop the car. All I want to do is run up the small hilly rock way and find Don Florencío sitting on his old wooden chair with the straw seat stuck together with twine, smoking his ironwood pipe with the little sculpted faces on the stem. The sun is to our left, midway up the sky. Don Florencío would say it's not a new sun, but one that woke up and is headed for the trillionth time to its appointed place in the center of heaven, a notch below God's throne. You can't look on its brightness for very long without hurting your eyes. Has anyone looked at the face of God and lived?

"You're right, Espi, they've made a mess of this place. Where's Don Florencío's mesquite tree?"

"*His* mesquite tree? He didn't own this land, Teresa. He just thought he did."

"He owned it all, Espi. Him and his ancestors."

"What did you see in that old man? What?" Espi's standing at the bottom of the small hill, and I'm at the top already looking to my right for La Cueva del Diablo stuck in the gray, rocky mountain ridge. Its dark, yawning mouth is boarded up with signs—NO TRESPASSING—DANGER! I remember Don Florencío's vision the night Jesse flew to Vietnam. Bats, he said, scattering wildly, screeching, following the trail of blood to Vietnam.

"You'll get trapped up there, Teresa! Get down! Somebody could find us."

Espi's voice is echoing off the rocks. I'm good at ignoring her. I know she'll get back in the car, lock all the doors, and wait for me.

The mesquite tree is gone but not its fragrance. My pores open in the warm morning air. My skin remembers the smoke drifting from Don Florencío's small wood stove. I take in a deep breath not minding the faint grimy smell coming from the landfill close by.

There it is, what's left of it. Don Florencío's adobe shack. The door facing east is hanging on one hinge. The tin can doorknob is gone. Where? Who took it? He was so proud of it. Three walls remain and one is completely gone, the one facing La Cueva del Diablo. Maybe the bats ate through it, snatched up what they could of the old man sunk deep in the adobe bricks. Maybe they did it on purpose, because he knew them, knew what they wanted that night.

There is silence all around me. It's spring, but there aren't any birds singing in the trees. We're far enough away not to hear the rush of traffic. I can see the Black Canyon Freeway in the distance, a concrete snail splitting El Río Salado in two. I sit on the crumbling adobe wall, and I want to start the wail again, the wail that Don Florencío said was the song of my soul weeping. *Pray for me, tlachisqui, pray that I'll do what God wants me to do. I'm afraid. It's always this way with me . . . my heart broken by men. My father, El Ganso, Jesse, Paul, Ricky, Ray . . . pray for me, pray for me.*

Nothing's the same. Don Florencío's not here, and Jesse's been gone forever. I stare at a bunch of old rags in a corner. Don Florencío's? I go check, barely touching the rags with my fingers. But, no, it's a pair of trousers, something too modern for the old man, and a blanket, something bought at a secondhand store, now torn and ragged, but not the old man's. His table is gone, the chair, his wood stove, his old cot, whatever it was that held his body or that he touched with his hands. I look up at the sun shining in through the missing tin slabs of the roof and breathe in the smell of mesquite. My nose tries to recapture the distinct fragrance of copal. I pick up a handful of dirt and pretend it's sacred meal. I throw it into the wind, spinning round and round.

"What are you doing?" Espi yells. "Are you crazy? Come down from there!" She's waving her arm, motioning for me to come down.

• I RETURNED a few days later to the house on East Canterbury with Manuel to move the rest of Lisa and Lilly's things to my mother's. Cisco was at one of his wrestling matches, and Ray had disappeared off the face of the earth; not even his buddy Steve, the fumigating con artist, could tell me where he was.

"I'll close shop, Teresa," Manuel said to me. By that, he meant he'd let his daughter Maria run his accounting business for a while. Manuel still wears glasses, wireless rims now. He's got less hair on his head, and a belly that hangs over his belt. His eyes still remind me of Orphan Annie's. He looks like he's searching for someone he lost in a crowded mall, and the whites of his eyes look bigger than his pupils. Regina's gone, his ex-wife, living with a mail carrier she ran away with. Manuel says they were meeting behind his back for years.

"You look as good as you did in high school, Teresa. Ray must be crazy!"

"Don't even mention his name. He's as good as dead to me, him and his girlfriend." Manuel is staring at me. The white part of his eyes looks even with the dark part for the first time ever.

"Been waiting for you, all these years." He winks, then smiles and opens his arms to me. It feels good to be held by Manuel, although I know holding me will only frustrate him. I know he'll never hurt me, I'm sure of it. Power between me and Manuel has always been in my favor. The only time it was different was the day Mom quit singing.

"Bendito" •

My mother's body was soft in the middle where she hid us as babies in her womb. I wanted her to live a hundred years and comb her hair in two white ponytails with a perfect part down the middle. I wanted to protect her as she stood leaning on the vinyl-covered rail that extended the length of the choir loft at our Saturday practice. She was poised like a little statue, holding tight for the first note of "Bendito." After Jesse left for Vietnam, Mom went on singing. It was her way of doing the same thing she did before he left, her way of clinging to the ordinary. She was in demand as a soloist for masses, weddings, quinceañeras, and whatever else was next on the agenda at St. Anthony's.

Mom's voice was so good she could have done a solo with the Two Doors Gospel Choir the night we went to see Brother Jakes. Her voice, full and luxurious, rose one note above the noisy organ at St. Anthony's Church. It jiggled the old-fashioned chandeliers and drifted up to the rafters of the church seeking out the cool, dark places where mother pigeons fed their young. Then it cascaded down like water dripping off a huge umbrella to bounce off candles, benches, people and the huge, carved altar where the priest served mass. The only reason the saints didn't smile and clap their hands was that they were made of clay.

Stand up straight. Catch your breath from deep down, under your ribs, not from your chest. That's singing. In through your nose, all the way down, let the air tumble out at your lips, easy, without straining. All you do is mouth the vowels, the air will do the rest. Your cheeks will tingle from the vibrations. Afterwards, your throat won't hurt. Will I ever learn? I practiced in front of a mirror watching my profile to make sure the air was going into the right places, pressing my hands on my cheeks to feel the vibrations.

On Saturdays, Yolanda Escalante looked closely at me, her big, moony face smiling. She was encouraging in her own way. She climbed the wooden steps spiraling up to the choir loft every Saturday afternoon to play the organ for our weekly choir practice. I'm surprised she didn't get caught in the narrow passage. She tested the ancient bench before she sat on it. Were the wooden legs as strong as they were last Saturday? If so, they would last through Sunday. "That's it, Teresa. Yes, you're learning, just like your mother." She was lying. I never sang like my mother. The most I could do was croak out a fight song with the other cheerleaders at Palo Verde High's football games. Priscilla could sing, but she never joined the choir.

It was six months after Jesse had left for Vietnam, June 6, 1968, when my mother quit singing. That Saturday afternoon Yolanda sat at the organ pounding out the chords of "Bendito," my favorite Spanish hymn. Yolanda was immense in her black skirt and flowered blouse. Standing at the balcony rail, my mother held sheets of music in one hand. Her lace veil lay back over her head, the last row of stitched roses barely touching her shoulders. She couldn't read music so she followed along by noticing the ups and downs of the squirming notes and memorizing all the pauses, the soft brushes of tones and the notes that painted a bold splash in the air. I marveled that she could move air from the middle of her body to her throat with the same precision Nana used to thread her silver needle.

Down below, the huge, ornate altar lay in shadows with hundreds of glowing candles reflecting off glass pictures and the shiny brass railing at the altar. Some candle wicks burned furiously like fervent prayers, undaunted by the darkness. Others sputtered tiny bits of light, old prayers dying, burning down to their glass bottoms. Jesse had written me, asking me to light a candle for him. One of those tiny flames belonged to him.

The altar harbored a collection of life-size statutes. There was Christ with a crown of thorns around his heart and Our Lady of Sorrows, His Mother, dressed in black, with a dagger piercing her heart, so sad, so wounded, and there was nothing I could do to help her. Men carried her statue on a platform in processions on evenings of Holy Week, marking the end of the Lenten season. Around the church she went, past el barrio that looked like it was suffering as much as she was. She swayed and lurched behind the big cross of Jesus that other men carried on their shoulders. Every woman wanted to suffer like she did, stoically, taking it all, not being chillonas, crybabies who wimped out with a little pain. Every man wanted to suffer like Christ did, carrying the cross until his shoulder ached from the burden. Then the man carrying the cross passed it on to another man who was waiting impatiently for the privilege of feeling the pain Christ felt on his way to Calvary.

The passion flower growing outside my mother's bedroom window unfolded in front of my eyes, white, purple, nails, crown, thorns, whips with blossoms that stuck out in every direction, crying out the pain of Christ. Christ stripped of his garments, half-naked rose on the cross in front of us common sinners, hopeless wretches who lit candles, pounded our chests, and burned smoky trails of incense His way. Were we afraid to suffer as He did? Was pretending enough for us? We ate no meat, we gave up gum, candy, dancing, cussing, thinking nasty things. Then on Easter Sunday, we went back to everything and decorated the altar with white lilies, self-inflicted sufferers, we had distracted ourselves for forty days not knowing that real suffering was with us every day. We were conquerors of a few discomforts, patting ourselves on the back, aligning ourselves with Christ and Our Lady of Sorrows. We were cheap imitations of the young mother who had watched her son die a brutal death.

Angels stood on either side of the altar, St. Michael with a hoofed and tailed devil at his feet and Gabriel ready to blow his trumpet. Stained glass windows sparkled with the images of St. Therese the Little Flower, St. Francis, St. Joseph, St. Martin de Porres, St. Ann, San Juan Caballero, solemn figures watching over the congregation from their lofty perches.

Above the figures of Mary and Jesus stood a statute of St. Anthony, patron saint of the church, holding the Baby Jesus in his arms. St. Anthony was famous for helping us find lost articles and bringing us sweethearts. I don't know how the saint bore responsibility for both, but he did. There were times I'd ask him to help me find a lost shoe or bracelet or ring and before long, there was the item, right in front of my eyes. Finding a sweetheart was something else. You had to be serious on that account. One woman got so frustrated praying for a sweetheart she threw the statue of the saint headfirst out her window, only to find that it hit her future fiancé on the head and knocked him out cold! The saint proved himself again, the caretaker of love affairs.

I was trying to capture music notes in my head that afternoon. Maybe if I thought about them hard enough, they would come out right. We were sweating. The electric fan barely moved the air around us. Father Ramon didn't like turning on the swamp cooler just for choir practice. Under my veil, my hair stuck to my scalp. I squished into my seat as I plopped down on the worn-out vinyl chair when we weren't singing. Yolanda blinked away sweat from her eyelashes. I looked around at the six girls and two boys standing in the shadows. None of the church lights were on, except Yolanda's lamp over the organ. The air smelled like smoky candle wax. Next to me, Espi was dripping sweat, pulling at her blouse and blowing down her neck when we weren't singing. "It's good I cut my hair," she said, showing me the back of her hair clipped above the neckline. I didn't have the heart to tell her the hairdo looked like a lopsided pancake on her head. Espi's nose curved into a smooth, brown knob. Her eyes were dark centers, set close together.

Tommy and Manuel, the only boys in the choir, looked like caricatures of grown men, dripping sweat after a hard day's work in the sun. Beads of sweat outlined Manuel's upper lip and mustache. I knew Manuel was there only because I was, and Tommy was there for Espi. Every few weeks, Tommy's face erupted with pimples. I told her he probably used rubbing alcohol to dry up his pimples. Espi didn't have much choice when it came to boyfriends. After she gained weight, Tommy was the only boy who really looked at her.

Manuel was taking classes at Phoenix College, where Jesse had been attending until he quit and made himself an open target for the draft. Manuel wasn't an altar boy anymore, except on special occasions when he joined the priest during High Mass at Easter. Manuel wore black horn-rimmed glasses. Sometimes light from the lamp reflected over one or both lenses, making Manuel's pupils disappear. He stared at me and smiled, and all I could see were two tiny spotlights for eyes. Manuel reminded me of a railroad man who waves at you and smiles when the train is rolling by, but never gives you a chance to take a good look at him. I never really looked at Manuel until that day, then it was all I could ever do to forget him.

That Saturday afternoon I was singing, but I was really waiting. It started then, and it hasn't ended yet. I'm still waiting. Back then, I was waiting for my mother to release the first vowel of "Bendito" into the empty church before all the statues and stained-glass saints. Everything stayed in my mind, a photograph I've carried in my soul; the heat and darkness of the church, my mother in her navy blue dress, facing the altar, Yolanda swaying over the keyboard, the light from the lamp holding us tight, and my mother's voice exploding on the first note of "Bendito," hushing the pigeons cooing under the eaves of the rooftop. Her voice was so beautiful, I swallowed hard and listened.

> Bendito, bendito, bendito sea Dios
> los angeles cantan y alaban a Dios
> los angeles cantan y alaban a Dios.

> Blessed, blessed, blessed be God
> angels are singing and praising God
> angels are singing and praising God.

This was the chorus. We sang it together. My mother sang the verses by herself. I was feeling a rush of pride, because my mother was a soloist for the church, but her voice was really mine. Mine when she sang in the kitchen, mine when she sang soft little lullabies nights I couldn't sleep. In the dim church, her voice searched out God's ear, yet something was crouching low, waiting to pounce like a jaguar snarling. I could sense it moving in the shadows. A chill went up and down my arms.

We knew Jesse's company had been ambushed. We had received the news on Tuesday in a telegram an Army representative brought over to the house. They called to make it clear Jesse was still alive, maybe wounded, but still alive. Nothing more had been sent, nothing. The information stopped abruptly. We called the office in Phoenix, no, nothing else from Vietnam. The veladoras at home flickered on the big oak dresser before El Santo Niño de Atocha and La Virgen de Guadalupe, waiting for Jesse to come home. El Santo Niño was known to walk from place to place in his little brown sandals performing miracles for the faithful. Sometimes people left tiny shoes for Him to wear to replace the ones worn out by His travels. My mother believed He could bring Jesse back. Bring our Jesse back from the other side of the world. Use your power to keep him safe. Keep him alive, Santo Niño. We didn't want to say "Don't let him die!" out loud, so we secretly shouted it in our minds, in our hearts.

The Vietcong had struck in all the major cities in Vietnam during the Tet offensive. Jesse's company, part of the 1st Infantry Division, was stationed outside Saigon at Bien Hoa. The news on TV was filled with pictures of wounded American soldiers. Magazines and newspapers were filled with photos of Vietnamese villages burning and children napalmed by American troops. I reached for Espi's hand and squeezed it hard. She shook it out. "What's wrong with you?" She looked at me, angry that I had caused her pain. I looked down at the altar and wondered why I had hurt her. "Sorry," I said. She turned away.

My mother's voice led the first verse of the song. Warmth exploded inside me. Her voice searched for me in the dark, making vibrations erupt between my shoulder blades and travel down my arms.

Yo creo dios mio que estás en el altar
oculto en la hostia te vengo adorar
oculto en la hostia te vengo adorar.

I believe my God that at the altar you reside
in the host you are concealed, I come to worship you
in the host you are concealed, I come to worship you.

Yes, God, we praise you, don't let me think of the ambush. The electric fan blew my hair. The rest of my body was one sweaty, sopping mess. My hands got cold, and I breathed into them like I was freezing to death. Espi looked at me, her eyes opening wide. "You're cold?" I only shrugged my shoulders.

The Secretary of the Army has asked me to inform you that the 1st Infantry Division, Company B has suffered an ambush in a battle outside Saigon. At this point no further information is available. You will be provided progress reports and kept informed of any new information concerning your son Sergeant Jesse A. Ramirez.

The telegram sent my mother into a panic, even though the messenger made it clear that it was not a death notice. Jesse's words scrambled around in my head, *I don't think I'm coming back, Teresa. Take care of Mom.* I was waiting, every nerve in my body held taut by Jesse's words racing through my mind like a flashing neon sign. What would I say to my mother if Jesse was killed? That I knew and didn't tell her? Kept it from her, didn't watch Paul close enough and he fell off a tree, scared her half to death almost drowning in the Salt River and she lost Inez, then El Ganso died at the Jones's Granary all because of me. Am I a hex, la muerte herself? Did Nana know? She had asked me what Jesse said to me as she looked at us through the rearview mirror on our way to the airport. "Un secreto? What did Jesse say to you, mija?" "Nothing, Nana, nothing important, just something about Chris." But I could see the truth in Nana's eyes. She knew. Nana had learned how to glide through the debris of life, floating through still waters, bumping shoulders with brambles and thorns, letting them sting her arms, her legs, then gliding away.

My mother's voice rose again for the chorus . . .

Bendito, bendito, bendi—

The last word punched the air like a fist that never stopped being a fist. My mother didn't finish the last syllable. Yolanda struck the keys with more power, looking over her shoulder at my mother, her brows gathering into a frown. We trailed unsteadily into the huge space my mother's voice had vacated, limping our way through the song, word by word. I looked at Espi, and all I thought about was Ray telling me Jesse would come home. "Jesse knows how to watch his back, Teresa." And I smiled like one of the women who watched him at the bars, open-mouthed. Espi poked me in the ribs. Her eyes said, "What's wrong . . . what's wrong with your mom?" I looked at my mother as though I had never seen her before. Everything about her had stopped. She had turned to stone. She was a ceramic statue. My mother's mouth was open, but there was no sound. I saw her lean over the balcony rail. The sheets of music slipped out of her hand and fell over, fluttering down to the empty pews below. I followed her eyes. The side door was open and sunshine was pouring in. Outlined in the light stood Father Ramon with a military man dressed in Army green. Messenger from hell. My mother's eyes were fixed on the military man. Yolanda's hands froze over the keys.

"What is it?" she shouted. She spun around on the bench, jumping off like an athlete.

My mother's voice ripped the silence apart. "MIJO! NO! NOT MY SON! NOT MY SON! PLEASE GOD, NOT MY SON!" Once, twice, many times . . . so many times, "NOT MY SON! PLEASE GOD, NOT MY SON!" I put my hands over my ears. I thought I saw the saints on the stained glass windows do the same. My mother's voice made me cringe. "JESSE'S GONE! YOU TOOK MY SON! GOD, WHY DID YOU TAKE MY SON?" I arched my back to hold in the pain. Her cries bounced off everything at the same time, making one loud echoing shout. Yolanda grabbed my mother and held her up to her huge breasts like she was a baby. The pigeons on the rooftop cooed wildly. Who can stand to hear the sound of a mother who knows her son is no more?

In one leap I was at the balcony rail. Manuel was right beside me. I saw the whites of Manuel's eyes gleaming, huge and empty behind his glasses. He held me in a big bear hug, pulling me away, afraid I'd jump. I grabbed a book of hymns and flung it with all my might over the rail, missing the military man by inches.

Gold of Asia •

January 31, 1968

Dear Sis,

It's unreal what's happening over here. At first we thought there were celebrations going on. The Vietnamese celebrate Tet, their New Year holiday. Incoming fire sounded like firecrackers. We didn't get the information on time. Just like these bastards. They cover their asses especially during holidays. I tell you it's like hell over here (don't tell you know who). Our squad has lost four men. Four. It sounds like 94 to me. One is too many. Guys ride on choppers with dead bodies in body bags. Sometimes the poor dead suckers don't fit in the bags and their legs stick out. Guys get nervous and start cracking jokes. They know it could be them. Did you light the candle? Don't worry I'm doing everything I can to stay alive. I don't want to ride in a body bag.

The people here are poor. You've never seen anything like this. Kids going through the garbage. They'll fight over a bone. Sis, this must be hell. What are we doing here anyway? Get this. Trucks here are made in Russia. They got Mitsubishi engines from Japan and Goodyear tires from the U.S. So what do you think this is all about? I look around and think the Vietnamese are right when they say "Dogs go home!" It's all about money and land for rice. I'm sending you the gold of Asia in this letter, rice, what else?

They have altars around here for the dead. Remember how we have El Dia de los Muertos? Well here they do it every day. They bury the dead in their front yards. I see these red candles burning in houses with pictures of the dead and statues of Buddha. Family members try to take everything down before the shooting starts. The Vietnamese don't like souls wandering around without a grave to hang onto. Even the homeless people get a grave. There's little altars along the roads for souls who don't have a regular place to stay. Can you imagine how these people think? There's a family here, a Mom, two daughters and a son, a little kid about Paul's age. They're Catholics, believe it or not. They fled from the north to get away from the Communists. They've been good to me. I even went to church with them the other day. One of the daughters looks like a princess. I mean it. They wear these beautiful dresses called ao yais. I wish the girls in the States could see their clothes. Now that's what I call women's clothes! I'll get you and Priscilla one. Guess what the sermon was on? The Good Samaritan! I couldn't understand a word but a Vietnamese who knows English told me. No better story to show us how wrong we are.

Hey, is Gates back? Last I heard he was in Nha Trang. And Willy? Where is he? I lost track. Chris is still with me. Check out the picture. Me and Chris posing with M-60 machine guns. We're standing on Ho Chi Minh's trail. All that's a lie. There's lots of trails over bridges and all kinds of ways. The U.S. protects the routes. They got a stake in the war like everybody else. We look at a trail and we automatically think Ho Chi Minh. Uncle Wes wouldn't know what to do if he found the real Ho Chi Minh, except to bomb him off the face of the earth. I wrote to Espi and she hasn't answered yet. How's Paul and Priscilla doing in school? Tell them they better study and hard too. Is Dad staying away from C? I won't even write her name. And Ignacio? Tell Julio about him if he bothers you. Julio will do business with him. Hug Mom and Nana for me and give them a kiss on each cheek. Tell them to stop crying. I'm OK.

Guess what? The moon's the same over here in Vietnam. I'll be damned if the sun don't shine just like it does back in the world. At night when I can see stars I think I'm nobody, a small speck, lost. Then in the morning I'm a soldier again. Play Solitary Man for me.

SWAK
Jesse

I shake out the remains of a fragile rice stalk into my hand. The gold of Asia weighs next to nothing.

• • •

• THERE ARE PLACES in El Cielito I've avoided all my life. Bars for instance, that attract vagabonds, drunks, and ordinary people who want to sit around and listen to music or do some dancing. Places I wouldn't be caught dead in, with pool tables in back rooms, green fabric seared by cue sticks and filthy lamps hanging overhead. I've glimpsed these things in passing, running, actually. As a child, I peered into these hovels of disrepute where people fought, howled, whooped, and issued out sometimes in couples to make love under the bushes in the alley next to our house. The bars fascinated and repelled me at the same time. Now I had to put all my feelings aside to hunt down Gates Williams in one of them. There was no other way to reach him to tell him my mother wanted him to go with us to the Wall.

"He hang over by Penny's Pool Hall," Blanche tells me. Her daughter, Betty, is standing next to her with two kids. She's dark like Franklin, taller than her mother by two heads at least. Blanche looks the same except her hair is white, and she's put on weight, not as much as Hanny, but still enough to make her move slower. I wonder if she still has the hat with the red pin. I open my mouth to ask and decide it wouldn't matter.

"Where's Cindy?" I ask her.

"She moved to Seattle with her husband and is miserable over there, because she says the sun don't shine much."

Betty's watching me. "Heard about all that money your mother got back. Saw it on TV. Now that's something! I tell you, when the government messes up, they mess up good. I wish they'd mess up on my child support money." I hear another child cry inside the house, and Betty disappears.

"I'm so tired of these kids," Blanche says. "I'd rather stay out here on the porch all day, Teresa. If it weren't so dangerous, I'd sleep out here. Why, I remember when . . ." She gazes off into the past, her eyes staring at nothing in particular.

"Well, I better go, Blanche. My mom is real excited about this trip."

"Your po' Mom ain't been the same since Jesse was kilt. Never come out of it. You go on now and tell her she be doing the right thing, that ol' Blanche sends her a big hug and kiss. Lord have mercy on the bunch of you . . . ain't she sick, Teresa?"

"Yes, she is. I've tried to talk her out of it, but she's made a promise to get to the Wall and won't let it go. Mom's stubborn. Remember when she went to see Brother Jakes and got healed of her migraines. There was no stopping her then either. I'm glad she went, because look what happened."

"Oh, I've never forgotten that night, Teresa. Nothin' like the power of the Lord to zap a sickness away! His son be preaching now, Pastor Rufus, but everybody call him Bear. He's 'bout as big as Gates and strong! That's the way he got Two Doors Gospel filled up. If he can't convince a man to turn to God by preachin' the gospel, he strong-arms him."

"Strong-arms him?"

"Oh, yeah, honey, he arm wrestles them! Bets a lot of money, 'cause he know he be winning. Men are greedy, you know, Teresa, they never say no. If they lose they have to come to church for a month! I tell you, that church is filled with men every Sunday. All the sisters are goin' crazy with so many men."

"I heard he plays a mean guitar, too."

"That too!"

We're both laughing. I can just see all the men who lost at arm wrestling, sweating and jumping around whether they like it or not.

"Well, now, you'll be fine, Teresa, baby. I'm prayin' for all of yous. If you find Gates tell him Erica's on his trail, that's his latest ex-wife. I can't tell you how I've lived with all the worry Gates has caused me. Franklin never gave me a bit of trouble. He lives in Mesa now, working as a probation officer."

It's hard to imagine that one of Blanche's sons bought into the system and the other one is doing all he can to stomp on it. Blanche opens her arms to me, and I curl up in her round, black arms. She feels warm, soothing.

"I miss Hanny," I tell her.

"Oh, so do I, and all that cookin', 'member?"

The name *Hanny* races across my mind. I imagine it on a headstone like a neon sign flashing. "I loved her ostrich hat."

"Hmm . . . you too?" There are tears in Blanche's eyes. "Everything's changed now, Teresa. You're so skinny, I'm getting s'cred. I'll send you some peach cobbler. How's that?"

"Like the one we ate when Brother Jakes was in town?"

"Yes, like that one." She kisses my forehead.

• • •

• I DECIDE TO VISIT Penny's Pool Hall before the sun sets, right before things get loud and wild. It's not far from Mom's house, located in a string of taverns, grocery stores, two barber shops, and a tortilla factory bordering Buckeye Road. Before I know it, I'm in the parking lot at Penny's getting out of my Honda and walking on gravel, loose rocks that get caught in the heels of my shoes. PENNY'S POOL HALL is painted in yellow letters and is punctuated by huge brown pennies that look like flying saucers. Some of the pennies are painted with their sides showing the bust of President Lincoln, others show the Lincoln Memorial in D.C. I've always wondered why the place was called Penny's but now, up close, I can see a connection between Abraham Lincoln on the pennies and the freeing of the slaves. They should have added a five-dollar bill or two.

This is an all-Black bar, and I'm definitely not Black. I walk into the place dressed in an all-white pantsuit. The doors are the push kind, worn out in the middle where most people push or fall through, whichever the case may be. I'm cursing Paul under my breath for not doing this himself. "I'll never get out alive," was his excuse. It was all I could do to stop my mother from running over to Penny's herself to invite Gates once she started thinking about how Gates and Jesse went to school together and boxed at the Golden Gate Gym with Trini.

"Help you?" asks a chunky man at the entrance. He's standing behind the bar setting up some bottles of beer. My eyes are still adjusting to the dim light, after the harsh sunlight of early June. There's music blaring from the jukebox, Janet Jackson. His eyes roam over my body and he smiles. "You'll need some help around here!"

"Yeah, I think you can." I offer him my hand. "I'm Teresa Ramirez, you remember my brothers, Paul and Jesse Ramirez?"

"Oh, hey, yeah! I'm Scotty. We lived over on the other side of Wong's. Sure do remember y'all! Your brother Paul out of prison?"

"Yeah, he's out. Trying to straighten up his life. I hope he does it this time."

"I seen him in there, over at Florence. Miserable in there, that's what he was. Me, I jest take it one day at a time. Say, you the ones who got all that money from the government? Didn't your mom get back a million or something?"

"No, not a million! A lot, though . . . about ninety thousand."

"Honey, throw some my way! How come you ain't dressed in diamonds? Lord knows you look like a movie star!"

"It's my mom's money, besides, you know how it is with money, it slips through your fingers, but listen, Scotty, maybe you can help me. Have you, by any chance, seen Gates around here? You know, Blanche's son?"

"That who you look'n for?" He throws back his head and roars with laughter. "You come at the right time, Teresa. Any later and that man be wasted. He's out back by the pool table."

I walk by a few men sitting at small, round tables looking at a baseball game on a TV monitor. They stare at me, turning their heads, measuring my steps. "Aren't you the daughter of that millionaire what got all that money?"

"I'm the daughter, but we're not millionaires." One of them smiles and winks. I smile at all of them. My heart is pounding, and I'm wondering what else will happen, as I see two other men walk into the place with a woman. She's dressed in a tight-fitting dress, fluorescent blue. She stares at me, then swishes her head to look at Scotty.

"Didn't know we were gettin' multicultural in here. I would have worn my sombrero."

"Shut up, Bea!"

The back room isn't as dark as the front, or maybe my eyes are adjusting. Everything I've ever heard about pool rooms is in front of me. A greasy orange lamp hangs over the center of the pool table. The room reeks with the odor of stale beer, cigarettes, and old wood. A smoky haze floats up over the lamp and trails toward the half-open back door. I catch a whiff of Pine-Sol from the bathroom nearby.

"Gates?" I haven't seen him in years and wonder if the man I'm looking at is Gates. He's sitting close to a young woman who has one of her legs curled around one of his. She's pretty, her hair pulled back, huge black eyes and a body that looks like it belongs to a model on the cover of *Vogue*. I watch as they both stand up, curious to see what they look like. She's wearing a midriff blouse and a pair of shorts so short they almost look like underwear. Her legs are shapely, the calves sheathed almost to the knees in sandaled leather straps. Gates is tall and stocky, hair graying at the temples, probably six-four. He lives up to his name, always has. He towers over her in a pair of worn-out black Levi's and a blue Chicago Bulls T-shirt. His light skin contrasts with her darker skin. Still handsome, he's lost weight, his face sags around his jaw and chin. His eyes are bloodshot.

"Hey, look what we have here! Is that you, Teresa? What you doing here?" He walks toward me unsteadily. "I knew you'd come lookin' for me someday, baby. Didn't I tell you, Kamika, I said, Teresa Ramirez is gonna come lookin' for a Black brother someday and there I'll be, good ol' Gates!" He gives me a big hug and Kamika glares at me.

"It's not really that way!" I say to her, "he's only kidding."

"Yeah, he's a big kidder all right!"

"Gates, did you hear about the money my mom got?"

"Yeah, my mom told me something about it. Man you guys hit the jackpot!" He motions me to sit down at one of the tables with him. "Kamika, go get us something to drink, darling. What you want, Teresa?"

"Just a Seven-Up. I gotta keep my wits about me."

"With all that money, you bet! Hey, baby, can you slap some here?" He extends his hand palm up, then laughs. "It's so good to see you!"

Scotty yells into the room, "Hey, Gates . . . your ol' lady's been calling! I don't want no trouble. That woman fights like a man!"

"No trouble . . . no trouble," says Gates. He looks over his shoulder at the back door. "Let's move, baby, where I can have a good look-see." He moves toward a corner where he's facing the entrance and the back door.

"Your mom told me to warn you that Erica's on your trail."

"Yep, that's the one Scotty's talking about."

My nerves are standing on end as I think of what will happen if Erica comes in fighting like a man while I'm talking to Gates or Kamika is wrapping her leg around his leg.

"Listen, Gates, did your mother tell you we're going to the Wall?"

"What wall?" He glances at the front door, then the back door.

"What do you mean 'what wall?' The Vietnam Wall! With the money we got, Mom's making the trip to D.C. I don't know how she'll make it, she's been so sick, but you know Mom, she believes God wants her to go there to touch Jesse's name before she dies, and there's nobody who can talk her out of it. She's made a promise, Gates, we call it a manda in Spanish, and she's inviting you to go with us, 'cause she remembers how you and Jesse were friends."

I hear Percy Sledge on the jukebox, "When a Man Loves a Woman," and wonder if Kamika put in the money to hear the song.

"I haven't heard a jukebox in years," I tell him. "All I ever hear are tapes. Well, what do you think?"

Gates lowers his head. His face has changed from smiling to somber. He is frozen in place.

"Gates?" I put my hand on his arm. "What's wrong?"

"Look at me, Teresa. Do you think I want to get to that Wall? I got brothers on that Wall, Black, Brown, and White! God, girl, look at me, I'm a fuck-up! I never got it together, Teresa. I can't let them see me like this." He shudders.

"Gates, they're not gonna see you! They're names on the Wall. They don't have eyes. You got as much right to be here as anybody else. Jesse would tell you that." Gates has his head in his hands and is shaking it from side to side.

"I can't go, Teresa! I just can't. All the medals and shit they gave us, for what? Last of all they built the Wall, like they were saying, There, now shut up! I saw my buddies shot over there like dogs. White guys made the plans on paper, but the blood was real, and they didn't give a shit about us. Body count . . . that's all they cared about, body count, body count, like they were counting toy soldiers and not men. Then at the airport when we got back to the world, people were crazier than we were—throwing shit at us, calling us baby killers!"

"Gates . . . Mom wants you to go with us. It means a lot to her. It'll be OK."

Gates looks at me, his eyes pleading. "Think about your brother, Teresa. He was the best ever. Now explain to me why he's dead and I'm alive? Can you give me a reason?"

"Me, give you a reason? I couldn't even figure out how we were gonna get to the Wall, but we're on our way! Life and death are all a big mystery to me, Gates. I don't know why things are happening the way they are. Nobody has the answers. Maybe earth is a place for questions, not answers."

Kamika is back with the drinks, a Seven-Up and two beers. She looks at Gates. "What's wrong? You look like you at a funeral."

"I am," he says.

"Somebody die?" she asks me.

"Kind of."

"What you mean 'kind of.' Either somebody died or didn't."

"Yes, somebody died." I take a drink of the Seven-Up. "Think about it, Gates." I put my hand on his shoulder. He keeps his head in his hands.

"I have. I'm not going."

"Going where?" asks Kamika.

I walk out the back door. It's easier than going all the way to the front, past the men at the tables, Bea and Scotty. The sun is sinking, out-lining a pale edge of violet orange in the sky. What am I going to tell Mom? She's so crazy these days she'll come looking for Gates herself. While I'm trying to figure out what to tell Mom, a gray, rusty Monte

Carlo screeches to a stop in the parking lot. As I open my car door, a woman jumps out of the Monte Carlo in a pair of faded Levi's, a tank top, and thongs. She's taller than Kamika, thick-boned with wide shoulders. She slams the car door shut and runs toward the back entrance. A piece of gravel gets stuck in her thong and she yanks off the shoe and shakes off the pebble without slowing down. I hear Scotty yelling for Gates, and I know I've just missed Erica. A glimmer of hope crosses my mind as I drive away. Maybe Erica will make things so miserable for Gates, he'll want to go to the Wall. I look through my rearview mirror and see a blur of fluorescent blue, short shorts, and faded Levi's as Kamika and Bea charge at Erica like two bulldogs protecting their territory. The whole thing looks hopeful for Gates slipping out of town.

Pilgrims of Aztlán •

t's five o' clock in the morning when I walk out into the front yard. We're ready to load up the vehicles we rented, two seven-passenger Chrysler Voyagers, one white and one gray, and a sky-blue Nissan Maxima, all brand new. It's the first day of June, 1997, and the last week at Jimenez Elementary. Lucky we're going in June, Irene says it's the month of the Sacred Heart of Jesus . . . all that love! We're bound to get there in one piece. I don't answer her. I'm learning to sit still and watch. Trying to figure out things hasn't done me any good lately.

I tried talking Mom into waiting until next week to leave, but she's convinced we should be on the road. This business of rushing makes me feel like I'm fighting to get ahead of something. I'm leaving things undone. The divorce is pending, the court date is next week, my kids aren't out of school, the house is still for sale, and worse still, I had to say goodbye to my second-grade class early this year. My attorney, Slick Sam, says he can't postpone the court date again. I guess he's not as slick as I thought he was. Sandra postponed it twice, saying she had new evidence. I've thought of a plea bargain but that would mean I'd incur guilt. How do I explain all this to my school district? Anything on my record could mean the end of my job, still I won't call up Sandra to try to reason all this away. I've got too much pride, Mom says. Pride that might cost me my job, maybe even a warrant for traveling out of state.

The smell of orange blossoms is everywhere, heavy, sweet. Then, like perfume behind my ears, I catch the faint scent of a rose bush that leans heavily against the fence. The fence used to be chicken wire, now it's chain link. The shiftless renters next door never water their lawn, and the yellow rose bush is the only plant that has survived. I remember Ricky Navarro's mother had flowers everywhere, front and back and in pots on the porch. I walk up to the rose bush and smell the huge yellow roses, carefully outlining the petals with my finger. I miss the tall stamen of the passion flower and its purple starburst middle. Something feels amusing to me and I can't explain what it is. A big joke in the sky, like God's got a marching band on hold just for us. I look up at the sky and catch myself smiling even though I tell myself I should be serious. Is it lack of sleep that's making me giggle, or the fact that soon we'll be in Albuquerque, and I'll see Chris Montez again? Is it all the money we have? Magic! Manuel's already invested some of it in CDs, a trust fund, and savings. He's got American Express checks and an ATM card for ready cash. Motel rooms have been prepaid all along the route we're traveling. My mother asks that Manuel give Irene, Willy—and Gates, if he shows up— $500 spending money, and $1,000 each for Paul and Priscilla. I'm wondering what Irene will spend her money on—more medallions? Manuel thinks Mom's too generous with her money and should be investing in a new house. I told him he's crazy. Mom will never leave El Cielito.

I'm trying to trace the source of the happy feeling I'm getting as I stare at the door of the shiftless renters' house. The door is cracked close to the hinges. The wood around the doorknob is black. It looks like it's been open and shut by a hundred greasy hands. A sudden longing to see Ricky Navarro comes over me. I'd convince Ricky to go with us if he was here and serve him tea and cappuccino in real china cups all the way to the Wall. We'd toast each other, his green eyes smiling over the lip of the cup.

I feel like the ballerina in the glass cabinet. I spin in a pirouette. I've got on my short black overalls with a white rayon top underneath, white socks, and tennis shoes. Manuel says I still look like the high school cheerleader he remembers. I know he's exaggerating, but it feels good to hear him say it. The sun is shining on me, already warm, its white light promising another scorcher. I feel good, tingly, like a kid on the first day of school. Something is about to happen that is more than getting to the Wall. My body is telling me, my mind is reacting, and I have no idea what it's all about.

I've talked with Dr. Mann, and have emergency numbers for physicians and hospitals in every state. He's concerned about Mom's heart condition. The left part of her heart doesn't function well, the artery on that side is hardening. Mom takes Lipitor to keep the blood flowing and her heart vessels clear. She's got nitroglycerin on hand for chest pains caused by angina. "Not a good idea to take your mother on such a long trip, Teresa. Her high blood pressure could lead to a stroke, or something else."

"Ok, Doctor, OK. You tell her. Maybe she'll listen to you." The doctor tried, I have to give it to him, he tried. It was the first time my mother looked through him like he was made of glass. She nodded, yes, yes . . . then when we left the office, she asked me if I had the shopping done for the trip.

Lilly calls me to the phone. It's Espi telling me that she and Tommy will be praying for us all the way. "Call me, Teresa, as soon as you get there," she says in a worried voice I can't match up with the funny child's face I keep in my memory. Hearing her voice reminds me how much I miss the crazy things we did as kids. It's that way every time I'm around Espi. We're still on the city bus, bringing home paper bags with creased-down sweaty handles filled with items on sale and layaway clothes our mothers paid on for a month. We're trying not to laugh, holding hands behind the organ as Tommy and Manuel hit the wrong note. Serves them right for standing there sweating under Yolanda's lamp just to be close to us. Espi is the keeper of my secrets, dark ones I don't understand that stand on sharp edges like razors in my soul.

Elsa, Julio, and Marisol are here to say good-bye. Elsa dressed Marisol in a pink summer dress with little sandals. I lift her up to rub my cheek against her dimpled face and kiss her. "Don't let the dog jump all over her," I tell Elsa. The baby walks up to Cholo as soon as I put her down. "See, there he is, already jumping on her new dress!" Elsa and Julio will be staying at Mom's as much as they can. Paul put out the word around the neighborhood that we're leaving. Everybody knows that means he's got eyes watching the house. Julio's from Las Lomitas and he's not the type that will let anybody from El Cielito sneak up on him. Everybody respects reputation in a barrio, strength and the ability to defend.

Elsa's cool with me, aloof. She makes a big fuss over Mom, ignoring me. "Take your medicine, Nana, don't forget. Tell my mom to call us every day." She looks at me, but doesn't say anything.

"I'll try to call as much as I can. Don't leave the house alone for too long. You know how Nana worries over burglars."

"I know what to do."

"Give your mother a hug," Mom says.

"I will, I will," she says, but she doesn't.

The neighborhood is coming alive, on a Sunday morning. Even the Ruiz clan, who hasn't seen a Sunday morning since they quit going to church twenty years ago, is up. Everybody thinks we're millionaires, and we are compared to everybody else. Irene's kids come over to see us off. Ray comes over to help the kids load up the cars. I'm glad he's wearing sunglasses, saves me the effort of having to look into his eyes. He picks up Marisol and turns around once with her in his arms. "Tata's princess," he says. He walks into the house with Elsa at his side.

I lose count of all the boxes of snacks being packed in, corn nuts, fruit roll-ups, Doritos, bean dip, and things that crackle and snap in your mouth, to name a few. We should invite a whole platoon, feeding them would be no problem. Willy and his wife Susie are partly to blame for all the extra snacks. Willy grabbed all he could from the store before the new shipment came in. He wanted his dad to think everything had been bought out.

"Gotta keep it simple for Dad, Teresa. If I tell him I brought all this stuff, he'll charge me for it!" Willy says. Susie is standing next to him, a pudgy, half-Filipino, half-Chinese woman. Her ethnic background confuses people all the time. In the summertime she gets dark and looks Hawaiian, in the spring she looks Filipino, and in winter, she looks Chinese. It gets more confusing as you hear her slip from Chinese to Filipino, to Spanish, then back to English!

I'm surprised Willy's running his dad's store. He always said the farther away from his folks, the better, but I guess the Chinese way won out. Xiu and Chong Wong are in their eighties now and live with their daughter, Helen. On holidays they dress up in their Sunday best and sit on two rockers in front of the store. They still talk in Chinese that sounds like they're arguing with each other and sip tea through toothless gums. General Custer, their dog, died years ago. He was poisoned by a piece of bad meat a thief left in the yard for him. After that, Xiu decided to get a dog that would bring out the Chinese in all of them. She didn't care about General George Custer and the Battle of Little Big Horn as her husband Chong Wong did. She bought a shar-pei with some of the money they hid in the walk-in refrigerator. They never kept the shar-pei at the store, it was too expensive. They named him Lin Chow, and I heard he's on his third eye operation to remove wrinkles that settle around his eyes. Without the operations Lin Chow would already be blind. Willy told me Lin Chow has cost his parents more money than all the kids put together.

I'm watching the twins and thanking God they're dressed in their baggy clothes. I don't want them stirring up Mom and Irene. I'm not in the mood to hear a description of the horrors that await disolutas who run around half-naked all the way to D.C.

Ray's already mentioned Cisco's earring several times. I think the Guadalupanas can't see it, which is why they haven't taken up on it themselves.

"How can you go to the Wall with that thing stuck in your ear?"

"Dad, some of the guys who made it through Vietnam wear earrings!" Cisco says.

"I don't wear one! Never will either."

Ray's ignoring me. "I can drive the van," he told me the night before we left. "Can't you put your anger aside and let me help you? Manuel doesn't have to go."

"My mom wants Manuel to go. He's handling all the money. Besides, where will you sleep, Ray? Won't you be lonely without Sandra? She'll get mad. Oh, and by the way, tell her the subpoena she sent doesn't mean a damn thing to me. We'll see what the judge says."

I said all this between clenched teeth. The part of me that wanted to reach out to Ray has shrunk to the size of a pea. Inside me, the cells that still remember him are floating loose, forming clusters of cells that send new messages to my brain, messages that are untangling knots I've held inside since the days of Consuelo and Dad.

Blanche and Betty show up with a tin of peach cobbler.

"Here, Teresa, get some meat on them bones," Blanche says to me. She gives Mom a big hug that lasts over a minute. "Alicia, don't you worry 'bout nothin'. 'Member when our Lord healed you from the migraines? Nothing to it, praise be to His name!" Both women are crying.

"Is Gates coming?" Mom asks. "We'll wait for him."

"NO! Don't wait!" says Blanche, alarmed. "That man don't know if it's day or night."

"But . . . I—"

"Mom, we don't know. He still might come," I tell her.

"Call him up, mija," she tells me.

"Oh, no, Alicia! Who knows where that man is!"

"Drive safe, Manuel," Blanche says. "My aunt lives in D.C., and she doesn't even own a car. She's so s'cred of driving up there she moves by subway."

"I'll be real careful, Blanche. Too many women looking over my shoulder," Manuel says.

Riding up the street in a black Riviera is Priscilla and her new boyfriend. I think his name is Albert. He's dark with broad shoulders. He drops Priscilla and the boys off. Priscilla gets out of the car wearing Levi's cut-offs, a black tank top, and wooden clogs.

Paul looks closely at Albert. "I think I saw him in the pen," he says.

"Got everything ready, Teresa?" Priscilla asks me. "I know how you crave organization."

"I'm sure I forgot something, if that makes you feel better."

"Here they go!" Paul says. "I hope the two of you make it to the Wall in one piece. I can just see one of you making a U-turn and coming back home."

Priscilla kisses Albert, and they say good-bye.

"Hey," Paul calls out. "You done some time?"

Albert ignores him and drives away.

"Shut up, Paul!" Priscilla says. "Just cause you've spent half your life in there, you think everybody else has, too."

"I never forget a pretty face," Paul says sarcastically.

Coming up the street is the Channel 5 van.

"Uh, look at this! Michael's got the news people out again," Paul says. "That kid's got a big head. Needs a little deflating, if you ask me."

"Don't start!" Donna tells him. "He can't help it if he's smart."

"Don't start with me, Donna!"

"Stop talking so loud. You'll upset your mom."

"He's my kid, Donna. Remember, I am his father. I can have my opinions about my own kid."

My shoulders slump. Already I'm tired of Paul and Donna, and the trip hasn't even started! By the time I walk up to the Channel 5 van, Michael is explaining the route we will take to the redheaded reporter, Holly Stevens. Michael's got a map of the U.S. with a dark, red line drawn across the center. The camera is rolling on Michael and the scene of us loading up the cars.

"We'll take Interstate 17 to Flagstaff, then Interstate 40 through Winslow to Albuquerque to pick up my uncle's friend Chris Montez. From Albuquerque we'll go on I-25, I means interstate, to Colorado Springs, running into state highway 24, then back to I-70 to Topeka, Kansas, and all the way to Baltimore and Washington, D.C."

"My, aren't you the little map expert!"

"This is nothing. I want to be a cosmologist when I grow up. I have to start somewhere."

"He wants to draw maps of the universe," Angelo says, folding his arms in front of him. He seems as if he's just made an important announcement to the whole world.

"Are you going to help him?" asks Holly.

"Am I gonna help you?" Angelo asks Michael.

"Of course you are! We're gonna have our own observatory!"

"My, what a mind-blowing idea!"

Michael's got his laptop computer in a leather case. He slings it over his shoulder. "This," he says, "is what's gonna keep us in touch with America. I made a web site for Nana." He points to the web site address pasted on the inside of the van window, www.jramirez68.com. Holly jots it down on her notepad. On another window, Michael pasted the words VIETNAM MEMORIAL WALL. WE REMEMBER.

"Your grandmother's lucky to have a grandson who's so smart! I'll send you messages, and you tell me how everything's going. Will you, Michael?"

Michael is beaming into the camera, "Yeah, yeah, I will."

Holly walks over to my mother. Mom's sitting in the van with Irene. Lisa and Lilly are behind her, adjusting their Walkman headphones and fluffing up their pillows. Mom's wearing her favorite pink blouse, dotted with bouquets of purple roses, a pair of black slacks, and Reebok tennis shoes. Her white hair is brushed back around her face, barely showing her ears, and smoothed down at the back of her head. From the back, she looks like she's wearing a white cap. She sets her cane up between the seat and window. Her eyes are full of the same look she gave me when she saw the photo of the Wall. She's got a surprise hiding behind her back, wouldn't I like to know! Irene's hair is dyed black and gathered into a bun. She's got a beauty mark, too, close to her bottom lip that Mom always said drove men crazy. I can't imagine either one of them ever making love, but I guess they did, they have kids. They're wearing their medallions of La Virgen and gold loops on their ears. I pick up the scent of bath powder, a surprising, newborn baby fragrance.

Irene's wearing a long navy blue dress with stockings and black-laced shoes. "You need tennis shoes," Mom told her before they got on the van. She lifted the edge of her pant legs and showed off her white Reeboks. "Never!" said Irene. "Imagine, tu Nana en tenis!"

The two old women sit stiffly in the back seat, ready for their trip across the nation. Their faces are transformed with excitement, turning wrinkles into faint lines curving gently around eyes, cheeks, and lips. We're all children off on an adventure, Americans who have never seen America.

"This is the big day, Mrs. Ramirez!" Holly says. She points the microphone toward Mom.

"Yes, I think so. Did he call you again?"

"Who?"

"The man on your phone?"

"Oh, him . . . yes, he did."

"Are you friends again?"

"No!"

"Good. You be strong, mija." Holly looks flustered. She picks up the thread of her story again.

"You'll be at the Vietnam Wall soon, Mrs. Ramirez. How do you feel?"

"I feel God is with us, nothing can stop us."

"You have so much faith!"

"We're moving into invisible parallels," says Michael, "The invisible has spoken!"

"Stop that kid!" Paul yells. "He's gonna put all the New Agers on us."

"You're so bright to come up with that!" Holly says to Michael.

"Yeah, he's a walking encyclopedia," Paul says.

"He's a genius, pobrecito," my mother says.

"I'm not a chip off the old block, that's for sure," Michael says pointing to Paul. "That's my dad."

"That's your father!" Holly says in amazement.

"You got a problem with that?" Paul asks her.

"No, of course not. It just took me by surprise. Tell me, Michael, do you believe your grandmother really is connected to a parallel universe?"

"That's one assumption. Nana has faith, and that's powerful, too. Subatomic particles are not independent energy. Everything's connected to everything else. What you do in one place affects the others, and that goes for the entire universe."

"Gee, I'm impressed. I'll have to think about all that."

"My mother is happy," I tell the reporter. "She won't rest until we get to the Wall. She's made this promise, a manda we call it in Spanish, and there is no turning back." Holly nods her head.

"Your mother is a beautiful woman. She inspired me the last time I spoke with her. I haven't been able to forget her and what she said to me."

"Lots of people won't forget her," says Michael. "She's the first nana with her own web page. We'll be talking to people we don't even know."

"Yes, you will!" Holly says. "And to think you did it all on your own!" She steps back and points to the flags, the U.S. flag and the Mexican flag, stuck on either side of the two vans. "That's colorful!"

"OK, who did this?" I ask.

"Cisco did," says Manuel. "And look over there, he put a U.S. flag and a flag of China on Willy's car."

"Yeah, Mom, people should know, we're not just Americans, we're Mexicans. We're Chicanos, Chinese too."

"What's the difference between a Mexican and a Chicano?" asks Holly.

"Chicanos are second, third generation in the U.S. They are a mix of the Indian populations of Mexico and the Spanish Europeans. They call us Mestizos. Chicano is an Aztec word that used to be spelled with an *x* instead of *ch*. Originally we came north looking for Aztlán," I tell her.

"What's Aztlán?"

"It's the mythical land of the Aztecs. They originated from Aztlán, from seven caves to what is now Mexico City, but was called Tenochtitlán in the old days. Many of them died wanting to find their homeland again."

"How interesting, how very, very interesting." She bores into my eyes as she did at the first interview. "Do *you* believe in Aztlán?"

"I believe in all kinds of things these days. Maybe we're standing in Aztlán right now. Maybe we'll be traveling through it to get to the Vietnam Wall. Can you tell me any different?"

"No, actually myths may have some truth in them."

"Or, the truth may be a myth, and a myth the truth. Have you ever thought of that?" She looks away from me to Mom.

"The truth is hard to figure out," she says, wrinkling her eyebrows. She starts waving. "Good-bye, Mrs. Ramirez, and everyone else!" she says brightly. "Ad . . . iooos amigos! Good luck, have a safe trip. Oh, and Mrs. Ramirez, don't forget my cousin, Robert O'Connor! Stay in touch, Michael!" Holly gives him a thumbs-up. She turns to the camera. "This is News Channel 5 with an update on the Ramirezes as they go cross-country on their way to the Vietnam Wall after receiving $92,000 from the U.S. government. This was due to the government's failure to award the full amount of money in 1968 for the death of their loved one, Sgt. Jesse A. Ramirez. The government's mistake has made it possible for the Ramirez family to make the trip to the Vietnam Wall. The family has its own web site, www dot jramirez68 dot com." She smiles into the camera and continues narrating as we finish loading up.

I check with Priscilla, Paul, and Willy to make sure they have the details of the route correct. Michael's made copies of the map with the route outlined for them. Manuel starts the motor, and my mother is still asking about Gates. The Guadalupanas make the sign of the cross over themselves, breathing prayers for our safety, acclaiming St. Christopher, the saint for travelers. I wonder if Chris Montez was named after him. Elsa runs up to my open window with Marisol in her arms. She gives me a kiss on the cheek and our faces touch. There are tears.

We start moving toward the freeway north to Flagstaff. I watch Elsa, Julio, Marisol, and Ray standing on the sidewalk. Ray's holding Marisol now and he's waving her little hand up and down, saying good-bye. The neighbors are all clapping, waving.

We're circling around the Central Park projects, the library, the park, another Chinese store, a Southwest Market, St. Anthony's Church. A few cars are parked along the side of the street in front of the church. Early morning mass is going on, the doors are open wide. I catch a glimpse of the altar and the huge statue of St. Anthony in the middle. I look back at Mom and her lips are whispering prayers, not songs.

Nana's image comes to my mind. She walks ahead of all the women, long strides leading them to the white, shining altar. She's hiding in the earth now next to Jesse. Father Ramon died five years ago in an old folks' home for priests. Father Clemente is now the pastor. The old Guadalupanas make the sign of the cross and implore the blessings of La Virgen de Guadalupe as we pass the church.

An old woman, holding on to a child's hand, walks down a twisted alley littered with glass. The sunlight bouncing off the glass is a carpet of diamonds under their feet. I half expect to see Tortuga come out of one of the Freeman Project apartments in an army fatigue jacket, hunting down his next bottle of wine. Mom told me he's on disability now and that his son, Mauricio, fell in love with a girl who only weighs ninety pounds. The girl made Mauricio lose over two hundred pounds, and now they're married. Mom says the girl steams everything and cooks like the Chinese to keep Mauricio slim.

It's too early for children to be playing in the streets. A few old men sit out in chairs drinking café con leche. They wave to us as we pass by. More neighbors come out to the sidewalks, sensing something important going by. Sunday morning in El Cielito is not the same, the air is different somehow, charged by an invisible current.

The ridge of the South Mountains is to my left, purple, blue in the distance. Bougainvillea vines and roses are blooming everywhere. Tamarisk trees and mulberries are in full leaf along the street, streets La

Llorona left when she found out about Vietnam. I look South to El Rio Salado to Don Florencío's old shack and see nothing, not even the tip of the twisted hill he lived close to. I make the sign of the cross over myself. Manuel sees me and puts his hand on my arm. I glimpse his eyes through his glasses, afraid he'll see the pain in mine.

The U.S. flags and Mexican flags on our vans are flapping in the wind, keeping time to the U.S. flag and Chinese flag on the Nissan Maxima. The old women are crying. I turn around and look out through the rear window and see the two vehicles in single file. Paul, Donna, Priscilla and the boys, Willy and Susie with the News Channel 5 Van trailing us, shooting its last footage. By the time we drive onto Central Avenue, other cars have joined us. Chevies, Fords, two pick-ups, a Blazer carrying Irene's kids, the Ruizes, the Valdezes, the shiftless renters, Blanche and Betty, Elsa, Julio, Marisol, and Ray. Without knowing it, we have made our own procession.

As we make the stoplight before heading down the Black Canyon Freeway, I hear a car honking. I put down the window on my side to get a better look. It's the same gray, rusty Monte Carlo I saw at Penny's Pool Hall. I see broad shoulders in the driver's seat and the profile of a woman. Erica's driving. Gates jumps out with a suitcase in one hand before the light changes to green and gets into Willy's car. Suddenly, I like Erica and don't mind if she fights like a man. My mother lifts her hands up to Heaven. . . . "Gracias, a Dios. Thanks be to God! I knew he would answer my prayer." Erica starts honking again as we climb onto the freeway ramp. Other cars join in, then horns start blaring on all sides from drivers who don't even know us. It's a noisy tribute for El Cielito's Chicano soldier.

• WE'RE PILGRIMS OF AZTLÁN, heading east, following the rising sun, on our own quest, una manda, searching out an invisible trek in a maze of voices calling, prayers, magical words, singsong chants of the ancient world, good wishes, broken promises, pain, traveling through the whiteness of Aztlán. My mother, the beginning of it all, is blind to all she's done. We're pilgrims on a journey to America's wailing wall. Only faith will get us there.

Changing Landscapes •

We stop at a rest area close to Flagstaff, in the middle of the Coconino National Forest. The bathrooms are brick structures with toilets that really flush. I walk around a huge pine tree, measuring its rough circumference with my hands, smelling the bark, hoping to catch a whiff of resin, copal for Don Florencío's fire. The kids start running around, punching each other, shouting. Other Sunday picnickers sit on wooden tables, preparing food, drinking coffee. The sun is moving to the center of the world, making the pine trees' shadows lean closer to their trunks. My lungs respond to the sweet mountain air. Manuel and I walk up a trail that leads into the forest.

An elderly couple approach us, smiling. The man has his arm around his wife. He's helping her walk over the uneven ground. She's reaching out, one thin arm extended in front of her, as if she's walking on ice.

"Are you folks headed for the Vietnam Wall?" the man asks.

"Yes, we are."

"I saw the signs on the window of the van."

"My nephew's idea."

"I had a son who served in Vietnam—James Kinney. He made it through, thank God. He's not on the Wall."

"He was lucky. My brother wasn't so lucky. He was killed in 1968."

"I'm sorry to hear that."

"It's sad," the woman says. "All the boys killed over there." She looks at me and I know she wants to cry. "Is that your mother over there?" She points to Mom, sitting with Irene at a picnic table.

"Yes, it is. That's why we're on the road. Mom made a promise to touch my brother's name on the Vietnam Wall."

"And all these other people?"

"Family and friends," Manuel says.

She looks around at everyone. "This is wonderful. Have a safe trip." She leans close to her husband, and her action reminds me of the time Dad picked up Mom in his arms at the airport after Jesse's plane took off.

"She's been ill," he says. "But she's a trouper, aren't you, sweetheart?"

She nods. "We'll be in touch with you. Barry will take down the web address."

"Barry and Eleanor Kinney. We'll be in touch," her husband says, and they walk away.

"Hey, Manuel, we're getting famous."

"Michael was right. A little publicity is good for us."

I stand still and close my eyes. "Breathe in the air, Manuel." I'm taking in deep, piny breaths. "Jesse would have loved this!" I look up. Manuel is staring up at the trees.

"There's lots of space between them. It doesn't look that way from the road."

"What?"

"The spaces between the trees. Some of the trees are burned."

"Who cares? Just smell the woods. Can't you feel the energy? Everything's alive!"

Manuel's staring at me. "You're so beautiful, Teresa. You look like a forest nymph."

"A Chicana forest nymph? Never heard of one!" We both start laughing.

Priscilla walks up to us. "Something I should know about?"

"We're laughing about forest nymphs," says Manuel.

"Getting into the spirit of things, are you? And I do mean *spirit*. All these voices calling Mom. What is this, a moving seance? What did the voices tell Mom? She doesn't know and neither do you, Teresa. I don't believe the dead talk to us."

"Who knows what the dead do?" I tell her. "The real question is, are they really dead, or just out of their bodies, and living somewhere else?"

"This is getting real spooky. Has it hit you that we're going across the country to prove Mom right?"

"Mom doesn't need anybody to prove her right. She believes anyway."

"Yeah, and now that I remember, you're a little weird yourself, chasing that old man over by La Cueva del Diablo."

Priscilla's wearing sunglasses. I see myself reflected in one lens, a distorted shadowy image.

"You wouldn't be saying that if you knew Don Florencío like Jesse and I did."

"People said he was a drunk! Smoked stuff he grew in his own backyard. He was nothing but an old Indian hippie. He should have set up shop in San Francisco, with your little boyfriend from next door, what was his name? Ricky Navarro. Don't you remember? Ricky joined a hippie commune."

"I never saw Don Florencío drunk. And if you're talking about peyote, you're crazy, I never saw anything but tobacco. He respected what nature gave him. And as far as Ricky's concerned . . ."

"Don't get so touchy. Touchy, isn't she, Manuel?"

"She can get a little testy sometimes."

"Whose side are you on?"

Manuel raises his hands, shrugs his shoulders. "Can't win between sisters, I better keep my mouth shut."

"How do you know Ricky Navarro turned into a hippie? He left town, that's all we know."

"Ricky was a pothead, an LSD freak, a total washout! Don't you remember all the rumors?" Priscilla starts to walk away.

"Just like you to say things, throw daggers, then walk away! Don't even start me on your men!"

My heart is pounding. I see the Guadalupanas sitting at a picnic table with the twins. Gates is smoking a cigarette, standing under a pine tree with Willy and Susie. I lower my voice. "Talk to me about your latest, Priscilla. He looks seedy to me. Isn't his picture over at the post office?"

Priscilla yanks her sunglasses off. She glares at me, her body stiffening. "You can't touch him, Teresa, and that's what bothers you! You always think you have power over men, all men—my men!"

"Que pasa?" my mother is standing, leaning on her cane.

"They're fighting, Nana," Lisa says.

"No, mija," she tells me. "Don't fight!"

"Don't think I'm on this trip because I want to be!" Priscilla yells over her shoulder. "If Mom doesn't make it, neither will you, I swear it!"

I look at Manuel. "Did you hear her? Threatening my life. There's a law against that! Blaming me for all this!"

Priscilla's already in the van. Paul and Donna show up with the boys. Cisco is wrestling with Michael, holding both hands behind his back. After traveling only a few hours, they're acting like brothers.

"Look Mom, chicken wings!" he yells.

"Leave him alone!" Priscilla shouts. She jumps out of the van and races toward Cisco, grabbing his arm.

"It's a wrestling move, Tía," Cisco says. "I'm gonna make him a tough guy."

"Not in my lifetime!"

"We're playing," Michael says.

Angelo grabs Cisco around the waist. "He's teaching us how to wrestle, Mom."

"Both of you shut up and get into the van!"

"Don't push my kid around, Priscilla," Paul says. "I can stand up for my own."

"You stay out of this, you loser! Where were you when Michael was a baby and needed you? Where were you when I hauled him around to all his dental appointments? Now you're back, and you want everything your way—well, it's not that easy!"

"It's OK, Tía," Michael says. "Dad just broke his own record. He's never defended me before."

Mom and Irene shuffle up to me, leaning on each other for support.

"Ya, behave yourselves, all of you! Look, everybody is watching us," says Irene.

"They'll say we're a bunch of Mexicans who can't do anything right," Mom adds.

"They probably think we're a delegation from the United Nations," Paul says.

My mother is distraught, her arm trembling from the effort of holding herself up on her cane.

"It's OK, Mom, don't get so upset. Priscilla has a big mouth, she doesn't really mean what she says."

"Ay, why can't you love each other? If Jesse was here he would know what to do."

"There you go again with Jesse!" Paul says. "Jesse this, Jesse that. Nobody can control these two, much less somebody who died thirty years ago!"

"Que nervio!" Irene says. "How dare you talk that way to your mother!"

Paul opens his mouth. "Don't say another word," I tell him. He turns away. I watch his back. One shoulder is slumped at an angle like Dad's. He's rummaging through his pocket for the car keys.

Donna wraps her arm around Mom. "Let me help you to the van, Alicia. Don't even think about all this. We'll be in Albuquerque soon."

"You ain't seen nothing, Mrs. Ramirez," Gates says, trying to soothe Mom. "My sisters used to run after each other with scissors and hatchets. And I don't even want to tell you about Erica, my ex-wife, you saw her today in the car. That big lady? She can crack somebody's head in two."

"Ay, Dios mio!"

"Sisters always fight," says Willy. "I have four and they almost started a fire in the back of the store. Remember the house we used to live in behind the store? None of them wanted to get up and turn off the stove."

"Your poor father. I know how much he loved his store."

"I never fought with my sisters," Susie says proudly.

"You're an exception!" says Willy. He takes his wife's picture, to record the "exception" for posterity.

Everybody is trying to make things right for Mom. I look at my watch and see it's time for her medications, Lipitor that helps circulate blood through her arteries, prescription ibuprofen for the pain, and another pill to regulate her blood pressure. Suddenly, I feel cooped up, as if the forest is turning in on me. The Wall seems a million miles away. How will we survive all this, and what if Mom dies before she gets there?

Manuel walks up to me. "Medication time?"

"Yeah, I gotta keep all these medications in order." I start counting out the pills.

"You're doing a good job." He pauses. "But you know what?"

"What?"

"You were pretty rough on Priscilla."

"I can't believe you just said that! Didn't you hear her threaten me?"

"She didn't mean it. She talks tough, but it's just because she's afraid."

"So what are you, Manuel? Her therapist? Priscilla doesn't let anybody get close to her."

"That's why—because she's afraid."

"Afraid of what?"

"Of losing, of not being what people expect her to be."

"And you know about that, do you?"

"I'm an expert on it."

"Gee, didn't know the two of you had so much in common."

Manuel and I get into the van and avoid looking at each other. Priscilla decides to ride with Willy and Susie to avoid Paul. Lisa pours water for Mom in a paper cup so she can take her pills. The cars start up again, and we begin climbing higher into alpine country. My mother is gasping for breath. The atmosphere is too thin. I'm looking nervously at my watch, to see how much longer before we get into New Mexico, closer to Chris's house.

"She'll be all right. We're almost out of the mountains," Manuel says. "How you feeling, Doña?"

"Never better, mijo, even though my children don't respect each other. No, they would rather fight. They forgot how to be a family. What is life without la familia?"

Manuel smiles, uncertainly. He understands better than all of us. He's Casper disappearing over the horizon in boxcars that never took him where he wanted to go, which was home, a real home, to a real family.

The blue-green of the forest is so rich I see spots of green when I'm not looking at the trees. Everyone's quiet. We pass by Montezuma Castle, old Indian ruins pressed into the side of a mountain, an ancient high-rise. Arizona is amazing. Huge saguaros grow next to spiny ocotillo and palo verde trees not too many miles from giant pine trees, maple, and aspen, and mountains capped with snow in winter. We have exited the heat of Phoenix, with temperatures that rise so high in the summertime you can fry an egg on the sidewalk. The sky is a perfect blue dome, cloudless, the day bright with sunshine, yet everything inside me has turned black. My mind is racing with things I'd like to say to Priscilla, hard things I've held inside me for a long time. I'm afraid when I look back and see my mother's ashen face, afraid of Priscilla's words. I want the trip to be over, and my mother headed safely back home. We're journeying to the Wall to touch Jesse's name. Does it matter anymore? Yet my fingers ache, anticipating the letters of his name. I've smoothed them down a hundred times in my mind, smoothed down his face in my memory, too, made everything fit into my thoughts, a flesh-and-blood jigsaw puzzle, but the pieces keep shifting and changing shapes the closer we get to the Wall.

• IT'S ASSUMED THAT when people travel together they will love and hate each other, be amused, be resistant, be irritable, show their bad sides, make excuses for not answering when spoken to, get drowsy and carsick and want to go back home. How much of this can we bear? Irene rests one leg on Mom's lap, and Mom rubs the painful varicose veins gently. Mom dozes on Irene's shoulder part of the way, while Lisa and Lilly fight over CDs. The other two cars are still following us, so I guess nobody has decided to go back home. Manuel surprised me by sticking up for Priscilla. Really, I didn't think he had it in him. Maybe I am like Priscilla says, wanting power over men, needing them to seem weak and limp, wanting to keep them home where my father should have been.

I look at Mom and wonder what it takes to keep a man home. She couldn't keep my dad. He was restless, beset with a wandering eye, looking for a new landscape to inhabit. Landscapes are changing in front of my eyes as we move from mountains to plateaus to flatland. In the distance, clouds hang low over purple, misty mountain peaks as we make our way to Gallup, New Mexico. Maybe I'm more like my dad. I need to have a landscape that's changing or changeable, moving, if nothing else.

La manda, my mother's promise, is changing our landscapes forever. It's suffering in motion. We're carrying our burdens on our backs as our Indian ancestors did, adjusting the weight every once in a while to make ourselves feel better. Suffering is our map, it's why we're on the road. Men and women in pain stand close to Christ, the man of sorrows; every procession at St. Anthony's taught us that. We wouldn't be on the road if it weren't for war and suffering. We're part of some unearthly plan to balance the scales of suffering, to release a spring in our souls that will free us from the fear of suffering.

We're moving back in time to '68, before it all started. Michael says every living thing in the universe creates a sound, the sun, moon, planets, the earth, trees, plants, animals, humans, everything emits invisible sound waves that ring, buzz, sputter and produce frequencies we can only pick up with radar instruments and some only with our spirits. My mother picked up Jesse's voice, vibrations that started in her ears, and traveled to her mind and heart. We're paying him a visit now where his memory lives in cold granite, behind the letters of his name. Each name is a story on the Wall, each story is a cry of despair, ringing, buzzing and sputtering pain throughout America. *War is real! War is death!* My mother listens to such things even when I wish she wouldn't.

Brown Berets •

B y 1968, rage against the Vietnam War exploded onto the streets of America's cities. Protesters, throats rubbed raw with shouting, feet blistered with marching, eyes blurred from not sleeping, took up the battle cry to end the war in Vietnam. War had come to America, and it wasn't bombs exploding, it was balled fists raised in signs of power, drug communes, and kids burning their draft cards. Sounds of grief for our dead boys rose like the mad cries of an animal caught in a hunter's trap. All over the world, the shouting was heard—students caught in dreams of building a perfect society were living out a nightmare. In Mexico, France, Italy, Russia, Germany, all around the globe students rioted and were beaten down by police, their lives crushed by heavy artillery, corrupt governments, the FBI, and the CIA. Finally, war was something we could hold in our hands, and it defied the American dream.

• THE BROWN BERETS came to Phoenix in late 1968, two years before Ray and I got married. Actually, Ray and I didn't get serious about each other until August of '69 on Little Lally's wedding day. Little Lally was one of Tío Ernie's daughters. Little Lally was so happy on her wedding day, nobody could have dreamed she would one day be divorced from

Demetrio. Ray's band played for the couple's wedding dance at the American Legion. That night was the first time I felt Ray loved me, although the idea surfaced after we fought in the parking lot and I tore up a pair of Jose Feliciano tickets in his face. In those days, I believed jealousy was proof of love. I saw it in Mom's face when she watched Dad walk out the door on his way to Consuelo's. This time the tables were turned. Ray was jealous of me, the suave, experienced man jealous of the girl still in high school who might run off with the star athlete. That was probably why we argued in the parking lot, but my memory is dim on this. It was torture for him to play on stage and watch me dance with other men. There wasn't much I cared about in those days. I was still wrapped up in Jesse's death, in the awful reality that I would never see him again.

By the time the Brown Berets came to Phoenix, I had decided to join in the protest against the war. My rage against the Army was so great I couldn't even see images of generals and politicians on TV without wanting to spit in their faces. Ray took me to the Brown Beret rally the night before Thanksgiving Day. The rally was held in one of the ramadas at South Mountain Park.

I remember the night was cold, starless, with a misty quarter moon dangling in the sky. Tall saguaros held up their arms in the gloomy night, like hands held up in prayer, or, as one guy said, looking like fingers, flipping off the world. The Brown Berets would have nothing to do with Thanksgiving Day, a gabacho holiday, they said—the story of the white man and his supposed conquest of America. What kind of picture did the white supremacists paint of the Indian Nation anyway? Not a pretty one—a servile people at best, aiding them, feeding them. Una mentira! The group said the story of Thanksgiving was all wrong and that los gringos wanted to prove they had befriended the Indians, when the truth was they were plotting to murder them all and take over their land, which is what happened in history.

We got there late. By that time, the group had built bonfires with dry brush to protect themselves from the chilly air. The flickering firelight reminded me of Don Florencío and the campfires Jesse and I danced around when the old man told us stories. As a child, I pretended I saw faces close to Don Florencío's fire, flesh-and-blood embers, grotesque forms, impish-looking fairy folk who hid in dark forests, chanting magic spells and unleashing dark powers to do their bidding.

Someone was talking over a bullhorn. I later found out it was Antonio Fuentes, the leader of the group. Antonio was dark like Jesse, but wide around the shoulders. He was slow-moving and sure of himself.

He kept fingering the brim of his beret as he spoke. I could see why he was the leader. He emanated passion like a hard, unyielding fist ready to swing. I was caught up in the aura he cast, eager to listen to every word he said, uncertain what I would do if I was ever alone with him.

In the dim light of bare bulbs dangling on an electrical line and the twinkling lights of Phoenix in the distant valley, I could see the rest of the group. Their uniforms were creased and pressed and they wore their infamous brown berets at a tilt. Men with dark mustaches, some with long sideburns, stood unsmiling, feet apart in a military stance. They had women with them, too, not much older than me. Some looked like Mayan Indian maidens, long hair, bold stares. They shouted slogans: Viva La Raza! Justicia! Somos La Gente de Bronce! Chicano Power! They clapped their hands and stomped their feet.

As the fervor rose, Antonio Fuentes jumped on a park table in one easy, fluid movement. He shouted, "PROTEST RAZA! PROTEST! Uncle Sam stole our land, now he's killing our boys in Vietnam. Two Latinos for every gringo! Is that justice? We're on the front lines, in artillery, blowing mines, the first to fire. We don't get no soft jobs, in offices . . . we can't get into no fancy officer's clubs, we can't get no deferments . . . NO! We're coming back in boxes, mi raza. They're wiping us out! My brother was killed over there . . . to make some fucking white general look good!" His voice broke.

"They killed my brother, too!" I shouted. My words were drowned in the noise everybody else was making. Ray was standing behind me with his hands around my waist. The rage in me was burning like the heat of the bonfires. I slipped out of Ray's grasp. "Take it easy, babe," he said. "This is a military demonstration. We don't want any trouble!"

"Trouble! The trouble is we haven't yelled loud enough. Ray, are you deaf? You went to Vietnam!"

"Look over there," he said.

There were two police cars, lights blinking in the dark. Suddenly, somebody turned on a stereo. A Mexican corrido came on, loud, dispersing the crowd.

I heard voices saying, "La chota, con calma raza . . . these assholes want to drag us all to jail."

I was more angry than afraid. I saw one of the cops talking to Antonio. Searchlights beamed over us. Somebody handed Ray a can of beer. "Nice party, que no?"

"Yeah," Ray said. "Some of you guys might end up partying in jail."

"We're ready! Hasta para morir!"

"Let's get out of here, Teresa," Ray said.

"I'm not leaving!" I shouted.

Ray put his hands on my shoulders, shaking me hard. "You're coming home with me. Right now! These cops are gonna start clubbing everybody to death."

Just as Ray said the words, somebody screamed. One of the girls had thrown a rock at a cop, and he had pinned her in an arm lock. There was a scuffle in the dark as two guys got into the fight. Before I knew it, Antonio was down, hands cuffed behind his back. Ray grabbed me and slung me over his shoulder. He ran between people, jumping over bushes in the dark. He threw me into the front seat of his car and locked the door.

"Let me out!" I yelled at the top of my voice. "You can't do this to me!"

He drove away, gunning the motor, making a dash for the paved circle that led out of the park.

"Cops are gonna be crawling all over this place like ants!" Ray yelled at the top of his lungs. We sped up to the exit, almost running over one of the park officials. Ray counted on the darkness to hide his license plate. We were all the way down the mountain by the time we saw four more police cars on their way in. I was crying, partly because I was angry at Ray, and more because Jesse was gone, and everything Antonio Fuentes had said was true.

• THE BROWN BERET rally was the first time I had ever publicly denounced the Vietnam War. Later, I joined one protest after another, with Ray or without him. I saw Antonio Fuentes again in East L.A. and wasn't surprised to find out Ricky Navarro was working with the Chicano Moratorium Committee. We were *Los Chicanos* back then, united, breathing the same air, sharing the same vision. People had to listen. By 1970 we were ready to protest the war in the biggest demonstration in the history of Aztlán, marching together, thousands of us, protesting the war, all the way to Laguna Park in East L.A. and the death of the *L.A. Times* reporter Ruben Salazar.

I found out in 1970 that a protest is a living thing. It's not just a word. It's made up of people who are filled with pain, anger, despair. It's something that has a life of its own, something that lives and breathes, shouts, cries, and groans.

Chicano! •

E
ast L.A. was hotter than I expected—muggy and over-
cast. George, Espi's uncle and his wife, Perla, dropped
us off at Belvedere Park. George was round and flat at
the same time, jolly most times, except the day of the
Chicano Moratorium. That day he was mad—mad at los gringos, at the
U.S. government, at Uncle Sam, who was nothing more than a murderer
of Chicanos, he said. "They killed Chayo, my cousin, and your brother,
Jesse." He stuck up for Jesse like he had known him all his life. I wanted
to frown and yell, pound my fist, kick walls, but I did nothing except listen to George blankly, letting his rage hit me in the face. I had too much
of my own and didn't know how it would erupt. I was sitting in the back
seat with Espi and her four-year-old nephew Fernando. Espi and I were
dressed in look-alike jeans and black T-shirts with the words CHICANO
POWER on the front. Between us, Fernando squirmed and wiggled, trying to poke his head out the open window.

"Don't let him get his head out," Perla said. "Next thing you know
he'll end up in the street." In the front seat she repositioned one-year-old
Frankie in her arms. Every once in a while Frankie popped a plastic bottle shaped like a bear full of grape juice into his mouth.

Chicanos from all over the U.S. converged in East L.A. that day.
Lining the streets were newborn babies in their mothers' arms, elderly
men and women who looked like relics of the Mexican Revolution, and

young people, lots of young people. I felt sorry for everybody. The march hadn't even started, and already some of the people seemed to be dying of thirst. I saw men sporting huge straw hats and women with purses dangling on their arms, as if they were walking down to the neighborhood grocery store to do some shopping. Flags were flapping in the breeze, the Mexican flag, the moratorium peace flag, Cesar Chavez's huelga flag, and flags bearing the image of La Virgen de Guadalupe. Banners announced in huge letters PEACE MORATORIUM AUGUST 29, 1970, BROWN IS BEAUTIFUL, CHICANO POWER, QUE VIVA LA RAZA, QUE VIVA CHE!

"Just like la raza," George said, "to make a fiesta out of the protest. Look at this, strollers, babies, nanas, tatas."

"What if there's trouble?" Perla asked him. "I don't want no trouble for the girls. We shouldn't let them march." My stomach went up and down like I was on an elevator when Perla said that. I started thinking what I would do if George didn't let us go. I was ready to jump out of the car if necessary. I had already been through hell talking Mom and Dad into letting me come to L.A. in the first place, not to mention all I had to do to convince Ray that I wasn't after Antonio Fuentes. If Ray had been any smarter, he would have been jealous of Ricky Navarro. It was Ricky I longed to see . . . the old Ricky, the one I knew before he went to Vietnam. I remembered, as a child, holding Ricky's hand, and leading him to our hide-out under the miguelito vines that grew like weeds over my mother's back fence. We'd carve out a spot under the thickest part, and play house. He was my husband, and my assortment of dolls, some of them in pathetic condition with eyes missing and hands and limbs falling off, were our children.

"There won't be any trouble," I told her. "I know some of the guys in the Brown Berets. The leaders of the moratorium got a license to march and all that. The cops can't do anything about it when it's legal."

"What are you, a Brown Beret?" George asked, half turning his head to get a look at me in the back seat.

"She's no Brown Beret," Espi said. "Don't worry about it, Tío, it'll be OK."

"I met them in Phoenix," I said to him. "They told me what the moratorium committee had planned." I didn't mention the cops taking over the meeting and throwing Antonio Fuentes and the others in jail. "Jesse was killed. You think I want them to get away with it?" My voice sounded loud. I might have shouted if George hadn't calmed me down.

"Take it easy. Just remember, the two of you—no trouble, heh?

Don't get into no line of fire. Run into the neighborhood if things get too hot."

"Too hot?" Perla asked as we jumped out of the car. I saw her turn around to look at us and knew she was still trying to convince her husband not to let us go.

"We'll meet you at Laguna Park," he shouted as they drove away.

It took a few seconds to get our bearings as we walked into Belvedere Park. Then, Espi and I became one with a crowd of hundreds walking in the same direction. Except for a few car radios blasting Mexican songs, and voices coming at us through bullhorns, the crowd was quiet, as if they were whispering or praying. We walked into the middle of the crowd, and I saw a sign that said, AZTLÁN SI, VIETNAM NO!

"What did I tell you, Espi. Look over there . . . Aztlán! Don Florencío was right about that. That's who we are."

Standing a few feet away from us was a group of Brown Berets. I walked up to them, "Do you know Antonio Fuentes?"

"Yeah," one of them said. "He's over there getting ready to march." He pointed Antonio out to me.

"What about Ricky Navarro?"

"Ricky who?"

"Navarro," I repeated, "Navarro."

"Oh, yeah," the guy standing next to him said. "El vato from Phoenix. He's around here somewhere. He never joined up with us. He works with the moratorium committee."

I grabbed Espi's hand and pulled her through the crowd to get to Antonio. If the guy hadn't pointed him out to me, I probably wouldn't have recognized him. They all looked more or less the same in brown khakis, light tan shirts, sunglasses, and brown berets.

I felt proud when I looked around me—proud that we were standing up for our rights and sad, too, as I looked closely at the Brown Berets and noticed most of them were skinny, knobby-kneed teenagers, not much older than Paul.

"Hey," I called out to Antonio. "Remember me from Phoenix?" He walked up to me.

"How could I forget? I would never forget somebody who looked like you." Just as he said the words, I saw a young woman materialize from behind him. She was a few inches shorter than me and dressed in the Brown Beret uniform. She walked next to Antonio, placed her hand on his arm and stood in a military pose, feet apart, glaring at me.

"This is Raquel," Antonio said. He looked down at her. "No empiezes, these girls are from Phoenix. They traveled all the way to march with us—so viva la raza, que no?" She didn't answer. Any thoughts of chasing Antonio Fuentes ended when I looked into Raquel's hard, unyielding face.

"Listen, where can I find Ricky Navarro? I remember you told me he was involved in el movimiento."

"He is. He's probably with that bunch over there." He pointed to a cluster of young men and women, some with papers in their hands, flyers or notes I couldn't tell. I thanked Antonio and half-smiled at Raquel. She stood stoic and unmoving.

"Maybe we'll see you guys later," I said to him.

"Chicano Power!" he said, lifting one balled fist into the air.

"Que viva la raza!" I answered.

"Boy! You're really getting into this," Espi said to me.

"Getting? I've been in it . . . where have *you* been?"

I saw Ricky Navarro's back before I saw his face. He had gained some of the weight he had lost and still wore his army fatigues, this time with a Mexican serape draped over one shoulder and tied at his waist. His hair had grown down to his shoulders. I went up to him and put my arms around his waist. He turned around with me still holding on.

"Hey!" Then he saw Espi and started laughing. I ran under his arm, and he held me in front of him, both hands on my shoulders. His eyes shone lime green in the sunlight.

"Look at you . . . look at you! Oh Jesus!" He held me in a huge hug. "We're here to do something about Jesse's death, Teresa. We're here to remember all our guys!"

"Please do something for Jesse . . . his life has to count, it just has to!"

"We will . . . we will. I was against the protest when I got back, you remember, but now I know there's no other way to end this thing. Your mom, Teresa, how's your mom doing?"

"She's heartbroken. And yours?"

"She followed me here. You know my ma, she's not one to let me go too far."

Ricky and I might have held on to each other longer, except the march was under way. Ricky motioned with one hand to a girl, a hippie with a long peasant dress and dark hair that went down to her waist.

"Who's that?" I asked him. "Your alter-ego? She looks gabacha."

"She's half and half." The girl stood next to Ricky, her eyes hazy and friendly.

"Groovy, is this another radical Chicana?"

"She's a friend from Phoenix. This is Faith, Teresa," Ricky said, reaching for the girl. Espi and I both looked at each other. All I could think of was LSD, flower children, and drug communes. Maybe it was true that Ricky had joined a hippie commune—here was the evidence. Any thoughts of going after Ricky ended that day too, as I looked at Faith put her arm around him. In my mind, I expected to see a line of tambourine-playing gurus come up from behind her.

"I'm a monitor," Ricky said. "We're gonna keep the people in line. Come on, let's get closer to the front. I'll keep an eye on you. Those are some of the leaders," he said, pointing to people at the head of the line. "Rosalio Muñoz, Ernesto Vigil, Roberto Elias, Gloria Arellanes—and over there David Sanchez, Prime Minister of the Brown Berets. Corky Gonzalez is gonna talk to us at the park. He's the big movimiento leader from Denver."

The march started down 3rd Street, slow, a Sunday stroll, moving in scattered rows that looked like we were crossing the street together. The monitors, lined up alongside the entire route, were telling the people to stay on one side of the street. I saw a little old lady who looked like Nana Esther. She wore a bright gold medallion of La Virgen de Guadalupe. I walked slowly up to her. "Eres Guadalupana, señora?" I asked her.

"Si, mija. Yes, forever. I've been a Guadalupana all my life." She lifted up her medallion for me to see.

"So was my nana, and my mother."

"And you?" she asked me.

"Not yet," I told her, surprised that I had left a door open, a possibility for becoming an aficionado of La Virgen in the future.

"Here," she said, handing me La Oración del Justo Juez. "This is for anybody who goes to the war."

I looked at the prayer card but wouldn't touch it. "My brother had that with him when he was killed in Vietnam. Why didn't God protect him?" For a few seconds, the woman's eyes locked deeply with mine. She muttered a prayer under her breath. A throbbing ache started between my breasts, a dull thud, Mom's pain stuck in my breastbone.

"No one knows. Quien sabe. But I know your brother went right up to God Himself. That's the way it is when you have faith. La fe . . . it will get you to Heaven." She put one hand on my arm, and it felt good. Her touch made the ache in my chest go away. In a few minutes, I lost track of the little old lady and figured she had stopped to get a drink of water.

People were chanting . . . *Chicano—Power! Chicano—Power!* over and over again, mixed in with cries of *Que Viva La Raza! Raza Si, Guerra No!*

Chale con el draft! Espi, next to me, got into the spirit of things, lifting one fist in the air with me every time we shouted *Chicano—Power!* Young people stuck up two fingers in the form of the peace sign.

As we moved, I began to feel full inside, as if the very act of march-ing was food for my soul. The louder the shouts became, the fuller I felt. The whole world might have ended for me at that moment, and I would have died strong, unafraid, the aching in my heart over Jesse's death only a memory. I looked on all sides of me, left, right, front, back at banners waving and at thousands of brown faces with features that told our his-tory—Aztec, Mayan, Olmec, Toltec, Spanish. There were black faces with us that day too and white, and all of them were believing the same thing—that the war had to end—and our boys had to come home. Here and there I saw the flashing lights of police cars, the L.A. sheriff, watch-ing us from outside the line of marchers, circling around us like buzzards, starving, desperate for death to own the living.

At Whittier and Atlantic I saw a man approach Rosalio Muñoz and give him a hug. I moved over to Ricky Navarro, walking only a few feet away from me. "Who is that?" I asked him.

"Ruben Salazar," he said, "the reporter from the *L.A. Times*. He's the director of the Spanish station, too. He's our voice to the nation."

Our voice to the nation. I looked closely as we passed him by, not knowing that it would be the last time Ruben Salazar would ever see his raza march. He was standing at attention as we passed by, as if he was watching a military parade. At his side was a cameraman. Ruben's face was passionate, kind. Not an hour would go by before he would be bru-tally murdered by the host of buzzards who now circled us.

Almost immediately after seeing Ruben Salazar, a ruckus began in the crowd. A young man threw a rock at a police car. Two monitors grabbed the guy, stonewalling him between them. Ricky whispered in my ear, "Provocateurs, people planted by the police to make us look bad. Some of them are even posing as Brown Berets." A chill went up my back. If there were troublemakers planted along the way . . . what could we ex-pect at Laguna Park?

I looked at the swaying, bobbing heads and bodies of thousands of protesters once we turned the corner onto Whittier Boulevard, the last stretch of the parade route. Hope rose in me—and pride so great it al-most burst through my skin. On either side of the street, businesses were decorated with flags and banners, showing their support. Some businesses were closed for the day. The protesters were so numerous, they now took up the entire street. The monitors cried out to no avail for the people to stay on one side of the street. A couple, newly wedded, happily joined the march. The bride's veil trailed behind her, white filmy lace so out of place in the crowd of black moratorium clothes, straw hats, ponchos, Levi's, and bare-chested men. Ricky pointed toward the back of the crowd. "Look, over there . . . those black and white buses. They're loaded with cops, sheriff's deputies." I looked behind me several times and could barely make out the white, cylinder tops of the buses.

We were in great spirits as we approached Laguna Park, shouting loud once we saw our destination was near. I heard music blaring, Mexican music, and flamboyant colors, dancers spinning on a stage. People were trying to find a spot on the grass to spread their blankets and food. The crush of so many brown bodies gave me a feeling that I was safe, totally protected. So many of us, thousands . . . there was nothing they could do to us. We were Aztlán. The power of the ancient world had returned to us, weaving a spell that made us think we were indestructible.

There were tables under trees with information on voting and other community events. People sold soda pop from coolers, but lines were long, and many started moving into the neighborhood to purchase drinks at nearby stores. One lone picnic table was set up under a huge tree with an image of La Virgen de Guadalupe propped up in the center. Photos of Chicanos killed in Vietnam were neatly arranged on the table, covering its entire surface. I reached in my purse and searched for Jesse's picture, a photo of him in his Army uniform. I added it to the rest. The little old lady I had seen en route to the park saw me and smiled.

Someone got on the microphone and said that we should rename Laguna Park Benito Juárez Park, and all the people cheered. Espi and I were ready to sit down on the grass when we heard Rosalio Muñoz introduced as the first speaker. We remained standing. I was close enough to the stage to see Rosalio. I remember he was telling us that we were like babies learning how to walk. "We fall, but we get back up," he said. "Time is on our side." He went on about how we couldn't live like familias separadas anymore. We were learning how to unite, how to speak up for what was right, and it was our unity that would make us strong.

"I wonder where Perla and George are?" Espi asked me. We looked at all the families gathered around us. There were hundreds of women there who looked like Perla and children everywhere who resembled Frankie and Fernando.

"They're probably over there," I said, pointing to the long line that trailed to the door of the bathroom.

Rosalio Muñoz's speech ended with the cry "Viva La Raza!" We all shouted the words together. Then I heard someone over the microphone say, "There's nothing happening back there, please everybody sit down. Everybody sit down. Stay still, por favor." People were standing up at the west end of the park, then more people started standing up. The man kept repeating the words. "Everybody sit down, please, remain calm. There's nothing happening." Someone else got on the microphone . . . "We got women and children here, no queremos pedo."

I stood on a park bench and looked over the heads of the crowd at a line of sheriff's deputies standing toe to toe with a line of monitors. Behind the deputies, the street was packed with police cars, lights blinking, sirens wailing.

"Oh, my God, Teresa, there's gonna be trouble . . . big trouble!" Espi said. I heard several men's voices over the microphone shouting, "POLICE HOLD YOUR LINE! HOLD YOUR LINE! HOLD YOUR LINE!" It was a loud chant that rang in my ears over and over again. "HOLD YOUR LINE! HOLD YOUR LINE! HOLD YOUR LINE!" Suddenly, the line of deputies attacked the monitors, beating the men down. The men got up and advanced toward them, some of them picked up rocks and threw them at the officers. Three times I saw the line of deputies advance toward the line of monitors, pressing on them, beating them brutally with their clubs. Then I saw smoke rising between the people. and people gasping, choking, their eyes red, watery. "Tear gas!" somebody shouted. "Run! Run!"

At that point, a great sound erupted from the people. The sound was like that of a terrible storm at sea when the waves of the ocean roar over the shoreline and earth wars with heaven. The sound grew louder and louder until it reached the peak of its momentum, then it turned into a solid, despairing cry, a huge, aching wound with a human voice. I was shouting, too.

I heard gunshots blasting in the distance. Espi and I took off running toward the bathrooms, searching for Perla and the kids. All around me was a great stampede of people, men, women, children. I saw babies crying, lost, unable to find their parents in the terrible confusion. I knew Ricky was one of the men the police had beaten up.

"Ricky! Espi, where's Ricky?" Everyone was running in between buses that were parked at one end of the park. Behind us, the police were pushing people up to tall chain-link fences, trapping them—everyone, men, women, babies. I saw an officer hit a boy on the side of the neck with his club. I ran up to the officer. "You fuckin' pig!" I yelled. He started chasing me, and I fell on the ground. He hit me once on the head, and I saw the world go black. Seconds later, I felt someone helping me up. It was Ricky. His head was split open on one side.

"My God! You're bleeding!" I said to him.

"So are you," he said. He rushed with me, holding me close as we ran between the parked buses to get out into the street. Laguna Park was a vision out of Hell. The police had overturned all the tables, kicking them down. Papers were blowing all over the place. Sacks of food were crushed underfoot, and here and there I saw shoes, clothes, an empty baby stroller. The table with the altar to La Virgen de Guadalupe lay upside down with the photos of all the Chicano soldiers strewn on the ground.

"Jesse's picture! I have to go get Jesse's picture!" I remembered the little old lady and looked around for her. I couldn't see her anywhere.

"No!" Ricky shouted. "We can't go back there." By this time, his girlfriend, Faith, was with us, crying, screaming. I looked at her and felt anger. She was white. This wasn't her fight, it was ours.

I saw Espi running toward us. "They threw tear gas into the bathroom! Perla and the kids are hurt. What are they, devils?"

Ricky led us all across the street and into the neighborhood. All around us people were running into houses and yards. Some people were throwing rocks at the police, hiding behind parked cars and buses. Neighbors were turning on their water hoses and letting us wash the tear gas out of our eyes. One lady handed me a towel for the cut on my head. I soaked it in water and held it up to the huge knot I felt at the top of my head. For an instant I felt dizzy. I held the towel tight around the wound until the bleeding stopped. A baby was crawling in the yard, crying as his mother washed him off. I heard the screech of car brakes—a woman had been hit running across the street. Sirens were wailing and more smoke was rising—now from everywhere, black, billowing. The air was filled with the smell of burned tires. Men ran out into the streets, cracking windows of police cars with sticks and rocks. All around me the world was a war zone. This is how Jesse must have felt in Vietnam—helpless, afraid, not knowing when the attack would stop, not knowing if he would live or die.

"Ricky—no!" I shouted as I watched him run back into the park and start fighting with a police officer who had just beaten up a teenage boy. Ricky took the officer's club away from him and hit him several times. Then I watched on in horror as Ricky was jumped by three officers. His body went limp after they put a choke hold on him and cuffed him.

Between the three of them, they picked Ricky's bruised and bleeding body and, swaying under its weight, they threw him into one of the black and white buses I had seen following us all the way to Laguna Park. I shouted from across the street, "You fuckin' assholes . . . you'll get yours!" One of the officers lifted his club at me from the distance, menacing. "You want some?" he shouted, smiling as he said the words. Espi had her arm around me.

"Teresa, don't!" she shouted. "Let's go!" We took off running down the street with Faith next to us. In front of me, I saw a young man with a torn shirt and a bloodied face. He turned around and yelled at two other guys behind us.

"Matarón a Ruben Salazar!" he said in Spanish.

"What?" I yelled. "What did you say?"

"They killed Ruben Salazar!" he repeated. "They killed Ruben Salazar!"

"Who . . . who killed him? Where?"

"The cops! The sheriff, over on La Verne at the Silver Dollar Café."

I spun around and grabbed Espi by the shoulders. "Oh my God, Espi! They killed Ruben Salazar! They killed Ruben Salazar!"

"Who? What are you talking about?"

"Ruben Salazar . . . the *L.A. Times* reporter . . . our voice to the nation! Oh, my God! Let's go, come on!" I was ready to take off running after the three guys. Faith said, "I'll go with you!" I looked at her with a new respect and thought about the little old lady who just that morning had told me that only faith could get us to Heaven . . . *fe* . . . that was this girl's name. Faith and I were ready to take off when Espi grabbed my arm again. "What are you, crazy? They'll arrest us. There's nothing we can do!" Just as she said the words I saw the cops grab a man and woman who were running out of a store. They beat them both down with their sticks and hauled them into a police car.

"See!" Espi yelled. "We're next!"

Across the street, Espi spotted Perla running toward the car with Frankie in her arms and Fernando at her side. George wasn't with her. We both shouted her name. Perla stopped and waved for us to cross the street. "Get over here, all of you! Get in the car!" she yelled. Her face was streaked with tears, her eyes red from the tear gas. Both boys were in hysterics, their eyes huge, red sores.

"I'm not going," Faith said. She took off running back to the park. I was ready to follow her, but Espi held on to my arm. "Don't do it,

Teresa! There's nothing we can do." Perla kept shouting at the top of her lungs for us to get into the car.

We ran across the street and got into the car. I held Frankie in my arms while Espi held on to Fernando. Perla drove like a madwoman, down Whittier, then she cut through the neighborhood because Whittier was blocked by cars, people looting, smoke and fires. I glanced back at the park and thought about the overturned table with La Virgen's altar on it and Jesse's picture trampled to the ground.

"Let me go back and get Jesse's picture!" I cried. Perla didn't answer me. She drove the car, jerking and screeching through stop signs and in between cars and buses to get us home.

• MONTHS LATER, newspeople investigating the Chicano Moratorium March and the murder of Ruben Salazar came up with evidence that the L.A. Sheriff's Department and judges hearing the case were unwilling to accept. News reports related that sheriff's deputies claimed they were chasing a burglar who had robbed the Green Mill Liquor Store the day of the march. Their story was that the burglar disappeared into the crowd gathered at Laguna Park, and that they had the right to pursue him. The owner of the liquor store later said he never made a call to the police, nor had he experienced a burglary. Sheriff's deputies also never explained their aggressive stance toward an unarmed crowd that included hundreds of women and children. They also never explained why they were out in high numbers that day, armed with clubs, tear gas, and buses for loading up protesters.

It was common knowledge among many in the Chicano community that Ruben Salazar had been on the police hit list for months. People closest to Ruben Salazar related that he knew his life was in danger, and that he had received several death threats before his murder. Salazar's co-workers said that he cleaned out his desk the morning of the moratorium march, as if he was never coming back. Salazar's sympathy for the protesters had grown as Chicano leaders pointed out the fact that Chicano youth were drafted to the war in numbers that were largely out of proportion to their actual population, and that once drafted, Chicano youth were most likely to serve in the front lines. Salazar's voice grew in importance, and the Latino population began to count on him to report their side of the story, which also involved numerous acts of police brutality.

It was at this point that sheriff's deputies took action. They chose the day of the Chicano Moratorium March, as they would be able to hide their actions under the disguise of keeping protesters in line and quelling riots. The Silver Dollar Café, where Salazar was killed, was nowhere near Laguna Park. It was about a mile and a half from the park, and the story from the police was that they were chasing a gunman who had disappeared into the café. A gunman was never discovered in the Silver Dollar Café, nor did the police give adequate warning before firing a tear gas projectile into the crowded café, which was aimed directly at Salazar. Upon further investigation, it was discovered that the device used that day was only used in cases when a criminal was firing from behind a barricade and police needed to destroy the barricade to apprehend or kill a dangerous criminal. The projectile beheaded Ruben Salazar, and his life ended tragically, while police outside the café hid the truth from the media for hours.

Ruben Salazar, the Chicano community's voice to the nation, was never heard again, and many years later, city officials renamed Laguna Park Ruben Salazar Park in an attempt to balance the scales of justice and end death's bitter memory.

Albuquerque •

A rriving at Gallup, New Mexico, we get off at a convenience store that doubles as a gas station and souvenir shop. The kids use their own money to buy juice and doughnuts, gummy bears, sunflower seeds, and whatever else they figure they haven't eaten yet. The men are outside filling up the gas tanks. Mom is intrigued with the Zuñi jewelry. It is silver and turquoise stone worked into fragile necklaces, bracelets, and rings. I'm amazed at the delicacy of the designs. It's all marvelous. A skinny white man with Indian tattoos on his arms tells me he's the owner. He makes a sales pitch, $400 instead of $600 for a necklace fit for a queen— well, what do you say? I say no, not because I don't want to buy it, but because I want to buy from the Indian merchants, not the white middleman. We're in honest country, country that dips abruptly into canyons and cuts into the horizon with jagged mountain peaks. It matters that what I buy is real. I want smudges on the silver made by brown, sweaty fingers, not polished objects sitting under glass cabinets in a souvenir shop.

The man at the cash register is Indian. "Hey," he says to me, "aren't you the family from Phoenix, Arizona, traveling to the Vietnam Wall?"

"Yeah. How did you know?"

"I saw your story last night on TV. That was great. I mean all that money. The government is a big screw-up. It always makes me happy when the government loses money." He leans close to me. "Listen, I got the best Indian jewelry around." He slips me a business card that reads *Leroy's Indian Jewelry*.

"You must be Leroy."

"Yep, and you must be Teresa. I remembered your name from the news report. I'm telling you, Teresa, I've got authentic stuff. My own grandfather makes it, and he saves the best pieces for family and friends. Call me, or e-mail."

"You've got computers on the reservation?"

He laughs. "I live here in Gallup," he says. "But yeah, I got a computer here and one over there, too. Business is business." He looks over at the white guy, and says out loud, "Anything else you folks need? The Wall is days away, you know. Hey, Byron, this is the family I saw on TV last night. They're headed for the Vietnam Wall."

Byron is showing Manuel and Priscilla some jewelry. "What family?" he asks.

"He never watches TV," Leroy explains. "Vodka, that's his company. Look, there's my wife," he says pointing to a middle-aged woman walking toward us. "Lovely, isn't she?" He lowers his voice and says, "Hey, hon, show these people what real Indian jewelry looks like." She raises up her sleeves and shows off her bracelets.

"Gorgeous!" I tell her.

"This is the family we saw on TV last night, hon."

The woman's eyes light up. "This is my lucky day! I've got a nephew on the Wall, Benjamin Rush, but his Indian name is Gathering Eagle Feathers. You won't see his Indian name on the Wall, though. Touch his name for me, please?" She presses my hand into hers, and holds it tight. "Benjamin Rush," she whispers in my ear, "Don't forget, OK? Touch his name."

"I'll remember," I tell her.

I check out with a cup of coffee and a pack of gum. I put Leroy's business card in my purse, and wonder if Michael knows anything about our story being shown on TV.

Gates passes me by carrying a white paper bag. "Something for Erica," he explains. "A dream catcher. To tell you the truth, I wish that woman would dream more, and leave me alone. But she's good to me, too, Teresa," he adds. "It's me that messes up her mind. Hey, you think they got nightmare catchers? I need one of those!"

"You have nightmares, Gates?"

"Yep, sure do!"

"About Vietnam?"

"Those are the main ones!" he tells me.

"After thirty years?"

"After thirty years. Time hasn't taken that away."

"I wonder if Jesse had nightmares in Vietnam."

"Believe me, Teresa, he did. We all did."

I notice Willy listening to our conversation.

"Do you have nightmares, too?" I ask him.

"Oh, yeah, once in a while, I still have one of those nightmares. I've got them all categorized by now. I guess it's not over till it's over, as the saying goes. Maybe this trip to the Wall will put an end to them."

"Yeah, maybe," Gates says, and walks away.

As I make my way out of the store with Mom and Irene, I notice people staring at us. They ask about the Internet address Michael pasted on the van's windows. Already Michael is getting responses from men who say they were there in '68, '69, '66, on and on. The war lasted so long there was always somebody there. Families are sending messages—*touch my son's name for me—my husband's—my cousin's—my boyfriend's—don't forget my neighbor's, he was only nineteen. I was there when they told his mother.*

Michael is sitting in the van working on the laptop. "Look, Tía! I've got over a hundred messages already, and the trip just started."

"Here's another name to add to the list," I tell him. "Benjamin Rush. The lady inside the store is his aunt. Her husband saw us on TV last night. Do you know anything about that?"

"Here's your answer," Michael says. He points to the screen on the laptop. I peer at the screen and notice it's a message from Holly Stevens.

"What does she say?"

"She sent a press release throughout the nation to hundreds of television stations. We're big news now, Tía!" I look around at a few strangers talking to Paul, Donna, Manuel, Priscilla, Gates, Willy, and Susie.

"Hey, Dad! Take a look at this. Holly Stevens sent our story everywhere!" Paul walks over to the van with Donna.

"*Dad?*" I whisper to Donna. "Did you hear that, Donna? Michael just called Paul *Dad.*"

Donna smiles. "Sounds good! Michael and Paul have been talking since Paul defended him in Flagstaff."

"She what?" Paul asks.

"Our story, Dad. Don't you remember the reporter?"

"The one you fell in love with," Donna says.

"Come on, babe, you know I only love you. What did the redhead do?" Paul asks.

"She sent out a press release on us!"

"I'll be damned."

"I thought you didn't want publicity, Paul." He turns and looks at me.

"A little publicity never hurt anybody."

"Now you're talking my language!"

"I can teach you how to get into our web site, Dad," Michael says. I watch as Paul listens to directions on how to get onto the Internet.

"They're finally talking," Donna says. "Something's working."

"I haven't heard Michael call Paul *Dad* for years," I tell her.

"It's about time," Donna says.

Manuel and Priscilla walk out of the souvenir shop together, and Priscilla is showing off a necklace Manuel bought her.

"Lots of other things are working, too," I tell Donna. We laugh together.

I notice that people treat the old Guadalupanas with respect. They understand old women in this part of the country, las Doñas, the age of wisdom. They understand not leaving them behind, bringing them with us like our ancestors did, traveling with everyone we know to reach a place we don't know anything about. Maybe that's why our ancestors traveled together. They huddled together, walking behind the hummingbird war god Huitzilopochtli all the way to Tenochitlán where they saw the eagle on a nopal with a serpent in its peak. It was there they settled together, always together at the mercy of the sun, moon, rain, of Huitzilopochtli himself, who turned on them and exacted human hearts so that he could be born anew each day in the heavens. He was the sun, dying each evening, fighting with the stars and moon in the day. Don Florencío said his own people were afraid of Huitzilopochtli and pined after Quetzalcoatl, the white, bearded god. When Quetzalcoatl appeared, looking like Cortés, they wept because he was a murderer, too. That's the story of blood and gore that shamed the history of the Aztecs. I'm wondering about the stories that shame the history of America, that lead us from one endless trek to another, chasing power and dominion, leaving our hearts in foreign lands, righting other peoples' wrongs while forgetting our own.

• • •

• WE ROLL INTO ALBUQUERQUE late that afternoon, and stop at Old Town to get our bearings. I feel we've traveled through a time tunnel back to the 1600s, the time of the Spaniards and Pueblo Indians. Los patrones from Spain took the land from the Indians, killed their leaders, known as caciques, and tried to destroy their gods, only to be treated in the same manner a century later by white pioneers. San Felipe de Neri, sitting in the center of Old Town, is one of the churches the Spanish built over two hundred years ago. In the distant sky appear the purple slopes of the Jemez and Manzano mountain ranges. New Mexico, the "Land of Enchantment." Now I know why. San Felipe de Neri captures the Spaniards' preoccupation for creating churches that rise above ordinary adobe buildings and small shops, to point man toward Heaven. Every plaza announces to the world that God is the center of the universe. He is at the heart of mankind's highest hopes and most terrible longings.

Enormous shade trees, lining the courtyard around San Felipe de Neri, are home to hundreds of birds that chirp and sing from dawn to dusk. A sign at the church door tells tourists they are entering a sacred place. Respect is demanded. Sunday masses have ended, and the church is quiet. I look over a church bulletin that advertises a celebration for St. Charles Lawanga and the Uganda Martyrs at St. Thomas Church in Rio Rancho.

"There's an African American community around here," I tell Gates.

"I'm not African American."

"Oh, really. What are you, then?" Gates looks at me, but doesn't answer.

Our cars are parked along the sidewalk, and the kids run into a grassy area across the street with a gazebo in its center. My mother walks unsteadily into the church with Irene at her side. We dip our fingers into small basins of holy water and make the sign of the cross, letting drops of water linger on our foreheads. The two old women pull lace veils out of their purses, even though I insist they don't have to wear veils anymore. I walk in behind them, adjusting my long steps to their short ones. We're walking over a centuries-old pathway in the footsteps of others who have crossed the wooden threshold and walked up to the ornate altar with statues of saints dressed in real robes. Candles flicker in dim corners, illuminating saints I know nothing about. The Guadalupanas join two old women in the pews. The four of them look like quadruplets. They finish saying a rosary. Their prayers are blunt echoes rising into the beams of the ceiling. There is nothing more consuming than sacred silence. It's space charged with energy, heaven touching earth. The old women are part of it all, the stillness, the statues, the candles, the smell of incense, the chants. I drop to the floor on my knees, conscious of everyone else behind me, sitting in the pews. Priscilla, Paul, Donna, Willy, Susie, Gates, Manuel, and the kids are waiting for me to finish, and I don't know what I'm supposed to be doing in the first place. I ask God please to get us to the Wall, ask Him, then tell Him in the next sentence. I can't decide if I'm ordering Him to get us there or pleading with Him for mercy. I look back at Mom who motions me over.

"Doña Rebecca tells me there is a chapel to La Virgen de Guadalupe close by." She points to one of the old women from New Mexico sitting next to her.

"Your mother should visit there. I see she's a Guadalupana. So am I."

"It's not far, mija. We want to visit there."

"Mom, we have to pick up Chris. I'll call him up as soon as I can. We don't have much time." Mom's eyes are tired, right in the center of her pupils where light should be shining, there is filmy liquid.

"Mom, are you OK?" I reach over and feel her forehead.

"Ya, mija. What are you so worried about? God wouldn't kill me in church! We have to pay our respects to La Virgen."

"What's wrong with Mom?" Priscilla is standing next to me.

"Nothing. She wants to go to some chapel that she says is close by."

"So now we're gonna stop at every church in this nation? We'll never get to D.C."

"Just this one, mija." Mom looks up at Priscilla. The boys, Lisa, and Lilly are walking behind the altar rail.

"Ok, kids," Priscilla says. "Let's go!"

"Keep your voice down," I tell her. "Didn't you read the sign?" Priscilla doesn't answer. She helps Mom get up and looks worried as she stares intently at Mom's face.

"She looks weak, Teresa."

"I know. I'll hurry and get in touch with Chris, so we can get to our rooms." We talk over Mom's head the way we used to, lying on either side of her when we were kids. Paul is waiting at the entrance.

"What's wrong with Mom?"

"Nothing, mijo," Mom answers. "All of you stop worrying. Can't you feel the power in this place? If I could take this power with me, I'd run all the way to the Wall and never get tired. Que no, Irene, like in the old days."

"I would run right behind you, cree lo!" Irene says.

Around the corner from San Felipe de Neri is La Capilla de Nuestra Señora de Guadalupe, an adobe structure with its door wide open. The chapel is simple, depicting the beauty of poverty. Flowers decorate a picture of La Virgen and there is a wooden kneeler for prayer. Light filters in from small, rectangular windows illuminating sayings on the walls. Michael reads the words out loud . . . *The zeal for your house has eaten me up . . . Love me and you will earn my love . . . My soul has desired thee in the night, in the morn will I watch for thee.*

Everyone crowds into the chapel, standing so close we brush shoulders. Willy is busy taking pictures. He's become our official photographer. I'm glad for that, he's got the fanciest camera.

"I've never been in a Catholic church before," Willy says.

"I have," Gates says. "Jesse took me there a couple of times, and I still remember all the candles, and big, old statues dressed like real people. Hey, Teresa, why do you guys burn so many candles?"

"They're prayers, Gates. Manuel over there can tell you more. He used to be an altar boy." Manuel walks in with Priscilla and the kids. He makes the sign of the cross over himself.

"What's that for?" Gates asks him.

"It's a blessing. You do that to remind yourself that this is a holy place," Manuel tells him.

"In China, they take off their shoes when they walk into a sacred place," Willy says. "I was there with my dad once."

Gates ducks down through an archway to go from one small room to the other.

"Didn't make them too tall, did they?" he says.

"You're too tall, Gates," Susie says. "You should see some of the houses in the Philippines. They're smaller than this."

Mom and Irene are taking turns using the kneeler. They cry and dab their eyes with Kleenex. Mom and Irene are mothers making their way back to their sons. Firstborn sons, hidden away from them all these years. Maybe that's another reason Mom's so tired. Her heart is beating as it did when Jesse was alive, except she's not forty anymore, she's almost eighty. Her heart can't decide what's making it come to life again.

Donna takes turns on the kneeler with the Guadalupanas. She's as reverent as they are, making the sign of the cross when she enters and leaves a holy place. I'm surprised she learned church etiquette so quickly. She's the first white woman I've ever seen who knows how to be a Guadalupana. Faith is what Donna respects. Faith is faith, no matter what the religion, she says. Donna is big on Mom, so it's easy for her to respect La Virgen. Her mother was a drug addict and gave Donna up when she was a baby.

I make a call to Chris while everyone is sitting at an outdoor restaurant eating. He answers the phone on the first ring. I know he's been waiting for me.

"You're real close to me, Teresa," he says. He sounds happy. His voice makes me long to see him. He gives me directions to get to Los Griegos, a neighborhood close to Old Town. "Everything here is named after some Spanish family, or Indian tribe," he explains. Manuel is watching me on the phone. I make a sign to him for a paper and pencil and repeat the directions out loud so Manuel can write them down. After I hang up, Manuel's still looking at me like I've done something wrong.

"Is there a problem?"

"No, just that your face changed when you talked to Chris."

"Changed?"

"Yeah, like you were real happy."

"I am happy! I haven't seen Chris in years, plus I want to get to our rooms."

Manuel stares at me for a few seconds, then reaches for his wallet to pay the bill. Outside, I notice a few tourists gathered around our cars, talking to the kids and taking pictures. One teenage girl is taking Cisco's picture. Once, twice, three times I see the flash go off, as Cisco strikes various wrestling poses.

"By the way, Teresa, where's Chris gonna ride? Isn't he bringing his wife?"

"He's divorced, Manuel. He's over at his mom's for now. Maybe he can help you drive. You can take turns." I regret saying the words as soon as I've said them. Manuel looks as if I just kicked him.

"Yeah, that's you, right, Teresa? You can do with one or the other. It doesn't matter."

"I can't believe you're saying this. All I care about is getting Mom to the Wall."

"Really? There's more to it, and I . . ."

I don't let him finish. "I'm not going to argue with you!"

Priscilla passes between us. "What's going on?"

"What do you do, spy on me?"

"Can't help it. You're big sis, the big cheese around here. The one who gives the orders."

"You mean the one Mom decided to put in charge."

"Let's put it this way. You planned all this, Manuel's got the money, and me and Paul are just here for the ride."

"So help me, when we get back home . . ."

"Threatening me? I think she's threatening me, Manuel."

"I don't think so. She's just a little nervous about all this."

"You don't have to defend me, Manuel. I can speak for myself."

"And you do, all the time," Priscilla says.

Mom is watching us, drinking a cup of tea. She stands up. "Mijas, let's go now. We can't keep Chris waiting. I haven't seen his mother in years, pobrecita. She was a drunk in the old days, but now she's too old for that. She was always after men, can you imagine, and her husband was so religious! She went after Pablo Jesús for a while. El nervio!"

I'm surprised to hear the passion in Mom's voice as she talks about Dad. "Doña Hermina was after Dad?"

"For a little while. She was just a big flirt. Pablo only had eyes for you know who, anyway. Sin verguenza!"

"Did you pay the bill, moneybags?" Paul asks Manuel.

"I got it."

"Crazy. My own mother doesn't trust me with the money!"

"Don't start all this, Paul," I tell him. "You've given everybody good reason not to trust you."

"Another lecture from you! I've paid my dues. Wait until there's a warrant out for your arrest! If I remember clearly, you got a subpoena for a court hearing, and now you're out of state. That's rule one, sis, you gotta stay in-state."

"To hell with the subpoena! I have more important things to do!"

Mom looks at me. "Don't cuss, mija!"

"Do you eat with that mouth?" Irene asks me.

Paul starts laughing. "It's getting to you, isn't it? I know the feeling. Run while you can, baby."

Paul's laughter makes me even more defensive. "I'm not running anywhere. The whole nation knows where we are. The cops can just come and get me." I say the words flippantly, then swing my purse over my shoulder, as if Paul's words don't mean a thing to me, and I'm ready to move on, no matter what happens.

Michael is already in their van with Angelo, connecting the phone to the laptop for incoming messages. He waves to me and gives me a thumbs up.

"It's working, Tía . . . the web page is a winner!" he yells.

"See, what am I telling you? It's no secret where I am."

As we walk out of the restaurant, a waiter catches up to us. He's a kid, not much older than Lisa and Lilly.

"Aren't you the Ramirez family? The ones headed for the Vietnam Wall?"

"Yes, we are," I tell him.

"Hey, Licos!" He calls another waiter. "I told you, man, these are the people I saw on TV last night. Can I take your picture? Right there," he says, "with your mom and her friend, and your daughters. Fine-looking! Your daughters are fine. Do they want dates? Just kidding!"

Manuel and I pose with Mom, Irene, and the girls. The waiter and his friend Licos are all smiles, clicking the camera, then shaking our hands, and giving the girls a menu with their phone numbers on it.

Los Griegos •

e're racing now, or so it seems to me. La manda is the iron in our bones, the Wall is the magnet. I'm wondering if it's Mom's promise or Jesse's we're keeping, maybe they both made a manda, that's why it's so strong. We can't go back, can't even stop to get Mom checked by a doctor. It would waste too much time, and we don't have any. I'm afraid of turning back and afraid of getting to the Wall. If the Wall reminds us of our pain, why would we want to touch it? Maybe la manda is breaking pain's power. We're in pursuit of pain, instead of the other way around. If we're pursuing, does that make us more powerful than pain?

The Spanish names on the streets in Albuquerque get blurred in my mind, Don Pascual, Isleta, Emilio Lopez, Don Jacoba, and villages like Atrisco, Los Lunas, Los Padillas, Peralta. Chris lives in a neighborhood that looks like El Cielito. We pass LA BOTICA, a pharmacy advertising herbs and medicinal teas. Irene tells me that orange flower tea is used to calm the nerves and help you sleep, and pecan tree leaves are for anemia. Fig tree infusion, she says, is used to bring in milk for nursing mothers. "That's how I got my big chichonas and fed all my kids, even the last one, the one the doctors said was deformed, you remember Santiago who was born blue?"

"Cornsilk tea," my mother says, "didn't I tell Matilde, that so-called mother of yours, to use it to clean out her kidneys, Manuel? No, she never listened to me, and now look where she is, on a machine that sucks up all her blood. God only knows what's inside her veins once her blood goes round and round in those plastic tubes. May God forgive me, but maybe she deserves it for all she did to you."

"No, Doña, don't think that way. She did take me in, after all."

"Matilde never was a believer in herbs," Irene says. "But look at this." She holds up a strand of gray hair. "I had the darkest hair by drinking rosemary tea. Dark and shiny, maybe that's why Lencho married me. Look, see right here." She pulls up her hair. "You can still see dark hair. Oh, and I used the rose of Castile to cleanse my eyes."

"Why are you trying to stay young?" Mom asks her. "Eres vieja. Why don't you admit it, Irene, you've got one foot in the grave."

"Don't talk to me about graves! My mother lived until she was one hundred and two."

"What a pity. I would never want to live that long. Don't you remember Doña Mariana and how she lived to be over a hundred years old? She had to be put in a cradle with a baby bottle in her mouth. Then her kids never cleaned her face and the milk dribbled down the sides of her mouth. Sugar ants, can you imagine? Ants ate off half her face!"

"That's a lie!" Irene said. "Doña Mariana died long before she was put in a cradle."

"Listen, the both of you," I tell them. "Who cares about Doña Mariana . . . she's gone, you're still alive. Make the best of it."

"That's the way it is with the young," Irene says. "They think they will live forever, but you'll see, Teresa. Someday you'll look in the mirror, and an old woman will be staring back at you." I look into the van's side mirror and see part of my sunglasses reflected back, a wavy, distant image. I wonder what my face will look like in twenty years.

I'm glad to see Chris's house as we turn into Los Griegos, his barrio. I wonder why they named the area Los Griegos, the Greeks. Chris's house is a framed adobe structure with a white picket fence circling the front yard. A stone flower pot extends the length of a large plate glass window. Wildflowers, purple, pink, and yellow catch my mother's eye. Huge shade trees dot the whole neighborhood and oblong strips of canals choked with grass and weeds run parallel to the streets. Mailboxes balanced on wooden poles line the dusty sidewalks.

"This looks like El Cielito," Manuel says. "If we weren't in New Mexico, I'd swear we were back home."

"It's greener out here," I tell him.

Chris comes out as soon as we drive up. He's shorter than I remember. His dark hair has turned gray at the temples. His face is still chiseled to perfection even though it's fuller. He's wearing sweats, a T-shirt, and a red bandana around his forehead.

"Why's he wearing that red bandana?" Manuel asks. "Is that the style around here?"

"I doubt it."

I'm out of the van and in Chris's arms before I know what's happening. The smell of his cologne mixes in with sweat and the sweet smell of newly cut grass.

"You made it! You made it! Oh, God, God it's so good to see you." He stands me at arms' length. "Look at you . . . more beautiful than ever!" He presses me up close again and we hug, swaying together. Both of us are crying. Instinctively, we wipe each other's tears away. "More beautiful than all the dreams I've had of you," he whispers. Hugging him is like touching Jesse again. I can't let go. The pressure of his hands releases energy I've stored in my body since I last saw him.

"Can I get a hug?" Priscilla is standing next to us. Chris is still staring at me. We're clinging to each other. "He—llo! Can I get in on the action?"

"Yes! Sorry, I'm dazzled by all this beauty." He gives Priscilla a big hug, lifting her up and turning her around. "Jesse's kid sister . . . all grown up!"

Manuel is standing behind me. He mimics my steps, moving just at the right time, to avoid my stepping on him.

"You remember Manuel, don't you, Chris?"

"Hey, sure . . . how's it going?" He shakes Manuel's hand.

"Sorry about the headband," he says, taking it off, "I was cutting the grass, trying to keep the sweat off my face."

"Hey, there's Gates and Willy!" The three men shake hands and pound each other's backs. "We're not old, are we, guys?"

"There ain't nothin' old about me!" Gates says.

"I should ask your wife," Chris says.

"Which one?" Gates asks. They both laugh.

Chris looks at Willy and Susie. "Are you running your dad's store?"

"Yep. Me and Susie, here. Just what I said I'd never do. But you know Mom and Dad. I'm the oldest. They'd die if I didn't do things the traditional Chinese way."

"Man, this is great, to see you all again!" Chris shakes his head, as if he can't believe it's really happening. "At ease, men, at ease," he says, laughing.

Mom is out of the van now, and Chris leaps to her side. "Doña Ramirez! How are you? How was the trip. Look . . . no wonder your daughters are so beautiful, you look like a queen!" He bends down and gently holds her to his chest. My mother is crying, her body shuddering with each sob.

"Ay mijito, all I can think of is Jesse when I see you! My poor mijito . . . how I miss him!"

"Yes, Doña, we all miss him—to this day!"

Mom introduces Irene to Chris. Irene is crying, too. Chris gives her a hug.

"Did you know my son, Faustino Lara?"

"I remember him when I lived in El Cielito. A great man, your son. Jesse said he was a good friend to him."

"My son is on the Vietnam Wall, too."

"Lo siento, I'm sorry," Chris says. He holds Mom and Irene, tenderly, one on each arm, and soothes them. Then he looks up at all of us, smiling. "Wow, what a mix! Jesse would have loved this! Hey, you guys are making big news! We saw you last night on TV. Who's the smart kid who started your web page?"

"That's Michael," I tell him, "Paul's son."

"Paul? Little Paul has a son?" He turns around and looks at Paul. He takes a step, then stops, stares, and shakes his head. "Man, your face. You got the look of Jesse in your eyes." He walks over, claps both hands on Paul's shoulders, and tousles his hair, "Jesse would have been proud of you! He talked about you a lot in Nam."

"He did?" Paul searches Chris's face. "What did he say?"

"What didn't he say? He remembered all the jokes he played on you, and what a good sport you were. The best, he used to say, mi carnalito, he's got some guts, gonna be a great man some day. So, are you?"

"Am I what?"

"A great man?"

"I've done some detours, but I'm working on it. Right, Donna? This is my girlfriend," he says.

"Good name, Donna. Isn't that the name of one of Richie Valens' songs? Nothing like a good woman to back up a man. And your son, Paul? Where's the whiz kid?"

Paul calls Michael over. "Mijo, get over here. Chris wants to meet you."

"Mijo?" Priscilla asks. "Did I hear right? That's a first!"

Michael gets off the van, minus the laptop. He stands next to Paul, smiling. Paul circles one arm around his neck. "What do you think, huh? Ramirez brains! My son could get us to Mars and back. He's got the right stuff!"

"Smart like your Tío Jesse," Chris says. "Man, Jesse would be strutting right now. Proud. Remember when he'd get into the ring, and do that little dance before a fight? He'd be dancing big time right now! Seriously now, Michael, you gonna get us to Mars and back? We'll be the first Chicano astronauts on the red planet. All we'll need to add is white and green, and we got the Mexican flag up there. What do you think?"

"Yeah, we'll do it!" Michael says.

"What about the web site? You getting lots of responses?"

"I've got over a hundred already, and we just started. Dad's been helping out, now that he knows how to send e-mails."

"Maybe I can help, too. I probably know some of the guys."

Chris's mother walks slowly out the door, a duplicate of the Guadalupanas, in a plaid dress and slip-ons. Following behind her, two heads taller, is her daughter, Queta. By now, everyone else is in the front yard, and there are handshakes and hugs all around. My mother and Doña Hermina are the same height, When they hug, their foreheads touch. Doña Hermina invites us into the house. I pinch myself to make myself believe we're not back home. Pictures of La Virgen, the Sacred Heart of Jesus, and St. Michael with his foot on the devil's neck remind me of Mom's house. There is a big pot of cocido, hearty beef and vegetable soup, simmering on the stove. In one corner of the kitchen is an old wood stove, a remnant of early Spanish days. I smell the aroma of freshly cooked tortillas and pause to think that Doña Hermina and her daughter Queta probably make them every day. It makes me feel guilty when I think of all the instant soups my kids eat. Both women are perfectly genteel, smiling, inviting us in. We just ate an hour ago, but there is no question that we will eat again, refusing to do so would be a slap in the face. The old women from Phoenix acquired the title Doña as soon as we crossed the state line. Now it's Doña this and Doña that. We're in New Mexico, where families follow strict traditions, and the way of our ancestors, los antepasados, rules.

Chris tells me Queta's never been married. She's broad and sturdy with bushy eyebrows and the handshake of a wrestler. She'd be a good ally in a fistfight. I'd like to set her up against Sandra in the near future. Queta motions toward Gates with her eyes. She whispers in my ear, "He's sooo cute!" I think of her and Erica and know they would be equally matched in a fight. I'm hoping Gates doesn't fall for Queta. She's already serving him a huge bowl of cocido and setting out hot corn tortillas for him.

I'm amazed at the chile in New Mexico. Tata O'Brien would have
already put some of the pods in his pocket to dry for seeds. Two wooden
dining-room tables are set with an assortment of chile and chile sauces in
ceramic bowls. A platter piled high with sopaipillas, soft, doughy bread,
is centered at each table. Tata often talked about New Mexico chile, examining chile pods and cutting slits into them to examine their interiors.
If the chiles were hot enough he'd keep his hands out of his eyes for days.

"Try them at your own risk," Queta says, laughing. "Really the
hottest are probably the serranos and the chipotles. No, Mama?"

Doña Hermina nods. "Chile de arbol is hot, too, and sometimes
jalapeños, depending on the crop."

"The rest of them won't put you into shock," Queta says. "They'll
just make you sweat." She looks over at Gates, and he looks back at her.

"I like that!" he says. They both smile at each other.

"Good for your sinuses," Chris adds quickly.

"My doctor says not to eat chile—what do you think about that?"
asks Irene.

"Don't listen to him," Doña Hermina tells her. "Los doctores told me
I was going to die last year. Imagine! Talking to me like they were God!"

We all sit at the tables. Manuel pulls a chair out for Priscilla, and I
move one chair over, and sit next to Chris. The last thing I want to do is
eat. I want to move. I want to chase la manda across America before my
mother's strength gives out. Chris's hand is within inches of my own. I
have to fight the urge to slip my hand into his. I can't believe he's next
to me. My mind is playing games with me. It's '68, and Jesse will walk
into the room any minute now. This is their going-away party. There's a
part of me holding onto the fantasy every time I look at Chris. Then
when I stare across the table at Mom, the fantasy dissolves, only to gain
strength when I see Chris again. Chris and I reach for the same bowl of
sauce at the same time.

"You first, Teresa." He serves the sauce for me. "Here, take a sopaipilla. Mom made them this morning."

I notice the kids using their spoons to pick out tender chunks of meat
and potatoes in their bowls of cocido, bypassing the onions and cabbage.
Michael and Angelo set aside their corn on the cob to saturate separately
with butter and salt.

"Ni lo pienses," says Doña Hermina. "Don't even think of leaving
tonight! I already have the beds ready, and the kids can sleep on blankets

on the floor. There's the cuartito out in the back yard too, the one my father used when he was still alive. We've got two beds in there for los muchachos. The women and kids can sleep in the house."

"We've already got the rooms," Manuel says. "What are we supposed to do, cancel out now?"

"Yep, exactly," says Chris. "There's no way my mom will let these ladies go. It would be totally disrespectful to her."

My mom looks so tired, I'm glad for Doña Hermina's offer. I don't think she can climb back into the van for the trip to the motel. We're all tired, except the kids. They're already making plans to go back to Old Town to listen to music in the park and go through the souvenir shops.

"What do you think, Mom? Should we stay?" Mom looks at Doña Hermina and sighs.

"You're lucky, Hermina," she tells her. "Lucky that your husband was so religious and never went out with other women. Mine? Well, you remember Pablo Jesús!"

"How could I forget?" The three old women exchange glances. Doña Hermina holds onto the edge of the table and stands up. "But he loved you, Alicia. He always loved you."

Mom surprises everybody by laughing out loud. Laughter explodes from her stomach, and makes her gasp for breath. "Love? What does any man know about love?" Irene and Doña Hermina start laughing, too.

"Well said, Alicia," Doña Hermina says. "I never thought they understood a thing."

Mom holds one hand over her chest. "Ay, but we outlived them all, didn't we?"

"And we got the last laugh, too," Irene adds.

"We'll stay, Teresa," Mom says. "It will be good for my health."

After dinner, Chris tells me he'll take the kids over to Old Town if I go with him. I'm rushing again, but this time it's to get my mother and Irene settled for the night so I can dress up and go with Chris.

Penitentes •

lbuquerque is a spin-off of an ancient world still under exploration. I see the Spaniards in my mind, soldiers in crested headdresses, searching for the Seven Cities of Gold in a land of stark beauty, pushing the borders of Aztlán for Chicanos like me who would come after them centuries later. I could have told them that the light bouncing off the sheer cliffs of the Manzano and Sandia Mountains is far more precious than gold. They could never capture the splendor of that light and take it back to Spain in a box. Maybe that's why they stayed. They saw how futile it was to want gold when beauty was priceless. I want to think that, even though I know they were greedy and wanted to own everything, like the white men from Pittsburgh. The Indians had their own wars, one village against another, but they never wanted to own everything. There's a difference in arguing over a blanket, and in thinking the sheep who grew the wool for the blanket, and the pastures and streams they live in all belong to you. Ownership, deeds, land titles, old names, lots of things in Albuquerque belong to somebody who died a long time ago, and now nobody's sure what belongs to whom. Family members fought each other for land, and the enemies of one generation became family in the next. Everything moves in cycles and seasons like Indian tom-toms beating slow and deliberate, making things happen whether we want to or not.

Chris tells me his family has owned the plot of land in Los Griegos for over a century. "El Camino Real used to go through here," he says, "right through Old Town. There were old families all over the Southwest Valley, we call it El Watche, big familias with a hundred kids who traced their bloodline all the way back to the Spanish crown. There was respeto, forced respeto for the Spaniards, los patrones who made the poor their servants. We had so much respeto, we didn't know we should have slit their throats. Los patrones ruled back then, then los gringos came, and you know them, they thought they owned the world."

We walk through the campus at the University of New Mexico in the moonlight. The buildings slope into each other, blending into a perfect Southwest symmetry. Chris's hand curves over mine, smoothly, his fingers lock into mine. We're replicas of the '60s, a movie that's been on pause for thirty years. God forgot us and now He's remembering us again. It's hard to find the words to say to each other when the only script we knew was buried with Jesse. There's a volume between us, *The History of the Vietnam War*. We're casualties. Our photos should be in the book with captions, "Survivors of the Chicano Bloodbath in Nam," words that would tell people we had our own holocaust in Vietnam. The volume is open between Chris and me, not by our own hands, but by la manda, my mother's magic.

"Remember el cochito, Teresa?"

"How could I forget. We stalled the plane to Vietnam."

"All the guys were looking out the windows trying to figure out what was happening. Nobody was saying a thing. It was like we were at a funeral. Any one of us could come back as a corpse. Then the stewardess came in and called out Jesse's name. 'I've got a little pig for you, Sergeant,' she said. Jesse looked at her like she was speaking Chinese. 'A what?' he said. 'A pig, from your mother.' All the guys were looking at him, then he opened the napkin. He saw the cookie and said, 'Hijola, I can't believe my mom!' It was funny, everybody started laughing, and that's the way we took off for Nam with the whole damn plane laughing their heads off over el cochito. I think they were really laughing off their fear. It was 1968, we were getting the shit beat out of us over there. Nobody knew if they would ever see their mothers again. We were happy in those few minutes. It was like your mom had touched us all."

"I wondered what was happening in there. I was the one who gave the stewardess el cochito. My mom was ready to faint. She did faint after the plane took off. It's been hard for her all these years. She blames herself for Jesse leaving, because my dad and him were always fighting. You remember my dad's lover, Consuelo? Jesse hated her, hated her son

Ignacio, too. Jesse stuck up for Mom all the time, but she never divorced my dad."

"That's the way it was in the old days, people didn't divorce each other, not like now. I'm a three-time loser myself, never thought I would be. Margie was my first wife. I don't know if you remember when we sent you a wedding invitation. We had two daughters, my girls Elizabeth and Lucia. Now they're married and on their own. Man, my head was messed up back then! But I loved Margie. You know how that goes. Loved her, and hurt her, loved her, and hurt her. I sure didn't take after my dad, he was a penitente."

"What's a penitente?"

"The penitentes are a religious cult. They're people who take religion to the extreme. They build moradas in small villages, like churches, except priests don't say mass in them. They can be masochists about some of their practices, sometimes wearing wreaths made of cactus thorns. They tap the wreaths with a stick to cause more pain, and according to them, no blood appears. They wear hoods on their heads right before Easter during La Semana Santa and carry real wooden crosses with splinters sticking out of them on their backs. Some of them tow la carretera de la muerte around. That's a real wooden cart with a figure of a skeleton representing death sitting in it, San Sebastina herself. Death has an arrow, ready to shoot the man should the purpose of his heart not be true. My dad's morada didn't haul la carretera de la muerte around, but they did all kinds of other weird things, like blacken all the windows of the morada during tiñeblas and carry on long hours of prayer. Who knows what else they did."

"What's tiñeblas?"

"Darkness. That's what it means. I guess the penitentes figure they're the ones who do penance for the darkness and sins of the world. Can you imagine my dad was a penitente and my mom was an alcoholic? Talk about opposites attracting! Sometimes they'd bring Nuestro Compadre Jesús for a visit at our house. I'm talking about a real wooden statue of Christ with movable hands and arms who was put up in people's homes like He was actually visiting. I can tell you we were real good when Nuestro Compadre Jesús was visiting us!"

"Unbelievable. I guess maybe everything combined helps us keep God in our minds . . . what do you think?"

"I don't know, but it kept us on the straight and narrow. And when we went off the trail, we knew it right away." Chris smiles and kisses my cheek.

"I've thought about you so much all these years, Teresa. I mean *really* thought about you . . . like wanting to kidnap you and bring you to Albuquerque."

"What stopped you?"

"It's a long story. After Jesse died, I didn't think I was worthy of you."

"I can't believe you said that!"

We stop and sit on the stony ridge of a flower bed. I rest my chin on Chris's shoulder. He clasps his hands in his lap.

"Jesse died, I didn't," he says. "Sometimes I wish I had."

"That's what Gates said."

"It's more than that with me, Teresa. I was there when your brother died. I saw the whole thing."

"What's that supposed to mean, Chris? Don't tell me you think it was your fault."

"I'm not saying that . . . it's just real complicated. I've never been able to clear my head."

"Do you want to?"

"I'm not sure . . . maybe I do . . . let's not talk about it."

He reaches in his pocket. "Forgot I quit smoking." He wraps his arms around me and holds me tight.

"Don't be a penitente, Chris. You don't have to do penance for Jesse's death."

We stand up together, and Chris kisses me, not like he did at the airport when he left for Vietnam, but with a fierce energy, a hunger that makes me believe he's really been waiting for me all these years. His energy ignites the part of me that watched him leave for Vietnam, watched the back of his uniform disappear into a sea of green. There's warmth slipping into a forgotten part of me that took off on the plane for Vietnam, finally it's throbbing, almost as if Chris never left at all.

• THE GUADALUPANAS huddle together in Doña Hermina's bed. The bed's their cradle, the moon shining in through the window is their candlelight. Maybe Jesse's spirit is burrowed in the atoms of moonlight filtering in through the window. I no longer expect to account for life in other dimensions. On Doña Hermina's dresser, veladoras flicker away in front of images of La Virgen and a collection of saints. I notice Mom and Irene propped up Jesse and Faustino's photos next to the pictures.

The old ladies fit together in the bed, as if they've been sleeping together for a hundred years. Mom sleeps in the middle, Doña Hermina and Irene on either side. The moon in New Mexico isn't the same as the one in Arizona. It's cunning, lighting up places here and there where Spanish gold was buried. Arizona's moon shines broadly and brightly over huge expanses of land.

My mother and her friends, so many old bones together in one spot, shriveled bodies outlined by a white sheet that looks like a shroud. I'm not one to visit nursing homes. They're too depressing. Where did the old ladies put their false teeth? Mom's are in a plastic container, a blue one that looks like the one Cisco used for his retainer when he wore braces.

Queta set up cots for the men out back in el cuartito. I wonder if Gates is with the other men or with Queta in her room. I can't imagine Manuel and Chris sleeping in the same room, but then again la manda's in control. Words that have stirred up the past and kicked up old memories are not as important as la manda. The boys are on blankets on the floor, the twins are sleeping with Priscilla in the next room. I sit in the dark for a few minutes and watch the old women sleep, listening to their uneven breathing, their light, trumpeting snores.

"Where's Chris?" My mother asks suddenly. Her eyes reflect specks of moonlight, small beams shining into mine.

"Asleep," I tell her. "He's asleep."

"I don't think so, mija. He's awake, thinking of you." Mom's words jar the darkness, tag it, make it impossible for me to say no. She turns on her side and moans in pain, curling one arm over Irene and turning her back on Doña Hermina. Is she still holding a grudge on Doña Hermina for going after my dad when they were young? I open my mouth to ask her, then decide not to, instead I walk into the living room and rummage through my suitcase until I find the plastic bag with Jesse's letters.

February 24, 1968

Dear Sis,

I've been thinking a lot about El Cielito and all the things we did. I'm already missing Mom's tortillas and Nana's tamales. There's not much to eat in the bush except C rations. Nothing is better than Mexican food, I'm convinced. I don't really care about eating these days anyway. We lost another guy, un mejicano from Detroit of all places. We called him Tiny. His family used to travel all over the place picking crops. The recruiting officer promised him a green card if he went for a stint in Vietnam. That's the way they work to build up the Army, with lies. Lies! This kid had never owned two pairs of shoes and all of a sudden he's getting an income for his family from the Army and he's got two pairs of boots. He couldn't understand English that well and I translated for him. They shot him, Teresa, while he was running out for some C rations that a chopper had dropped. We're supposed to be helping the Vietnamese people with food and protection, but all I see us doing is scaring them and making their lives miserable. If you can find out what the hell we're supposed to be doing out here, write me and tell me cause every time I turn around there's one more order that doesn't make sense. Like the other night, it was raining so hard, we were almost swimming in our holes, but the captain sent us out on patrol. Lots of guys around here are high on pot, booze or speed. I'm not saying I haven't tried the stuff. Believe me after you're out here a few nights, you start getting desperate. Damn, I've seen some stuff. I wish I could tell you the rest but it's more like I would be telling you a nightmare.

The word for sun in Vietnamese is mat trang, *the word for day is* ngay, *the word for morning is* buoi sang, *the word for love is* ting yeu. *I can't make sense of all the accents, they have more than we do. I can't believe it that I'm in this crazy war on the other side of the world and people have words for everything we know. Remember that family I told you about? Well their daughter is the one teaching me Vietnamese. I wish I could tell you more about her, but when I think about her my mind goes blank, like I'm trying to reach something and I don't know what it is. Is it love? I've never been in love so I don't know. I would hate to be in love now, but I guess nobody controls love. Gotta go. I'm up for patrol. Search and destroy, that's our mission. I wouldn't want to meet Jesus Christ some night and have to explain what I was doing here. Do you think He would understand?*

Have you seen Trini? Tell Mom to get Paul to Trini's gym. That old trainer is the best ever. He'll be good for Paul with Dad the way he is. I guess our old man is still after what's her name. Right? Gotta go. This stinking hole smells like shit, maybe some guy went in his pants. The pills for malaria do that to us. Did you get Chris's letter? I got one from Espi and it felt good to hear from her. Pray for me. Light another candle.

SWAK,
Jesse

I had forgotten about the woman who taught Jesse Vietnamese and about Trini, the one-eyed trainer who ended up shadow boxing at an old folks' home.

El Gato •

Jesse changed his name to El Gato when he started boxing for Trini Bustamante, the best trainer south of the river. Trini was a nino, a godfather to all his boxers. He worried about them, scolded them, made them eat, made them sweat, and taught them to pick out his voice in a crowd of hundreds shouting at them during a fight. Trini was short like Jesse and could be loud or quiet to match the thoughts going through his head. He had trophies galore he collected from his vatos, the swinging, swaying dudes of the Mexican world. Alert, alive, fed on jumping beans, jalapeños, and tortillas made by their sainted mothers, his boys took championships all the way to New York City. Trini had them practice to the music of the Mexican Hat Dance to stir them up to their calling.

"Ramirez, Ramirez! Your mommy smells like tequila! You look like you're playing with dolls! Come on, ballerina, shake a leg!" He yelled all kinds of things at Jesse to test his concentration. "One wrong turn and you're a goner. See this eye?" He would take off his sunglasses to show everyone the slit of eye on the left side of his face. He had refused surgery and wore the eye like a badge of courage.

"The crowd will hound you! Los jodidos! That's the way people are, bloodthirsty. They want you to look at them just to mess you up." Trini danced away jabbing at the air, fighting an invisible opponent for his eye.

"POW! POW! One for your precious momma who smells like tequila. One for your grandma who smokes marijuana, ha, ha!"

Trini trained his boys at the Golden Gate Gym across the street from ol' Perez's Dry Cleaners. I always waved at ol' Perez when I saw him standing outside his cleaners in his wrinkled clothes. "Es la verdad," Mom used to say, "whatever a man knows how to do he never does for himself or his home. Look at your dad, works in construction and our house is falling down all around us!"

I went to the Golden Gate Gym on afternoons Jesse practiced to watch him spar. "You've got to stay loose, ballerina," Trini shouted. "Loose but quick . . . loose, loose, jab, jab . . . you're getting it. Stay inside, stay inside . . . loose, loose, jab, jab." It was a chant.

Jesse taught me the four main punches, jab, right hand, uppercut, left, right hook. Jesse's best combination was the overhand right, left hook. Drops of sweat dribbled from El Gato's forehead and down his face when he was in the ring. His normally slender jaw bulged under his mouthpiece like a jack-o-lantern's. His perfectly straight teeth were hidden underneath it. "Don't forget your mouthpiece, Jesse. Your mouthpiece, your mouthpiece." That was my worry. I didn't want a toothless brother. I knew we didn't have any money for dentists.

The crack of leather on leather sounded like a firecracker had gone off under a pillow. It made me nervous, especially if Jesse was getting the worst of it. Usually he wasn't. He took the name El Gato. It fit him because Jesse was dark, quick, and sly like a cat with its ears flinching and its body ready to leap. Trini gave him an old speed bag to practice on at home. Gates, Willy, Faustino, and Chris would come over and spend hours, taking turns on the speed bag hanging from a wooden beam in my dad's old garage. I brought out towels for them to wipe their sweat and water to drink. I practiced my cheerleader moves with Priscilla while they boxed. Ricky Navarro from next door came over a few times but said he was a lover, not a fighter.

I liked watching the guys, especially Chris. Of all Jesse's friends, he was the best-looking. He was taller than Jesse, light, his jaw square, his hair dark, wavy. His face looked chiseled, like the faces I had seen on Greek heroes in my history book. His dad didn't let him box, because he said there was already enough fighting in the world. In high school, Chris moved to Albuquerque, and I didn't see him again until the night before he and Jesse left for Fort Benning.

The last time Jesse boxed was at University Park where they set up a ring for the Metropolitan State Tournament. Frank Rodriquez, a famous boxer, came by to hand out trophies. The winners were slated to go to Las Vegas and fight national champions. Mom and Nana came that night to watch. It was the first and last time they ever sat in the audience. Jesse boxed featherweight against Andres El Animal, who was known to let loose in such a way that the other boxer had to fight for his life. Nana held onto her Virgen medallion the whole time Jesse was in the ring, holding it up to her lips every once in a while. Dad had bought popcorn for Paul and Priscilla. Somehow Mom got so excited she ended up flipping the popcorn bag into the air. Some of it landed in her hair and still she kept yelling, "Get him, mijo! Ay, Dios mio, I can't take another minute!"

Actually, the fight didn't last very long, but Mom said it was the longest fight of her life. When Jesse went down, Dad had to tackle Mom to keep her from rushing into the ring. Jesse left for Vietnam with the scar Andres El Animal gave him over his left eyebrow. It was the only fight Jesse ever lost, until he got to Vietnam.

• ALL THE GUYS from the Golden Gate Gym showed up the night we said good-bye to Jesse. Trini came by showing off his bad eye, telling the guys that's what happens to you when you don't concentrate. Los vatos wanted to take a few shots at El Gato before he left, teasing, jabbing him right and left. A mass of relatives, primos, tías, tíos, crowded around Jesse, toasting beer cans for his safe return and making speeches about everything crazy they remembered about him. His gabacho friends from college were there, burning their tongues on Mom's hot tamales and loving it. Mom, Nana, Irene, and Tía Katia piled up tamales, rice, beans, salads, filling up bowls with menudo. Even ol' Duke got into the act, knocking kids down in the backyard for scraps of food.

Music was playing, playing like crazy. "Solitary Man" over and over again, "Blue Velvet," "Louie, Louie," "Respect." Jesse laughed, talked with his friends, Gates, Willy, Chris, and Manuel, who had a deferment to stay in school. Manuel said he loved me, and I ignored him. I wanted to pull on his ears like a puppy dog.

Chris came by from Albuquerque to leave on the same plane with Jesse. His breath smelled like Doublemint and beer, lots of beer. "Your sister, the cheerleader. Sing me a cheer, Teresa!" I was afraid of him, afraid of the urgency I sensed from him, afraid of life and death. I might never see him again. We might cling too long, cling too strong. They were both going so far away. There was a thud in me. Something that hit a brick wall when I thought of Vietnam. The word *Vietnam* rose in my mind, and I pushed it away, flesh and blood was still real to me. I ran up to Jesse all night, touching him, his face, his shoulder, sparring with him, playing tag, he was home base. I tell you I was crazy. Jesse was slipping away from me. I'd have to watch the news every night to try to catch a glimpse of him on TV, where figures were only six inches tall.

It was at Jesse's farewell party that I started to repeat words in my head like a singsong chant, like El Ganso who sang instead of talked. I didn't want to feel like me, like Teresa, named after Saint Teresa, the patron saint of Avila, Spain who ran around building convents, levitating in the air, and her nuns had to grab her by the heels to keep her grounded.

Jesse was this skinny kid, in my mind, with bony elbows that stuck up under his shirt and knobby knees that bulged under his Levi's. It was impossible that he'd carry an M-16 and use it to kill somebody.

It was winter outside, January. The house was warm, too warm, from the steam made by big pots on the stove. I wanted it to be the celebration of La Virgen de Guadalupe all over again so Jesse and I could run up and down the steps at St. Anthony's and breathe hazy circles in the frosty morning air.

Nana Esther sat in the bedroom with the veladoras flickering around her, the matriarch, queenly. She wanted to give Jesse her blessing, the blessing of a holy woman, a Guadalupana who had won the favor of the Mother of God. She didn't turn on the ceiling light, only the candles, she knew the prayer, La Oración del Justo Juez, the Prayer to the Just Judge, by heart:

Santísimo Justo Juez, hijo de Santa Maria, que mi cuerpo
no se asombre, ni mi sangre sea vertida. Que mis enemigos
no me vean, ni sus ejercitos me dañen.

Con el manto que cubijo a Jesucristo cubre mi cuerpo
que mis enemigo no me ataquen.

Con las bendiciones del Padre, el Hijo, y el Espiritu Santo
concedeme paz y alegría. Amen.

*Most Holy Judge, son of Saint Mary, do not let my body be
harmed or my blood be spilled. Let not my enemies see me
nor their armies hurt me.*

With the robe that covered Our Lord Jesus Christ, cover my
body so that I will never be attacked by my enemies.

With the blessing of the Father, the Son, and the Holy Spirit,
bring me peace and happiness. Amen.

"Keep it in your wallet, yes, please, mijito. God will protect you. The prayer won't fail you." Later she gave it to Chris, to Willy, to Gates. Jesse knelt in front of Nana, and she extended her hand over him. "I bless you in the name of the Father, and of the Son, and of the Holy Spirit. May God get you safely to Vietnam and bring you back home again!"

Her voice broke. She held him in her arms, his head on her lap. He was her baby, still. Mom and Dad knelt down with Jesse, crying, hugging him. I stood over them, tears falling, looking at the throbbing heart of familia.

Yellowhair •

t Doña Hermina's I place a call to Elsa in Phoenix. It's early Monday morning, the second of June. The day is pleasantly warm. A breeze is blowing, stirring up the treetops and clumps of tall grass that grow along the canals.

"You got a call from your lawyer, Sam Diamond," Elsa tells me. "He's mad at you because you left town without telling him. He says he can't postpone the court date, and that a warrant might be issued for your arrest."

"Tell him he better get me out of this! What am I paying him for? Slick Sam! He knows I had to take this trip."

"Wanna talk to Dad?"

"What for? He's going to court with Sandra, for God's sake."

"Mom, he still loves you."

I laugh, remembering the old ladies, and how they laughed when they thought of men and love. "Loves me? If he loved me, he'd try to get me out of this trouble. Most of it is his fault anyway. Nice try, Elsa. I tried all kinds of things, too, that I thought would make my mom and dad happy, and nothing ever worked." I feel angry with myself, and wonder why I wasted my time fighting over Ray in the first place.

Elsa tells me she's been watching us on TV, and that some news stations are charting our route. "Get ready, Mom," she says. "It looks like everybody in America is going on this trip with you."

"That's scary," I tell her. "I wanted publicity, but this is too much." We say good-bye, and I'm left worrying about the publicity Elsa just told me about. One thing is certain. If there's a warrant out for my arrest, they won't have any trouble finding me.

I call Jimenez Elementary to ask Shirley how things are going, and Clara answers.

"Where are you, Teresa?" she asks. "Everybody in Phoenix is watching the news about your family. The kids at school are excited. Your class is writing you letters."

"Letters? That's wonderful! But where will they send them? We're in Albuquerque. We'll be heading out today and stop for the night in Colorado Springs. Have Lorena Padilla, my assistant, collect the letters. I'll pick them up when I get back to Phoenix." I stop myself from saying any more, remembering I'm talking to Clara, the rumor queen.

"Guess who's not here anymore?" Clara asks. Her voice rises with excitement.

"Mr. H., who else?"

"Oh, you should have seen him at the last faculty meeting! He looked so pathetic, but you know he's a back-stabber. I never liked him."

"He didn't want me to tell Jesse's story to my class. That's what I remember."

"Well, good riddance then! Maybe they'll send us somebody who can lead the school, but I doubt it. Everything is politics, you know that as well as I do. Anyway, let's get to the good part. Met anybody interesting yet, Teresa? You know the saying . . . so many men, so little time!"

"Huh, no. Listen, is Shirley there? I want to ask her if there's anything else I have to do. I handed in my report cards and my end-of-year check-out form. Lorena Padilla's got the classroom keys."

"Oh, Shirley? She's visiting her mother in Wisconsin. She should be back next week. Everything's in order, Teresa. But let's get to the good part. Any new man on the horizon?"

"Listen, I gotta go. Say 'hi' to everybody for me." Ending my conversation with Clara is like springing out of a trap. Now I'm worried thinking who we'll get to take Mr. H.'s place. I can see Annie Get Your Guns and the rest of the teachers cheering their victory. It might be short-lived after they see Mr. H.'s replacement.

• • •

• BEFORE BREAKFAST is served, we get a call from a local news station.

"How did they find out where we're staying?" I ask Michael.

"They saw us last night in Old Town. I couldn't tell if they were reporters or tourists. I guess they were reporters."

"Yeah, right, you couldn't tell who they were."

"They asked us questions," Angelo says, "lots of questions, and Michael showed them our itiner . . . how do you say it?"

"You mean our itinerary?"

"Yeah. The map of where we're going."

"Oh, great!"

Chris walks in with a newspaper in his hand. "Look, Teresa, here's a story about your family." I look at bold letters taking up one side of the front page: RAMIREZ FAMILY VISITS ALBUQUERQUE. There are pictures of our vehicles and of the kids shopping in Old Town.

"I'm getting nervous about all this, Chris."

Mom and Irene walk in. "What's making you nervous?" Mom asks.

"Stories about us, Mom. Publicity. People talking." I look out the front window and see a pick-up with the words NEWS CHANNEL 10 on its door. "Here we go."

"Don't worry," Mom says. "What can they do to us, pobrecitos, they have to make a living. Remember that poor girl who talked to me at the house?"

"You mean Holly Stevens? She's the one responsible for all this. And she's not a poor girl, Mom. These people are out to sell their stations and newspapers." Lisa and Lilly run in from the front yard.

"Mom, the news people want to know how Nana's doing," Lilly says.

"See, mija, they care."

"Yeah, right."

"Here, Alicia," Irene says, helping Mom to the window. "Stand here, and wave to them." Manuel and Priscilla walk in. "What's going on?" Priscilla asks.

"Nana's waving at the news people," Lisa says.

"Oh my God! How are we ever gonna get to the Wall with the whole country chasing after us?"

"Don't get excited," Manuel says. "They'll tire out. The media is fickle. Something else will attract their attention."

"I hope you're right," I tell him.

We sit down to breakfast, and Queta already has a plate ready for Gates. They look at each other as if they're schoolkids who just came in from a first date. Doña Hermina watches her daughter closely, but doesn't say anything.

Paul and Donna walk in with Susie and Willy. Everybody's taking a place at the tables. Priscilla and I help Queta set out the huevos rancheros, potatoes, ham, salsa, sopaipillas, juice, and coffee. The food smells delicious, and everybody digs in. For dessert, there's pan de huevo, a variety of Mexican pastry, fruit empanadas, rolls, and gingerbread cochitos like the one Jesse ate on the plane to Vietnam.

After breakfast, I get a call from Espi.

"I just talked to Elsa," she says. "Your attorney called and told her he just got word that Sandra's dropped the charges on you."

"She did?" A sense of relief flows through me.

"Yeah, she said she didn't want to be blamed for putting the daughter of a hero in jail."

"The daughter of a what?"

"A hero! Don't you know? Your mom is being called a hero, the first Nana hero this country has ever known, publicly, that is."

"My little stubborn mom is a hero? What makes her a hero?"

"Are you kidding me? She's taking her life into her own hands by making this trip. She's answering her son's call to get to the Wall. This is a life-and-death situation. Then there's the whole thing about the money. How many other families did the government cheat? Poor families, minority families, victimized. That's what the stories are saying. Your mom's a symbol of all the other moms who lost their sons in Vietnam." She pauses and waits for me to say something. "Teresa, are you still there? This should make you happy. What's wrong?"

"We're a week away from the Wall. I don't know what's gonna happen. She might make it, she might not. All these memories coming at us! Is Mom strong enough to take all this?"

"You told me not too long ago, not to be so uptight, and to stop worrying. Now I'm telling you, Teresa, get a hold of yourself. Things will work out. You're doing what your Mom wants you to do. Now, what about Chris? How's he doing?"

"He's OK."

"He's OK, and you're crying?"

"It's a lot more than that, Espi. It's everything. Like the stories say, it's life and death."

• • •

• BEFORE WE LEAVE ALBUQUERQUE Queta tells me her mother wants Mom to meet Palmira, la curandera. The old woman is famous all over New Mexico, Queta says, for the cures she works on people. Even she has gone to her to do a plática, which is a conversation, and can be compared to a therapy session. La plática centers in on patients' needs, physical, mental, and spiritual. A curandera never heals without taking into account the whole person.

"We had Doña Carolina in El Cielito. She was our curandera," I tell Queta, "and I knew an old man who claimed he was a tlachisqui, a seer, like a wise man of the Aztec nation. Jesse and I used to visit him over by El Río Salado. He told us about our history, and all kinds of stories about the ancient world. He had lots of cures, yerbas, teas, you know, like they use in healing. When he looked at you, it seemed he was looking right through you."

"Palmira could be his twin."

"That mystical?"

"Yeah. Spooky sometimes, if you ask me."

One hour before we set out for Colorado Springs, Palmira, la curandera, shows up. I notice people don't call her Doña Palmira, just Palmira, as if she's some kind of goddess. This is a special visit, Doña Hermina explains, because Palmira never goes to anyone's house. People come to her, and many do, hundreds every year.

Palmira walks in, and she reminds me somehow of the reeds that grew along the banks of El Río Salado. There is a quality about her that bends this way and that like the movement of the reeds when the wind swept over them, or when El Río Salado overflowed, drowning them for days. There is power in the old lady. She could bend and rise again, drown and come back to life. I'm two heads taller than she and have to stoop to give her a hug. She's wearing a simple dress with tiny black and white half moons all over it, and black shoes with white socks. On her finger, where her wedding band should be, is a ruby-red ring. Around her neck is a chain with a medallion of La Virgen and a gold crucifix. Her white hair is pulled up into a crown of braids piled on top of her head. She reaches out with freckled arms to hold me briefly.

"You've touched the ancient world," she says to me. "How have you done this?" Palmira's eyes, shiny, black pupils, look deeply into mine, and I don't know what response to give. Once again, she says to me, "What power have you met? Cual poder?"

Finally, I realize what she's asking. "Don Florencío," I tell her.

"Don Florencío, who?"

"A tlachisqui of the Aztecas."

"I haven't heard that word since I was a child. Tlachisqui." She repeats it softly. "Tlachisqui."

"He gave me a tea to drink, yoloxochitl."

"Como no, of course, to heal a broken heart. The loss of your brother, no?"

"Yes. And my voice. I couldn't speak. He healed me so I could talk again."

"Muy bien, very good, always good to regain something lost por un susto. Susto is trauma to the soul. The soul will hide and be unable to grow until it is recovered and the trauma is healed. Voice comes not only from the throat, but from the heart and soul as well." I want to ask Palmira about the susto my mother suffered when I almost drowned in El Río Salado, but without understanding how, I know the time is not right.

"Teresa, you are named after a great saint. Teresa of Avila. She is my patron saint. My middle name is Teresa. Teresa of Avila, tan poderosa! I rely on her many times to guide me to know God's will, for as you know, all great healing comes from God. We are only instruments." Palmira is silent for a few seconds. She looks at me intently. "There is still a part of your soul you must bring home. La alma needs to be coaxed sometimes." Palmira turns to Mom.

"Come with me, Doña Ramirez," she says, and leads Mom to Doña Hermina's bedroom, where they can speak in private.

Later Mom told me Palmira gave her a limpia. She swept a bunch of fragrant herbs over her body, romero, and ruda, rosemary and rue, while she recited various prayers. Then she passed an egg over her body, to uncover the root of Mom's problem. The egg was cracked into a bowl, and its elements read by Palmira. She told Mom she was suffering from una tristeza grande, a great sadness which came about through susto. Jesse's death cost my mother the loss of the part of her soul that was joined to Jesse—the mother's love that wanted to protect him from all harm. Guilt was the consequence, and great regret, and the song in my mother's heart was snatched away. All this, Palmira read of my mother's life. I marveled that she could be so right. An image of Don Florencío emerged in my mind, arms outstretched, sprinkling sacred cornmeal in the four directions, a gift to the gods, he would say, for sharing such knowledge with mere mortals.

• • •

• OTHERS ARE TRAVELING with us now, Yellowhair and his mother
Sarah. They're Zuñi Indians from the reservation west of Albuquerque.
Chris knows Yellowhair from his days in Vietnam. Yellowhair's brother,
Strong Horse, known by his American name, Eddie Bika, was killed in
Vietnam in 1970. It's a miracle, Yellowhair's mother says, that her son saw
Chris only two days before we arrived in Albuquerque. She claims God
answered her prayer, maybe it was even El Santo Niño. That intrepid
child again! The Zuñis hold celebrations in honor of the Christ Child,
making new shoes for him every year and guarding Him in their homes
against members of the tribe who attempt a kidnapping of the Child if
given the opportunity. All is done in the spirit of good play.

Of course we'll let Yellowhair and his mother go with us, my mother
says. Why not? We have enough money. Manuel doesn't like the idea of
renting another van for the Bikas. We'd need another vehicle anyway to
make room for Chris. Manuel's angry that Chris has volunteered to drive
Mom's van to keep her company the rest of the way. Really it's me he
wants to keep company, but Manuel says nothing more about it. He's
good at isolating, and I'm good at letting him do it. Priscilla says Manuel
can help Paul drive the van they're riding in. There's nothing strong
enough to separate me and Chris.

Everything has an appetite, Don Florencio always said. I'm understanding appetite the longer I stare at Chris. This never happened to me
with Ray. Ray was the one who unwound the bandages I wrapped my
soul in after Jesse died. Once my soul was free again, there was nothing
else for Ray to do. The Guadalupanas sense how things are between
Chris and me. They're old women who led strange love lives. I don't
know if they ever got excited or went to bed with no underwear. It's almost blasphemous to think these thoughts about them when I see them
sitting in the back seat, dressed in their old ladies' clothes, their gold
medallions shining on their flat chests. Then I see Irene whispering to
Mom, and I don't think they're talking about La Virgen.

Yellowhair's mother tells me she got her name from a missionary
who lived on the reservation. Her mother named her after the first person who walked into their house after her daughter's birth. "I'm glad it
wasn't a man," she says, "or I would be Samson instead of Sarah!" Her
son was named Yellowhair because his grandfather had a dream the night
before his birth of a stalk of corn with a child's face on it. He figured his
grandson wanted to be named Yellowhair in honor of the cornstalk.

Now we really look like a United Nations entourage. Gates and
Queta found an African flag at a souvenir shop and now that's sticking

out the side of Willy's car, flapping in rhythm to the Chinese flag. I didn't realize the South African colors are red, white, and blue like the U.S. flag. The Chinese flag is solid red with yellow stars on one end. The flags wave together as we travel, U.S., Mexican, Chinese, South African, making bold splashes of color everywhere we go. Gates bought a book on Nelson Mandela and suddenly claims an allegiance to South Africa. He says he'll finish reading the book before we get to the Wall.

Queta would have gone with us to the Wall, but her mother went into one of her dizzy spells, and she had to stay home. I'm wondering if her mother's dizzy spell is the way Doña Hermina keeps Queta home. Gates promised he'd stay in touch by phone. I'm hoping he's staying in touch with Erica, too. I don't want her appearing in D.C. unexpectedly.

Yellowhair is displaying two feathered wands on their gray Toyota van. One is blue for the Sun Father, the other is yellow for the Moon Mother. He says the Zuñis were never conquered by the Spaniards, or anyone else for that matter. Fray Marcos de Niza, the Spanish missionary, believed the Zuñi villages were the fabled Seven Cities of Cibola, the cities of gold. His famous guide, Esteban, was killed at Zuñi for his big mouth and insulting ways. Other Spanish explorers stayed clear of the Zuñis, once they discovered the Indians didn't take much to strangers.

Yellowhair and Sarah look more like siblings than mother and son. Their brown faces are smooth, almost wrinkle-free. I can't tell if they ever squint in the bright sun, or frown when they're angry. I look closely at them, and wonder who else will join us.

• THE NIGHT BEFORE we leave Albuquerque I have another one of my Río Salado dreams. This time I see Jesse's body coming home in an airplane, flying over the Pacific. The plane has a single engine like the kind used in World War I. The bottom of the airplane opens and his coffin drops into the sea. It's so real, I feel the water splash on my face. I jump on his coffin, as if I'm riding on El Ganso's neck and nearly fall off when I see the lid open just a crack and blood ooze down the side of the coffin and into the sea. I wake up trying to save myself from falling into the sea. The dream reminds me of my baby sister, Inez. I'm running away from her again. I never meant to give my mother el susto, the fear that caused Inez's death.

Time Warp •

n our way out of Albuquerque, I spot a sign on a local church, a framed wooden structure sandwiched between a residential home and a parking lot overgrown with weeds: PARE DE SUFRIR (Stop Suffering). I point it out to Chris.

"See, they want us to stop suffering."

"How?" he asks. "Suffering is in our bones. It's the fatalism of the Indians. The Indians are selfish about suffering. They've made an art of it."

"Why does it appeal to them?"

"You mean why does it appeal to us? We're Indian, too. I guess we've done it so long, been oppressed so many years, we're fish out of water without it. There's beauty in it, too. How would we know joy if we didn't suffer? There would be no measuring rod."

I hadn't thought about that. Stoicism, silence, and laughter belong to those who know both joy and suffering. Hiding from suffering will not make it go away. Native Americans are wise to make it a part of life. It's there whether we like it or not, an ongoing Purgatory that keeps us reaching for grace, a bit confused, unsure why we're suffering in the first place. Hell's suffering, I imagine, is jagged pain with no end in sight. Our suffering is jagged pain with a purpose. We know we'll come to the end of it and learn something.

We pass through New Mexico's capital, Santa Fe, a city of classic colonial architecture and vivid colors created by the mingling of Spanish and Indian blood. History is alive here. Spirits inhabit stone and mortar, luring tourists to come closer, to touch and feel the world they knew. Beauty becomes a coveted souvenir. Visitors buy it in the form of trinkets and works of art they can pack into their luggage.

The Guadalupanas are talking about stopping at Chimayó, which is not far from Santa Fe, to see el santuario with a miraculous little well, known as el posito, in one of the chapels. Chris says a man named Don Bernardo Abeyta saw a light shining on the ground during Holy Week around the hills of Potrero sometime during the early 1800s. He was a member of the penitentes, like Chris's dad. As the story goes, he saw a light shining near one of the hills close to the Santa Cruz River one night when he was out performing penances. He dug in the dirt with his bare hands and found a crucifix. He called the neighbors together to venerate the crucifix with him.

The local priest took the crucifix twice to the church at Santa Cruz, but each time the crucifix returned miraculously to the hole in which Don Bernardo had found it. They ended up building a church at Chimayó to house it. Chris says the church is a humble structure that hasn't changed much since the time of Don Bernardo Abeyta. It is surrounded by a rural community of small farms and winding roads that resist the march of progress. The sacred posito in the church is never empty of holy dirt. Visitors take and take from the hole, and still there is more to take. Some people claim to be healed at Chimayó, and to prove a healing, they will often leave behind crutches, canes, and other items related to their illness. Another attraction for the Guadalupanas was the fact that there is a chapel to El Santo Niño de Atocha in the same location, and they wanted to go pay their respects. Chris tells me there are shoes left there for El Niño by people who claim that He walks to the homes of the faithful at night and wears out His shoes.

"How can anybody believe all this?" I ask him.

"There's so much history here, so many stories, that I think people say things to keep their faith growing."

"Do *you* believe all this?" When I ask him the question it reminds me of Holly Stevens looking into my eyes, asking me if I believed in Aztlán.

"Personally, I think it's superstition, but then again, half the time scientists don't know what they're talking about either, and they're supposed to know the facts."

That puts me back to square one. Nobody has any straight answers.

I convince my mother that we can't go to Chimayó, or to the miraculous stairs in Santa Fe built for the Sisters of Loretto supposedly by a mysterious stranger, whom the nuns claim was St. Joseph, the carpenter. The stairs were built so the nuns could climb up to the choir loft. I ask Chris if he's seen the stairs.

"Seen them three times," he says. "Amazing. Two 360-degree turns with no supporting pole through the center! Now that one really makes me think. I can't figure how anyone working alone with a few tools could have created such a thing, but there they are for all the world to see. Experts say the whole thing should have crashed to the ground a century ago. Then, the man who constructed the staircase never even waited to get paid."

Lisa and Lilly are pressuring me to take them to see the stairs. They have images of themselves flying down the banisters.

"You won't be able to," Chris tells them. "The whole area is roped off."

I look back at Mom and Irene sitting in the back seat. Their faces are like Lisa and Lilly's—fresh-looking, wanting to see something nobody can explain, to cheat a little and get closer to Heaven.

• WE TRAVEL UP I-25 and stop at Raton, New Mexico, to buy some groceries. The name is amusing. I don't know too many towns named for a rodent, the rat. The smell of a small town gets stuck in your nose like incense. The place is beautiful. A light drizzle of rain makes the hills surrounding Raton look misty. In the distance, the Sangre de Cristo Mountains tower over the countryside, deep purple, stately.

As we walk into the store, I look back to make sure the Guadalupanas are OK. They have refused to walk out in the rain, claiming the rain will cause us all to catch frío, cold air that settles in different spots of the body and causes cramps and pain. Michael and Angelo are whipping around the store with a grocery cart, loading up on packages of corn nuts, sunflower seeds, Squeeze-Its and everything else that makes it impossible for them to sit still. Cisco's walking behind them, flirting with the girls from Raton, pretending he doesn't really know Michael and Angelo.

One of the package boys asks me if we're the family on the Internet who's traveling to the Vietnam Wall.

"My dad's a Vietnam vet," he says. "He saw your web page on the Internet." He calls another package boy over, "Hey, Scott, here's the family my dad was talking about the other night. They won about two million dollars from the government!"

"Actually, it was only ninety thousand," I tell him. "We didn't win it, they owed it to us."

"Where's your mom?" asks the first package boy, whose name, I find out, is Jeffrey. "Nana . . . is that what you call her?"

"No, her name's not Nana! That word means grandmother in Spanish. She's in the van outside. She's not feeling well."

"Can I meet her?" I tell him they can both meet her and her friend. The boys start packaging our groceries and refuse to allow anyone else to help them. Jeffrey says he wants to tell his dad he packaged food for the Ramirez family. Lisa and Lilly are standing close by and the two boys are doing all they can to keep their eyes off the girls and to finish packaging the food. Before long, several people gather around us, talking about the Wall. One lady says it's like going to church.

"You'll feel like praying, after you get through the tears," she says.

"Everybody should go there," says the girl who's checking us out. "A once-in-a-lifetime experience."

The store manager comes over, a robust, red-faced man with a quick smile. He asks if we are the Ramirez family. Manuel tells him we are, and he asks if we wouldn't mind waiting for the news people to get to the store. They'd like to take pictures of us with the store personnel.

"These things don't happen in Raton every day. Your mother is teaching us all about faith," he says. "And I understand that she heard voices?"

"What voices?" I ask him.

"That's what the news report said. Your mom heard voices calling her to the Wall."

"Well, it might have been a dream."

"I don't think so. When my mother died a few years ago, I swear I heard her voice a couple of times. Don't you believe the supernatural world can send us messages?"

I look across the store's aisles, and notice at least twenty people gathering around us.

"Don't you believe in supernatural occurrences?" the manager asks me again.

"Well, of course, I believe in invisible forces. I wouldn't be on this trip if I didn't."

Michael walks up to me with Cisco. "Parallel universes," he says. "Other worlds that reverberate one thin line away from ours. That's what we're experiencing. There's lots of things we don't know anything about."

"Is this the young man who set up the web page?" the manager asks.

"That's me," Michael says.

"Well, congratulations on such a great idea!" As the manager finishes his sentence, two newsmen come in with a camera and a huge lamp they shine in our direction. "Here they are, come in, gentlemen. Yes, the Ramirezes are visiting our humble store!" The camera lens sweeps over all of us.

"Anything you'd like to say—any of you? Teresa, Priscilla, Paul, Manuel, Michael . . . and who else? We know your names by now," one of the newsmen says.

Paul answers. "We're doing what my mom wants, heading for the Wall. The money, all that doesn't really matter to us. What's important is getting to the Wall so Mom can keep her promise. But there's a problem."

"A problem?"

"Yeah. Jesse's not with us. This should be a family vacation, but it's not. We never had a family vacation, we were too busy surviving, and now that we have this money, we're still not on vacation. Nothing can make up for the death of my brother—or anybody else's brother, for that matter."

Chris looks at Paul. "I think Jesse was right," he whispers to me.

"I've never seen Paul like this," I tell him.

I look out the windows and see Gates on the phone. I wonder if he's calling Queta or Erica, or even Kamika. We end our talk with the newsmen, and walk out to our vehicles, followed by the manager and the newsmen. The drizzle has turned into a light rain, slanting through sunlight. My mom would say the does are bearing their young in the forest when it rains like that. Before we reach the van, the rain stops. I introduce Jeffrey and Scott to the Guadalupanas. At first, the boys are surprised to see the two old Doñas. I don't know what they were expecting. They're courteous and shake the old ladies' hands. They are two blond, blue-eyed boys making contact with two matriarchs from another world.

"God bless you both," my mother says, and to Jeffrey she says, "Tell your father I'm glad he came back from Vietnam, because today I met you, his son." Jeffrey is moved by this and raises my mom's hand to his lips.

"That kid's a real charmer," Chris says.

"My mom loves it," I tell him.

The manager introduces himself to Mom. "I'm Emery Billings, Mrs. Ramirez. I was telling your daughter here that I believe you heard the voices. Why shouldn't you? I heard my mother after she died."

"The voices, yes. They were whispering to me. I don't know what they were saying, but I know it was my son, and the other men on the Wall."

"You keep the faith, Mrs. Ramirez. Nothing's more important than doing what you think is right." He shakes Mom's hand, then reaches over and shakes Irene's hand. He looks at me.

"Have a safe journey. I wish I was going with you. I've never been there."

"Don't say that too loud," I tell him. "My mom wants to take the whole world with us. Look over there." I point to Yellowhair and his mother Sarah. "Zuñi Indians. The woman's son, Strong Horse, known as Eddie Bika, was killed in Vietnam. Strangers to us, but they're traveling with us."

"Wonderful," he says.

Jeffrey and Scott stand out in the rain with the store manager, Emery Billings, waving to us and giving us a thumbs-up as we drive away. Other people wave to us from the entrance of the store, some come out into the parking lot, holding umbrellas or paper bags over their heads, protection against the rain that has started up again. The newsmen are filming us as our vehicles get back on the highway.

The day has been an exhausting one. Traveling in and out of the rain has taken its toll on us. Dark clouds make me feel like going to bed, and with Chris next to me, the thought of going to bed is so strong I have to start massaging my neck to deal with the pressure. Chris puts his hand on my arm. "Maybe you could spare a little neck rub for me," he says. I smile. "Sure." His hand has left a hot spot on my arm. Irene sighs, even though I thought she was dozing off.

Late on Monday afternoon, June 2, we arrive in Colorado Springs and head for our rooms in the TraveLodge. Manuel had a good experience on one of his business trips with people from India who run the motel chain. Now he wants to return the favor by giving them our business.

"I mean it," Chris whispers as we're unloading. "I have a room to myself, and I need a neck rub." I feel like shouting "WHERE'S THE ROOM?" but all I say is "After dinner, I'll see how Mom is doing." I say it nonchalantly, like nothing's happening inside me. Manuel is watching us while he's helping Priscilla get her things into her room. He brushes past me with two suitcases. One of the suitcases hits my knee.

"Sorry," he says. "Did I hurt you?" He pauses to look at me, then stoops down to take a closer look at my leg.

"No, I'm fine."

"I should be more careful, or you should be more careful, or we both should be."

"Never mind, it's OK."

WE'RE CONTROLLED by time. The hours, minutes, and seconds of our lives tick away in regimental order. We try to catch up to time, but it eludes us and forces us to spill over into tomorrow. There are times when we want nothing more than to stop the world and demand that time stand still. Michael says time is relative to how fast we're moving. Objects traveling at the speed of light have a different experience of time. This poses a problem for astronauts who will travel in outer space for long periods of time. If the voyage is an extended one, the astronauts may come back younger than their own grandchildren! Time on earth is dictated by the forces of nature, the aging process, and the way we live our lives. It's true that when something is important to us, time seems to pass too quickly, and when we are going through great suffering, time passes too slowly.

We're in a time warp traveling to D.C. We've entered an orb that's propelling us to the Wall like a boomerang. We'll come back, but we won't be the same. When we get to the Wall, will that be the beginning or the end? Are there really parallel universes as Michael describes, whole images reverberating in the universe, defying our concept of space, location, and substance? And last of all, are we moving closer to Aztlán, or did we already pass it by?

Blue Doors •

hris's socks are hanging on the back of a chair in his
room. They look like white Christmas stockings. He
says he always gets his socks and shoes ready. You
never know when you'll have to run out somewhere.

"It's from my old war days. It stayed with me. We never took off our
shoes when we were out in the field no matter how bad the jungle rot
got on our feet. To take off your shoes meant you were half dead and
they were taking them off so you could die in peace."

I position Chris's socks on the nightstand and sit back on the chair.
He's sitting on the bed wearing corduroy walking shorts, a T-shirt, and
no shoes. I've never seen his legs before. They're hairy, pale, thinner than
I expected. The bed is a king-size with a glossy, orange comforter. It's
bigger than the queen-size I shared with Ray at our house on Canterbury
Street. It makes me wonder if people really need all that room.

"I hope someday you won't have to put them out at all," I tell him.

"Someday." Chris looks closely at me. "Relax. We're adults, not
kids."

"I don't think anybody saw me come in here."

"And what if they did?"

"You know how people are."

"Yeah, I can imagine Manuel, busting in here to rescue you."

"He's always had a crush on me."

"He better get over it."

"What's that supposed to mean?"

"The vato's gotta learn to take 'no' for an answer. You'd think he would have learned after all these years. But I can see how he could fall in love with you."

I'm watching every move Chris makes, slow, deliberate moves. He walks a few paces to lock the door. His bare feet pound softly on the carpet. With my eyes I measure what his body might mean over mine. He's taller than Ray, with more angles, and firm muscles. He sits on the edge of the bed and leans close to me. It's strange how faces change, but eyes never do. Chris's eyes are the same. I see myself reflected in them, the high school girl he said good-bye to at the airport and the look in his eyes, mournful, afraid. The appetite I felt earlier in the day is filling up the space between us. It makes me shiver.

"Are you cold?"

"No, not cold." I want to smile, but can't.

"Don't be so nervous," he says. The middle of my chest starts to ache the minute he says the words, as if somebody ignited a match inside me. He kneels at my feet, switching off the lamp. Now we're encased in inky darkness.

"Leave the light on, I can't see you."

"That's the way it was in Nam, Teresa. So dark I swear I could see black atoms floating in the air."

"You must have been afraid." I notice numbers glowing, bright red, from the digital clock on the TV, 12:31 A.M. I watch the numbers change . . . 12:32 A.M.

"After a while that went away," Chris says. "Then you became part of the darkness, like a tree or a rock—you just stayed there and tried not to move. The night didn't care what side we were on, it covered us all, except Charlie knew the place with his eyes closed, and we didn't. We were in his backyard. Imagine being in somebody else's backyard at night."

I feel Chris's forehead and he's sweating, cool drops of sweat on my hand.

"You're sweating, Chris—are you all right?"

"It happens sometimes. I guess my body's got the nights in Nam recorded like a history lesson. I wish it didn't, but never mind about that, take off your shoes, Teresa, and I'll rub your feet."

"I'm here to give you a neck rub, remember?" My voice sounds like an echo in my ears. I feel like I'm talking in a cave.

"Forget it. I want to do this for you," he says. The flame in my chest reaches my stomach and groin. It makes me sit up straight in the chair.

Chris starts taking off one of my sandals and can't undo the strap. His fingers feel icy cold against my flesh. He's fumbling, trying again. It's comical somehow, like we're two kids in the back seat of a car.

"Chris, turn the light back on."

"I can see in the dark. I learned how to do that in Vietnam."

"This isn't Vietnam."

"Are these shoes glued to your feet?"

"Maybe you're nervous. Let me do it."

"No, I can do this." He tries the other shoe.

"Chris, you're making the straps tighter . . . you're hurting my ankle." I feel for his face in the dark, and it's wet with tears.

I kneel on the floor with him. He puts his arms around me, and I lay my head on his shoulder.

"You smell like you did when I left for Nam, Teresa. You were so beautiful, so beautiful, still are. I swear I carried your smell with me all the way to Nam. I guess I want to do for you what I didn't do for your brother—take off your shoes, give you peace. All I did was cover Jesse's face with my shirt. God, I regret not riding with him in the chopper!" I hold Chris tight in my arms. He's crying on my shoulder, into my hair. Our tears get mixed up in the dark. We stand up together, holding tight.

"Lie down, Chris." I lead him by the hand, like a drowsy child, gently, slowly to bed. His teeth start chattering. I cover him over with a blanket. His body twitches. He groans. I take off my shoes, thinking of El Santo Niño's sandals and how worn out they would be if He walked all the way to Vietnam. I lie next to Chris, encircling him in my arms, resting his head in the middle of my chest where the match ignited an ache in me. I stroke his hair.

"Jesse told me he wasn't coming back, Chris." I whisper the words and swallow back the sound that wants to erupt from my throat.

"He knew more than I did. Jesse was like that. His mind moved through space, like he could figure out things we didn't know anything about. Me? I thought I would die, and Jesse would come back."

"Is that why you went back . . . to see if you would die?"

"Maybe. There were so many Chicanos over there, and even more when troops were being pulled out and only certain companies were left. We had front row seats. You know no Chicano is gonna do the rear when his buddies are up front. Maybe I wanted to join them. It was worse staying alive—all the nightmares, the whole mess here. People accusing us of killing babies. I let my hair grow long, I hated anything that made me remember the war. I didn't even tell people I had been there, it got so bad. I started to march with the protesters for a while, then I couldn't stand it, because I thought they were a bunch of cowards, going the gabacho way and burning their draft cards. Sorry m'fer's, I thought. Then I'd feel bad cause I really didn't want them to go to Nam. I knew the war was sick—so sick, and we still kept fighting. Your nana gave me that little prayer, remember? I kept it with me next to my mom's picture, and it was the only thing I didn't lose. We were like that, los Chicanos, holding on to crucifixes and prayers, pictures of La Virgen de Guadalupe, and our moms. We were in a man's world, but we hung on to our women. I never told Margie any of this. I came back to Albuquerque and married her, and I didn't know why."

"Ray never told me anything about Vietnam either, and he wasn't even fighting in the front. He was a mechanic."

"It's like we were chained up together, Teresa, like all of us went to Hell and nobody else would understand. I had my two daughters with Margie. She finally divorced me, and I don't blame her. I still love her. Margie could have had anybody she wanted. I don't know why she waited for me. After Margie, I went two more rounds with other women, and they did the same thing. I didn't really care, because I didn't love them. I looked at myself in the mirror one day, and I couldn't stand what I saw. I was disgusted with myself, because I couldn't get Nam out of my system. That was the day I almost turned a gun on myself. If it hadn't been for thinking about my two daughters, I probably would have done it, but I remembered all the kids I saw in the war with no parents, crying, sleeping on the streets, some of them raped, or made into prostitutes and drug dealers. I saw their faces in my head, so small. They were these tiny people and I was a giant, 'number ten GI' they used to call me cause they knew I wasn't into torture and all that shit. I was ashamed of myself, watching what other guys did to them. And they still called me 'number ten GI'!"

I hold Chris tight until the pain is a pinpoint in my chest. Chris is still mumbling about the kids in Vietnam, a baby who was paralyzed by a bullet in his spine, a young girl raped by one of the ARVNs, an old woman beaten by an American with the butt of his gun, running—wanting to find Salt and Pepper, the fabled Black and White soldiers who deserted the American forces and joined up with the VC.

My throat is aching. There are questions I want to ask Chris. What did Jesse say before he died? And the woman he wrote to me about, the one who taught him Vietnamese—who was she? It won't make any sense to Chris, not now. He finally falls asleep, and I sleep, too.

I wake up with a jump. Chris is bundled in a blanket next to me. We're curled up in the middle of the bed. The room is ice cold from the air conditioner running all night. It makes me wonder if there's winter in Vietnam. I want to get up before everybody else does.

I slide quietly to the edge of the bed. Chris rolls over and puts his hand on my thigh. It's warm. Deep in my pelvis, I sense an ache. I want to rush back to the middle of the bed and let his hands find the rest of me, but the room is already bathed in early morning light. The light illuminates the truth. I'm not the high school girl Chris said good-bye to at Sky Harbor Airport, and he's not the young soldier who walked backwards alongside my brother to get to the plane that would fly them away to Vietnam and change them forever.

He strokes my hair gently, and lets his hand run smoothly over my shoulder. "Don't leave, Teresa."

"I have to." I put my sandals back on. "You don't have to help me with my shoes. I'll be all right."

"I'm sorry," he says.

"For what?" I ask him. I lean over him, arrange the blanket under his chin, and kiss his forehead.

March 6, 1968

Dear Sis,

Most of the houses over here have blue doors and shutters. They say blue stands for hope. I don't know what there is to hope for. President Johnson came over here and left, promising more troops. What is he thinking? Can't he see the handwriting on the wall? These people have been fighting for years. Yesterday, Chato, this guy from Texas, said he was gonna do whatever it takes to get home. I don't think he'll succeed, outside of having himself killed. Two White guys got shipped out the other day, one because his mom knew a senator back home and another because he was sent to keep accounts at the base. Los Chicanos don't have mommys who know senators and none of them I know of have more than high school, if even that.

Mostly the races keep to themselves over here. When we're fighting, well, that's the time to kick ass and not care who's next to you, but when we're back at base camp or on R & R, it's back to who you belong to. I tried shooting dice with los negros. They reminded me of Gates. It was cool until a couple of them accused me of cheating and playing like a Mexican. They called me a taco. I told them I was from the States but they wouldn't buy it. It's hard around here. I don't want to be too Mexican, cause the Chicanos get mad, and I don't want to be too Chicano cause then the Mexicans say I'm going white. It's as bad as north and south Vietnam. The people are so mixed up over here, we can't tell who's from the north and who's from the south. The ARVNs we got with us are supposed to be from the south and they're more trouble than they're worth. Sometimes the VC shoot at them and pass us by. I already saw that when it comes to saving somebody, we'll save each other before we get to them. That's a double-cross if you ask me. Some of the guys say the ARVNs are a bunch of queers. They pat each other all the time, sleep together, stuff like that. I told them that's the way it is around here. Father John told me that. He studies up on all the customs. The other day Father said a mass out here with a box for an altar. The gospel was about the man who lived out in the tombs and was full of demons. Jesus took out all the demons and sent them into swine. There were so many, they called themselves Legion. It was weird because later that day I saw a farmer herding a bunch of pigs to the city. It was the first time I've seen that. I've seen water buffalo but not pigs. I'm surprised somebody hadn't killed the pigs for meat. I wonder why Christ sent the demons into the swine. What do you think, sis? To me, we're acting like devils and the pigs are only being who they are. Maybe demons need to destroy something on their way out. Is that what we're doing?

I think I know what this war is all about. It's about body count. Everytime there's a firefight we have to go out and check to see how many VC we killed. Lieutenant McCoy, this guy I've learned to hate, asked me the other day for the body count. Well I had none to give him, but he called in 21 anyway. He told me to always give an odd number as that sounded more like the truth. All this goes to base camp and nobody ever checks up on the numbers. Some guys get carried away and start cutting off ears and fingers when they find bodies. One guy said he saw an American Special Forces squad that had been ambushed by the VC. The VC had cut off the guys' you know what and shoved them into their mouths. Sorry if this makes you sick, sis, but this is what is called war. Some of our guys hack away because they know that's one of the worse things you can do to a Vietnamese. They have this thing about burying the bodies right away. Some of them get killed trying to get one of their dead buddies back to their camp. Father John told me they house the dead souls in tombs. I've seen the graves, here and there. I told you about them. Remember? The tombs aren't in straight lines like in our cemeteries. They stick up wherever the person was buried. Some of the families have taken down their tombs for now because they don't want their ancestors disturbed by foreigners. They believe the ghosts of the dead will haunt them if they don't build a house for them, even prostitutes and the homeless get something.

There's a kid who hangs around with us. Chris has buddied up with him. I saw him sharing his poncho with him yesterday when it was raining.

The Vietnamese word for rain is mua *and for rainy it's* co mua. *We got plenty of that over here. I've been thinking, sis, how the U.S. prays for peace, then turns around and arms itself to the teeth for war. Are we Legion?*

Write to me as quick as you can. There's nothing worse than not getting mail out here. Tell Paul and Priscilla to do all their homework. I'm not there to check it for them, so do it for me. Give Mom and Nana a kiss and check up on Dad.

SWAK
Jesse

I go over Jesse's letter in my room before the girls get up. I didn't know blue was the color of hope in Vietnam. I make a plan to paint our front door blue when we get back to Phoenix.

Little Saigon •

e gather at the Denny's for breakfast on Tuesday morning, June 3. Chris isn't with us.

"What did you do to him, Teresa?" Priscilla asks.

"Wouldn't you like to know."

"I knew it! All these years talking about me . . . making it sound like I'm—"

Mom stops her. "Priscilla, don't let the boys order food they won't eat, mija. They waste everything."

"Are you listening to me, Mom? Your little angel isn't so holy after all!"

"They're fighting again," Lisa says.

"We're not fighting," I tell her.

"Look, all the people are staring at us again," Irene says. "You two girls stop all this, y ustedes, you boys," she says, pointing to Michael and Angelo, "stop arguing about what you want to eat. If you were at my house, you'd eat chorizo and beans, y ya, cree lo!"

A waitress comes over. "You've got to be the Ramirezes. Are you?"

"Yes, that we are," I tell her.

"Is that your mother?" She looks at Mom. I nod. "Señora, you are a hero," she says. "Would you give me your autograph?" The girl pulls out her order pad and cuts out a page. "I'll keep this as a memory of you."

My mother looks at her. "What do you want me to do?"

"Sign your name, please," says the girl. I look at Mom to see if she's really gonna do it.

"Teresa, do you have a pen?" I fumble through my purse and find a pen. Mom takes it and signs her name with a flourish. "There," she says, "pobrecita, what a beautiful girl!" A second waitress comes over, and Mom signs a page of her order pad, too. People from all over the restaurant are watching.

"Oh, man," Priscilla says. "I hope there's no media in here."

I notice a woman walking toward us. "You must be Teresa."

"Yes. And this is my mother, Alicia Ramirez."

"Of course, we've been hearing all about you. I'm Corina Ybarra. My husband served in Vietnam." She sighs as she says the words. "I'm proud of it, no matter what people said about the war. He's gone now. He died of skin cancer. There were tumors that showed up on his skin. The doctors would remove them, then others would show up. I know it had something to do with Agent Orange. You know, the chemical they used during the war. We tried to sue the government, but nothing ever came of it . . . nothing. He was young, only fifty-three, and over there is our son and his wife. See that baby?" She points to a child sitting with the couple. "My husband won't ever see him grow up. There are so many casualties of the Vietnam War, and lots of them aren't on the Wall." She turns to Mom. "Te acompaño en tu sentimiento," she says, I accompany you in your grief. She says the same thing to Irene. Mom and Irene respond with the same words, ancient words used to comfort the bereaved. She walks back to her family, and they all wave at us.

"I had never thought about guys who died here in the States from what they went through in Vietnam," I tell Priscilla.

"It never occurred to me either."

"What about those who died of alcoholism and drugs?" Manuel says. "There must be plenty."

The two waitresses are back again, taking our orders, smiling, telling us what the best deals on the menu are. I sense new energy in the air. The sun is shining, the light is white, warm. My mother just gave someone her autograph. She's a hero, for God's sake. Two men have joined Willy, Gates, and Yellowhair at their table. They may be Vietnam veterans, or the brothers, cousins, and friends of somebody who served there. Willy told me the Vietnam War was the longest war in the history of America. Thirty years long, he said, and $500 billion spent. I reach for my coffee cup and tell the kids they shouldn't order more than they can eat. My voice is too loud. "I heard you," Lilly says, "you don't have to shout."

She edges close to Priscilla and whispers something in her ear. Priscilla smiles. Are they talking about me and Chris?

Another thing is happening. Priscilla and Manuel are suddenly close friends. I've never seen them talk so much in all my life. I don't know if they're talking to avoid me or if they're really interested in what they have to say to each other. Manuel is teaching Michael how to keep accounts on the computer. People stare at Michael when they see him pounding away on the computer. They think he's a poor Mexican kid who doesn't speak English and wonder what he's doing on a computer.

Donna is sitting next to the Guadalupanas. Paul's outside in the van, chain-smoking. My mother tells Donna to ignore him. He's mad about Manuel handling all the money and says he's being treated like a child. He's sick of Donna preaching to him and is ready to hitchhike back to Phoenix, except I know he won't because he'd never forgive himself if something happened to Mom. He's like Jesse that way. There's a part of Paul that wants nothing to do with Jesse, and another part that still has Jesse on a pedestal. It must be crazy to be the kid brother of a man who's perfect in the eyes of his mother.

My mother is coughing this morning. None of her prescribed medications are for cough, and I'm wondering if I should stop at a local fire station to have her blood pressure checked and her lungs listened to. Paramedics will tell us if she needs to be hospitalized. She's stubborn, just as Irene says. Palmira gave me the cure, she says. She cleaned out my system, starting with my soul. I'll be all right. And why bother the firemen anyway with another old lady's problems? Irene wants to go to the fire station because all the firemen are handsome, she says, and she needs somebody to help her with her legs.

"They're not sobadores," I tell her, "all they'll do is tell you to go see your doctor." She's disappointed and still wants to go.

I listen to snatches of the men's conversation talking about their war days, R&R, the food in Vietnam, the flight over and back, the marijuano officers who got stoned, the kids who swarmed them on the streets. Nothing about battles, blood. They're keeping everybody at bay. Willy says the Vietnamese kept speaking their language to him, they figured he understood. He had to keep reminding them he was Chinese American. Gates tells them there was a whole street in one of the cities where Black men lived with Vietnamese women, and they were treated like gods. The people were good, he says. What were we doing there anyway? Yellowhair remembers that his brother left for Vietnam when he got shipped back to the States. They didn't want two brothers from the same family serving at the same time. "It should have been the other way around," he says. "I should have gone, and he should have come back."

My mother's listening to the men talk, tilting her head this way and that like a bird listening to flight instructions. She'd wear wings if that would get her to the Wall faster, feathered wings she could flap and not annoy God by defying gravity on a Boeing 747.

I see Chris motioning to me through one of the windows. He's pretending he's holding on to a car wheel, spinning around in the air, showing me he's ready to move on. I smile and wave back. It feels so good to see him clowning around. I didn't know what to expect from him this morning.

"There's Chris," I tell Priscilla. She doesn't say anything.

By the time we're ready to leave, we have attracted more attention. People are watching us board our vehicles. "The Vietnam Wall or bust!" one man shouts. My mother's walking, swaying on her cane. I hold on to her elbow. Priscilla walks close behind us. People are wishing us well. The two waitresses and the men who joined Willy, Gates, and Yellowhair all join us in the parking lot.

Michael catches up to me and tells me he's got a Vietnamese man who got on the web site this morning. "He's from Little Saigon in Orange County, Ca—lifornia," Michael says. Michael holds the first syllable in the word *California*, and it sounds like he's announcing the word over a loudspeaker.

"I didn't know we had a Saigon in the U.S.," I tell him.

"Little Saigon," he says, "the biggest Saigon besides the one in Vietnam."

"Who's the man?" I ask him.

"I don't know, but he says we'll find out pretty soon."

"What's that supposed to mean?" Michael passes me by, racing with Angelo to get back to the van and the laptop.

Déjà Vu •

e pass red, jagged mountains in Colorado. Some have tops that look like mesas. Chris tells me the Garden of the Gods is close by. A sacred place, he says. The red rocks of Colorado converge in the spot to form a place of astounding power, so real it makes the air thick. Maybe it's like walking on Jupiter, Chris says. The earth's gravity weighs you down, tugs at your feet, and you get stronger because you have to work harder to lift your feet off the ground so you can walk.

Chris and I don't talk about what happened last night. I can't tell if Chris regrets not making love. I don't. I didn't realize he was still in love with Margie. Just the thought that I could be anything close to somebody's Consuelo is enough to stop me from anything romantic with Chris. Is he ashamed of the tears he shed? I can't tell that either. Chris is so easygoing this morning, it makes me suspect it's just an act. There's something we have to say to each other, but neither one of us knows how to start. There are tiny pockets of space between us. Some of it is Margie, some of it might be Ray, but most of it is Jesse.

At Denver we pick up Highway 24 for a short distance as we cross the state line into Kansas, then pick up I-70 that leads us into Topeka. We're heading for the middle of America, and things are looking foreign to us. All we've known is the Southwest. Every once in a while a motorist or a truck driver will honk at us. Sometimes they wave, or stick their hands out of open car windows and give us a thumbs-up. Maybe they've seen us on TV or visited the web site, or read about us in newspapers. I haven't seen the news people out here. They like the excitement of the big cities.

There are flashes of lightning in the sky. We hear thunder. Rain starts, pattering on our windows at first, then it turns into hail. The hail is as big as golf balls. Chris tells me it must be cold somewhere in the higher elevations and the hail has traveled down to us by way of wind currents. My mother and Irene pull out their lace veils and wear them as scarves. It's a protection against lightning, they say. I explain that the rubber of the tires protects us from the electrical currents, but they pretend they're not listening. I'm glad the flags waving on the vans are plastic. Mom tells me to block off the rearview mirror, because lightning might hit it and bounce back to them. Irene says her grandmother was afraid of lightning, too. She worked out in the fields all her life and ran from bolts of lightning to hide under tents made of cardboard and canvas. This was the suffering la raza bore before Cesar Chavez won rights for the poor and forced rich landowners to provide decent housing. "Before that they were treated worse than animals," Irene says. "My grandfather's appendix burst, pobrecito el viejito, and there was no doctor around for miles. My family was too poor to pay a hospital, so he died right there under a tree."

The landscape has changed to Kansas flatlands I've only seen in pictures. Grassy plains spread out on either side of the highway, disappearing into the distant horizon. There is no farmhouse or building to obstruct the view of miles and miles of green, rolling hills. The smell of rich, wet earth is everywhere. We're in Dorothy's land, straight out of *The Wizard of Oz*. I'm expecting her house to whiz by any minute with the Wicked Witch of the West flying after it on her broom.

Chris tells me the landscape of Vietnam was like no other he had ever seen.

"We were on the asphalt streets of the U.S. one day, and out in the jungles the next. There was no middle point. Nowhere to catch your breath. The jungles were so green, so beautiful. Then you'd run into a place where the U.S. Air Force had bombed or sprayed with Agent Orange and the place looked like a landscape from the moon. When we first got there we were the FNGs, Fucking New Guys." He looks back to make sure the Guadalupanas aren't going to ask him to redefine FNGs. His voice is almost a whisper. He wants to keep what he says to me private. "And the guys were so young! Kids out of high school. Me and

Jesse were the older ones at twenty. Can you imagine?" He looks out over everything as if he's looking beyond the edge of the horizon.

"The heat, I can't explain the heat over there. It suffocates you, then squeezes every drop of water out of you, until you swear you'd shoot your own foot just to get the hell out of there. And the smells, people doing the bathroom outside in the open . . . the stench. The people so poor you get sick to your stomach." He stops himself like a recording someone clicked off. My mother's listening.

"They were very poor?"

"Yes, Doña, very poor, except some of the people in the big cities."

"And Jesse, what did he do?"

"He felt sorry for them, Doña. He wanted to help them, not fight them. He made friends with some of the families over there. They brought him little gifts, mostly fruit, good fruit. They brought him dragon fruit and lichee nuts, and lots of others. I can't remember the names."

I see Jesse in my mind with his teeth colored red from the pomegranates we ate in the summertime. Summers when he played the part of King David, and we shot rocks at targets in the backyard, Goliaths we wanted to get even with.

"The fruits in Vietnam . . . were there any pomegranates?"

"I never saw any, but there could have been."

"Jesse had friends there?"

"Yes, a few families he got to know in Bien Hoa, actually a little suburb right outside the city of Bien Hoa."

"Is that close to Saigon?"

"Very close."

"Tell him, mija, about the call I got after Jesse was killed."

"Someone called my mom from Saigon two years after Jesse was killed. Do you know who it might have been?"

"No, but it could have been one of the people he knew. They're very friendly, and when they like you, it's usually for life."

"Whoever it was hung up on Mom. Why would somebody do that?"

"Everything's controlled by the communists over there. Maybe they were forced to do it."

"My mom suffered a lot over that call. She thought Jesse was still alive, or captured by the Vietcong. We even thought maybe he went after Salt and Pepper, and joined the Vietcong. It still haunts us. And now, there's a Vietnamese man sending messages to Michael on the web site."

"That could be someone who knew Jesse during the war, and somehow made it to the U.S."

Chris squeezes my hand and looks at me, lifting his eyebrows. I understand there's more he wants to say but can't in front of Mom.

"Tell him, mija, how they sent my poor son to the wrong address." Mom starts to cry.

"Take it easy, Mom." I reach over and put my hand on her knee. "It's true, Chris, the Army sent Jesse's body to the wrong address! Can you believe such a thing? That's why they owed us all the money, because of the mistake they made on the address."

"That's what they do," Mom says, "to us, los pobres. Our sons weren't the gringos' sons. They didn't care about us!"

"All I have of my son is an American flag," Irene says. She's crying, too.

"Jesse was very brave, Doña Ramirez. I know. I was there when he died," Chris says. "He wasn't afraid." His voice sounds hollow as if he's talking from a great distance. He shifts in his seat and grips the steering wheel with two hands instead of one.

"Don't cry, Nana," Lisa says. She reaches over the seat and gives my mother a hug. "Tío Jesse doesn't want you to be sad."

"Si, you're right, mijita. I should stop, but I can't."

"Don't cry, Mom," I tell her, "you'll start coughing again." She starts coughing as soon as I say the words. I reach into my purse and find a cough drop for her.

The flatlands seem endless. Panic hits me. There's no place to take Mom if something happens out here. I look out the back window of the van and catch a glimpse of Yellowhair's van with Paul at the wheel. Behind him is Willy's car. I can't see Manuel and Priscilla, but I figure they're last. I want to tell Chris I'm afraid, but can't. We're passing small towns that don't look like they even have a hospital, much less an airport to get us to civilization. I'll have to depend on La Virgen and El Santo Niño out here. What other hope do we have? A tornado that would whisk us away to Oz?

"Ay, how much more can we bear?" Mom asks.

"Con fe, Alicia," Irene says. "Our faith is what will get us to the Wall."

Pain starts in my forehead and travels to my eyes. I reach with my fingers under the lenses of my sunglasses and try to press the pain away. The pain spreads to my cheekbones. I keep my eyes closed for a few seconds. I open them, and the landscape is still wide, grassy plains, with hardly any cars in view. Dark clouds are floating away, and spots of blue sky are beginning to show.

The old women stop crying and begin to doze off. Suffering has exhausted them. I remember the sign we saw pulling out of Albuquerque— PARE DE SUFRIR. I wish the old women would sleep all the way to D.C., so they wouldn't keep fanning to life the pain of Jesse's death, old suffering still so fresh. It's bad enough I'll have to help them at the Wall when we get there. I take off my sunglasses and put my face in my hands.

"It'll be OK, Teresa," Chris says. "I'll tell you more about it tonight."

We pass Bunker Hill and see a sign advertising the largest prairie dog in the world and a cow with five legs. Lisa and Lilly want to stop and see the creatures, and I know probably the other kids want to do the same. "No time," I tell them. "They're probably fake anyway." Abilene, Kansas. It sounds familiar to me for some reason. Chris tells me President Eisenhower was born there. Maybe I saw the town's name in a history book.

At Salina, we stop at a gas station with a convenience store to buy sandwiches and gas up. There are only a few people around. An old man sitting at the entrance of the store asks Gates for a cigarette. Gates gives him one, and they start talking about the Vietnam Wall. The old man tells Gates that he served in World War II. He says when they came back to the States from the war, they had parades and parties, and it was too bad that the Vietnam veterans got nothing. It's all because of those long-haired hippies, he says, who protested and made the military look like fools. Nobody could control them, the old man says, they were running around smoking pot in Central Park and burning the American flag and their draft cards. "Cowards," the old man says, "that's the word for them. And Nixon watching them, threatening them, then all he does is end the war just like that, and everybody pulls out."

"We were lucky we finally pulled out," Gates says.

"Lucky? We shoulda bombed the hell out of 'em and gotten it over with! What the hell's an army for if it don't do what it should?"

"Have a nice day," Gates says and walks away. I can tell he's angry by the way he starts washing the windows of the van, scrubbing them with all his might.

"Take it easy, "I tell him. "People don't understand what was going on over there."

"Then they shouldn't talk."

Paul and Donna walk out of the convenience store holding hands. I guess they made up. I look at the tattoo on Paul's arm with the *A* made into an *O* and almost laugh. A woman talking at a public phone stares at them. Maybe she's never seen a Chicano guy holding a white woman's hand.

Paul's driving the gray Toyota van with the Zuñi feathered wands. Donna's with him, Yellowhair, and his mother Sarah. Paul's in the lead as we leave Salina, which I found out is pronounced with a long syllable sound of the letter *i*. Our van is behind Paul's. Manuel, Priscilla, and the boys are behind us, and last is Willy and Susie in the Nissan Maxima. We're traveling over a desolate stretch of Kansas highway. Monotony takes over as we drive over a road that stretches bare and lifeless before us. Once in a while, we spot the faint mound of a hill in the distance. Chris looks in the rearview mirror several times.

"What's wrong?" I ask him.

"Kansas Highway Patrol behind us, that's what's wrong."

"They won't do anything. I'm sure they've heard of us."

"You never know. This is bush country compared to the cities. Some of these cops are rednecks, they don't know anything about who we are, and some of them don't care."

"Mom, there's lights blinking behind us," Lilly says.

"Where?"

"Behind us, it's a police car."

"Trouble," Chris says. "Here comes trouble!"

"Déjà vu! I haven't had trouble like this since the moratorium march in East L.A."

Chris looks at me in surprise. "I didn't know you had gone there."

"Oh, I can tell you some stories about that!"

The police car passes us by, and presses close to Paul's van. It's obvious they want Paul to stop, but Paul keeps moving.

"What's Paul doing?" Chris asks me. "He better stop before these rednecks get pissed off."

"Who knows what's going on in Paul's mind? Our luck they picked on the only one of us with a prison record!"

Paul's van continues to move for at least two minutes that seem like an eternity to me. The siren on the police car goes on. It makes me jump.

"Stop, you idiot! What does he think he's doing?" I roll down the window to yell at Paul to make him stop. He finally moves over to the side of the road with the police car glued to his bumper. Chris eases our van in behind the police car. The lights on the police car are flashing red and blue against the green prairie grass. In the distance, the sky has suddenly turned black just over the ridge of mountains where the sun disappeared.

The officer driving the police car gets out first. His belly hangs over his belt. His pant legs barely cover the top of his black boots. The officer who stays in the car looks like a rookie. He's talking on the radio. The first officer struts up to the van like he's king of the prairie. He motions impatiently for Paul to roll down the window. After Paul rolls it down, he yells into Paul's face.

"Where's your green card, homeboy?"

"Fuck you!"

"Oh, shit!" I open the door and start to get out. The rookie is out of the police car, shouting at me.

"Ma'am, stay in the vehicle!" The rookie's a tall redhead, with pale skin. He's wearing sunglasses that have blue lenses in them. He plants himself between our car and theirs.

The first officer throws the van door open and yanks Paul out. "Lean on it, homeboy, lean on it!" He shoves Paul up against the van. "Spread 'em," he shouts, taking out a billy club and hitting Paul's legs.

"Que pasa, mija, what's happening?" My mother is on the edge of her seat.

"It's OK, Mom, Paul knows what to do."

"The police, Alicia. The police are arresting Paul!" Irene is almost in tears.

"No, Irene," I tell her. "They're only asking him questions."

"When have the police asked Mexicans questions? They throw us in jail, that's what they do." Mom puts her hand on the handle of the car door as if she's going to open it.

"Mom, stay in the car. Didn't you hear what the officer said?"

"Mom, they're gonna take Tío Paul away!" Lisa is shouting.

"Be quiet! You're making everything worse," I tell her.

The rookie starts radioing for backup.

"Where'd you get your tats?" the first officer asks Paul.

"Where your momma got hers," Paul says.

"A smartass! Hey, Harry, we got us a smartass!" Donna says something to the officer I can't hear. "Stay out of this, or you'll join your boyfriend!" yells the officer. He twists one of Paul's arms behind his back, up to his shoulder.

"How you like that, huh, talkin' shit about my momma!" He slaps on a pair of handcuffs.

"Wait a minute. Ease up on him," says the rookie. "I just got the word. This is the Ramirez family. They're on their way to the Vietnam

Wall. Look over there." He points to Priscilla's van and the signs Michael put up on the windows.

"They're a bunch of fucking illegals, and you know it! Vietnam Memorial Wall! Shit, these people don't know nothin' about that."

"I'm telling you, there'll be hell to pay," says the rookie.

Chris opens the car door and is ready to get out when the first officer reaches for his gun. "STAY THE FUCK IN THE CAR!" he shouts at the top of his lungs.

"Chris . . . what are you doing? The guy's crazy!" I tell him.

"He's a psycho, the son-of-a-bitch!"

Mom opens the back door and is out before I can stop her.

"Mom, stop! Mom, no . . . get back in the car! Look at her! Where's her cane?"

My mother doesn't answer. "I'm warning you, ma'am," says the first officer, "get back in the car or I'll . . ."

"You won't do anything to me," my mom says in a voice so calm, the officer doesn't say another word. "This country already took one of my boys, Mr. Policeman. You can't have the other one."

"Mom, go back!" Paul shouts. The rookie steps aside and lets her walk by.

"No, mijo." She walks up next to Paul and leans on the van, her arms raised over her head. "Take us both," she says.

"What is she, a Chicana Rosa Parks?" My mother holds her head so high, the curve in her spine disappears. I'm out of the van, rushing to get next to her. I hear sirens approaching and the two-way radio is turned on full blast.

"I'm fine, mija. No es nada. I've seen this all my life. We have to teach these gringos something."

Two more police cars rush to the scene. Traffic is slowing down in both directions and three cars have stopped on the opposite side of the street.

"We got a mob resisting arrest!" yells the first officer.

"We got nothing!" shouts the rookie. "They're people traveling to the Vietnam Wall. I already told you. My kid looked them up on the Internet. Don't you see the address on the windows?"

Michael's out of the van, shouting at the officers. "My dad has constitutional rights! You can't do this to him. You'll see—I'll take this case all the way to the Supreme Court. You can't harass an American citizen!"

"Shut that kid up!" yells the first officer.

"No," my mother says. "He's a genius, officer. He can't help himself."

Everybody's out of the vans and lined up around Paul's van. Irene stands at Mom's side.

"Where's your green card, officer?" Yellowhair asks. "You're standing on my land. My family's been here for forty thousand years. I think these cops are descendants of the fuckin' Texas Rangers."

"Don't you know, Yellowhair," says Gates, "he's one of the white masters who wants everybody to bow down to him? They did all this shit in South Africa to Nelson Mandela himself! Mandela had to carry identification papers to travel in his own country! Don't you know we all look the same to this guy? This guy's so stupid, he can't tell his ass from a hole in the ground!"

"Shut up!" yells the first officer, "or I'll arrest you for harassing a police officer."

"Gee, I'm terrified," Gates says, laughing. "And to think I risked my life in Nam for your white ass!"

Willy is snapping pictures. "Wow! Won't this make interesting news. 'Kansas State Police Arrest Family on Their Way to the Vietnam Wall.' Is nothing sacred anymore?"

"No need for that," says one of the backup officers. He's holding a clipboard in his hand. His voice is somber. "The officer, here, just made a little mistake. He acted a little too quick. He's got you confused with a group of illegals we're trying to stop from running over the state line. It's obvious you're not them, so you can go on your way. You're the Ramirez family, aren't you?"

I ignore his question. "Just like that? You're gonna let us go after you harassed us and embarrassed us in front of these two elderly women and our own children? I don't think so!" I turn around and ask Manuel if he's got something to write on. He hands me a notepad and pen. I start writing down badge numbers while the first officer unlocks Paul's handcuffs. The Guadalupanas are whispering prayers, anticipating our final escape.

Chris helps me write down the badge numbers. "You'll hear from us, all right," he says to the officer with the clipboard. "That you will!"

Priscilla's shouting, "Don't have much to do out here, do you? Need to play games with people's lives. Well, you messed up real good today. We're Chicanos, been here before your grandpappies were born, and we'll see your asses in court for this! This immigration scam is an old story, man."

"Calm down, Priscilla," Manuel tells her. "These guys should learn their history lessons before they get to be cops."

"I apologize to you, ma'am," the rookie says to Mom. "I hope you don't think all Kansas state police officers are the same. Trust me, I'm not like that."

"There is good and bad everywhere," my mother says. "I've seen this all my life."

Paul holds Mom in his arms. She lays her head on his chest. "Mom, why did you do this? Here, let me help you back to the van."

"I have to be here for you, mijo. What do you think—that I love Jesse more than you? I love you both, con poder, but different because you're different people, but you're both my sons." She looks into his face. "Don't you know, mijo, that if you were on the Wall, I would be making this trip for you—yes, I would!" They're both crying. Paul is stooping down to hug Mom, cradling her in his arms.

Paul walks Mom back to the van, with Irene at her side. Suddenly, Mom is left with no strength. She used it all up to defend her son.

At Topeka, I hear Paul and Michael talking about police brutality and the Rodney King case while we're unpacking. Seeing them together is getting to be normal. I watch them move in unison as they unpack the van, and smile to myself. Michael is almost as tall as his dad. Lisa helps Mom and Irene out of the van. The Guadalupanas are holding on to each other, making their way to their room. The day has wearied them.

The sun is setting over the horizon, and a veil of gray, wispy clouds appears. There's moisture in the air. I breathe it into my lungs, aware that I am at the heart of a nation I know nothing about. Rays of the setting sun turn the sky bright orange. Don Florencío used to say Chicanos are descendants of the sun people, and I'm not sure that's what I want to be. I'd rather follow the moon and hope not to be sacrificed to an angry god. I'm not amused by obsidian knives. I'm baffled by the brutality of my ancient ancestors. Violence and the oppression of others is a mystery to me. Could I have done what the Kansas State Police did? Could I ever be as brutal as the sheriff's deputies were on the day of the moratorium march? Playing with violence and power is familiar to all of us. That's another reason we're on our way to the Wall. We're victims of the lust for violence and power that led this nation to the madness of Vietnam.

April 1, 1968

Dear Sis,

Thought I'd write you on April Fool's Day, except I don't have anything to fool you with this year. I hope you played a trick on Paul and

Priscilla, just to keep up family tradition. Remember when I told them I had caught a real alligator in the sewer, then when they paid me a quarter to see it, it turned out to be a lizard I had trapped in the yard? I had them convinced it had shrunk to the size of a mini-alligator because it didn't have enough water—boy I had them going! Then I yelled "April Fool's Day!"—and they both jumped me, but I was laughing so hard I couldn't even push them off of me. I was rolling around in the yard laughing until my stomach hurt. Those were the days, que no?

I think Don Florencio played a joke on me over here in Vietnam. I dreamed about him on April 1st and guess what? I saw him dressed up like a woman! It was him, I swear it was. He had on this headdress that looked like one of those Aztec warriors, he was smoking his ironwood pipe, but he had on a dress, a long dress. I looked at him and asked him, "Is that you, Don Florencio?" "Yes, mijo," he said. He looked at me like he always did, like he was looking right into my heart. There was a light shining behind him, real bright, but it didn't hurt my eyes. "If it's you, why are you dressed like a woman?" I asked him. "Men and women don't live where I am," he said, "only spirits. It doesn't matter anymore if you are male or female, it only matters how you lived your life." Then he sucked on the end of his pipe and I swear I smelled that sweet tobacco he used to smoke. The smoke made a big circle around us and held us together, and there we were, him dressed like a woman, smoking a pipe and me in my Army uniform with this light all around. It felt so good, I can't explain it. I felt powerful, like I had just won a prize. Then I stooped down to clean my boots, but they weren't boots, they were a pair of sandals, brown sandals, like huaraches. And I thought it doesn't matter anymore, sandals will get me where I have to go, I don't need my boots anymore. Doesn't El Santo Niño wear sandals?

Write me back real fast. We're moving out all the time so I don't know when you'll get this letter. We're trying to stay out of the killing zone, but that's hard to do because we don't know where it is. It could be ten feet away from here. Charlie's a guerrilla so the whole place is a battlefield. The other day I passed this little altar set out on the road. It looked so pitiful, a house for wandering souls. Maybe somebody will put one up for me. Don't worry, sis, it can't be that bad. I saw a guy die the other day. I didn't really know who he was, but man he was hurting, then all of a sudden his face got all soft and peaceful, like he was looking through everybody, and then he died. Maybe death is just a change of view. We see things one way over here, and we'll see them dif-

ferently on the other side. Do you think God is male and female? I never thought I'd ask anybody that. I know one thing. He understands Vietnamese, cause these people are praying all the time. I haven't seen the family I told you about lately. I guess they moved all their village out. I'm trying to find them because of their daughter, she's the one teaching me Vietnamese. I miss her. Any guy would, but I'm the lucky one even though the whole family has to be there every time I talk to her. I'll tell you more later.

I'm looking at some farmers working in a rice paddy. These people are unbelievable. They go on working no matter what's happening. The rice seedlings need lots of work, planting, transplanting, until the rice is full grown. I didn't know that. So much of the country is destroyed by bombs, Agent Orange, and napalm. It's weird to see one side of a hill all green, and the other side burnt off. It's like the U.S. can't make up their minds to kill them or let them live. I guess maybe that's peace to our country, that they can go to another country and take over. In other words, let us destroy you, then we'll have peace. One of the colonels said the other day that the way to end the war was to haul Vietnam out into the middle of the ocean and bomb the hell out of it. They should haul his ass out to the ocean see how he likes it.

I'm tired, sis, so tired. Maybe I'm not making sense. I haven't slept for two days, lots of shit happening. Give Mom and Nana a kiss, hug dad. Be sure Priscilla and Paul eat their Cheerios. What I would give for a box of cereal right now. I'd take this letter out to the mailbox for you, but there aren't any. Sorry if it gets to you late. We're on a special mission, whatever that means.

Some old man is waving at me. These people look at us los Chicanos like we're one of them. We look more Vietnamese than American, that's for sure.

Hey, did I tell you, they got rubber trees out here, giant trees. It reminds me of that song, what did it say that an ant can't move a rubber tree plant, but we've got high hopes or something like that. So add that to the list of why we're here. Rubber trees, another money maker.

I think a chopper's coming in. The old man is waving and jumping up and down. We'll give him some C rations if it's the relief flight. Tell Espi I'll write when I get a chance. I'm glad I finished this letter, maybe it's the last thing I have to do.

SWAK
Jesse

It was May by the time I got Jesse's letter. I was finishing up my junior year at Palo Verde High. Reading his letter made me laugh and cry. Laugh because Don Florencío was dressed like a woman, cry because Jesse was embracing the other world. He was right, it was the last thing he had to do. After that, his letters stopped.

Thom •

t Topeka it's all I can do to keep myself from running into Chris's room to find out what he knows about Jesse. I want to switch the lights off in the room for us so the night can get inky black again. We're at another TraveLodge built close to the freeway.

Cisco tells me Chris went out with Willy, Gates, and Yellowhair and said he'd be back in a couple of hours.

"They went over to the Highlander Lounge, wherever that is," Cisco says.

"He didn't tell me he was going out."

"Mom, he doesn't have to tell you everything. He can do what he wants. Right?" Cisco looks closely at me. "Mom?"

"Yeah, you're right, of course he can." Cisco's not convinced I mean what I say. "I guess the veterans want their own night out."

Paul says we should go to the lounge next door for a drink. Donna, Susie, Priscilla, and Manuel decide to go with him. They invite me and I tell them maybe I'll go down a little later. Sarah, Yellowhair's mother, is asleep in her room. Lisa and Lilly have a room to themselves tonight. They say they want to watch movies and call their friends back home. Cisco's decided he can take care of the two boys and they don't need to room in with anybody else. I know Michael will be busy for hours on the laptop, answering e-mails. He says the Vietnamese man from Little

Saigon is telling him all about the real Saigon in Vietnam. He says his family lived in Saigon during the war.

I've just settled the Guadalupanas in their room. They were saying the rosary the last I heard of them. They set up two veladoras on the dresser and put up photos of Jesse and Faustino. The photos now have plastic gold-colored frames around them. Mom seems like she got over her cough and looks stronger than she has in months. For some reason, the fight with the Kansas State Police has energized us, made us jovial, like we won at a picket line, or finished doing a sit-in and got what we wanted. There's power in facing something together, a sense that everybody did the right thing at the right time.

I'm in a room by myself and call Elsa to find out how they're doing. She was asleep, and I could barely hear her tell me everything is fine. I dial Espi's number and her answering machine goes on. I have so much to tell her, I don't say anything. I know she'll know it was me.

A restlessness is taking over me. Maybe I should go to the lounge next door. I decide that's not what I want. I want to find Chris, but there's no way I'll hunt for him in Topeka. He has the nerve to leave when he knows I want to know what happened to Jesse. Maybe that's why he's gone. Men! Why did I think I'd hear the truth from one of them? I reach for the phone and dial the front desk. A man answers, and I ask him for the address of the Highlander Lounge. He gives me directions, then tells me he's gotten two calls from news stations in Topeka asking questions about us. He asks me if I want their numbers and I tell him no. I repeat our web site address and tell him to have them send us e-mails.

The name Highlander makes me think of a country-western place. I take a shower and dress up in black Levi's, short black boots, and a red silk tank top. I drive no more than a mile before I get to a bar that is probably one step above Penny's Pool Hall in Phoenix. It's got strings of white Christmas lights shaping an arc around the entrance. A bronze statute of a cowboy stands on a man-made hill in front of the place. The bar is built to look like a huge log cabin. I'm surprised it's packed on a Tuesday. I make my way around rows and rows of cars in the parking lot, and finally find an empty spot in the last row. I walk as fast as I can. Two guys whistle. "Hey, baby. Don't go in there. I'm over here!"

I'm relieved when I spot a broad-shouldered security guy walking toward me. He's wearing a T-shirt with huge orange letters: HIGHLANDER SECURITY. A woman at the front counter, dressed in western clothes and hat, tells me there's a $10.00 cover charge. She explains that it's a $10.00

charge tonight because the Bronco Brothers, Billy and his brother Buster, are playing. They're famous all over Kansas, she says, that's why the place is so packed. Billy and Buster are jamming away on their guitars as I walk in. There's a woman with them on stage, playing an electronic keyboard. I take a few seconds to adjust to the dim light. Several men are looking at me. One of them almost falls off his bar stool and has to rearrange himself on the seat. I feel like running out, but there's nowhere to go except back to the motel. I spot Chris and the others at one of the tables. There's a woman talking to Chris, a brunette with her hair pulled back into a ponytail. She's wearing a tank top that reveals her midriff, and the smooth, ample curve of her breasts. Chris sees me and motions me to come over. They've got drinks on the table.

"Hey!" Chris says. "What a surprise!" He kisses my cheek. His breath smells like whiskey. The brunette is watching.

"Did Cisco tell you?"

"How do you think I got here?"

"What? I can't hear you, the music's too loud."

"Yes, he told me!" I'm almost shouting.

"Are you mad at me?"

"You told me we were gonna talk about Jesse. Don't you remember? It's not like we have all the time in the world." Chris ignores me.

"Hey, Pamela, this is my friend from Arizona. This is Teresa."

"The famous Teresa Ramirez?" Pamela's got one hand looped over Chris's neck. She takes a sip of her drink.

"None other." Chris looks at me. "Everybody's buying us drinks, right, guys?" He looks at Willy, Gates, and Yellowhair. They're talking and laughing. Gates has a small, blond woman sitting on his lap.

"Yeah, I can tell."

"Order a drink, Teresa," Willy says. He calls the waitress over. I order a margarita.

"Loosen up, Teresa. Let's have some fun," Chris says.

Pamela stands up. Her skirt shoots up to her panty hose line. "Well, excu—ooose me! Don't want to get into anybody else's action." She puts out her cigarette in the ashtray, then looks at me and laughs.

"What action?" I ask her.

"Oh, no, honey. You got the word *fight* written all over you! I ain't been laid in weeks, and I need some—if you know what I mean?" She laughs and walks away.

"Bitch!"

"Loosen up, Teresa. Can't you take a joke?"

"A joke? I'm not in the mood for jokes."

"What?"

"I said, I'm not . . . never mind!"

"Come on!" Chris grabs my hand and we start dancing a country-western polka. "You feel good, girl." People are waving at us, smiling. I start smiling back. "That's it!" Chris says.

Drinks keep coming to the table, compliments of the guests. I take a couple of drinks, and get dizzy right away. Next time the waitress comes around, I ask her for a Seven-Up. I dance with Willy and Yellowhair. Gates is dancing with the blonde. Pretty soon we're all sweating, and the management sets up huge fans to cool the place down. Yellowhair does a jitterbug with a woman to "Rock Around the Clock," and wins first place. People are clapping, hooting, and whistling. Yellowhair wins a bottle of tequila.

"I'm getting out of here," I tell Chris. "It's almost midnight. Aren't you driving tomorrow, Chris? Remember, the trip?"

"All that's under control," Chris says. He's got a stupid grin on his face. "Stay, maybe tonight? What about tonight?"

"You're in love with Margie."

"That was yesterday," he says.

"You're sick! I'm getting out of here."

I walk out expecting Chris to follow me, but he stays behind. I wonder if Pamela will end up back at his table. As I drive up to our motel, Susie comes out of her room.

"Where's Willy?"

"They're down at the Highlander Lounge." I don't tell Susie anything about the Bronco Brothers, Pamela, and the blonde on Gates's lap.

"Boys' night out! This shit isn't gonna work with me."

"He'll be right back."

"He better be!" Headlights turn into the parking lot, and it's Willy.

"It's about time!" Susie yells at him. "What the hell are you thinking? You're not in the Marines anymore, buddy."

"Sorry, babe, I just got a little carried away."

"Where's everybody else?" I ask him.

"Oh, they're still going strong." Susie and Willy start arguing as they walk to their room.

I check up on Mom before I go up to my room. She's sitting up in bed, propped up on pillows. She's draped one of her flowered shawls around her shoulders. Irene is on another bed sound asleep.

"What time is it?" she asks me.

"One in the morning."

"And why are you up?"

"Why are you?"

"You're not fighting in bars again, are you?"

"No, I'm not fighting in bars! What do you think I am?"

"Don't talk so loud, you'll wake up Irene. Ay, that woman snores!"

"I don't hear her snoring."

"She'll start any minute. Now, there, you hear that?" Irene starts making a noise that sounds like she's gurgling water in her throat.

"Don't listen to her. Lie down, Mom. Try to sleep."

"I have too much to think about." She looks at Jesse's photograph on the dresser. "I don't know what Jesse wants to tell me. There's something he wants to say, I know it."

"How do you know?"

"How does any mother know about her child? A mother just knows. Words aren't the only way we talk. How many more days, mija?"

"Three, if nothing goes wrong. We should be there by Friday. Why? Are you feeling bad?"

"I'm always feeling bad. What does it matter? I wonder if El Santo Niño walks around these places."

"Mom, how, can you believe in that?"

"Don't talk so loud. If Irene wakes up, she'll never shut up. God is everywhere."

"Walking around as a child, in little shoes? Mom, that's a joke."

"You don't understand, Teresa. El Niño is a symbol. Everything is a symbol of something else. Un símbolo. El Niño teaches us the humility of God, a God who would walk through all kinds of danger to find His people. A God who would wear out His shoes, searching for those He loves. He teaches us. Learn, Teresa, learn, to see more than what you see."

"I don't know how."

"Listen, that's all you have to do. Your soul will do the rest." Mom takes a drink of water from a glass on the nightstand. "Sleep now, mija. We have to leave here in the morning."

"Mom, do you think you're strong enough to—" She doesn't let me finish.

"Who cares who's strong or weak? What does it matter?"

Irene wakes up and rolls over. "Who's weak?"

"Never mind, Irene. Everybody's weak. Go back to sleep."

Walking to my room, I notice the moon over Topeka is silver-gray.

There's a halo around it. The night is warm. I hear crickets in a thicket of hedges nearby. The rush of cars whizzing across the freeway is constant. A loud honk sounds from one of the diesels.

I notice Chris standing by the motel office.

"Hey," he says. "Don't they sell any coffee around here?"

"They're closed. What are you trying to do, sober up?"

"Still mad at me, huh?" He walks up to me and puts his hands on my shoulders.

"Where's Pamela?" I ask him.

"How should I know?"

"You smell like a brewery."

"Let's talk. Your room or mine?"

"Mine."

We walk into my room. I close the door and darkness takes over us.

"Don't turn the lights on," Chris says.

"I wasn't planning to." Chris sits on a couch. I take off my boots and sit on the edge of the bed. There's a sliver of light shining in through a crack between the drapes. I can make out the white oval of Chris's face and the outline of his body.

"Why did you run away?"

"I'm here."

"But you ran before you got here."

"You don't understand. You people who didn't go, just don't understand! You were back here in the world taking it easy!"

"And you people who went just don't understand how we felt either!"

"OK . . . where . . . do . . . you want me to start?"

"The beginning would make sense."

"I feel like I'm in a confessional. Fond memories for the son of a penitente, I can tell you!" Chris says. He shifts around in his seat. I can't see him in the dark, but I figure he's crossing his legs and leaning heavily on the back of the couch. He pauses, then begins. "Anyway, here goes. There was this one night in Saigon just before Jesse was killed. I want to tell you about it, because the guy Jesse fought with that night was the same guy he saved before he died. Can you imagine the kind of man your brother was?

"We were in this hole in the ground. It was a dive. It didn't even look like a real bar, it looked like somebody's house with tables and chairs in it. All kinds of guys were there, mostly Army. We were together, a bunch of Chicanos from all over the States. Frankie from Denver, Pete from Long Beach, and a bunch of others. Most of the Chicanos weren't bookworms like your brother. They couldn't get no deferment for going to school. We hung out together, you know, 'cause we were all los vatos, los camaradas trying to get through the war, looking at los pinches gringos, knowing they had it made. The whites covered up for each other all the time. Lots of them were freaks, stoners, right down to the officers, y los negros, the Blacks, they were in the same boat with us. But you know, when we were out on the hills, nobody cared what color you were. Some of the Chicanos were marijuanos, I admit that, but we didn't go out of our way to beat up on the Vietnamese. How could we? Some of us came from migrant familias. We saw them out on their little plots of land, and so help me God, they looked like our nanas and tatas. Some of us had come from the cotton fields to the foxholes of Nam, there was nothing in between. I got to hate some of the Vietnamese after a while, just because we lost so many men. Some of them were sneaky. We couldn't tell nothin' in their faces. They could have a bomb down their pants and be smiling and bowing. I hated like hell to hurt them, though, especially when there were kids around.

"That night, we were boozing it up, playing cards and our whole thing was, a la chingada con todo, you know, fuck this shit. Jesse was with us, but you know him, he was always a cut above us. He didn't lose control like we did, even if he was high. There was this whole table of gabachos in the place, and this girl, a real pretty Vietnamese girl Jesse knew, was waiting on them. Her name was Thom. She showed me and Jesse her name on a piece of paper once, and she spelled it with an *h* but she pronounced it Tom. She said it meant beautiful smell. She wasn't one of the whores, just a girl who cleaned the place up and helped out when it got busy. Well, this big ol' white guy, we called him Tennessee, 'cause that's where he was from . . . anyway, he starts grabbing Thom, and she starts screaming and telling him to let her go. Jesse's watching the whole thing. All of a sudden Jesse throws his cards down on the table and yells at the guy, 'Leave her alone!' He yelled real loud, like he was roaring at the guy, you know in his sergeant's voice. The guy grabs Thom one more time, and Jesse stands up. 'I said, leave her alone!' By this time the guy's pushed Thom away and is standing up. He must have been over six feet two, and you know Jesse, he was short. 'Did somebody say something?' he asks, playing all dumb. He shakes his head like there's a bug flying around. 'I thought I heard a fly buzz.' All the white guys start laughing like they're gonna piss in their pants. Tennessee looks at Thom again, and Jesse says, 'Don't touch her, fucker.' Then Tennessee says, 'Who's gonna stop me?' And your brother says 'I am.' I tell him, 'Calmate, Jesse, we don't want no trouble with these jodidos, they'll call in the MPs, you know they're a bunch of fuckin' crybabies.'

"Tennessee walked over to Jesse, and Jesse looked so short next to him, I thought the guy was just gonna hammer him on the head. By now everybody's standing up, all the Chicanos and the white guys. 'A la madre,' Pete says, 'get ready to kick ass, vatos.' And that's what we were gonna do, back Jesse up, protect his back, no matter what happened. One thing los vatos didn't know was that Jesse was El Gato. I told them . . . hey watchale, you're looking at El Gato. They didn't know what the hell I was talking about. Everything came down in a couple of seconds. Before Tennessee could blink, Jesse swung a right-left combination to his body and landed him flat on his back. El pendejo gabacho just lay there with all the air beat out of him. Jesse jumped on a chair like Superman and yelled, 'COME ON, FUCKERS! COME ON! WHO'S NEXT? WE'RE IN THEIR COUNTRY, FUCKERS, AIN'T YOU GOT NO RESPECT?' The white guys just looked at him like they were in the twilight zone. We were ready to wipe them out, now that their main man was down. We were all pumped up, and it was gonna be a scramble when we heard this whistle and the MPs showed up with Lieutenant Hopkins. The MPs were ready to rumble too, they had their billy clubs out. They lived on shit like this. But the lieutenant was cool, a todo dar, he didn't give a damn what color you were as long as you were doing what you were supposed to do. He looks at your brother on the chair and yells at the top of his lungs 'RAMIREZ!' . . . the whole place freezes, then he yells, 'Sit on it!' and Jesse says, 'Yes, sir,' and sits on the chair like he was innocent as a lamb. Lieutenant Hopkins looks at all of us, then he looks at Tennessee on the floor and gives him a dirty look and all he says is 'Gentlemen, as you were.' Then he walks out, like he didn't give a shit if we burned the place down. When the white guys saw we had back up from him, they sat down and left Tennessee rolling around on the floor."

"The overhand right-left hook was Jesse's best combination. I wish I could have seen him do it on that guy! El Gato . . . the winner!"

"Well, he used his combination that night. And that was the night I found out Thom was Jesse's girlfriend. Her family lived just outside Bien Hoa on this little farm. They were Catholic and Buddhists mixed, but mostly Catholic, because I remember Jesse and Thom went to church one Sunday. Her father was with the South Vietnamese Army, and that's what got the whole family in big trouble when Saigon fell."

"She's the same one Jesse mentioned in his letters, but he never told me her name. He told me she was teaching him Vietnamese."

"What could he say about her anyway? That he fell in love with a Vietnamese girl, not the kind of girl he could bring back home to Mom? Not that Thom was a whore, or any of that, just that it took guts to get married to one of their women and to bring her back to the States. If he had lived, I think Jesse would have brought her back. That's all he talked about before he was killed, about Thom, and he told me to take care of her if something happened to him. But you know me, I never did anything for anybody. I just lost track of her, even when I went back the second time, I couldn't find her."

"Remember, Jesse always wanted a girlfriend. He loved Neil Diamond's 'Solitary Man,' cause he was always looking for the right woman, and never found her. Do you think this woman . . . Thom, was the one who called Mom?"

"Could have been."

"What happened the day my brother was killed?"

"The day Jesse was killed. I wish I could forget that day forever!"

"Tell me how he died. Did he say anything?"

"No, nothing. There was no time. I was walking point the day Jesse was killed, and the guys were depending on me to lead us over this hill, but it wasn't a hill, it was more like a big mound. I later found out it was a place where people buried their garbage.

Can you imagine what we fought for? The officers would always say 'Pack up, we got some humping to do!' We were the grunts, doing all the shitty work. We were made of flesh and bone, but the officers back at headquarters only saw us as pins on their maps. They never told us where we were going, how far we'd come, nada. We were running in circles, chasing our own tails.

"I stood for a minute thinking what the bad smell was, and looking at maggots crawling through the dirt, when Jesse was hit, right through the neck. I didn't even know, 'til Pete screamed like he was half-crazy, 'Jesse's down! Jesse's down! Call the medics.'

"Tennessee was in the middle of it again. I heard Jesse was hauling him over to a trench 'cause he was hit in the stomach. That's when Jesse was hit, right there, after he rolled Tennessee's body into the trench.

"Man, it made me sick just to think about it! Me? I would have said let his buddies roll his white ass into the trench! I didn't give a shit about him. That's what I would have done after what happened at the bar. But you know Jesse, he wasn't like that. The medics came in a Huey, but it was too late, Jesse died before I got to him. All I did was take off my shirt and cover his face. I couldn't stand to see him for the last time like that. I remember somebody was yelling. Later, the guys told me it was me . . . I was yelling. I can't even remember what I was saying."

I think of Jesse with Chris's shirt over his face. "Oh, God, I wish I had been there to touch him one last time!"

The silence between Chris and me is greater than the darkness. I think of Li Ann in my second-grade class and her mother Huong and wonder if Thom looked like Huong, delicate, fragile, almost a child. The women exchange profiles, hands, feet, until Huong's face becomes Thom's. I wish Jesse had told me more about Thom. Is it jealousy I'm feeling or anger that Jesse left me out of this part of his life? Having a girl-friend was one of his dreams. The stuck-up American kind didn't attract him, and I could see how a gentle woman like Thom could have won his heart.

We hear voices singing outside our door. Chris opens the door, and it's Yellowhair and Gates singing and doing the stroll. They're dancing through an imaginary line, then back again.

"Hey, you two, hold it down! Don't you have any respect? Everybody's asleep."

Yellowhair notices me standing at the door. "Hey, Teresa, you and Chris come on out here and do the stroll with us! Come on, don't you remember how to do it?"

Chris closes the door, and reaches for my hands in the dark. He's holding my hands so tight my fingers ache. "OK, that's all I know, Teresa. I lost track of your brother that day. Then to make it worse, I didn't ride with him on the plane back to the base. I've been kicking myself for it all these years! Forgive me! Will you?"

Chris wipes the tears off my face, and I do the same for him. "You lost track of my brother! Then you just let him go off by himself. In a body bag? I don't even want to think about it!"

"You don't want to think about it? How do you think I felt? I'm ask-ing you to forgive me."

"I'm not blaming you. There's nothing to forgive you for, Chris. You were a kid yourself. You didn't know what to do. You didn't do anything wrong." I press my forehead into Chris's shoulder. He holds me in his arms.

"Say it again," he says.

"You didn't do anything wrong." Chris cups my face in his hands, then with one finger he traces over my lips. He presses his finger up to his own lips.

"Your tears taste sweet."

"Liar." We both laugh.

The singing outside gets louder. Chris opens the door. Security lights have gone on in the parking lot.

"You guys are gonna get us thrown out—shut up!" Chris turns around and kisses me. "Wanna stroll, Teresa?"

"Yeah, been waiting thirty years." I brush away new tears, and slip into my shoes.

Yellowhair and Gates make a line and Chris and me do the stroll through the center. We're all singing and clapping. The guy from the office comes out.

"I know you're the Ramirez family," he says. "But so help me, if you guys don't get into your rooms, I'm calling the cops."

"We've already met them," Gates says sarcastically.

Priscilla comes out of her room, "What are you, crazy? Teresa, have you flipped?"

"Come on, Priscilla," I tell her. "You and Manuel. Let's stroll."

"Hell, no!"

I hear Manuel's voice from a distance. "You guys better settle down. This guy's serious. He *will* call the cops."

"All right, everybody," Chris says. "Let's go to bed." He walks off with Gates and Yellowhair. I see lights here and there in the motel windows. One man yells, "Shut up out there! Can't a person get some sleep around here?"

"It's over," I tell Priscilla and Manuel. "They didn't do anything wrong."

Priscilla's got her hands on her hips. "What's that got to do with this mess?"

"Everything," I tell her.

• WE'VE GOT MORE COMPANY as we drive out of Topeka on Wednesday, June 4. Pepe and his brother Gonzalo are tagging along in their Dodge pick-up. They're two men Chris and the others met at the Highlander. Their long-bed is packed with cases of beer. I didn't even know there were Chicanos in Topeka, but they assure me there are plenty. Some of them work on farms like they do. Both men are short and stocky, their skin tanned dark brown from hours of labor in the sun. They tell us their mother died of a broken heart one year after their brother's death. She never got to go to the Wall, and now they want to go pay their respects to their brother.

I'm proud that the boundaries of Aztlán are getting wider and wider. Don Florencío would be glad to know just how far we've come from the seven caves our ancestors lived in. The Indian huehues would have applauded, saying la raza was right to return north, to Aztlán, the place of their origin.

Manuel refused to rent another vehicle for Pepe and Gonzalo and told them if they wanted to join us to use their own car. Mom told Manuel to let them come. They're poor boys, she says, who lost their older brother, Gustavo, in Vietnam. And then, to make everything worse, their mother died, too. Can you imagine such suffering?

I don't say anything to Mom about Chris losing track of Jesse the day he was killed. It doesn't matter what happened on the field that day. Jesse went after Tennessee, and if he hadn't, he wouldn't have been the brother I knew. I want to know more about Thom, the woman Jesse loved. Beautiful smell. Did she love him back? Is she still alive?

This morning Chris is like a kid wanting to please me, like Manuel when he gave me chocolate valentines.

Stable Light •

ichael tells me light runs in waves that don't interfere with each other even when they cross paths. How can this be? You'd think the elements would merge, yet everything remains distinct, every electron orbiting separately from the others, yet "conscious" of everything else around it. Our reality is really only stable light. In another dimension we might be traveling at the speed of light and our concept of time would be eternal. We wouldn't look at things horizontally or vertically because all points in space would be equal. That's the way it is with us, we're traveling in one light beam all the way to the Wall, an unbroken web with Jesse somewhere in the middle. Still, we're separate from each other, thinking our own thoughts, connecting with him in a hundred different ways.

I think the Guadalupanas wanted Chris and me to fall in love. They know it's not happening. How they know, I can't say. I think they're disappointed with us, even though I know they stayed with their husbands and slept all their lives in their marriage beds. There's a sad frowning in their faces, lines that yesterday were anticipating some new love story unfolding before their eyes are now back in place.

Chris is still in love with Margie. Maybe he's thinking the bad times between them weren't so bad and the good times were better. I'm always remembering bad times between me and Ray. I don't want to think about the good times. Maybe I chose Ray to satisfy my craving for suffering and appease the Indian blood coursing through my veins. I'm wondering if I'm an addict for suffering, a freak who looks for the wrong choice to make, the wrong step to take. My mom and Irene memorized the formula for suffering before they were born. They have accepted it the way they accept their swollen feet and aching knees. Cold, uncaring men, traitors, are part of their plan to prick their own flesh with pins.

I think of Thom and Huong, Li Ann's mother, one and the same being, little women who bear great secrets and great suffering. Where is she, this woman who held my brother's heart in the palm of her hand? Chris is of no help. He never found Thom. There's a part of me that wants to fly from D.C. to Saigon.

• WE LEAVE TOPEKA later than we planned. By the time the men got up and dealt with their hangovers, it was almost noon. Passing through Kansas City, Kansas, we pay a toll before we get into Missouri. This is new to us, and something we'll have to get used to. People everywhere recognize us. Sometimes they follow us in their vehicles for a short distance. At times, we spot a helicopter flying overhead, signaling another news story about our whereabouts. It's as if America is caught up in a mystery story: "Where are the Ramirezes?"

We stop at gas stations and people ask us how Mom's doing. Some people want to shake her hand, others take her picture. It's unbelievable, I tell Chris. Mom's getting famous in her old age. At a gas station in Kansas, Missouri, I get on the laptop with Michael, and see messages from the man in Little Saigon who calls himself, lnrlittlesaigon@aol.com. Several people are standing close to the van. They spot Mom and Irene through the windows, and start waving. Mom and Irene smile and wave back.

"Hams," I tell Chris. "These old Guadalupanas are two big hams!"

It doesn't take us long to cross over the Kansas River and drive into Missouri. Truman was born on the Missouri side. Still, who is he to me? Another unknown I read about in history books. There's a sign advertising a prairie house, and it reminds me of Laura Ingalls Wilder, the author who wrote about her days as a child in the 1800s. Chris tells me part of the Civil War was fought in Missouri. The Battle of Lexington, he says, was a big one. I'm wondering if the men and women of Aztlán, who walked as one and huddled together in circles at the end of the day, came this far. Is it just my family who's passing through to remind the world that Aztlán existed?

On our way to St. Louis we pass a restaurant owned by someone named Ruiz-Castillo, Everybody wants to stop there and have some Mexican food. We park our cars along the road to talk about it, and finally decide that it wouldn't be worth it. The food's not the kind we have in Phoenix, Manuel says, and just think of the time we'll lose.

At St. Louis, the Guadalupanas want to stop at a church to say a rosary, and almost make us stop as we cross over into Illinois and they see a sign advertising Our Lady of Snows shrine. Chris tells me we'll lose two hours by the time they get out of the van and into the shrine and everybody else stops to take pictures and buy souvenirs. Then there are tourists to contend with, and people who want to get Mom's autograph, as if she's a movie star. He says we have to keep moving so we can get to Richmond, Indiana, before dark. My mother's face is pale today, and she's complaining of an upset stomach. Irene gives her half a lemon to suck on, telling her this will stop the nausea. I'm worried it's more than that, maybe her heart condition is disguising itself as indigestion. I tell her we can stop at a hospital somewhere, and she says that will make us lose even more time. I'm tempted to call Dr. Mann, but Mom says he'll only scold her, and why should she listen to him, since he's in Arizona and she's in Missouri? The road through St. Louis leads us into Illinois. We cross over a bridge into Illinois, and spot gambling boats at Station Casino. There are ferryboats like the ones in Mark Twain's stories, chugging away through the water. St. Louis boasts buildings with huge spires, and a gigantic metal arch separating Missouri from Illinois. Everywhere there are buildings constructed in French Colonial style.

We're finally in Indiana, the Crossroads of America. I'm not impressed with what I see of Indianapolis; most of the buildings we pass are old and look small. I'm amazed at the history all around us, though, places that look like scenes out of an English colony. We pass a town named Terre Haute, and I wonder if it's a British name, French name, or Indian, or a combination of all three.

By the evening of Wednesday, June 4, we reach Richmond. The Guadalupanas are sleeping on top of each other in the back seat. Mom's using Irene's shoulder as her pillow, and Irene is leaning on a real pillow propped up against the window. The motels in Richmond are packed, and the TraveLodge where Manuel made our reservations lost our paperwork. The manager was very upset when he realized who we were, but there was nothing to be done, outside of driving miles from where we were to another motel that had room. Chris and I suggest the Sheraton or the Hilton to Mom, and she says no. That's for rich people, she says, and what if the kids break something? Now we're stuck driving up and down the main street, searching for another place.

We find out the reason everything's so crowded is that medical people have descended upon Richmond to attend, of all things, a convention on aging and geriatric care. A convention called the Intergenerational Communication Link is going on. That might be lucky for me, if they could help me understand the two old women I've been traveling with these days, help me understand why they had to make this journey now, when they both know my mother's heart condition could lead to her death. Why don't they go back home and grow passion vines? They'd see the story of suffering each day in the palm of their hands. Mom and Irene don't tell me what's going on inside of them. They're keeping secrets they only share with La Virgen, the mother of all mothers. I want to shout at them, "Dying is real!" but it's no use. They would just look at me, and ask how many more miles to the Wall.

We finally manage to get rooms at the Budget Motel, a place with lopsided mini-blinds and frayed carpet. The guys we picked up in Kansas, Pepe and Gonzalo, say they've stayed in the motel before, which makes it all seem worse. Management is scurrying around spraying air freshener and supplying us with extra towels. The woman, who tells me she runs the motel at night, says she read about us in the newspaper. Her uncle went to Vietnam, she says, and now he's in a veteran's hospital suffering from diabetes, which isn't connected to the war, but keeps him in a place that reminds him of the war all the time.

Our room smells of cigarettes, and there's nothing we can do about it. The kids take a room upstairs and Cisco almost flips Michael over the balcony rail when he tries his fireman's carry hold on him. It's a hold that means the opponent gets thrown a few yards up in the air. A fellow motel resident ran out to stop the fight and found out it wasn't really a fight, which made him mad. He looked like a Hell's Angel, and I think he was disappointed when he couldn't use the knife he had unsheathed. The Wall is only one day away. We'll be in Frederick, Maryland, before nightfall tomorrow, and there's nothing left to do after that but turn our faces toward the Wall. We've decided to do laundry at Frederick and get things ready for our entrance into D.C. Mom says she doesn't want Jesse to see her in dirty clothes. I remind her that Jesse can't "see" her, but she says she wants to look nice.

At two o'clock in the morning, I still can't sleep. I'm sharing a room with Lisa and Lilly. The girls went to sleep without turning off the TV. I find the remote and turn it off. The room goes dark, except for light from the lamppost illuminating the window. I hear people in their rooms, a man and woman arguing. Thumps on the wall, a TV still on. I get up and open the door, looking up into a moonless, starless sky. Scattered raindrops are falling with big spaces between them, reflecting colors from cars and dark specks from puddles on the asphalt. Everything is dreary. I miss Ray. I miss Chris. Maybe I miss being held in the arms of a man and lying back to pretend the world belongs only to us, that the magic between us will keep until morning.

I walk out the door and regret taking a deep breath. The smell of the city streets gets caught in my throat. I look up at the balcony and see Chris at one end, leaning on the rail smoking a cigarette. He doesn't see me in the dark. He finishes his cigarette and flicks the dying ember to the ground. He stands looking up at the sky with his hands in his pockets. I want to walk up the stairs and put my arms around him, but I don't. It will only open up all the pain, and tonight I'm so weary, if I hear anything more I'll burst. I wonder if he's talking to Jesse.

Crossing El Río Salado •

There's something about getting closer to a place that makes you want to turn around and start all over again. It's unexplainable. I don't want the journey to end, even though that's all I've thought about for weeks. Endings start new things and I don't know what this one will start. We've touched Jesse in so many ways already I wonder if we still need to touch his name on the Wall. Nothing can convince my mother we don't.

We pass the Mad River as we loop into Ohio on Thursday, June 5. So far I've counted two Springfields, one in Illinois and one in Indiana. I'm wondering if there are more. We stare at places that look like German villages. Everything is so green I imagine we're in a giant greenhouse. People at a gas station tell us the land has been reclaimed and re-planted where it was overused by industry. Miles of forests bordering the highway are covered with wildflowers. We spot farmhouses built so close to trees, I wonder if the family has enough room to park their cars and open their doors.

At a rest stop, we meet a couple of truck drivers headed for California. "Ohio's nice country," they say, "but the snow gets too high for us. We hate driving in winter." It's hard to imagine that snow piles up so high people can get lost in it. The truckers have picked up a hitch-hiker, a guy who claims he was in the DMZ as a Marine in 1969. "Saw so much action up in Hue, it was hard to come back to sanity," he says.

Donna tells me the guy still looks pretty insane, and both of us are hoping he won't want to go to the Wall with us. It's too late. By the time we leave the rest stop, Pepe and Gonzalo have convinced the guy to travel with us to the Wall, telling him he'll never get another chance. Of course, my mother says it's OK, and Manuel throws a fit because he says the guy's a crackpot. "We might get in trouble taking him, Doña," he explains to my mom. Mom doesn't even respond. We know no matter what we say, the answer for Fritz, that's what he calls himself, will be "yes." Fritz says his grandparents settled in Ohio in the late 1800s. They were German, Scottish, hard workers, he says, the kind who lived by the sweat of their brows. His parents were the same way. Fritz says he didn't like to sweat, so he left home at age fifteen and broke his parents' hearts. "Then look what happened," he tells me. "God got even. He sent me to Vietnam, and I sweated so much over there, half the time I thought I was standing in puddles of water."

We've got mainstream America traveling with us now, and he's taking a good look at Donna. Donna's already preached to him, telling him if he hasn't found the Lord yet, it's still not too late. Paul puts on his red headband, which means he wants to look dangerous. He's mad-dogging Fritz, and I guess Fritz thinks Donna's not worth a fight, especially after he hears her preach. Paul teases Fritz. "Hey, I met your cousin Fratz the other day," he says. Fritz just smiles and doesn't seem to mind.

Irene gets into an argument in Ohio over hand cream. She says she has some lotion made from aloe vera that causes skin to get soft and white. Mom says that's not true, because aloe vera is better for your hair and not that good for your skin. She says she bought vitamin E cream from a drugstore once and that it is proven to seep in through the skin and restore moisture. I never even knew Mom cared about her skin. I turn around and notice her skin is clear, smooth, almost wrinkle-free. I try to imagine her as a young woman, her skin supple, her breasts fully formed, the creamy skin held taut around the nipples. It surprises me to think that way about my mother. I've always seen her as sexless, someone who couldn't make my dad stay home. She catches me looking at her.

"Don't be so hardheaded, Irene," Mom says. "What would you know about creams, your family worked out in the fields most of your life."

"Forgive me for saying this," Irene answers, "but I lived around herbs all my life and I learned from the very best, my abuelita, who was a curandera straight from the mountains of Jalisco."

"Don't start on curanderas!" Mom says. "My mother held the degree on that one!" She grabs her purse like she's gonna fly out the van door while the car's still moving.

"Ay, both of you, stop!" I tell them.

"You're right, Teresa," Mom says. "Who cares who uses what? Our skin is as dry as a snake's back, nothing could make it look good."

"Speak for yourself," Irene says. "My skin is soft because I use aloe vera cream. Here, touch my arm." She moves her arm up against Mom.

"Esta mujer! You are unbelievable. I don't want to touch your arm! I told you, I don't care about skin anymore."

Lilly's sitting in the seat directly behind Mom. "Touch *my* skin, Nana," she says, putting her face next to Mom's.

"See, now here's beautiful skin, mijita has perfect skin!" Then Mom's eyes fill with tears. "I remember when I saw Jesse after he was born, ay, I thought I was looking at an angel. His face was so soft, I couldn't stop kissing him, and now look, all I have left to touch is his name! The war has never ended for me!" Irene takes out a Kleenex and admits the war's never ended for her either. The fight over hand cream is over.

We pass through Columbus, and the land is resplendent with acres of trees in full bloom, ash, white pine, oak.

"Let's live in Ohio, Mom!" Lisa says. "The forests, they're so beautiful!"

"What do you think, Chris?"

"If you can take the winters," Chris says.

"She can't even stand the winter in Arizona," Lilly says.

"Look who's talking."

"Come on, girls," I tell them. "We're not moving to Ohio, unless you want to come here on your own, someday."

We stop at Newark to eat at a busy family restaurant. Newark news people descend on the place. They talk with Gates, Yellowhair, and Willy. They ask Priscilla and me about Mom, and start counting how many people are with us. "We keep growing," I tell them. "No telling who will join us next." One woman hands Mom a St. Christopher medal.

"To go with your other medallion," she says. "To protect you all the way to the Wall." Tears start in her eyes. "My boyfriend was killed there," she says. "We were high school sweethearts. Look." She shows Mom a picture of a handsome young man in a Marine uniform. "Good-looking, huh?"

"Very handsome!" Mom says. She shows the woman a photo of Jesse.

"Very handsome too!" the woman says.

Michael tells me to come look at all the messages he's getting on the laptop. I ask him about the Vietnamese man from Little Saigon, but Michael says he's not sending any more messages.

Paul's helping Michael answer e-mails, and is making up messages like a whiz. "Like son, like father," I tell him, "or is it the other way around?" I am stunned when I see lists and lists of names sending messages to our web site: Adams, Acosta, Lane, McMillan, Shubert, Tan, Redding, Alarcon, Yusef, Vital, Stein, Ortiz, Johnson, Williams, about thirty Smiths, lots of Garcias and Hernandezes, Hendrix, Jordan, the list goes on and on. I see one from Barry and Eleanor Kinney, the elderly couple we met in the Coconino Forest in Flagstaff who had a son who served in Vietnam. The messages are pleas, good wishes, prayers, heart-breaking stories, blessings, and many requests: *Touch his name, my son, my husband, my brother, my cousin, my uncle . . . touch his name, touch his name.* There's a message from Holly Stevens, the reporter from Phoenix. *Get ready for Frederick*, she says.

"What does that mean?" I ask Michael.

"How should I know?" Michael says. He looks flustered, irritated because he doesn't have time to answer all the messages.

"Don't worry, mijo," Paul says. "Just do what you can."

We head up to Wheeling, Ohio. Pepe and Gonzalo weave past us with Fritz sitting in the back of the truck. I'm worried they're doing more than drinking.

"If we all make it in one piece it'll be a miracle," Chris says.

"Don't say it too loud," I tell him, "there's people here who believe in miracles."

Wheeling is old brick buildings with white-trimmed windowpanes. Two-story houses face the street. We've passed Livingston, Lancaster, strong British names, then drive by Egypt Valley. I wonder if people from Egypt settled there. I can barely imagine the descendants of the pyramid builders living in the magical green forests of Ohio. I can only see them in deserts. Wheeling is the last city we drive through to get to West Virginia.

"We're almost there, Mom," I tell her. "We're crossing into West Virginia." My mother sighs and makes the sign of the cross over herself. I look back at her. She's thinner than she was in Arizona. Making her eat is a lost cause. She always puts it off for later, then I forget if she ate or not. It's all I can do to keep track of her medications. One by one the pills have disappeared, and my mother looks the same.

There are days I don't want to give medications to her because nothing seems to work. Priscilla thinks I should stop at a hospital and have Mom checked in an emergency room. She's threatened twice to take her there herself. Mom won't hear of it and keeps saying La Virgen will protect her. She says la manda is her whole life.

We travel through the tip of West Virginia and cross over into Pennsylvania. The country is lush green with banks of green grass that look almost blue growing up the sides of the highway. We pass Jessop Place, and it reminds me of Jesse. We drive through a tunnel built right through the Allegheny Mountains. The mountains are bluish-green, tall, mystical. Don Florencío would have loved to explore those mountains, maybe even live there in a cave. In Pennsylvania we see the first sign advertising D.C.; 127 MILES TO D.C. Chris starts honking, and all the others echo the same. It reminds me of Erica when she dropped off Gates at the freeway right before we climbed up the ramp. Other motorists honk, too. I look back through the rear window, and everyone is still trailing behind us. I glimpse the Zuñi feathered wands, and the flags of the U.S., Mexico, China, and South Africa flapping in the wind.

"Wow, what a trip," I tell Chris. "Can you imagine the beauty of this country? I never knew how beautiful it really is. America was just a word before, and now it's something I can feel—I can hold it, and I don't know where I'm holding it. My mind? My heart? My spirit? I don't know, maybe it's all three."

"Yeah, the guys in Nam felt the same sometimes. We'd think of the world back here, and we'd get homesick, just wanting to come back and watch a baseball game or eat a hot dog. Me? I wanted to climb up the Sandias. You know, the mountains you saw in Albuquerque. I used to take my daughters there on Sundays. We'd watch the sun set, and the mountains would turn dark purple, then darker and darker, until they disappeared, and all I could see were shadows. Huge mountains, and they disappeared."

"Jesse must have felt the same way. He wrote to me about the Salt River. We used to call it El Río Salado. I almost drowned there when I was a kid, but it was still a special place. Jesse remembered it when he was walking through the Mekong Delta."

We pass the Mason-Dixon Line, and the history I read in high school classes takes on a new form. These were places where the American Revolution and the Civil War were fought, places with great meaning for millions whose children would one day travel through the U.S., eventually meeting up with us, the children of Aztlán.

It's dark as we drive into Frederick, Maryland, but I can still make out wildflowers growing along the roadside, white, violet, yellow. Surprisingly, the evening is cool. My mother wants to stay at Frederick for the night to wash clothes and pray. She says she can't go see her mijito with her clothes all dirty and no clean socks to wear. I want to move through the night and get into D.C., but I also want to turn around and wish this all away, like a dream after I wake up in the morning.

• IN FREDERICK we meet a girl who's washing clothes at a laundromat. She helps Sarah load up a washing machine. Sarah tells her that when she was a girl on the Indian reservation, they used to go to the river and beat their clothes on wet rocks to get them clean. "For soap, we used Borax," Sarah says. "That's all the missionaries had to give us. Then my mom got a washing machine with a wringer for rolling clothes through. She hated that machine. She used it three times, then filled it with rainwater for our horses. After that, we went back to beating our clothes on the wet rocks."

The girl tells Priscilla and me that her name is Bridget. Thank God she's not a Vietnam vet, she's too young. I don't think anybody will be tempted to invite her to go with us to the Wall. She only remembers the war in schoolbooks. She tells us which machine to use, because she goes there every week. She just got married, she says, and is happy with her new husband. I tell her she's the first happily married person I've seen in a long time. "It's easy," she says, "we treat each other like we're boyfriend and girlfriend. It makes us do special things for each other all the time." I think about that and wonder how long they'll be able to do this. I feel like a pessimist and only smile at her and congratulate her for such a lovely way to live. Privately, I think she's living in a bubble that will burst some day and drop her to the ground.

The Guadalupanas are back in the motel getting ready for their big day tomorrow. They have an upstairs room this time and have to use the elevator. Mom says the upstairs room is better than the ones on the bottom where you have to put up with cars parking at your front door. They've decorated a coffee table with white linen and added a couple of vases with silk roses. They light candles and set up the image of La Virgen and a small statue of El Santo Niño. They prop up Jesse and Faustino's pictures in front of the images. Pepe and Gonzalo have given Mom a picture of their brother, Gustavo. It shows how much they love their brother, Mom says. Irene says she almost died like Gustavo's mother after her son's death. Maybe it would have happened, Irene says, except she had so many problems with her other kids, she had to stay. Gustavo's picture is un-framed, and leans up against Jesse and Faustino's framed photos. His photo shows a young man in a shirt and tie, dressed for a wedding or a party.

One of the flickering candles is scented, and makes the motel room smell like a miniature church. The two heavenly figures look back at the old ladies, unblinking, silent. "They've brought us this far, they won't fail us now," Mom says. "Dios obra en todo, God works through all things."

Later, Priscilla and I come back from the laundromat with the clothes folded and ready to be put away. We find the Guadalupanas kneeling be-fore their makeshift altar reciting a litany of praise, a chant that moves in circles around their heads, breathing over the flickering candle flames. Bendito sea Dios, bendito sea su santo nombre, bendito sea Dios en sus an-geles y en sus santos, Blessed be God, blessed be His holy name, blessed be God in his angels and in his saints. Blessed be this, blessed be that—the chanting goes on for fifteen minutes at least. It reminds me of the song my mother never finished the day we found out Jesse had been killed. Bendito, Bendito, Bendito sea Dios, los angeles cantan y alaban a Dios. Blessed, blessed, blessed is God, angels are singing and praising God, an-gels are singing and praising God. A deep nostalgia for Mom's voice goes through me like an electric shock that makes me drop the clothes I'm put-ting away. The Guadalupanas are so caught up in their prayers they don't even look my way. I want to shout at Mom—SING THE SONG—SING "BENDITO"! It's been so long, too long. I don't say anything. I just freeze in position behind them and listen to their chanting, mesmerized by the weariness of the journey and the feeling that la manda between Mom and Heaven will be finished before another day goes by.

Jesse looks like he's smiling at all of us from his position between the heavenly figures. I know Jesse. He'd probably say "Get me out of here" if he really found himself caught between the two old women. He wouldn't say anything about La Virgen and El Santo Niño, he had too much respect for that.

Priscilla is out the door before I am. "Mom shouldn't be kneeling like that, it'll put pressure on her knees."

"Forget it," I tell her. "She's got more strength than the two of us when it comes to praying and believing."

"That won't help her in D.C.," Priscilla says. "Have you thought about what's really gonna happen there? Do you think Mom can handle all this? We'll see his name on the Wall." Priscilla says the last words like she's whispering a prayer. *We'll see his name . . .*

"And we'll touch it," I tell her.

"God, why did all this happen to us? Did we do something wrong?" Priscilla asks. "Maybe we didn't love God enough, or each other. Maybe God got mad at us and took Jesse. He was the best our family had to offer. Do you think God's like that?"

"He's not the Aztec god! What are you talking about? Christ sacrificed Himself, what does that tell you?"

"I still miss Annette, Teresa!" Priscilla says suddenly. "God, this trip is killing me! I'll never touch my baby again! Mom gets to touch Jesse's name, and all I have is Annette's headstone." Priscilla is crying, wiping her tears with the end of her T-shirt. I haven't seen her cry in years and forgot what it was like to smooth her hair back and blot out her tears with my fingers. "Maybe I'm being punished for all the wild years. You remember . . . the times I wouldn't listen to anybody."

"I told you, God's not like that. He's not standing around wondering how he's gonna hurt us. He doesn't think like a human being. He knows we're hurting, but there's some hurt He can't take away from us just as we can't take our kids' pain. Those two old ladies in there, they know what it means to suffer and still believe that God is good. Just because we go through pain, doesn't mean God isn't close by—that He doesn't love us anymore. All these years I've known how much you hurt for Annette. I've always known, maybe that's why I'm glad you're close to Lilly. I thought maybe one of my own girls would give you comfort."

"She does. Lilly's part of the reason I've survived all these years. She's given me the chance to see what it means to have a daughter."

"Think about it this way, Priscilla, we were with Mom all the way. She has to do this, she has to finish la manda." We hold hands as we did when we were kids and get ready to walk downstairs. Before we take a step, we hear Michael and Angelo racing up the stairs, out of breath. They tell us that Yellowhair and his mother, Sarah, have started a bonfire behind a garbage bin and are chanting and moving around in a circle.

"It's some kind of Zuñi ritual," Michael says. "A cleansing ceremony from their tribe."

"Can I put on feathers like Yellowhair?" Angelo asks.

We hurry down the stairs before the motel manager calls the fire department on Yellowhair and his mother. By the time we get there, Yellowhair is smoking a peace pipe and sitting before a fire smoldering in a tin tub that looks like the old-fashioned kind we used to bathe ourselves in when we were kids. He's wearing red and white feathers as a headdress. I'm glad there's high oleander bushes all around, blocking

Yellowhair and his mother from the parking lot behind us. Sarah is sitting next to her son, dressed in a black and white jumper, flowered scarf, and white leggings, holding a white eagle feather in her hand. The fragrant smell of sage reaches me and instantly my body relaxes. I remember Don Florencío and pretend he's the one who lit the fire.

"Jesse would love this!" I tell Yellowhair.

"My ancestors wouldn't like us to approach a place like the Wall without a ceremony cleansing us and getting us ready for what the invisible world is preparing."

"And what is it preparing?" Priscilla asks.

"Who knows?" Yellowhair answers. "It's best not to ask too many questions. The answers will come by themselves. My ancestors hid for years from the white man, in kivas to worship in secret. So much of what is revealed is in secret. My mother, here, knows so much, she's wise, but she doesn't say much because she knows the gods will do what they want anyway."

"Gods?" I ask him.

"Gods, like beings who guard us, but there is only one Great Spirit. We have Shalako who dance, six of them with huge masks. They tell the story of how the Zuñis came from the center of the earth to a resting place on a river. Later the white man swallowed up the river with a dam, and now we live in villages."

Yellowhair sprinkles sacred meal on the fire and it turns the fire to tiny sparks.

"Jesse and I knew an old man named Don Florencío, a descendant of the Aztecs. He used to sprinkle sacred cornmeal in fire to cleanse the air of evil spirits. He believed our ancestors came from seven caves, somewhere in a land called Aztlán, which was north of Mexico."

"The Zuñis believe they are at the center of the earth," Yellowhair says. "I think all people believe themselves to be located in sacred places. My brother, Strong Horse, now lives in a sacred place, maybe in the center of the earth, who knows?"

Michael and Angelo adorn themselves with feathers and start dancing around the smoky tin tub. They attract attention from other motel residents and pretty soon a maintenance man comes by with a hose to spray the fire down. He splashes water into the tub, and the fire turns to gray smoke.

"This is against city code!" he says in a loud voice. "What are you people trying to do, close the place down?"

Manuel, Chris, and the others come down to see what's going on, and the maintenance man tells us if we're going to do a war dance to go to another motel. Pretty soon we've got an audience of motel guests.

"We're not doing a war dance," Manuel says. "We're against war! We're the family traveling to the Vietnam Wall. Haven't you heard about us?"

"Oh yeah," the man says. "Yeah, I heard about you, and frankly I don't care where you're going as long as you don't burn this place down."

"It doesn't matter what happens now," Yellowhair says. "The ceremony is over. Great Spirit protected us." The man dumps the water from the tub into the oleanders as we walk away, then hoists the tub into the garbage bin.

"Buncha crazies," he says. "The whole goddamn world is going to hell."

I think about the Guadalupanas in their room with the flickering candles, the silent images and the prayers spinning circles over their heads, and decide I don't believe the world is going to hell anymore. I did once, after Jesse was killed. I smile at the man, and it surprises me. He's so unhappy, his whole body is an angry fist.

• I'M GLAD CHRIS is sharing a room with the boys tonight. I'm tempted to crawl into bed with him. There's also a part of me that wants to call Ray on the phone just to hear his voice. The Wall is bigger than life in my mind, an immense structure, bigger than the Wall of China Willy talked about the other day. He said the Great Wall of China was one thousand miles long. "Is it a wailing wall like the Vietnam Wall?" I asked him. "No, of course not, except thousands died to build it, so that makes it a wailing wall of sorts."

About one o'clock in the morning Irene knocks on my door to tell me Mom is upset and crying. I walk into their room and Mom is sitting up in bed, her hair like a wispy halo on the pillow. My first thought is that she's heard the voices again. I sit next to her hoping it's not the voices. A chill goes through my body.

"Did I do right, mija?" she asks as she catches her breath between sobs.

"About what, Mom?" I sit next to her, smoothing the sheet around her, arranging her hair on the pillow.

"Staying with your dad. He was so mean to all of us—to Jesse—then Jesse left. I know it was to get away from your father. But I still stayed with him! Ay, can Jesse ever forgive me? Maybe he hasn't—maybe I came all this way, and Jesse doesn't want to see me!"

"Mom, his name is on the Wall. There are no eyes on the Wall."

"You don't understand, mija. Spirits see without eyes."

"Jesse's not mad at you, Mom. You know how he loved you and Dad. He couldn't stay home when other guys were paying with their lives in Vietnam. But let me ask you this. Are *you* mad at him?"

"Ay! For leaving me, yes, for leaving me! Why did he do that to me? I told him stay in school—but no, you see he didn't do what I asked."

"What about me, Mom, are you mad at me?"

"Mad at you? For what, mija?"

"For not telling you that Jesse told me he'd never come back. I knew even before he left."

"Your nana told me. I knew, but I didn't let myself believe it. You should never blame yourself. I hid everything inside me, and I didn't want to see it."

"Mom—remember when you lost Inez, because I almost drowned in the Salt River and gave you el susto?"

"El susto?"

"Yeah, the fear. Doña Carolina said fear could freeze you in place, even kill you. I'm sorry I made you lose Inez. It was all my fault!"

My mother looks at me, her eyes opening in surprise. "Mija, you didn't make me lose Inez! I was sick from the moment I got pregnant with her. There was something wrong in the womb, that's why Inez didn't hang on. You blamed yourself all these years? My poor mija! Nothing has been your fault—ever!"

I bend down and kiss her forehead. We're both crying. I don't let go until she stops crying, and Irene starts talking to her, promising her that Jesse will be happy to see her. "He's over there smiling with Faustino and Gustavo," Irene says, pointing to Jesse's picture. "Our sons know we're here."

I sense Jesse standing by watching us, the atoms of who he is merging with us, not floating aimlessly, but in a distinct spot. I put out my hand to touch him and grasp only empty space.

• THAT NIGHT IN FREDERICK I dream I'm stepping on bodies in a river in Vietnam. The jungle is like pictures of Vietnam I've seen in books and on TV, except the trees are huge shade trees with birds' nests in the trunks. I'm calling out for El Ganso to come get me across El Río Salado, and he doesn't come. I see bodies floating all around. I keep pushing them down with my feet trying to sink them. The water is blood-red. Then, I try to step on the bodies to get across the river. The shore looks so far away, and I'm so tired. I can feel my feet sinking, but I keep walking on the bodies like they're solid ground and make it to shore with no one helping me. I'm on the shore, waving my hands in ecstasy. I made it! The worst is over. I wake up and remember what my mother said, "Nothing has been your fault—ever," and I smile in the dark, because I'm not drowning in El Río Salado anymore.

Frederick •

riday morning, June 6, we're still in Frederick. It's as if we don't want to leave. The sun is shining, and the day is incredibly clear. We have breakfast at a diner that looks like a train. It's got all kinds of artifacts related to the era of trains and trolley cars. Mom looks strong, and her energy spreads to all of us. We've been traveling, hypnotized by the sun rising and setting in a country so beautiful it makes your heart long to hold it all in your arms. We've seen so many landscapes they've blurred into one. Deserts look like forests with fewer trees, and the pattern of stars at night is the same over Denver as it is over Pittsburgh. American families look alike whether they eat in a McDonald's in Raton, New Mexico, or Topeka, Kansas. It's the same tradition of moms, dads, grandparents, single parents with kids.

I've never seen the bloodied fields of Vietnam. Jesse did. I've been protected, spied on by Heaven, seduced by the winds over the flatlands and mountains of America, seduced to believe that the American way of life is the only reality. We're foreigners, still, the remnant of Aztlán, issuing from caves, blinking in white sunlight, rounding the detours of America to get to its wailing wall, clearing the underbrush to find a straight path to D.C., the city of pain, straight to the warrior's heart that charmed the sun into moving across the sky in the splendid empire of the Aztecs.

• • •

• WE FINISH BREAKFAST and head back to the motel. By the time we get there, the motel parking lot is crowded with cars and vans from local news stations. There are reporters with cameras and microphones standing in the motel office.

"Oh, man, take a look at this! Are we celebrities, or what?"

"So, this is what Holly meant by 'Get ready for Frederick,' " Chris says.

"Is this a press conference, Mom?" Lilly asks.

"I guess that's what it is."

"Is something wrong?" Mom asks.

"Just people, lots of people, who want to talk to us. Don't get nervous, Mom."

"I don't think she's nervous at all," Chris says. "What about you, Teresa?" He eases our van into the parking lot, takes his sunglasses off and looks closely at me. "Well? Are you OK?"

"I don't know. All this delay. We need to keep moving."

"These reporters will be hard to shake. They've been waiting for us. We're probably their six o'clock news report."

A man approaches our van as Chris comes to a stop. I put my window down and he leans into the open space. "How do you do? My name is Diego Mendoza." The man's Spanish name surprises me. He's light-skinned, someone who could pass for white.

"I'm from News Channel Ten, and we'd like to do a story on your mom." Behind him are at least ten more reporters with cameras rolling.

"The question is, does she want to do a story with you? We're pretty much in a hurry to get to the Vietnam Wall. As a matter of fact, we're running late."

"I realize that, and it won't take long, I promise!" He puts his hand over his heart, briefly, as if he's making a pledge. "The nation is caught up with your family's journey, Teresa. You are Teresa, right?"

I nod. "Your mother's faith, and the love for her son that's caused her to risk her life to come this far is what's keeping the nation on your trail." He smiles broadly. "You understand?" Then he looks over at Mom. "Señora Ramirez, will you talk to me?"

"Are you a mejicano?"

"Yes. My family's from Guadalajara."

"Do you know any Mendozas from Phoenix? There was a Mendoza

family who helped us when we had no money for food. Do you remember them, Teresa?"

"No, Mom. I don't."

"I do," Irene says. "It was a big family. Fifteen kids!"

"Your dad was so proud, Teresa, even though he had nothing to be proud about. He wouldn't let us get on welfare when he was out of work. The Mendozas helped us by giving us government food. Era comida, it was food, and I sneaked it into the house so your dad wouldn't see it. Si, of course, I'll talk to you!"

Diego Mendoza helps Mom and Irene off the van. "Were you named after Juan Diego—the one who saw La Virgen at Tepeyac?"

"The very same one."

"La Virgen must be sending us a message. What do you think, Irene?"

"She is miraculous," Irene says. "She must be telling us we'll be at the Wall very soon."

We walk with Mom to the motel lobby. We're followed by the reporters and cameramen. Everyone else catches up to us. "Are you gonna let Mom do this?" Paul asks.

"She wants to do it. Ask her yourself."

Paul walks up to Mom and the reporter. "Excuse me," he tells Diego Mendoza. "I need to know if my mother wants to do this press conference."

"She gave me the OK."

"Mom, is that true? You want to talk to all these people?"

"Si, mijo. Don't worry. This man's name is Diego Mendoza. There was a Mendoza family who helped us when we were starving."

"He's not related to them!"

"We're all related. Somos familia."

I look over at Paul. "Told you."

Questions start, as all of us settle into the lobby. Mom and Irene sit together on a flowered couch. I sit next to Mom. Paul stands behind her, and Priscilla sits on the armrest next to me. The kids sit on the carpet. Everybody else locates a space on a chair or couch, and in most cases, just stand wherever room can be found. The bright camera lights make me feel as if we're on stage.

Diego Mendoza starts the questions. "You're almost in D.C.," he says, looking directly at me. "What thoughts do you have to share with us about your trip, Teresa?"

"It's been hard traveling, and there were times none of us thought we'd ever get to the end. But it's all been worth it, such a beautiful country we have, and all the people we've met along the way have made it all worth it."

"And to think it all started with you, Mrs. Ramirez." He looks at Mom. "You heard voices?" I scan the faces around the room to see what reaction his words have made. Nobody flinches. It's business as usual.

"Voices? Yes, but I didn't know what they were saying. I never heard them before."

"How do you know it was your son?"

"Do you have children?"

"Yes."

"And you know their voices?"

"Yes."

Diego Mendoza smiles.

One of the women reporters asks, "How do you feel now, Mrs. Ramirez? Now that you're almost there?"

"My mijo, that's Jesse. He didn't call me here for nothing. I feel strong. I could walk the rest of the way!" Everyone laughs along with Mom. "It's la manda, my promise that's making me strong. I made a promise to get there, and I'm going to keep it. God is leading the way, and La Virgen." She lifts up the medallion. We will get there. My friend, here, Irene, has a son on the Wall, too."

Irene leans into a microphone. "My son's name is Faustino Lara," she says. Irene says her son's name slowly, as if she wants everyone to hear it correctly.

One reporter wants to know how many messages we've received on our web site. Cameras turn to Michael. "Over two thousand," Michael says. "Some people send two or more messages, but there's always somebody sending us a message."

"And you are how old, Michael?"

"I'm twelve. There's my dad over there." He points to Paul.

One reporter asks Paul, "How does it feel to be the father of such a bright boy?"

"It feels good. My whole family is smart. I'm proud of my son."

"Your brother, Jesse, did he win the Congressional Medal of Honor?"

"No. He won a Purple Heart, a Bronze Medal, a Silver Star, and other medals. It's not the medals that make a soldier, it's the kind of person he is. You can't forget somebody like Jesse because of who he was.

He was my only brother, but he was more than that. He was like a dad to me, a friend I could always count on. He was my hero."

Priscilla whispers in my ear, "Wow."

One woman stands up and asks, "These voices, has your mother ever had this experience before? Could this phenomenon be related to medication or to her health?"

Priscilla answers quickly, "If you think Mom needs Prozac, you're wrong! She's the sanest person I've ever known." There is a pause, as the newspeople talk among themselves.

"I'm sorry, I meant no offense," the woman says.

One man addresses the vets. "You men who served. Have any of you visited the Wall before?"

They all respond that they haven't. I notice Pepe, Gonzalo, and Fritz standing just outside the front door. I signal them to come in, and they shake their heads—no.

"I didn't even want to come on this trip," Gates says.

"Why was that?" the man asks.

"I didn't think I was good enough. My life has taken some detours, you might say." Gates smiles. "But things have changed. I'd like to thank the Ramirez family, and especially Mrs. Ramirez, for inviting me to come. Being here is making me realize how lucky I was to have friends like Jesse."

"We're connected to the guys on the Wall," Chris says, "whether we know it or not. When we were out on those hills, I can tell you we fought for each other. We couldn't depend on the government. None of it made any sense." I look at Chris and nod my head.

"I'm hoping to meet other Chinese Americans at the Wall who served in Vietnam," Willy says. "The Vietnamese thought I was one of them when I wasn't in my uniform."

"Any comments from you? I'm sorry, your name?" One reporter is looking at Yellowhair.

"I'm Yellowhair. This is my mother, Sarah." He puts his arm around his mother. "My brother Strong Horse was killed in Vietnam. We've always sent warriors to battle. It's no new thing for us."

"Or for any of us," Manuel says. "Chicanos are another group who have been drafted left and right, along with the Blacks, and other minorities."

"So, it's the government's mistake that made all this possible?" one woman asks.

"Yes," I tell her. "Money, long overdue. They sent Jesse to the wrong address, that was a nightmare for us."

Diego Mendoza looks at me and says, "I understand President Clinton is sending some White House aides to meet you at the Wall."

"This is the first I've heard of that," I tell him.

Our press conference ends with some comments from the kids. The kids wave to their friends back home, and I wave to Elsa, and my granddaughter, Marisol. I sigh out loud in relief. "I never want to do this again," Priscilla tells me. My mother and Irene sit like two queens, totally poised, waiting for someone to lead them to their royal coach. "They probably wouldn't mind it," I tell Priscilla. "Did you ever think Mom could do all this?"

"Surprises come in small packages, I guess," Priscilla says.

• BEFORE WE LEAVE the motel, I get a call from Lieutenant Major William Prescott, who tells me the Army would like to have a ceremony for us at the Wall on Saturday morning. He tells me the president would like to pay tribute to the men who served in Vietnam, and especially Hispanic soldiers. I tell Mom the news, and she looks at me, her face weary. "Era hora," she says. It's about time.

The Wall •

We're driving into D.C. at dusk on Friday, June 6, 1997. The press conference made us late. What should have taken us no more than two hours' travel time has now extended to a whole afternoon. We drive past green, rolling hills, thick foliage, wildflowers, and huge trees. Picturesque homes, some with red barns, and tin roofs dot the landscape. We move slowly, waiting for the vehicles to line up so nobody gets lost. We've decided to go big and stay at the Capitol Hilton, only blocks away from the White House.

"Did it rain?" I ask Chris.

"No, why?"

"All the cars look washed." He looks through the rearview mirror and laughs. "They're just shining in the sun, Teresa. We're at the end, that's what's making everything so clear."

Traffic is picking up, fast cars that move helter-skelter all around us. Some appear to be following our vehicles, making us look like a cavalcade of at least fifty cars. The flags and Zuñi feathered wands on our vehicles are fluttering in the breeze, waving a colorful salute.

"Look, Mom! Look at all the people following us!" Mom turns to look out the back window.

"Ay Dios mio! Will we all fit at the hotel?"

"Mom, they're not staying with us! They're probably people who live around here. People who have been reading about us, or watching us on TV."

"God bless them all!"

"Can you imagine if they all stayed with us?" Chris asks me.

"Don't say it too loud. Mom might get the idea into her head."

We're driving down Georgia Avenue on the northeast side. We see Black people everywhere, crossing the street, walking the sidewalks, kids playing out in crowded apartments.

"La capital!" Irene cries with joy. "We're here, Alicia, here to touch our sons' names! What would they say to see us here? Ay mijitos!"

Then without warning, my mother begins to sing in a voice so clear and crisp, you'd think she was thirty, instead of seventy-nine.

Bendito, Bendito, Bendito sea Dios
los angeles cantan, y alaban a Dios
los angeles cantan, y alaban a Dios.

I turn to look at her and her face is radiant. If I could have taken her picture in that instant, I would have framed it and put it into one of the stained glass windows at St. Anthony's Church. I wave at Manuel and Priscilla in the van following us. Their images blur through my tears.

Yo creo Dio mio que estás en el altar
oculto en la hostia te vengo adorar
oculto en la hostia de vengo adorar.

Bendito, Bendito, Bendito sea Dios
los angeles cantan y alaban a Dios
los angeles cantan y alaban a Dios.

My mother's voice is rushing in my ears, and I never want her to stop, not now, not ever. Her voice is my lullaby again, caressing my soul. We round the corner onto Constitution Avenue and see the Capitol loom ahead of us, imposing, regal. On either side are buildings that belong to the Smithsonian, some with American flags waving from entrances and front lawns. The cavalcade of cars curves behind us with my mother's voice announcing to the nation's capital that we are here, the Mexicas of Aztlán, to pay honor to their fallen warriors.

• • •

• WE DRIVE BY the memorials, but don't stop to get down. We barely glimpse the pathway leading to the Wall, and the Wall itself, off in the distance. There is anxious energy in all of us, we want to run to the Wall, and we want to run the other way. We decide to get to our rooms and wait for the ceremony promised by the Army in the morning. My mother says nothing when I tell her we're staying at the Hilton. I expected a lecture about the cave Christ was born in, and how La Virgen didn't even have a decent blanket to wrap Him in, but she only nods, and asks me if I got rooms for everybody, including Pepe, Gonzalo, and Fritz. Pobres, she says, they probably drink to stop their pain. That's the way it is with men, she says, always wanting to hide their pain.

Mom looks so strong, I swear she's gotten ten years younger. Her appetite is good. She eats dinner for the first time in weeks and finishes the meal. Mom and Irene tease each other like girls in school, laughing about what they've been through to get to this city. I imagine them teenagers, giggling behind their hands, wearing miniature copies of their Virgen medallions. They've arrived to where their sons are immortalized in granite, etched in silence, reflecting back light from the sun shining overhead.

That night Chris and I decide to go dancing. There's a sigh of relief between us, a coming together that makes us feel comfortable with each other. We're los peregrinos, the pilgrims who made it through valleys, hills, and enchanted landscapes to come to the end of an old woman's promise, la manda she made to God, a compact that could never be broken, except by death. We should have set our sights on Magdalena, Mexico, at least we could have lifted San Francisco's head from its stiff pillow and know our prayer was being answered. I don't know what we're supposed to do at the Wall, except touch Jesse's name—all this way to touch his name.

• MANUEL, PRISCILLA, PAUL, DONNA, AND GATES decide to join us for the evening. The kids, Willy, Susie, and Sarah stay back at the Hilton with the Guadalupanas. Yellowhair, Gonzalo, Pepe, and Fritz decide to go off to the seamy side of the city to look for action.

Visits to the web page have tripled the closer we get to D.C. It takes all Michael's time to man the web page and answer as many requests as he can. We've taken rooms on the Towers floor of the Hilton and get our own concierge who provides us personalized service. We get our own fax machine, which Michael and Cisco are using to send faxes to some of the people who have visited our web site.

The old women set up their makeshift altar on a coffee table draped in white linen. The image of La Virgen, the statue of El Santo Niño with Jesse, Faustino, and Gustavo's photos propped up in the middle, are becoming familiar faces glowing between the flickering candles.

The Hilton staff is looking in on us every hour. They heard about the money we got from the government and know our names from stories they read about us in the newspaper. The whole place makes the Guadalupanas nervous. They're not used to being served. The rooms are too rich for them, they say. I'm glad it's late, and we can't go off hunting for another hotel.

We ask a cab driver who looks like he's from some foreign country to recommend a nightclub. He's wearing a turban wrapped around his head. We barely make out his English and finally end up having to trust him to drive us to a decent place. We pack two taxis to the Club Noche Libre. We're together in the nation's capital, Chris, Gates, Priscilla, Manuel, Paul, Donna, and I, spruced up, dressed to the hilt, out to celebrate the end of the journey of our lives.

Everybody in Club Noche Libre looks foreign. There's a hundred dialects of English going on at the same time. Most of the people seem to be from Central America. The place is jammed, smoky, small and lighted by dim violet lights. The music is hot salsa. I can't believe how small it is! Nobody seems to mind, they just stack up closer together. I imagine people's drinks get mixed up with others. From the looks of things, I don't think people care much what they're drinking. We're ushered in after paying ten dollars a head, and sit in dark corners, close to the door. Manuel and Priscilla are holding hands. They look so proper, almost conservative. I'm convinced Priscilla and I have changed roles. I'm the daring splash, and she's Miss Prim and Proper. How did this happen? I'm wearing a red silk dress I picked up at Dillard's, the ritzy fashion store in Phoenix. It clings to me, outlining my body.

• I DON'T SEE HIM at first, Gates does. They're giving each other back slaps and El Cielito high fives before I know who it is. I almost tip the table on Chris's lap when I jump up to run to him. It's Ricky Navarro! Not even the excitement of getting to D.C. matches the way I feel when I see my boyhood prince, the kid next door, who should have been born rich, glowing like an amethyst in the violet lights of Club Noche Libre.

"Teresa, you're real, you're real!" He's saying this, holding me in his arms, spinning me until the violet lights look like a halo over the place.

"Is this real?" I keep asking him, over and over, "Is this real?" I almost sit down on the floor so we can exchange teacups and secrets. If I could frame this scene, we would be in an empty nightclub. All I can see is Ricky. Everybody else is only looking at us through windows.

"Put her down," Chris says. "What do you want to do, make her dizzy?" Ricky puts me down and reaches over to shake Chris's hand, still holding me by the waist. He looks at me again. I stare back at him, at his elegant face and green eyes. He's let his beard grow, perfectly trimmed around his face. He's wearing a black coat, black tie, and everything else white.

"I've been sending messages to your web site, but I didn't want you to know it was me. I wanted to surprise you! I called the hotel, and your son, Cisco, told me you were on your way to the club."

"What are you doing in D.C.?"

"I work for the Veterans Administration. After I got my head straight, I decided to do something for all the vets who never got it together. I worked in California for years as a counselor for Vietnam vets, then they transferred me here."

"With your family?"

"My ex-wife's back in San Jose with our daughter."

"What ever happened to that hippie girl, Faith?"

"Who knows. We lost track of each other years ago."

"And your husband, Ray?" he asks me.

"We just got divorced." He smiles big.

Then he whispers, "Old Ray couldn't keep you after all. He didn't deserve you, Teresa, nobody does but me."

Manuel, Priscilla, Paul, and Donna are shaking Ricky's hand, talking to him, hugging him. Ricky never moves from my side, not that night, and not ever again.

• I SHOULD REMEMBER magic is short-lived. It doesn't replace reality for very long. The prince finds the princess locked up in a tower and then has to fight the fire-spitting dragon to win her. Am I forgetting my fairy tales, dancing with Ricky? I want to control myself but can't. Every time I get close to Ricky, I want to hug him with both arms and elephant-walk on his shoes. I want our bodies to meet, splendid, warm curves fitting into each other. There's a scent that flows from both of us, as if we've just created a new perfume.

Even as I'm dancing, it's easy to spot Sarah, Yellowhair's mother, when she comes into Club Noche Libre. She's ancient, and everybody else is modern. She's wearing her Zuñi clothes and has her hair back in a bun. Sarah is walking toward me with a man who looks like the owner of the club.

"Excuse me," he says. "This lady is looking for you." Sarah's eyes are big. She's looking intently at me.

"What is it, Sarah?"

"Your mother, Teresa. Willy took her to the hospital. She's very ill." She says the words so quietly, I don't react at first. Then my knees bend like Mom's did at the airport when she said good-bye to Jesse. Ricky scoops me up by the elbows.

"It's OK, Teresa, I'll take you to the hospital."

"Which hospital?"

"George Washington University, the paramedics took her there," Sarah says.

Manuel and Priscilla are already running out the door with Donna, Gates, and Sarah. They jump into a taxi before Chris and I get into Ricky's car.

We get to George Washington University and find out Mom's in the critical care unit. The words wreak havoc inside my brain. *Critical care.* I'm glad Chris and Ricky are with me. I need them both to make it into the elevator and up to the fourth floor. When I get off, I see Irene huddled in the corner of one of the couches, a grounded sparrow, her wings broken. The kids are with her, sitting around on other couches and chairs. The twins sit on either side of Irene, and the boys are together, their faces gloomy. Angelo is leaning on Cisco, half asleep. Willy and Susie are standing together. Willy walks up to me.

"I'm sorry, Teresa. I took her as soon as I could. She was having trouble breathing, and I didn't want to take any chances."

I give him a hug. "Thank you, Willy. You were there for her."

I look over at Irene. She's crying. "Tu Mama, Teresa. She will have to fight to keep la manda now."

"Never mind about la manda. God's not gonna send her to hell for not keeping it." Thinking about God makes me angry. Is all this a joke? Are El Santo Niño and La Virgen accomplices? Miraculous figures who sent Mom on her way to the Wall only to trip her up just before the fateful day?

"Where is God now?" I ask Irene.

"Everywhere," she says.

"You're impossible," I tell her. I walk down the hall and see Sarah leaning up against the wall next to Mom's room. Priscilla, Paul, Manuel, and Donna are inside Mom's room, standing around her bed. Mom is hooked up to a heart monitor and an oxygen tank. She looks ashen, her hair disheveled around her.

Prsicilla walks up to me and whispers angrily in my ear, "I told you, didn't I? I told you Mom wouldn't make it. Damn you, Teresa! You never listen to me." Priscilla's words go through me like the thrust of a knife—sharp, cutting.

The nurse comes in and tells us there's too many people in the room. "What happened?" I ask her. She draws me out into the hall.

"Your mother's had a heart attack," she says, "and we think there may be a blood clot going through her left artery."

"That side's given her trouble for years," I tell her. "I can give you her doctor's name in Phoenix."

"We got that from your daughters and have already spoken to him. The doctor can't operate at this point. She'd never make it out of surgery. We're doing the best we can for her." Then she looks at me and holds my hand. "I'm sorry. She'll get the best care here. If there's anybody else you have to call . . . would you like a priest or chaplain to come see her?"

The tips of my fingers are icicles. "Now?"

"Yes, now."

"Ah . . . a priest. We're Catholic—she's very traditional—from the old society of Las Guadalupanas, that's what they call themselves."

"I see. We do have a priest, but he's gone for the evening. I can call him to come back tonight."

"Yes, do that." I'm shivering. My lips are trembling. The nurse tells everybody we have to take turns in Mom's room. Donna says she'll stay with me in the room. Priscilla doesn't look at me as she walks out.

I take Mom's hand in mine. She opens her eyes and looks at me like she's searching for me in a crowd. She struggles to focus.

"It's me, Mom. Don't try to say anything. Everything will be OK. The doctors here are very good, remember we're in la capital, where they have the very best."

She whispers, "God is the very best. Whatever He wants, He'll do." I want to tell her to stop talking about Him but decide not to.

"Stop crying," I tell Donna. "Mom doesn't need to hear all that." Donna blows her nose on a Kleenex.

"I can't believe this is happening," she says.

"Well it is," I tell her, trying to sound strong.

Paul is standing at the door of Mom's room. He motions me to come out.

"We just got a call from the Vietnamese man from Little Saigon. He's here in D.C. He's on his way to the hospital."

"He's coming here? Who is he?"

"He doesn't say. Just that he'll be right over."

"What do we do?"

"Nothing, just wait. We'll listen to whatever he has to say."

I return to Mom's room and sit with her in silence. She has gone to sleep. I hold her hand, and it lies limp and still in mine. I smile as I see her fingernails, polished red by the twins. I'm wondering what the visit from the Vietnamese man means for all of us. Did he know Thom? How will all this affect Mom?

I look at Donna and whisper, "The man from Little Saigon is on his way to the hospital."

Donna's blue eyes get big. "Who is he?" I shrug my shoulders. Mom's eyelids flutter, and Donna starts to cry all over again. I put my finger up to my lips to make her stop, but it's no use. I shake my head, and watch Donna cry softly into her Kleenex. Not more than an hour goes by before Paul walks into Mom's room.

"They're here," he whispers to me.

"They?"

"You'll see."

Chris meets me as soon as I walk out of Mom's room. "She's here!" he says. "She's really here!"

"What are you talking about? Who's here?"

"Thom!" The name causes a chain reaction to go through my body. It's as if I've said her name every day of my life. It takes a few seconds for me to speak again.

"You mean Thom, Jesse's girlfriend from Vietnam?"

"His wife! She just told me they got married over there! And their son!"

"*Their* son?"

"They had a son together."

"Oh, my God!" Chris leads me out to the lobby area, and standing before me is a Vietnamese family. The woman is beautiful, petite, with short black hair brushed in waves around her face. She's wearing a pair of loose-fitting dark pants and a flowered blouse. Next to her is a man that looks so much like Jesse, my knees bend all the way this time. I stumble forward, and Chris blocks my fall.

"Take it easy, Teresa. It's them, it really is!" Chris leads me by the hand, as if I'm sleepwalking.

"Thom, this is Teresa, Jesse's sister." I see crinkles in Thom's neck and a gold necklace with a small jade elephant hanging at her throat. Her face is silky smooth, her voice calm, refined.

"I'm so glad to meet you," she says. Her eyes fill with tears. She nods her head slightly. I reach over and hug her, a soft hug that makes me know I'm not dreaming. We look at each other and see Jesse between us. He's in the pupils of our eyes, two women who loved him. With one look, we know more about each other than if we had lived as neighbors all our lives.

"Yes . . . I'm so glad to meet you, too," I tell her. "You have no idea how happy I am to meet you!"

"Jesse's son," she says, drawing her arm through her son's. "This is Lam."

"Lam." I say his name, and it sounds so strange on my lips. "Lam . . ." I look at him and see the smile I recognized from my cradle. The dark features, the eyebrows straight, not curving, the perfect teeth. He's several inches taller than me.

"Jesse was my father. This is my son," he says, holding the hand of a child about four years old. "This is Joshua Ramirez! Say hi to your aunt, Joshua."

"Joshua Ramirez! Oh, my God, you've carried on the family name! Jesse must be clapping his hands in heaven!" I look deeply into Lam's and Joshua's eyes, and for the first time Don Florencío's prophecy makes sense . . . *a new form—your brother will come back in a new form. Our ancestors have always walked the earth.*

Joshua looks solemnly at me, "Hi," he says, and I go down on one knee and kiss both cheeks. Already, Lisa and Lilly are standing around him.

"Mom, how cute! He's adorable!"

"We flew in from Little Saigon in Orange County, California," Lam says.

"Yes, my nephew, Michael, told me you were sending us messages from there."

"My wife is visiting in the real Saigon, in Vietnam, but now it's called Ho Chi Minh City. Look, there he is," Lam says, pointing to Michael. "That's the boy I've been talking to on the Internet!"

Michael walks over and Lam shakes his hand over and over again. "Good job! You helped me find my father's family! Good job! Very smart boy!" Michael is smiling big, puffing up his chest. "I work for a computer company, we can talk . . . very smart boy!"

"See, I told you, Tía, Nana's web page is a winner!"

"Yes, it is a winner! You were right, Michael. But Lam," I ask, "how is it that you never knew where Jesse lived?"

"Well, that's a sad story in my family," he says. "You see, when my mother left Vietnam her father forbade her to look for him. My grandfather was an officer for the South Vietnamese Army and was already in big trouble with the communists. To make matters worse my mother was pregnant with me, the baby of an American soldier. Her whole village was burned to the ground, everything destroyed. She wasn't able to save even one letter with my father's address on it. Her family barely escaped Vietnam with their lives. They had to climb on river boats to make their escape."

"But what about the marriage? I thought they were married."

"My father never accepted my marriage," Thom says. She shakes her head sadly, "Never. Over the years, I accepted my fate, and yet, I prayed for the day I would find Jesse's family. And now look, here we are all together—a miracle!"

Everyone standing around us looks like still-life pictures to me. No one is moving a muscle, as I turn around and announce, "This is Jesse's family from Little Saigon in Orange County, California!"

Everyone comes up to shake hands. Thom and Lam walk up to Irene, and hold her hands.

"Si!" Irene says. "I can see that this is Jesse's son! And Jesse's wife is so beautiful!"

Thom and Lam turn to Paul, looking at him closely.

"He looks like your father!" Thom says to her son.

"Jesse was better-looking," Paul says with a wink.

"I'll be right back," I tell Thom.

I walk into Mom's room with Ricky and Priscilla. Priscilla stands on one side of the bed, Ricky and I stand on the other. I take one of Mom's hands in mine.

"Mom, there's something I have to tell you, something very important." She opens her eyes and sighs, then looks at Ricky standing next to me and recognizes him. Tears start.

"It's me . . . Doña . . . It's Ricky."

"I know it's you, Ricky," Mom says. "Your mother," Mom whispers, "how's Juanita, mijo?"

"She's fine, Doña. She's in San Jose." Mom smiles and closes her eyes.

"My old neighbor—your mother, such a hard worker. I never knew I would see you here, mijo. You and Teresa used to play together. I thought someday you would marry her, but then you went away."

"I'm here now, Doña."

"Mom—there's someone else you have to meet tonight!" I tell her. "She came a long way to see you. It's someone who knew Jesse in Vietnam. Mom, are you listening?" She nods her head. "Mom, she came with someone else, too." Mom senses the electricity in my voice and opens her eyes.

"Who? What are you talking about?" She looks closely at me. "Why are you all dressed up, mija? Am I dead yet? Is this my funeral?"

"No, Mom, you're not dead! Listen to me . . . keep your eyes open. You'll see something . . . but don't get scared, OK? Remember you said Jesse was calling you here? I believe you now!"

I walk to the hall and motion for Paul to bring in Thom, Lam, and Joshua. The nurse sees what's happening and doesn't say a word to us. I hold Thom's hand and lead her to Mom's side.

"Mom—open your eyes. Here she is." Mom opens her eyes and sees Thom. She stares at her, surprised. Her eyes take in Thom's face.

"Mom—this is Jesse's wife—he married her in Vietnam!"

"Jesse's wife?"

"Yes, isn't she beautiful?" Mom nods. Tears are streaming down her face. Thom puts her arms around Mom's shoulders and kisses her forehead.

"Mother-in-law," she says. "I loved your son. He was a very good man. He treated me with love. He was a good husband for me." She brings Lam to her side. "Look!" she says. Mom stares at Lam and sits up in bed, propping herself up on one elbow.

"Jesse!" she cries. "You made me a grandmother!" She leans back on the pillows and reaches for Lam. Lam tenderly hugs Mom, then lets her kiss each finger of his hands as she kissed Jesse's when he left for Vietnam. She traces a cross over Lam's forehead.

"Ay está mi Dios, there is my God, a witness to this miracle. I came without knowing what I would be given today! This is what Jesse was telling me that night—that he had a wife, a son, a grandson!"

Lam brings Joshua over. My mother is laughing and crying at the same time, holding onto Joshua. "Mira no mas, I'm a great-grandmother too! Así es, mijo! Well done, Jesse!"

Ricky wraps his arms around my waist, standing behind me, letting me rest on his body. Priscilla is crying. She comes over and puts her face into my shoulder.

"I'm sorry. I was wrong. Mom had to be here." I hold my sister, and we both balance on Ricky. Manuel walks in, and puts his hands on Priscilla's shoulders.

"It's OK, Priscilla—how you felt," he says. "It was only normal."

My mother is talking to Lam. "Now I can die in peace," she says.

"Don't talk about dying, grandmother," Lam says. "I barely met you. I don't want to lose you now."

"Tell me," my mother says to Thom. "Tell me about my son, about the things he said to you."

"He told me he loved you very much. That you held up the plane going to Vietnam with a cookie you wanted to give him. That you were so good to him—such a good mother." She smiles gently.

"Did he talk about his father?"

"He only said he had a father that forgot him sometimes, but still loved him."

"Was he happy—my son? Was he ever happy in Vietnam?" Mom is holding Thom's hands, pressing her hands up to her face, wanting to touch the woman who touched her son.

"Yes. Together, we were happy. We were married by a priest, Father John. I am proud to have him for my husband."

"Gracias, thank you Santo Niño, Virgencita. God was with my son in Vietnam. What more could I ask for?" Mom closes her eyes and her face relaxes into a perfect smile.

Irene goes back to the hotel with Sarah and brings the things on their altar to set up in Mom's room. The nurse gives permission for one candle to be lit. Then Irene does what Guadalupanas have done for ages. She sits at the head of Mom's bed and directs Donna and Sarah to take turns at the foot of the bed. In this way she lives out the tradition of Las Guadalupanas by providing guardians stationed one at the head and one at the foot of the dying Guadalupana until the bitter end. They drape el listón around Mom's neck, the ribbon of the Society of Las

Guadalupanas. It's red, white, and green, the colors of the Mexican flag, symbols of La Virgen. And they wait . . . and they pray.

• MY MOTHER DIED Saturday afternoon, June 7, at 3:24 P.M., on the day she was to complete la manda to touch my brother's name. Just before she died, she clung to Thom's and Lam's hands. The perfect smile she had relaxed into stayed on her face after her death. So much was happening to all of us it was like rain falling from everywhere, I had no time to break down. There was nothing left for us to do but release my mother's body to be prepared for the trip back to Phoenix. Irene chose her burial clothes and sent along Mom's Virgen medallion and el listón, the red, white, and green ribbon, to be draped over her shoulders. They say God will see the ribbon and recognize her as one of His own. Mom packed a dress in her suitcase, white with a fringe of lace at the collar and sleeves. The twins ask me to tell the funeral people to take the red polish off Mom's fingernails. They say it was only for the Wall, and they don't think their Nana would want to wear it at her own funeral. I tell them, maybe she would, after all.

"Look at this!" I tell Irene, holding up Mom's dress. "Did she know she was going to die?"

"Who knows? Your mother listened more to God's voice than she listened to any of us."

Only death could break the promise, end the bargaining between my mother and God. Before my mother died she looked at me and said, "You will touch my mijito's name for me, Teresa—you will do it for me—yes, mija?" It was a question and a command. Yes, do it for me? The invisible only asks of us what it knows we are ready to do.

I'm not one to break la manda. I don't want to end up like the man who swallowed the needle. I looked at my mother's eyes, gray, colorless, I looked closely into them. It was important to lock eyes with her. The power of la manda demanded it.

"Yes, Mom, yes, I will. Don't worry, go ahead of us if you have to. Say 'Hi' to Jesse, tell him we miss him and that we're glad we came all this way to touch his name, to meet his family. Tell him I love his wife and son and grandson. Tell him to say 'Hi' to Don Florencío for me, Nana . . . and Dad, too."

My mother lay her hand gently over mine and never said another word. I still feel the pressure of my mother's hand over mine, cold, hard.

I let my mother take the heat out of my hand, and in exchange, she laid the burden of la manda into mine.

• LIEUTENANT PRESCOTT and another military officer come to the hospital to offer us condolences on behalf of the U.S. Army. The lieutenant tells us the ceremony at the Wall has been postponed until Sunday. He asks if we will still be willing to attend, and tells us that honoring our men is very important to the U.S. Army. Yes, of course we will attend, I tell him, my mother's promise will be carried out, no matter what.

After they leave, Ricky tells me the ceremony is media propaganda to give the Clinton Administration credit for recognizing the 191,000 men of Latin descent who served during the Vietnam War, and that's not counting all the others with Latino roots who don't carry Spanish surnames. He tells me we don't have to acknowledge any of it, but I tell him the more publicity, the better. I'm only quoting Michael on that one. Los Chicanos are a huge part of the Latinos, and we've come a long way to be heard.

The Army tells us they will provide a military escort to fly my mother's body back to Phoenix. My mother would die twice if she knew we had plans to fly her back to Phoenix, or she may not mind it anymore, considering she's flown ahead of all of us.

We return to the hotel to make plans for Sunday's visit to the Wall. I call Elsa in Phoenix, Espi, and Ray. Elsa cries the whole time I talk to her. Priscilla and I cry every time we see each other. Paul is stoic, his face sullen, pale and unsmiling. Donna is crushed. It's as if she had lost her own mother.

"We have to be strong," I tell Priscilla, "We have to do this for her." Strong, strong, strong . . . I say the word so many times it becomes a battle cry. Nobody has anything left to say to us. Suddenly, everybody's quiet. Not even the excitement of D.C. attracts our attention.

Michael tells me the web site is buzzing constantly. Our story has been picked up by news stations, local and national. Cards and flowers arrive at the Hilton. The Hilton staff is hard-pressed to find places for the floral arrangements, and resort to setting some of them out on patios and terraces.

I don't remember eating on Sunday, don't remember brushing my teeth. I have only one thing on my mind—my mother's death and la manda. We arrive at the Wall at 9:30 A.M. The sun is shining overhead. The morning is warm, and a bit humid. Cars line the streets, and everywhere there are people milling about, watching us as we get out of our cars and begin our trek to the Wall. Photographers are snapping our pictures, cameras are pointed our way. I notice a marker with the words VIETNAM MEMORIAL WALL.

We walk through a pathway under trees and green grass all around. Hundreds of birds are singing in the trees. Every now and then we spot a squirrel in a tree. We walk slow with Irene between us, taking one labored step after another. We're in procession, the sacred stance of the Sun People led by El Santo Niño and La Virgen. Don Florencío would be so proud of us.

I notice teenagers skating up and down the streets. People are sitting outside the White House protesting nuclear weapons. IF THE BIG ONE GOES OFF, WE ALL GO WITH IT, one of the signs says. The words DON'T SELL OUT PEACE are written on a huge banner hanging between two trees. It looks like a scene out of the sixties. Some of the nuclear protesters wear tattered Levi's and headbands. I've always wondered about our philosophy of promoting peace and building weapons of war at the same time. It doesn't make sense. It's like going to the doctor to get well, then going back home and drinking poison.

We're grassy yards away from the Wall. I'm walking now with Priscilla, Paul, Manuel, Thom, and Lam with Joshua in his arms. I turn to Priscilla.

"Does your breastbone hurt?"

"Yes."

"So does mine."

Everyone else is trailing along behind us. Lisa and Lilly are helping Irene. Cisco and Michael are walking together. Michael's got the laptop and cell phone in his backpack and is already anticipating meeting some of the people who have visited our web site. *The Vietnam Wall forms a chevron-shaped angle like a V that connects the Washington Monument and the Lincoln Memorial.* The Wall looks exactly the way my second-grade students described it in their report. The whole place is even bigger and more impressive than I've seen on postcards of D.C. The waters of the Potomac are gray, serene, reflecting back sky, trees, and glimpses of the memorials. The Washington Monument and the Lincoln Memorial are bold markers, hemming in the Vietnam Wall. I'm catching my breath. It's like I'm getting ready to climb a mountain.

We see cameras and a podium set up some distance from the Wall. There's a sign on the podium, WELCOME RAMIREZ FAMILY. Now I'm nervous.

"Oh, my God . . . Ricky, look at the crowd!" All around us are people, White, Black, Brown, Yellow, Red, every nation represented. In spite of their numbers there is silence, as if we're all in church together. Some people are wiping their tears away.

"What are we supposed to do?" I ask Ricky.

"Just be yourself," he says, "that's what they want to see, all of us here, saluting our men."

We're getting our picture taken as a park ranger walks up to us and tells us we can look up Jesse's name in the directory and find out what panel he's on. We walk around the sidewalk to several stands set up with books in which you can look up a soldier's name. We look up *Jesse A. Ramirez, born April 23, 1947, died June 7, 1968.* Chris is helping Irene look up Faustino's name. Gates is at one of the directories with a woman who looks like Kamika. He must have met her last night. I'm glad Erica is 2,300 miles away. Gates got over his "poor me" attitude. He's gotten stronger on the trip, reading about Mandela and the struggle of Black people to gain respect, which is their due. Yellowhair and Sarah are looking up Strong Horse, alias Eddie Bika. Pepe and Gonzalo are looking up their brother Gustavo. Fritz is looking for names of his friends. Michael doesn't forget to look up Robert O'Connor for the redheaded reporter, Holly Stevens. I tell Cisco to look up Gathering Eagle Feathers, who is on the Wall as Benjamin Rush, nephew of the Native American woman from Albuquerque. We get slips of paper on each man that look like cash register receipts, and papers with small pencils for making rubbings of their names.

Now we're ready. People are milling around us, and Lieutenant Prescott is at the podium. Ricky's talking to him, and he motions us to come. Lieutenant Prescott shakes my hand.

"On behalf of the Secretary of the Army, I welcome you, your family, and friends to the Vietnam Memorial Wall."

"This is Jesse's son," I tell Lieutenant Prescott, "and his wife and grandchild." He looks surprised.

"Pleased to meet all of you!" Later, speeches were made by the Army, Air Force, Marines, and Navy, congratulating veterans of color and their families for serving their country during the Vietnam War.

Cameramen move in on us, and I see a couple of reporters talking into their microphones . . . "The journey is over for the Ramirez family, recipients of ninety thousand dollars owed them by the U.S. government for the death of their loved one, Sgt. Jesse A. Ramirez. Tragically, the family has lost their mother, Alicia Ramirez, who passed away yesterday afternoon at George Washington University Hospital. They have journeyed for a week from Phoenix, Arizona, bringing with them other minority families, victims of the Vietnam War."

I'm glad the reporter said "victims," because I feel I'm on the Wall with Jesse. I look at Thom and Lam and wonder if they have a wall in Vietnam to honor all their victims. Mothers cry in the same language the world over. I notice Angelo is wearing a Zuñi feather stuck in a headband. He's walking with Sarah, dressed in her Zuñi clothes and Yellowhair in his buckskins. There are gifts all along the Wall set on the cobblestone path, small flags, flowers, teddy bears, caps, a baseball, pictures.

Just before we get to the first panel a tall white man approaches me.

"Teresa?"

"Yes."

"I'm Ronald Bradford—but Jesse knew me as Tennessee."

"Tennessee? Oh, my God, Tennessee!"

"Hi, Tennessee," Chris says, walking up and shaking his hand.

"Good to see you!" Tennessee says. They hug and pound on their shoulders at the same time.

"Your brother saved my life," Tennessee says to me, "and ma'am—I mean, Teresa, I'm so grateful, my heart is breaking, has been for years!" He starts to cry and holds me in his arms. I'm holding the man Jesse died for, but it could have been anyone else. Jesse would have done it for whoever needed him. That's the way it was for the guys in Vietnam. They fought the war for one another.

"Are these your children?" I point to two teenagers standing behind him.

"Yes, and if it hadn't been for your brother, well, they wouldn't be here. Please accept our love." The kids hug me and Priscilla and shake hands with Paul. Tennessee turns to Thom. "I'm so sorry," he says to her. "Your husband was a great man." Thom looks so small next to Tennessee. She stands on the tips of her toes and hugs him. Tennessee turns to Lam and hugs him. He gives Joshua a kiss. "Look at this! Never would believe the day!"

So much has happened that Priscilla, Paul, and I are becoming experts at accepting whatever comes our way, like the Guadalupanas, accepting life, death, love, sorrow, joy. Who's next? What's next? The journey has tried us, sifted out our fears, made us warriors like the men on the Wall. Maybe that's why my mother wanted us to journey together for days and days so we would get to the heart of who we are.

We walk up to the first panel and someone whispers to us, *God bless you Teresa, Priscilla, Paul . . . God bless your mother, your brother Jesse . . . We love you . . . We're here for you.*

We reach the first panel. It looks so small. I don't touch the Wall. I'm waiting to get to Jesse's name. *Angel Luis Sanchez . . . Robert Cinosa Gonzalez . . . Aurelio Garza Herrera . . . Pedro Caudillo . . . David Esequiel Padilla . . . Anibal Ortega Jr. . . . Miguel Pagan . . . Ernesto Coto . . . Frank Alday . . . Arturo Barriga . . .* As I walk by I see more and more men with Spanish last names.

"Oh, my Christ . . . look at all the Spanish names! They cleaned out the barrios for this war!" I cry out the words. A reporter puts them down on paper. Priscilla and I are holding hands. Ricky has his arm over my shoulder.

"Lots of the men were from Puerto Rico, too," he says. "Others were from Mexico, Central America, South America, but they're all Latinos."

"I can't believe it!" Priscilla says. "Oh, my God Teresa, I can't believe this!"

Frank Navarro . . . Bobby Joe Martinez . . . Juan Marcos Jimenez . . . Filiberto Chavez . . . Paul Galaniz . . . Leroy Valdez . . . Rudy Lopez . . . Robert Lopez . . . Arthur Castillo Tijerina . . . David Urias . . . Pablo Duran . . . Wilfredo Reyes-Ayala . . . Francisco Diaz . . . Joe Hernandez. . . . Steve Garcia.

The panels get bigger. *Juan Martinez . . . Jesus Martinez . . . Antonio Lopez Jr. . . . Steve Gomez . . . Tom Galvez . . . George Ramiro Sosa . . . Juan O. Sanchez . . . Encarnasion Rodriquez Jr. . . . Dennis J. Rodriquez . . . Cristobal Figueroa-Perez . . . Jaime Rivera Lopez . . . Leandro Garcia . . . Felix Alvarado Ruiz . . . Paul A. Miranda Jr. . . . Ernesto Soliz Cantu . . . Juan Macias Jimenez . . . Rene Zaragoza Hernandez . . . Manuel Martinez Gonzales . . . Joseph A. Mena.*

"Jesus, God . . . no! God, how did this happen? This isn't real—I'm in a nightmare!"

The panels now tower over us. *Tony Cruz . . . David Moreno . . . Pedro Valenzuela . . . Anastacio Gomez . . . Agapito Gonzales . . . Daniel M. Arizmendez . . . Pedro A. Rodriquez . . . Rudy M. Oliveras . . . John Salazar . . . Luis A. Lopez-Ramos . . . Julio A. Hernandez . . . Juan F. Garcia-Figueroa . . . Ricardo R. Tejano . . . Luis G. Gomez Mesa . . .*

Geronimo Lopez Grijalva . . . Felipe Herrera . . . Jesús Mejia . . . Joseph A. Padilla . . . Octavio Molina-Rosario. Each man has a story to tell and perhaps, a little old lady like my mother who mourned him all her life. I can barely look at the Wall, but I have to. I notice an airplane flying over us swaying in the clear blue sky; its white wings disappear in the distance. *Carlos Cruz Aguirre . . . Felipe Cantu . . . Manuel Herrera.* I don't have to walk very far to see another Spanish name. *Joe Gutierrez . . . Joaquin Castro . . . Joel Gonzalez Velez . . . Vicente Ramirez Gonzalez . . . Tony Valdez Nastor . . . Felix F. Flores . . . Eligio Rice Gonzales Jr. . . . Angel L. Gonzalez-Martinez . . . Arturo Serna Rodriquez . . . Ramiro Lopez Salinas . . . Pedro JT. Mota . . . Benito Contreras Jr.,* and then I see our own *Francisco Jose Jimenez* from Arizona. This is a massacre, a travesty. Each name is alive. I turn to the crowd, hundreds standing on the cobblestone walkway, on the lawns, under the trees, and by the waters of the Potomac River in the distance.

"Why did we let this happen?" There is silence.

We reach Jesse's panel, and right over us, a few inches above our heads, is his name . . . *Jesse A. Ramirez.* Priscilla and I stare at it as though we're looking at Jesse's face. We see ourselves reflected in the Wall. In my hand, I feel the pressure of Mom's hand over mine, the exchange of la manda. Her promise empowers me to do what I have to do. I reach up and touch my brother's name, feeling my hand turn warm as I trace the letters of his name, rough, uneven under my fingers. Cameras are flashing. I stand there for what seems like a long time, caressing Jesse's name. "Hello, I've missed you . . . hello, I love you. We made it. You called us, and we're here," I tell him. "I took care of Mom like you asked me to, Jesse, now she's over there with you. Take care of her for us. Your family is beautiful! It meant the world to Mom to see them before she died— thank you so much for that, Jesse. You always thought of her first, always."

Priscilla is next, then Paul, Thom, Lam, and Joshua held in Lam's arms, reaching up to touch his grandfather's name. Then Chris, Gates, Willy, Manuel, Tennessee, and the kids touch Jesse's name. All around me everyone else is touching their man's name. The Wall is reflecting our faces like a mirror. We've journeyed through Aztlán to the place where our warriors are immortalized in stone, their names, their stories hidden in atoms of granite. We've crossed paths with them, exchanged orbits, let their spirits dance.

Epilogue •

We flew out of D.C. on Tuesday. The Army kept its promise this time. We were flown by military escort back to Phoenix. On our plane were the words FREEDOM BIRD in bold blue letters. I glimpsed people looking up at us, as our plane hovered over the Wall. The Air Force backed us up, too. They sent two Air Force jets to guide us out of D.C. Dad would have been clapping his hands. The Air Force jets flew in unison with our plane in the middle. A couple of times they charged off into the distance, looping back in huge circles, spewing white, foamy gas into the sky. Once out of D.C., they flew one more huge loop around our plane, and disappeared into the distance.

We bought plane tickets for everyone else to fly back to where they needed to go. The Army gave us special permission to have Mom's coffin on board with us, resting behind our seats. Irene positioned herself at the head of Mom's coffin and Donna sat at the foot. They stayed with her the whole trip, and again in Phoenix, until her coffin was lowered into its grave. Irene removed Mom's Virgen medallion, and gave it to me. She told me Mom had asked her to do this. Donna says she wants to be a Guadalupana, and Irene says she'll be the first white Guadalupana in the world.

Michael and Lam sat together, enjoying each other's company. Lisa and Lilly decided to take turns holding Joshua on their laps. Thom sat in silence all the way to Phoenix. She's invited us to visit with her in Little Saigon.

As we flew out of D.C., we made a turn in the sky that led us straight over the Vietnam Memorial Wall. I looked down at the Wall, glittering below us in the sunshine. The plane shook.

"Turbulence?" I asked Ricky.

"Who knows?" he said.

"Look, Tía," Michael shouted. "Look at the light over Nana's coffin!"

For a few seconds Mom's coffin was bathed in a spotlight that engulfed it, outlining the grain of the oak wood.

"It's Jesse!" Irene said. "He's touching his mother!"

I didn't answer. I've learned not to doubt the impossible. If I've learned anything on this journey, I've learned that. No one knows if a spirit can balance on the point of a pin, or send light beams when we least expect. I looked down at the Wall. Light shone from it like a laser beam reaching us flying overhead. It's OK that I knew my brother wasn't coming home. I was supposed to. It got me to write this book, to tell his story to the world.